THE DARK ISLES
CHRONICLE BOOK 1

ARTHUR

L.K. ALAN

For Paula.

BONUS

Don't forget to claim your free bonus chapters at www.lkalan.com

This book contains graphic scenes of violence, strong language, and fantasy horror.

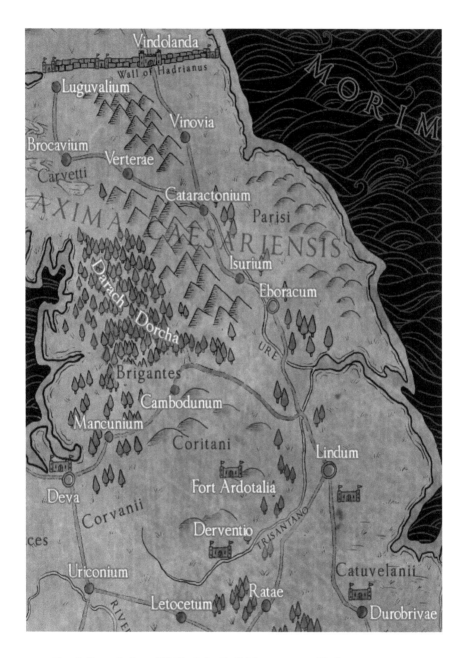

Get A Free Colour PDF of the Full Map at www.lkalan.com

THE DARK ISLES
CHRONICLE BOOK 1

ARTHUR

CHAPTER ONE

The horsemen thundered through a rich land of green valleys and ancient forests bathed in silvery moonlight. They raced toward another evening of slaughter and cruel death. One killer amongst them stared into the night sky, feeling the pulsing heartbeat of his steed, Amicus, beneath him. He struggled to recall his existence before the clan, but those days were as much a mystery as the star-studded void above.

The Raven clan had filled his every waking moment and nightmare for as long as he could remember—a never-ending torment he'd learned to endure. The clan pillaged, the clan raped, and the clan fed on the weak and avoided the strong. If it wanted gold, the clan took it. If it needed women and children, the clan enslaved them. They destroyed lives and property which they deemed worthless. This was their way. And as the empire's grasp loosened, their attacks grew ever bolder.

The band drew to a stop at the prearranged signal of a raised hand, then dismounted and removed the sacking from their saddlebags. They wrapped their mounts' hooves before continuing on the last leg of their journey in near silence, nothing more than ghosts upon the plain.

Arthur glanced along the line of riders and glimpsed the form of Drest at the far end. As always, he sat astride Duthas, a shaggy-haired brute of a stallion with a swirling red firebrand on its flank. The creature's wicked temperament, alien even to its own kind, rivalled its master's. The older men whispered that their leader had once been a noble of a far northern tribe, cast out for necromancy. Arthur's best guess was that the carrion halls of the nether had spewed him forth, such was his malevolent presence. He feared Drest like the others. None would dare challenge him.

The settlement emerged against the inky backdrop. By the outline of the roundhouses within, Arthur guessed it was one of many farming villages scattered throughout the province. Behind the dwellings loomed a large wood, and he wondered if any of the unfortunate inhabitants would live long enough to flee into its depths. Those who could not run faced enslavement or worse.

They closed upon their prey and halted, the warm breath of their mounts misting into the cool air. Arthur waited for the signal, knowing the crushing attack would follow the same pattern as their previous exploits.

The mimicked sound of a nightjar trilled from Drest, prompting torches to spark to life amongst the riders. A dog's urgent barking rang out from the settlement. No matter, it was too late for the villagers to organise a credible defence.

Trotting along the muddy lanes between the homes of the slumbering inhabitants, the warriors positioned themselves near the entrance of each modest house. As well practised in this tactic as his comrades, Arthur tightened his grip on his sword and waited. The dog's yelping reached a hysterical pitch before being silenced. Still, the villagers continued to sleep through the last peaceful moments of their lives.

The silent attack started with the torchbearers tossing their faggots onto the heather-woven thatch of every home. Flames spread across the rooftops, baked as dry as kindling during the summer months, releasing the scent of burning flora. Moments later, the first audible signs of alarm emerged from within the dwellings.

To Arthur's left, a naked old man staggered from the nearest hut and gazed around in stunned confusion. The young warrior unsheathed his blade and nudged Amicus toward the oblivious elder, whose rib-lined back betrayed his lack of value. It would be a kindness to kill this one and spare him the sight of his loved one's desecration.

Arthur emerged from the shadows behind his target, ready to strike the farmer in the skull. He'd ended many lives this way. With a flick of his wrist, he would cleave him, revealing the strange white matter that resided in all men's heads. Job done.

The elderly man froze in terror upon seeing the bandits move between his neighbours' homes while hurling fiery death about them. Arthur raised the blade above his target's hairless pate, then chopped down with force. But his hand stilled, the sword's edge only a finger's breadth from the man's skull, for a vision had overwhelmed him: a child clutched at its mother's golden hair while flames surrounded them. The waking dream was so vivid that he saw her sad blue eyes glistening with unshed tears. The red-cheeked baby's screams echoed through his being. Time slowed, as did the roaring conflagration about to engulf the helpless pair.

Confused, Arthur shook his head and glanced around him to see if any of his clansmen had witnessed his moment of shameful weakness. Although he'd been lucky to escape notice, a short distance away loomed Festus, a dark-haired thug from Epirus. The former legionary had grasped a stocky woman by the arm while he stabbed a balding man through the throat. Unlike Arthur, he enjoyed his work and was too engrossed in the act to see his comrade's hesitation. Grateful for the reprieve, Arthur returned his attention to the old man, who'd turned to notice the stalking figure of death behind him.

Their eyes met. Flames, mixed with strange defiance, danced within the red-rimmed whites of the man's gaze. Despite his exposed fragility, the farmer radiated pure hatred. Unnerved, Arthur nudged Amicus forward a step, then raised his sword once more, willing himself to deliver the fatal blow, yet it refused to come. The impasse stretched for an eternity until his wrist quivered with the effort of restraint.

To Arthur's further dismay, his intended victim did not go, but remained motionless, his jaw thrust forward in contempt. He shook his head again to clear the fog, but the image of the mother and child was seared into his mind. His focus shifted to his reflection within his prey's eyes. A young man with an unkempt beard and piercing blue eyes looked back. His formerly broken and crudely-set nose provided a lasting reminder of the childhood he tried to forget. Fear sat upon the coward's face.

No longer able to keep the blade aloft, Arthur's arm dropped, doubt gnawing at his confidence. Frustration turned to impotent rage, and he roared a battle cry to make the elderly man flee.

'Go—run!' he growled, his tone halfway to a scream.

The man did not move.

'Run, damn you!' he shouted again.

Nothing. Instead, the farmer fell to his knees and raised his head to the sky. 'Hear me, divine lady!' he called through toothless gums. 'Hear me, mighty queen of vengeance!' He pointed a gnarled finger at Arthur. 'Punish this creature! Let me rest knowing we have justice!' He spat at Arthur's feet.

Flames bathed the once quiet village in waves of shimmering blue and orange. The dancing colours transfixed Arthur. Such was the power of the dread spell that he did not notice the old man's gaze shift to his left until it was too late.

A shuddering blow, then sudden agony speared Arthur's side. Alarm screeched through his senses. The force had pinned his torso in place, forcing him to turn his head toward the source of the devastating attack. A woman—no, a girl had driven a pitchfork into his side. She stepped back, as if in disbelief of her own action, then yanked the fork out. A torrent of paralysing pain coursed through Arthur's tortured body.

At the edge of his awareness, he experienced the dim sensation of falling, then, blessedly, the pain receded, as did any semblance of strength. Before sweet oblivion took him, he watched the girl thrust the pitchfork into Amicus's belly. Arthur tried to raise a hand to help his friend, but he couldn't move. He cried out for the animal he'd raised from a foal, the only being in his life he remembered showing him love.

* * *

ARTHUR FLEW UPWARD as the world below burned. He felt no fear, only exhilaration. Up, and still up, faster and faster, until an azure horizon bloomed before him. He surged through dark clouds, marvelling at their wisp-like substance as the heavens embraced him.

The horizon's mighty curved line stretched above a vast globe surmounted by endless night. He had become comfortably numb, immune to the incredible speeds buffeting his body. To his surprise, he could move his neck and view the moon, daughter of Aeon, looming above him, a thousand times more brilliant than he'd ever seen her.

The blue band shrank to a tiny strip of light as he ascended into the dark heavens. Below, the world was a great orb covered by wondrous swathes of brown, green, and white. His ascent slowed, allowing him to look ahead as the brightest star emerged from the void and moved inexorably toward him.

The heavenly body swelled and took form. At first, Arthur could not discern the gathering shape, but it soon resolved into the unmistakable figure of a woman. The glow surrounding her transformed itself into a billowing white dress that accentuated her feminine contours. What had begun as a blank oval above her shoulders took on the most beautiful countenance, lovely beyond description, yet foreboding. Her alabaster skin was flawless, but unlike a statue, life radiated from her presence. She had a blind wrapped around her head, covering eyes that Arthur longed to gaze upon. But he knew if he did so, it would drive him mad.

She approached with a corona of fire illuminating the blackness of the starry abyss surrounding her. Arthur's will dissolved before such perfection.

'Am I dead?' he asked, though his lips did not move.

You have not yet lived, child. The reply came from within him.

The lady frowned in disapproval, filling his soul with misery. *You, unwanted by the universe, lowest of all—you will serve me now.*

The command filled him with both hope and dread.

'Can I ever be forgiven?' he asked.

His answer came in the form of icy pain flooding his lungs. Arthur gasped and tore at his neck, unable to breathe the airless night invading his body.

CHAPTER TWO

The boy turned the spit roast, his skin scoured red from the constant heat. He looked around from his squatting position beside the fire and noticed the fat cook still slept off the wine he'd been consuming all afternoon. Although he risked a flogging, the child ripped strips of meat from the carcass, then wolfed down the hot scraps with relish, ignoring his burnt fingers. This was the way he'd survived longer than the other children—a shadow of a life, always out of sight and mind. Such was the lot of a slave. To share was to starve, and to be weak was a death sentence, so he grew strong instead.

* * *

CHOKING, Arthur woke to a red dawn. Merciless waves of agony surged up and down his body, while his stomach churned with writhing serpents. He forced his eyes open, only to be greeted by a vision of smoke and ruin. A tortuous throbbing in his fingertips demanded his attention, so he looked down and found them blackened above a smoking ember. With a cry, he pulled them aside.

Around him lay the wretched bodies of settlers, burned beyond recognition, with only patches of raw, red flesh clinging to their bloated carcasses. His clansmen had hewn others where they stood, their blood running in thick rivulets through the dirt. He saw no sign of the old man or the girl. Whether they'd escaped, he knew not. This place was a tomb.

Arthur drifted through a waking dream until the smoking ruins greeted him again. When he shifted his legs, pain flared in them with a ferocity that left him as breathless as a fish out of water. Fearing that hostile survivors might hear his laboured groans, he bit his arm, then inspected the mess of mangled flesh and leather that had been his torso. He stifled a whimper as he lifted himself into a crawling position and dragged himself forward. But after several minutes of shuffling through the scattered wreckage, he'd moved only a dozen feet.

The morning breeze blew through the settlement's remains, bringing with it the sickly stench of burning flesh. Arthur retched up a mixture of blood and mucus. The evil smell triggered his most primal urge to flee, and he staggered upright while cupping the wound in his side with his right hand. It took every ounce of strength he'd earned from years of struggle. His vision swam.

Following a terrifying moment when he thought he would pass out, the view of his surroundings firmed. What had been a dark shadow earlier was now a visible tree line to the south. Although the wood offered respite from the surrounding charnel house and the attention of survivors, it also put him beyond the aid of any returning clansmen. He could stay and risk torture or find shelter elsewhere. If he lost consciousness, the beasts of the wild would feast upon his helpless flesh.

His parched throat made him delay the decision. Arthur staggered into the heart of the slaughtered village, where he found Amicus's corpse lying across the opening of the main well. When the girl had injured him, the horse must have charged into the deadly trap in sheer panic. Blood dripped from the stallion's flanks into the shaft. Resolved to die rather than drink here, he wiped his brimming eyes with a trembling hand, blackened by soot. All he could hear was Amicus's life essence hitting the water below. No voices called, and no birdsong permeated the air, as if nature abhorred the evil afflicted upon this place.

He endured many a grim spectacle as he picked his way over shattered beams and twisted filth. At the edge of the village facing the wood, he resolved that anything would be better than to stay with vengeful ghosts, so continued toward the gloom of the thicket. The stench of butchery lessened, and he took in a great lungful of fresh air, but this small mercy was short-lived because his thirst had become a torment greater than the pain. He searched in the hollows for moisture, but the undergrowth slowed his movements and drained his exhausted reserves, leaving him utterly spent.

Arthur rested against the trunk of a huge oak and closed his eyes. A breeze stirred the leaves above him. How he longed to collapse there, listening to that soft sound, waiting for the inevitable, but something within him refused to give in to the embrace of oblivion.

The sun peeped through the canopy and touched his face. He sobbed, not knowing if he could endure much more, but the compulsion to live forced him to search for water again, so he rummaged through the fallen foliage beside the oak, uncovering a small pool at its base. A shudder of elation swept through him. With desperate speed, he plunged his head into its stagnant surface and drank deeply, before spewing back the rancid liquid. Arthur reached in and felt a slimy, bony texture. He lifted the grisly thing from the depths and choked with disgust at the skull of the rotting rodent.

Dismayed, he threw the carcass away and drank another

mouthful, forcing himself to retain the vile stuff. Regardless of its putrid nature, the water ran down his throat like the finest wine, returning a small measure of strength to his battered body.

After one final swig, he pressed on, but soon lost track of his direction, confused by blood loss and the impenetrable wall of foliage. The world became a green blur. His mind wandered into a semi-conscious state while he battled the lulling beauty of this ancient place. Light danced through the patchwork of dark hollows surrounding him in a hypnotic display, and then coalesced into a woman in white ahead. He followed her, wondering if his mother had come to take him from a hated life.

She led the way, her pace quickening until she drew further and further ahead. He called out, but she did not turn. Then she vanished, and with her leaving, so his hope faded. He dropped to his knees. The last thing Arthur remembered was the green wall parting, and the light of the world returning once more.

CHAPTER THREE

Arthur could feel his life ebbing. It would soon end. His long vigil of pain through the night had passed, and now the numbing embrace of oblivion neared. A faraway place called to him, and with every passing moment, the pure note of its song grew stronger, urging him to let go of the mortal plane and follow. He somehow knew that once he accepted that calling, there could be no return. What started as a gentle pull became irresistible.

The bandit prepared to leave and used the last of his strength to shift his head and take one final look at the world. Through his dim awareness, he noticed the looming form of a cart trundling toward him. Although the possibility of aid was welcome, the wagon would soon roll over his prone body. He tried to alert the driver, but only a hollow gasp emerged from his throat.

The rickety vehicle meandered from one side of the road to the other. Its single occupant, an elderly man with a shaved head and a thick grey beard, lounged in the driver's seat, his outstretched legs resting on the rump of the nearest mount. Unaware of Arthur, he snored in loud contrast to the morning birdsong. The two old nags harnessed to the transport, one a speckled grey and the other pure white with a black mane, appeared to have only a few more trips left in them.

Although the driver remained oblivious of their precarious progress, the cart avoided the many potholes dotting the Roman paving, well overdue for repairs. When the hoofs of the animals came within a few feet, Arthur could only close his eyes and thank the gods that his suffering would be at an end. But his prayers went unanswered, for the wagon creaked to a stop. Having decided his skull had stayed intact long enough, he peeked once more and found a stationary equine leg, only inches away from his head.

The sudden jerk must have stirred the driver from his doze, because Arthur heard a loud snort.

'What's up, girls?' a sleepy voice asked. Through the fog of his awareness, the voice sounded hollow, as if spoken from a great distance. Two booted feet hopped from the pedestal onto the road and strode to the front of the wagon.

'Hmm. Well, now, ladies, have you been running folk down again?' the elderly man asked. Again, his companions chose not to answer, although one nickered at the accusation.

Arthur grunted in pain as someone turned him onto his back. A striking, grey-eyed gaze regarded him over bushy eyebrows. Soon after, two rough fingers pressed against the side of his throat.

'You should be dead, my friend,' the carter said. His frown deepened as he noticed something else. He placed a palm against the young man's forehead, and the strangest sensation came over Arthur, as another presence touched his mind. All the while, those nearly translucent eyes regarded him. The stranger's brow furrowed. 'What's this?' he muttered, like he'd encountered something unexpected. The driver stared at him as if pondering. '*Codladh*,'[1] he said in Gaelic. As

14

THE DARK ISLES CHRONICLE BOOK 1

he did, Arthur's mind drifted toward oblivion. 'I think you're better off out of it for a...'

* * *

ARTHUR EXPERIENCED no emotion as he looked down upon the old man tending to his broken shell. In fact, he felt nothing at all—no pain, no guilt, and no sorrow. He floated pleasantly above, a mere spectator as the carter lifted his leather jerkin to examine the three bloody puncture wounds in his side.

'Not the most challenging diagnosis,' he commented before reaching into a satchel and taking out a cloth bag. He unrolled it on the gravel next to his patient, revealing a neat row of implements: knives, spoons of various shapes, and cutting shears. Then, taking a pair of thick blades from the bag, he swiftly cut into the leather surrounding the clogged gashes. He ripped the stiff padding apart and inspected the festering flesh.

'If I didn't know better, I'd say you'd been diddling a farmer's daughter.' He winced at the three puncture marks. 'And her dad didn't approve.'

Arthur's floating consciousness thought nothing of the comment. It only felt a sense of detached curiosity upon watching the old man work.

The carter put the shears aside and held his right hand above the mangled flesh. '*Ionúin, Airmed,*' he called, raising his head to the sky. '*Le do thoil cabhrú leis.*'[2] As he spoke, his eyes rolled back, then returned with irises transformed from pale grey to a deep crimson. He lifted his outstretched hand over Arthur's bare torso, and a cleansing blue fire burst from his palm, forcing black filth to bubble from the weeping sores while cauterising them. When he'd sealed the wounds, he opened his patient's jaw, then parted his own mouth a few inches above it. '*Fuil,*'[3] he commanded.

Great gouts of blood spewed into the young man's mouth. Light steam rose from the flowing lifeline into the cool morning air as it transferred from one man to the other, without a single drop missing its mark. The torrent ceased once the last precious drops had passed between them, and the carter's gaze returned to their previous grey hue. He curled his hand into a fist and beat it hard upon the younger man's chest. With each blow, Arthur was yanked back into his waiting host.

CHAPTER FOUR

Arthur knew he must be dead. Clouds floated across a perfect blue sky, and his pain had faded, as had the sickening stench of death. These pleasant sensations came as a surprise, for only the just earned entry into Annwn.

Finding he could turn his head without difficulty, he noticed the grain sack beside him. The mundane sight prompted him to wonder why the spirits needed food. Even more curious was the unmistakable sound of one of his ethereal hosts breaking wind.

'They'll be no cabbage for you tonight, Fionna!' an aged voice said in a lighthearted tone. The nicker of a horse answered the observation. 'Agreed, my sweet Aina. 'Tis a fearsome waft she inflicts upon us.'

Satisfied that he was no longer in the blessed lands, Arthur sat up with much effort and looked on a long straight road passing into familiar rolling hills. Someone had placed him in a cart. Panic flared within him at the thought of being captured by local militia, having secretly witnessed the fate of those exposed to the wrath of Roman justice. All had been big men. All had begged for their mothers before the end.

17

He thought it odd that his limbs remained unbound, leaving no obvious impediment to his escape. Looking toward the driver, he could see the back of the lone man steering the vehicle. Perhaps the carter had learned of the attack, found him nearby, and tended to his wounds in promise of a hefty reward. The fool was no soldier, for none would turn their back on a clansman so.

Did he see the branding? Arthur wondered, inspecting his chest. The telltale scar would give him away for certain. Although the old man had removed his jerkin, his blood-stained undershirt covered his upper torso. Still, the stranger could've lifted his garment and glimpsed the mark. A linen gauze bound his stomach. He fingered the wound expecting pain, but to his amazement, he barely felt anything. A strange smell emanated from the dressing, sweet with the distinctive aroma of vinegar.

'Don't fiddle with it,' the driver said without turning.

Unnerved, Arthur went to leap from the rear of the wagon, but his weakened limbs didn't respond, and he flopped out the back. The hard landing knocked the wind out of him.

The cart stopped, then came the sound of approaching footsteps. 'Hmm. You've a real desire for that road, don't you, my stupid friend?'

Arthur lay prostrate, panting and spitting dust. The pair of boots beside him looked patched and well worn. He flipped onto his back and squinted into the sunlight. Shading his vision, he got a glimpse of the older man staring at him with a twinkle of mild amusement in his disconcerting grey eyes. He'd never met anyone who possessed the unusual colour, but he had heard such folk were evil fay.

'You aren't the brightest star in the sky, are you, boy?' He placed his hands on his hips. 'Had I known you loved eating dirt so much, I'd have left you the first time.'

There was something familiar about him that Arthur could not quite place, other than the fleeting vision of watching himself die while the carter sat beside him.

'Bollocks!' he replied and spat out more muck.

'Yes, I'm sure that's where your brains reside, lad. Now, are you getting off your arse or not?' The driver offered his hand. Arthur glared at the gesture. 'It's up to you,' he added with a seriousness his earlier jovial ridicule had lacked.

Too weak to argue, Arthur took the older man's hand. The carter lifted him, then grasped him by the waist, allowing his reluctant passenger to place an arm around his shoulder for support. Instead of returning him to the rear of the wagon, the driver aided him to the driver's pedestal and hefted him on board with surprising strength. He then retrieved his satchel and climbed on himself.

'Can you sit up?' he asked.

Determined to show he was not helpless, Arthur pushed himself upright with much discomfort. He wobbled like a drunkard for a moment, his head swimming.

'That'll do,' the carter observed and tapped the reins to set them trundling forward once more.

* * *

'How long have I been unconscious?' Arthur asked, curiosity overcoming his distrust.

'Nearly two days.'

'Two days? But I…'

The carter shot him a grey-eyed glance. 'You—were all but dead.'

Arthur reached down, the memory of the pitchfork plunging into his belly flooding into his head. 'My stomach.'

'Aye, that was quite a wound, lad. I've seen healthier looking things stuck to the bottom of me boots,' the driver replied, fixing him with another disconcerting look. 'Someone took a serious dislike to you.'

He did not respond.

The old man broke the awkward silence, asking, 'What's your name?'

'Boden,' he lied.

The carter shrugged.

'Where are we?'

'About ten miles north of Ratae.'

The prospect of being so far away from the ravaged settlement and any vengeful survivors was a welcome one.

'Where are you going?'

'Derventio, then Ardotalia.'

Arthur hid his alarm. Both Derventio and Ardotalia were fort towns. It would only take an accusation for the locals to haul him in front of the local court. A simple examination of his body would uncover the crude bird mark. Certain death would follow.

The day of his branding had been the worst of his life. Of the three boys scarred that night, he'd been the only one to survive the following infection. Despite the high mortality rate, the cruel ritual ensured they recruited only the strongest. The surviving few were bonded to their masters for life because the Raven mark cursed its bearer to be hated by the populace and subjected to a merciless end if caught.

Had the old man spotted the brand? The dilemma gnawed at his guts. The fool had done nothing but mock him since they met, yet he detected no guile in him. True, he might risk trying to kill him and steal the cart, but the wily old goat was stronger than he looked, and in his weakened state, Arthur doubted the outcome. He decided to bide his time, for now.

'What did you say your name was?' he asked, deciding an air of civility might lower the other man's guard.

'I didn't.'

Irritated by the rude reply, Arthur pressed him further. 'Well, what is it?'

'What is what?'

'Your name!'

The carter stared back. 'You can call me Amadán.'[1] He did not recall hearing the old-fashioned name before.

Hours into their journey, the sun fell over the horizon, trailing a brilliant magenta display amongst the darkening clouds. Amadán steered them off the road and into an abandoned field as the shadows lengthened. They stopped beside the crumbling remains of a small roadside shrine. The worn face of a female deity wearing a headdress filled with snakes adorned the stone block. She would soon lose her battle against the elements and fade into obscurity forever.

'Well, I'll be—that's an old one,' the carter noticed with a smile. He stepped onto the flower-filled meadow and approached the shrine at a measured pace then picked a bunch of daisies and lay them before the effigy.

'Why bother? The old gods are dead,' Arthur said, unable to resist provoking the sanctimonious fool. Something about the fellow's casual mockery made him bristle with anger.

To his further annoyance, however, Amadán smirked at the barbed observation. 'Is that right?' He strode back to the cart and untethered the horses. '*Baois óige*,'[2] he added to the white nag, patting her neck. She nickered her approval.

He unloaded blankets and camp gear with a practised manner while Arthur watched, still stewing with indignation. The old man appeared unconcerned.

After building a small fire, Amadán laid out his bedding and tossed his sullen guest a threadbare blanket and patched woollen tunic. Without comment, he settled for the night and was snoring within minutes.

The young bandit looked down at the tattered, bloody

shirt clinging to his torso and conceded he must accept the miserly gifts. He stepped off the cart with difficulty, then hobbled to the fire, where he threw the bedding and new attire in a heap. In truth, he was exhausted, but he could not sleep yet, having resolved to kill the carter before dawn.

* * *

ARTHUR LAY for more than an hour, staring at the sky while doing his best not to dwell upon the strange disaster that had befallen him over the past few days. No matter. Soon, he'd return to his comrades with some booty to compensate for his absence. Although he felt a passing regret at the prospect of cutting the driver's throat, he'd learned many years ago that trust was a fatal flaw.

His resolve firmed as the regular breathing of the old man deepened. Arthur rose silently and paced across the makeshift camp to the thick branch he'd spotted beside the fire. Though not elegant, it would make a perfect murder weapon. Wincing, he reached down and grasped it before testing its weight. Satisfied it could crack a man's skull, he crept beside his intended victim. Amadán faced the shadows, which was good because Arthur was oddly reluctant to club him in the face.

He raised the branch above his head and prepared to strike, grimacing with anticipation. This time, he would not hesitate.

'I wouldn't do that if I were you,' Amadán said, yawning.

Arthur shrugged off the bizarre command and swung hard, but immediately staggered backward as a blinding flash of pain burst across the bridge of his nose.

'Argh!' he cried, eyes filling with tears. The blow had somehow landed upon himself.

One of the horses whinnied at his evident distress.

Infuriated, he charged at the prostrate man, intending to kick him to death, but just as he was about to lash out, he found himself running in the opposite direction. He stopped dead and fell to his knees, panting.

'Fuck!' he roared in impotent rage.

'I'd rather not,' Amadán said, sounding more annoyed than afraid. 'Now—do you think I might get some bloody sleep tonight!'

Arthur cupped his pounding nose and staggered back into the light of the camp, astonished by the unseen force thwarting his attacks. 'How did you do that?'

'I used my brains instead of my fists.'

'Magic?' the young warrior asked, agog. He'd heard stories of a time when men performed uncanny acts with their minds alone but had believed such tall tales to be nothing more than myth.

The carter grunted. 'Some call it that. It is what it is—a power given to some by the gods.'

'Why did you save me?' Arthur shouted. The idea of being indebted to this mocking old goat was unbearable.

The carter turned to face him. 'Why do you find that such a strange thing?'

'I'm not going to Derventio!'

'That's up to you.'

Arthur blinked in confusion. 'I'm not a prisoner?'

'Should you be?'

The uncomfortable response gave him pause. 'Why haven't you asked what happened to me?' The question had bothered him all day.

Amadán turned away once more. 'I know enough to know I don't want to know more.'

'What does that mean?'

'It means I don't appreciate being woken in the middle of the night while you run around like a howling banshee!'

The grey nag snorted in agreement at her master's rebuke.

'Are you going to sleep or not?' the old man asked.

At his words, a wave of sheer exhaustion washed over him.

'Oh, and add more wood to the fire. It's getting chilly,' Amadán added, before he could reply with a suitable insult.

Arthur shuffled back to his bedding and flopped down, his mind numbed by fatigue.

'Boy?' the old man said just as sleep had begun to creep over him.

'What?' he muttered.

'You forgot the wood.'

CHAPTER FIVE

Arthur slept well that night and awoke feeling refreshed. He opened his eyes to find that dawn had long gone, with the sun riding high in a clear blue sky. A gentle breeze blew through the abandoned field. Sitting up, he noticed Amadán had already risen and was preparing the horses to leave. He waited for the tirade of accusations sure to greet him.

'Morning,' the old man said cheerfully instead. 'There's some bread and cheese in the sack beside my seat.' He popped a carrot into the mouth of the grey horse, who swished her tail appreciatively. 'You can either come with me and eat, or stay here and run around, howling at the sun.'

Arthur felt ravenous. Until now, he'd not considered how he would keep himself alive in his weakened state. With his plan of murdering the carter no longer an option, the possibility of starving to death in the middle of nowhere arose as a likely outcome. He baulked at the prospect of abandoning his only source of sustenance, but the risk of the old man betraying him for money was real. Why else would Amadán so casually dismiss the attempt on his life? Groaning with pain, the young warrior rose and changed into the ill-fitting tunic.

After pulling on his boots, he strode to the cart and rummaged through the cloth bag for food. He ripped off chunks of bread and shoved the pieces into his mouth. The taste of soft dough was enough to make him want to cry with pleasure. He further contemplated his dilemma while he chewed, eyeing the carter with suspicion. The man pottered around, paying no heed to his hostile guest.

There was something odd about him, and not just his fey ways with magic. He didn't have the bearing of a simple tradesman, and his fearless wit betrayed a more complex character than his humble appearance would suggest. Whether that made him trustworthy was for the gods to decide.

He finished the food in several large mouthfuls, then reluctantly rolled up his blanket and placed it in the back of the cart before sitting on the driver's pedestal. Without comment, the old man sat beside him, imparted an approving wink at a sullen Arthur, and then nudged the horses.

* * *

THE JOURNEY to Derventio was uneventful, and just as the sun started to wane, they spotted the river Derbentione and the imposing fort on its far bank. On the near side, a vicus lay huddled beside its military neighbour, supplying the garrison with goods and services in return for protection. An ancient wooden bridge connected the two, probably older than the settlement itself.

Arthur knew little about the fort, but he recalled some veteran clan warriors speak of it being on the front line of the occupation three hundred years ago. It marked the boundary between the quelled tribes of the Coritani and the fierce Brigantes to the north. Now, the fortification was at the centre of the province the Romans called Flavia Caesariendis and served as a tenuous reminder of who ruled here. The inhabitants generally regarded the militia's harsh presence as preferable to the chaos that much of the diocese endured. Few of the old network of forts remained, with only those occupying critical strategic locations still functioning. The empire had saved Derventio because of its position at the heart of Britannia.

They emerged from the last valley of their journey and came upon a group of plebs toiling in the wheat fields surrounding the settlement. It was uncommon these days to see free citizens supporting themselves in this way. Most of the food produced in the diocese came from a patchwork of vast estates, ran by slaves on behalf of rich patrons who'd never set foot on British soil.

As the cart trundled past one ploughing team, a voice called out, 'May the blessings of Danu be upon you— *Tighearna Myrddin!*'[1]

Amadán raised a friendly hand to the elderly farmer and grinned at Arthur as if his morose companion would share his enthusiasm. The greeting had partly been delivered in Celtic which grated on the young man's ears, as he'd never learned the native tongue of his ancestors.

They continued down the narrow roads of a bustling village, with people going about their daily routines. Derventio was an unattractive mess of contrasting architecture. Thatched hovels sat cheek by jowl against brick supply buildings. The local population paid the newcomers scant attention, engrossed with the many tasks of the working day. Muddied infants ran amongst their elders, chasing each other with sticks and adding a counterpoint of childish giggles to the sounds of hammering and scraping. When they entered the centre where a great forge bellowed smoke, Amadán exchanged welcoming comments with an ageing blacksmith who pounded the mailed rings of an auxiliary's *lorica hamata*.

They headed toward the river's edge and a small freshwater wooden dock, where Arthur expected Amadán would sell his goods before either leaving him to his own devices or claiming the reward on his head. If the latter, he vowed to slit the old fool's throat before the soldiers dragged him to his own bleak fate.

The air here was thick with flies and the stench of the nearby tannery situated away from the domiciles of the locals. Teams of children and a few old maids stamped on the skins immersed in human and animal urine. Following several hours of this back-breaking work, the remaining hair clinging to the skins could be easily scraped off. Others pounded dung into the leather to soften it further. He guessed they would transport the finished hides up river to the seaport of Deva.

To Arthur's alarm, however, the cart did not stop at the dock, but carried on toward the bridge and the waiting fort.

'We're not stopping at the docks?' he asked, suppressing his concern.

'Not with this cargo—too valuable,' the old man replied, which gave him no comfort as he had seen nothing of obvious worth amongst the grain sacks. That was, other than himself.

Indecision paralysed him, and his senses prickled with alarm as the two bored-looking auxiliaries guarding the double-tower gatehouse of the fort eyed them. If he were to run now, it would surely provoke their curiosity. He remained as still as a corpse as they rolled onto the bridge. A moment later, he reached the panicked realisation that his opportunity to flee had passed. His fate rested in the hands of a stranger he'd tried to murder the previous night. Again, he berated himself for his suicidal madness, but a darker part of him was relieved his days of hiding in constant shadow were over. At last he would find a measure of peace—even if it came at the price of pain.

The fort itself was a perfect rectangle, with white-washed walls twice the height of a tall warrior. This fortification was smaller than others he'd seen at a distance and lacked the more elaborate defences available to the empire, such as the massive ballistae that could shoot a bolt large enough to cleave a man in two. Above the central iron cataracta gate sat the effigy of the Aquila. The great eagle glared down at Arthur with its gold-painted wings spread wide, surrounded by laurels. Stamped upon its breast was the phrase every member of the clan feared: SPQR. As they drew closer, however, he saw cracks on the painted surface of the ancient symbol, giving it a pockmarked appearance.

They stopped a respectful distance from the gate. One of the guards, a big, unshaven man with food stains down the front of his crimson tunic, swaggered over with his chest thrust out, then stood with his legs wide apart. Arthur had the urge to kick him right there.

'Halt,' the soldier mumbled, while removing his battered *galea* helmet and scratching his scalp.

'We already did,' Arthur could not help but comment aloud.

'You what?' the guardsman snapped, stiffening.

'Greetings, legionary,' Amadán intervened, hailing the soldier with a flattering choice of words. In truth, this garrison was little more than a local police force.

The other man scowled at Arthur before continuing. 'Business?' he asked, mollified for now.

'I bring grain from Ratae and wish to meet Caeso Aetius.'

Despite the spark of interest on the soldier's bristled face, he sneered. 'Even if he wasn't nailed to a tree by now, I'd not let a vagabond and his bum boy see the commander.'

L.K. ALAN

Arthur shifted to step down, intending to confront the rude bastard, but a sharp glance from Amadán stopped him.

'He will want to see me,' the old man insisted, his tone cooler. 'And what do you mean by *nailed to a tree*?'

'None of your fucking business is what I mean,' came the helpful reply.

Amadán seemed unperturbed. Smiling, he answered, 'I think you'll find it is—my friend.'

Regardless of the less than cordial exchange, Arthur's anger faded back to fear. He had no doubt what the meeting request was about, but he took comfort in the idea of killing this arse hole before the end. As he prepared to snatch the soldier's sheathed gladius from his tarnished belt, however, the guard's companion, an older man with a less shoddy appearance, hurried over, eyes wide with alarm.

'Listen, you old goat,' the big guard began, poking Amadán in the chest, but his comrade interrupted and urgently whispered into his ear.

Realisation dawned over the flushed militia man, and he retracted his finger as if he had placed it on a hot stove. 'M-my apologies, Lord Merlin. I d-did not know...' he stammered.

'No bother,' replied the 'old goat' with a wicked twinkle in his eye.

The guard looked relieved.

'I find goats to be pleasant creatures,' the carter added.

The guard's neck turned a deeper shade of crimson. 'I did not mean to offend.'

'Lord,' the man formerly known as Amadán finished for him.

'Sorry—lord.'

Arthur listened in stunned disbelief.

'Like I said, it's no bother,' the man no longer called

Amadán replied, 'but I'd suggest you have a shave before referring to others as goats.'

'Erm, sorry. My thanks for the advice, erm, lord,' the guard said, looking like he wanted to crawl under the bridge.

Arthur struggled to understand why these men believed they were speaking to a mythical figure, then recollections of the previous night's encounter and his own miraculous recovery hit home. His guts churned at the realisation.

The guards opened the gate with an undignified amount of haste and allowed the unassuming cart to trundle forward again.

'And if you need any instruction on grooming, my bum boy here has legs smoother than an Egyptian whore!' the so-called Merlin added with a parting wave of his hand.

At this, the fat auxiliary gave Arthur a speculative look, much to his disquiet.

'That was for waking me last night,' the old man muttered from the corner of his mouth.

CHAPTER SIX

Talorc, King of the Picts watched as the reptilian creature drove the rusty nail into his father's wrist, pinning his frail body to the filthy wooden crucifix. The old ruler groaned in pain, the sound no more than a hoarse whisper, as a crimson gush erupted from the wound.

His son took another swig of the good Roman wine, then placed the goblet back onto a silver tray held by a female southern slave. The dim light within the cavernous viewing chamber highlighted the swirling blue eagle tattoo on his thick bicep. The memory of his sire inking that ancient symbol of their line into his skin, dulled his cheerful mood.

'Fuck tradition,' he told the girl. Wisely, she averted her eyes and gazed impassively at the grisly spectacle instead. Only a single trickle of sweat running down her bare chest betrayed her fear. He liked that.

Talorc turned to the cowled figure of the emissary beside him, as it watched the lizard beast continue to hammer. 'You assure me he is already dead?'

'His spirit has passed through the veil to us, yesss.' The

creature shuddered, the sound reminiscent of a bird rustling its wings. 'But his flesh remains in this realm.'

'And his shade thinks it still lives?' The king asked, suspicious that what he saw was an illusion.

'Yes–to it–the pain is real.'

The answer satisfied him. 'Do you think the wretch suffers as much as the first time?'

'I assure you, he suffers exquisitely, my lord,' came the rasping reply.

'Still,' the young ruler muttered, 'perhaps your creature could torment the old bastard more often. How about twice a day?'

As was its custom when declining a request, the dark prince's envoy did not answer.

Upon completing its gruesome task, the reptilian imp sneered in the face of its victim, then loped away on bent legs toward a passage behind the execution platform.

'Tell me, servant of the nether world, did I select a fitting punishment?' Talorc asked, suppressing his anger at the envoy's refusal.

'Fitting, my lord?'

'Did I pick an end worthy of your world?' He enjoyed the way the slave flinched as he reached for the goblet once more.

'Truly, sire.'

He could never be sure if the envoy lied, finding its servile demeanour irritating.

'I spent weeks thinking of a way to reward his kindness but couldn't decide. Then it came to me, the thing he hated even more than his son. Do you know what that was, creature?'

'Enlighten me, lord.' The emissary's countenance was so alien that it was impossible to discern whether he'd heard a note of impatience in its sibilant whisper.

The young king rolled the goblet in his palm while

restraining the urge to rebuke the demon. 'He hated the empire more than anything—spent every day of his miserable life whining about the Romans.'

The creature ignored the comment.

'So, the Roman way it was!' Talorc raised the cup in a mock toast to his suffering elder.

His father peered back through hate-filled eyes, then puffed out his cheeks as if struggling to speak.

'Go on, old man! Call me a wee useless shite. I dare your arse!' Talorc roared, throwing the goblet at the splayed figure. The cup hit the old king in the chest, then clattered onto the cave floor, where its contents mixed with the congealing blood at the base of the stake.

The burst of violence caused the slave girl to step away, the silver tray slipping from her grasp and clattering to the ground. She gaped in horror at the mistake and pressed trembling fingers to her mouth.

Talorc switched his attention to the woman, smiling, even as her fear aroused him.

'Would you like to join him, whore?' he asked, stepping toward her. He ran a calloused hand down her cheek. 'Hmm?' The caress ended in a sharp slap.

'No, my lord,' she whimpered, flushing an angry red.

'Or perhaps it would amuse me to watch the snake imp hump you.'

'Please...' she sobbed.

He shoved her away, sending her skidding along the floor, where she remained, paralysed with terror. Talorc's groin stirred further. With his anger sated, the king turned to resume his conversation with the envoy. It met his gaze through a polished black ebony mask, resembling a smirking cherub. The impenetrable facade reflected his own handsome features, framed by the great golden torque of Abergairn around his neck, an ancient birthright of his family from times immemorial.

'Have you any word on the forces your master will lend us for the coming campaign?'

It gave the same evasive answer as always: 'Our legions will be as the stars.'

'I count swords—not stars!' the king snapped. 'I can raise six thousand, but that won't be enough to breach the wall! You must match this number at least.'

'Patience, my lord. He shall bring much to our endeavour.' The envoy's robe undulated as it spoke.

'Smoke and shadows!' Talorc scoffed. 'I value strong arms and hard steel. Tell him that!'

The flawless surface of the child mask contorted into a pout. 'You can tell him yourself, mighty king.'

Talorc found himself discomforted by a sudden tightening of his throat. 'He comes himself?'

The mask became a smirk once more. 'My master comes to your aid.'

The king rubbed a pensive hand over his thick black beard, unsure what to make of this news. There was much afoot and little certainty. The dark prince would prove a formidable general, and yet...

'What of Merlin? He has caused mischief to the fortunes of my people. I want him up there.' He pointed to his weeping father. 'The pair of old turds can keep each other company.'

'As do we, sire, but capturing the drui is not a simple matter. We must show guile to ensnare him.'

'What do you speak of? I am in no mood for riddles today.'

Its robe shimmered, turning a deep purple before settling back to black.

'There are ways to crush the soul of one such as he... with great sacrifice.'

The king grunted in distaste, knowing where this conversation led. Growing tired of such matters of state, he eyed the supple legs of the slave. They were a good pair. Only the tattooed designs of the Brigantes marred her left thigh.

'My master has a request,' the emissary hissed.

Talorc sighed. 'What is it?' he asked, knowing what the 'request' would be.

'We need more offerings. Both to further aid your cause and to destroy the Drui.'

'More!' Talorc snapped, the colour rising on his cheeks. 'First, you ask for dogs, then horses—and now we've slit the throats of every slave from here to Aberardour! I've barely enough hands to run my own palace!' He crossed his arms. 'There are no more lives to give!' The impulse to strike the mocking grin off the visage before him grew. 'Your master can be displeased as he likes, but I can't produce blood from stone.'

The envoy's robe shimmered purple again. 'We have whole realms where men are rendered as lifeless as stone, yet they experience each agony as we harvest their blood for an eternity.' It delivered the statement as coldly as death on a winter's day.

Talorc found his anger checked by a finger of dread running down his spine.

It did not speak while the image sank in. When Talorc raised no further objection, the approving smile upon the creature's mask broadened. 'Fear not, great king. He merely asks for the lives of your blind and crippled.'

The king's eyes bulged. 'Merely, you say! Why such wretches?'

'To forge a bridge between worlds that will support a great host requires much—even for my master,' it hissed. 'Such an offering would attract the most powerful of our underworld allies to join your cause.'

Talorc rubbed his furrowed brow, exasperated by the constant demands. In the past six months, he'd suppressed two revolts by clans still loyal to his father. And the excessive tributes demanded by his dark allies had only fanned the flames of sedition, requiring him to make increasingly extravagant promises of war spoils to keep the clan chiefs loyal. Fulfilling those vows, and so avoiding the fate of his predecessor, called for nothing less than total victory. 'Just the blind and the crippled, you say?'

'Yes, my lord.'

'And if I agree, your prince will give me knowledge of the force he raises?' he pressed. 'My clan generals need assurances.'

'He will—and more. The offering will be sufficient to free our legions from the shadow lands.'

'Hmm, good. Finally!' Talorc exclaimed with relief. 'So, can your master conjure this army into the lands of the empire?' The idea that he could summon warriors at the rear of the enemy was tantalising.

To his disappointment, the thing shook its head. 'No. The crossing must be forged close to the source of sacrifice. It must be in your lands.'

Talorc frowned. To get a force of a dozen, a few hundred even, across the wall without notice would not be difficult. They had already done so for nether scouts and saboteurs. 'We cannot slip such a large army past the wall unnoticed. Even now the lazy bastards are garrisoned and half asleep.'

'Then we will support your assault as you progress south,' it said. If the prospect of his people attacking the most extensive fortification in the whole of the Isles bothered the emissary, it did not show it.

'Very well. Is that all?' Talorc said, eyeing the slave.

'We have one final requirement,' it replied. The lifeless sockets of the cherub's gaze burrowed into his own.

The envoy had not uttered the word 'final' since it had made the pledge of shadow amongst the great Ring of Brodgar nine moons ago.

'Speak, for I grow weary of your presence,' he said between clenched teeth, although inwardly, it relieved him this would be the last.

'The offering must come from your own bloodline.'

'My own?' His mind raced with the implication. 'You mean my family?'

The mask shuddered as a thick black tongue emerged from beneath the hood and licked the cherub's lips. 'Yeesss.'

In spite of his skin crawling at the unnatural display, Talorc considered which fitting candidate would cost him the least politically. There was no one, for the great purge of the past year had left no rival to the throne. Eventually, he reached a disturbing conclusion.

'My mother?' he asked in a near whisper. Years ago, when he'd been young, his father had blinded the dowager queen and left her with the mind of a child following a drunken rage. The last he'd seen her, she'd still thought him a boy.

Talorc slumped into a chair, thirsty for more wine. 'Your master asks too much.'

'The queen is old and suffers greatly, lord.' The nether creature's words of comfort were delivered without emotion. 'And the victory you seek requires much power... much, indeed.'

'Is there another way?' The king asked, fleetingly recalling a sun-filled morning upon the shore of a great loch, where he'd picked wildflowers with a tall woman. They'd known happiness together that day. 'What of my father?' Talorc asked.

'Even a king cannot give what is already given, my lord.'

Again, the king suppressed the growing urge to grab the thing by its neck and squeeze.

'Our enterprise risks the gods themselves intervening. We need surety, as do your generals,' the emissary pressed. 'With this… personal gesture, we can raise a mighty army indeed, one that will bring great misery to your foes, both Briton and Roman alike. With it, your victory is assured.'

Talorc imagined the glorious slaughter to follow. His clans would sweep all those before them, freeing the peoples from the tyranny of the empire and returning the land to glory. At the vanguard of this triumphant force would be himself, the great war chief, conqueror of Albion.

'It shall be done,' he whispered.

CHAPTER SEVEN

'They called you Merlin?' Arthur asked, still stunned.

'Yup.'

'You're named after the myth?'

'Something like that,' Merlin replied distractedly, his attention on the dilapidated state of the inner fortress around them. 'The rot has truly set in,' he grumbled, tapping Fionna onward.

'Then Amadán was a lie?' He felt cheated by the old man besting his own deception.

'It was a fool's name for a fool's game—Boden.'

Arthur bridled at the old man treating him like a child. 'I'm sick of your insults.'

Merlin directed a furrowed brow toward him. 'Ignorance makes a man easy to mock. You should know your own language, boy.'

'But I was never taught!'

'Aye, that is so for too many of the young these days,'

Arthur had never been inside an imperial fort before this, as such a visit could only mean death. The interior's straight lines and ordered layout struck him. Rows of faded white barracks stood on either side of the road, but many were abandoned and covered in crude graffiti, written in a dozen different languages that he didn't recognise. The lewd intent was unmistakable, as some scrawls featured figures encumbered by huge genitalia engaged in various acts of sexual congress.

They continued along a cobbled road toward a walled compound at the centre of the fort. Oddly, there was little activity, the silence only broken by the clopping of hooves and creaking cart. While they remained alone, Arthur brooded over his prospects of escape. But the events and actions of the enigmatic man beside him at the gates had left him uncertain which course of action presented the most risk.

The storage buildings and workshops beyond the barracks were similarly devoid of people, one building having suffered unrepaired fire damage.

'*Conas an mighty tar éis titim,*'[1] Merlin muttered to himself, unimpressed.

As they approached the compound at the centre of the fort, cheering and whistling erupted from within.

'Looks like we're in time for the entertainment,' Arthur commented without enthusiasm.

A red-painted plaque above the walled compound proclaimed it as the *principia*, the headquarters of the fortification. They trundled through its northern gate and entered the inner plaza. Arthur's gut dropped at the sight of the hundred or so soldiers gathered before him, enjoying a leisurely afternoon of drinking and playing dice. Few wore their uniforms and most sat at ease, attired only in loincloths. The stink of sweat, vomit, and unwashed bodies filled the air.

A legionary standard hung on the far wall above the gathering, its crimson banner flapping in the breeze. Another Aquila eagle sat at its centre, gazing sternly upon the frivolity below.

'Great, this is all we need,' Merlin said, pulling the horses to a halt. 'Wait here. I'll find out if someone is leading this mob.' He hopped from the wagon and strode into a side building with the look of an administrative block, leaving Arthur alone to curse his poor luck.

Another wave of cheering broke out as three leather-clad handlers holding a taut pole ending in a noose dragged a strange beast by its neck onto the raised wooden platform dominating the southern half of the plaza. A second handling team followed, using the same brutal method to wrestle a similar animal. Continuous roars of approval greeted the struggling duo's entrance.

Arthur had never seen the like. Each was the size of a large dog, but reptilian in appearance. One had a bright green-scaled body, the other blue. Upon seeing each other, they exploded into a frenzy of aggression, flailing and hissing to escape their bonds. With their salivating maws agape, they glowered at each other through beady eyes burning with hatred and extended the leathery gland under their chins in a dazzling display of colour.

A reedy man holding two leather bags and wearing the tarnished breastplate of a *decanus* stepped onto the platform and edged around the straining beasts before facing the crowd.

'Any more for the green, lads?' he bellowed, shaking the bag marked with a green X, the other bag denoted with a blue X.

A scruffy audience member ambled over, his feet none too steady from booze.

'Hurry up, Chrocus, you fat tit! We haven't got all fucking day!' his thin superior berated.

The chastened private hurried his pace, then placed a few more coins in the green bag in exchange for a token issued by the *decanus*. The crowd jeered at the interruption.

'Right then, ladies!' the junior officer announced, quietening the onlookers. 'What do you reckon we warm up with a bit of local justice?'

The men roared in agreement while Arthur's blood ran cold with fear.

The old man betrayed you...

But how? This lounging mob seemed unaware of his presence, let alone ready to lynch him. Perhaps the wily old bastard had secretly signalled a sentry at the main gates, and the men had gathered after that?

When the answer came, relief flooded through him. Two soldiers entered the plaza, carrying a manacled prisoner between them. The man's head drooped with exhaustion, having experienced the unwanted attentions of his captors. He limped heavily, and bloody clumps of matted hair hung from his scalp. Arthur shuddered to think what this pathetic shadow of a man had already endured and still faced. The capacity of their Roman overlords for inventive cruelty was a common tale used to frighten Celtic children across the land.

The guards threw the prisoner onto the platform before the two beasts, just beyond the reach of their flying claws. He sagged to his knees, but they forced him to stand and face the crowd. The strange creatures continued to struggle against their restraints, oblivious to the human between them and more intent on getting at each other.

Having collected the last bets, the *decanus* placed the two coin bags on the floor and removed a worn papyrus scroll from under his breastplate.

'*By the authority invested in me by the divine first citizen, the most—*' he read from the parchment in a booming voice. One man blew a raspberry in response, much to the delight of the other spectators. The master of ceremony gave his comrades a stern, albeit half-hearted stare of disapproval until the barrage of abuse ended. '*I hereby order this tribunal into session*

—*ex aequo et bono*.'[2] He cleared his throat then continued. '*We are gathered here today to pass judgement against the defendant…*' He peered down at the scroll. 'What's his name?' he asked in annoyance of the two guards holding the prisoner.

One handler slapped the wretch around the face. 'Speak, dog!' he roared, pulling back his head.

Arthur's breath stuck in his lungs, for he recognised Festus, whom he'd last seen massacring plebs on the fateful night of the attack. Such a fate was common for those who acted without care when out foraging or while indulging in their own private acts of plunder.

The big Epirian did not respond and spat into the face of his interrogator instead; the act of defiance earned him a punch to the gut. While he gasped for breath, the *decanus* cut away his blood-stained vest to reveal the crude image of a raven seared onto his chest. Arthur instinctively raised his hand to his own breast, realising he'd soon witness a fate that might befall him.

'*This nameless wretch has been charged with being a member of a prescribed group on this day, the twenty fifth day of September,*' the officer continued, a grin appearing on his bearded face as he warmed to the occasion. 'What's the verdict, boys?' he bellowed.

'Guilty!' roared the crowd.

The same joker who'd blown a raspberry followed the unanimous proclamation with his own 'not guilty!'—to the general amusement of all.

'You, murderer and thief, have been found guilty by this tribunal!' the *decanus* pronounced with gusto, widening his arms in a theatrical flurry. This prompted whole new levels of wine-fuelled joy in the gathered men.

Festus urinated upon the stage, not sharing their anticipation.

'I therefore sentence you to death—*executio juris non habet injuriam!*[3] the officer concluded with the ancient customary proclamation, not disguising his enthusiasm.

The two guards restraining the prisoner drew wicked-looking hatchets from their belts. More cheering followed.

'Paratus!' the decanus ordered.

Festus did not resist as his left-hand captor lifted his right arm, then poised the axe blade over his trembling flesh.

An expectant silence fell.

'Unus!' the gaunt ceremony master announced after a suitably long pause.

The guard chopped off the prostrate limb, and it flopped onto the boards. A torrent of blood spurted from the severed stump.

Festus screamed. In his agonies, he lifted his head to see the crowd, as if trying to gain one last view of the world. Then in a horrific moment, his red-rimmed gaze met Arthur's. Despite his ordeal, his comrade's eyes widened in recognition and wild hope.

'Spare me!' he screeched. 'Spare me and I will give you our leader. He is here amongst us!' Festus raised his remaining hand at a dumbstruck Arthur. 'Look! Drest is there, on the cart!' The cunning lie only drew loud derision from most spectators. But to Arthur's dismay, a burly veteran playing a dice game nearby shot him a narrow-eyed look of suspicion, then rose and strode toward the cart. Even worse, his companion followed him.

'Who the fuck are you?' the big man asked, pointing a calloused finger at Arthur.

Stunned by the turn of events, he could not respond.

'You 'erd him, maggot. Why are you 'ere?' his squat comrade added, drawing a nicked *gladius* from his belt.

Arthur glanced around for Merlin, but only saw more of the bloody drama unfold onstage. One executioner picked up Festus's dismembered limb and tossed it to the blue beast.

Enticed by the smell of fresh blood, the creature switched its attention from its opponent and devoured the arm, ripping great chunks of meat off the bone while its owner watched in tear-filled horror.

The gladius poked Arthur in the ribs none too gently. 'We asked you a question, pleb.'

'I'm, erm… I'm,' Arthur hesitated, unable to take his eyes off the ghastly spectacle.

The second guard beside Festus lifted his remaining arm while his partner steadied their ward's flagging body.

'I'm with Merlin.' he said, pulling his gaze away to look upon his interrogator.

'Lord Merlin?' The soldier looked puzzled, then sneered. 'Well, isn't that a fine circumstance, seeing as Brutus 'ere is the Queen of Bethinia.' To emphasise his disbelief, the auxiliary increased the pressure of the blade tip to the point of becoming painful.

'*Duo!*' Arthur heard the command ring out, then the second limb hit the boards. Festus's screams receded to a feral howl.

'Let's see your chest, maggot,' the brown toothed trooper pressed, speaking the words he'd dreaded to hear his entire life.

Arthur tensed, intending to go out fighting.

'Touch my apprentice, and I promise your fate will be worse than the wretch's up there.'

The voice was Merlin's.

Arthur turned to face the old man, now glaring at them.

'Who the f—' the squat soldier began, then cut himself off, his eyes widening with recognition. 'My apologies, lord,' he said. His companion opened his mouth, about to say something, but his shorter comrade gave him a slow shake of the head, and the duo left to resume their game.

'By the tits of Áine, lad—I leave you for one minute!'

Merlin grumbled as he took up his seat again, but his demeanour soon changed to profound distaste on seeing the butchery unfolding before them. 'We are to go straight to the commander's quarters,' he said after a time, his tone subdued.

'*Crus!*' the officer demanded, and the guards shoved a deathly white Festus onto his back, upon a platform awash with gore. One pinned his blood-drenched torso to the ground while the other lifted his left leg and stretched it out.

'*Trēs!*'⁴ the scruffy *decanus* shouted with relish.

In response, the executioners hacked at the limb in rhythmic, workman-like fashion. Regardless of their skilled strokes, Festus was a well-built man with muscular thighs, so it took many blows to bite through flesh, sinew, and bone. With their work done, the captors tossed the prisoner's leg between the two creatures. They snatched it up in unison and began a gruesome tug-of-war over the grim trophy.

'What are they?' Arthur asked, to distract himself from the bile rising in his throat.

'Basilisks,' the old man responded. 'They nest in the peaks north of here.'

The executioners prostrated his second leg, but Festus had become so slippery with blood they struggled to wrestle his right thigh into position. Eventually, they were ready, and the junior officer called out, '*Quattuor!*' The last limb flew.

It never ceased to amaze Arthur how much of the crimson life force a man's body contained.

In a final act of contempt, the guards picked up their prisoner's twitching torso and threw it to the feasting beasts. Incredibly, Festus remained alive. His eyes rolled one last time in their sockets, just enough to see the widening throat of the green basilisk as it took his entire skull in a crunching bite. The crowd went wild.

Job done, the executioners hopped from the stage to a

smattering of applause. This allowed the beasts' handlers more room to loosen their grip on the neck tethers of their wards while they remained distracted by their grisly meal.

When the basilisks' feeding frenzy had subsided, their awareness of each other returned. Finding themselves unrestricted, the beasts leapt at each other, biting and raking claws into flesh as they locked into furious combat. They kicked Festus's corpse around in the melee, and the creatures gashed more hideous wounds into his broken remains. Following the first flurry, the two battling foes backed off, spitting and hissing. Then circling each other, they searched for weaknesses to exploit. The crowd roared with glee at the spectacle.

The basilisks went at it again, with such vigour that the handlers struggled to hold the tethers. For a frenzied second, the blue team was dragged forward, freeing their competitor enough to take a swipe at a drunken auxiliary standing too close to the action. Luckily for him, he ducked just in time, only to have his dexterous achievement rewarded with jeers from his comrades.

The ensuing carnage was brutal but brief, with the green creature securing a bite hold on the blue creature's wind pipe. The battle concluded with an audible crunch, and the life faded from the burning gaze of the defeated. Although vanquished, Arthur could not help but feel the blue beast was the luckier of the two, for at least its suffering had ended.

'*Codlata deartháir beag*,'[5] Merlin whispered.

The green beast clambered on top of its rival's corpse and hissed at the crowd in triumph. While it revelled in its victory, however, its gaze fell upon Merlin. When their eyes met, Arthur saw the rage drain from it. Then, as timid as a lamb, it stood down from its bloody perch and retracted its throat display, visibly diminished into hopeless desperation once more.

CHAPTER EIGHT

The shadows were growing as they halted outside the *praetorium* quarters of the commander. The grandiose villa appeared new, incorporating the latest fads of the elite. Apple trees and statues of the gods adorned the columned entrance, where a short guard with an ugly pockmarked face stood picking his nose while observing them.

'What do you want?' he asked, still rummaging in his nasal cavity as they stepped from the driver's pedestal.

'My patience wears thin,' Merlin grumbled to himself, then continued in a louder voice, 'Tell the commander, Merlin of the Trinobantes expects his hospitality.'

I This explained the grudging deference of the Romans. If Merlin was a noble of the ruling tribe, it meant he was related to the governor. And it was common knowledge that the embattled emperor had entrusted the administration of the dioceses to the dubious loyalty of the old Britannic noble families. Better that than to allow a true rival to set up a power base at the farthest edge of his sprawling territories.

The guard removed his finger, perhaps weighing the dilemma of confronting a man claiming to be an ancient hero against his superior's security. In the end, he nodded before opening the polished oak door of the villa and gesturing them inside.

They entered an opulent greeting chamber, dimly lit with expensive oil lamps. The walls were painted red with black borders in the Roman fashion. A mosaic floor depicted a leering legionary standing over the naked form of a prostrate Celtic woman. The crown upon her head was tilted, about to fall to the dirt.

Against the far wall, a set of stone heads gazed back at them, each rendered in fleshy, lifelike tones. Arthur recognised the likeness of a few of the emperors from the many coins he'd plundered over the years, including the weasel-like visage of the incumbent.

Their reluctant escort instructed them to wait and disappeared through a side door indistinguishable from the surrounding decor.

Merlin took a seat and tapped upon its arms. He'd been in a thunderous mood since witnessing the impromptu display of Roman power. After waiting several minutes, he gestured at the walls and said, 'Always red! You'd think they'd tire of the damn colour considering the butchery they've inflicted over the centuries!'

Deciding nothing good could come from replying, Arthur paced over to the busts of the emperors. On closer inspection, the craftsmanship was impressive, even down to the iris colour of each bust. Some had the square-jawed appearance of military men, while others appeared haughty and aloof. As he walked along the royal line, he realised these must be the true likeness of their subjects, for many were decidedly ugly. Considering the infamously vain nature of the Roman elite, he found such an honest portrayal an odd affectation. One gnome-like character with a heavy brow and protruding ears caught his eye.

'Claudius,' Merlin said from across the room. 'Smarter than he looked. We learned that to our cost.'

'What do you mean?'

'Is your head entirely empty, boy?'

Arthur returned the inquiry with a dark look.

The old man rolled his eyes, then stood and strode to his side. 'This misshapen toad is the reason you don't speak Gaelic.'

'What?'

Merlin sighed with impatience. 'He conquered the Isles,' he said, staring into the long-dead man's brown eyes. They appeared dull and unintelligent compared to the striking grey gaze regarding them.

'He doesn't look very impressive,' Arthur observed.

It was strange to imagine this carbuncle as the leader who'd subjugated the tribes of Britannia. He'd always imagined the famed conqueror as a giant with the strength of three men.

Merlin's expression turned reflective as he touched the emperor's narrow chin. 'Many men underestimated him—including me.'

Arthur could not help but challenge the implication. 'You mean, our ancestors underestimated him?'

To his inner amusement, the jibe provoked a disapproving glare. 'We bandy too many useless words—Arthur.'

The bandit's stomach clenched. It wasn't possible for this so-called Merlin to know his identity. 'How do you know my name?' he asked. His mind raced with the implication. Perhaps he'd uttered as much while delirious with pain when they'd first met?

The old man gave another exasperated sigh. 'You flounder like a bull in a potter's shed while the very bones of the hills trumpet your arrival, boy.' He let his hand slip from Claudius's stone countenance and eyed Arthur. 'I'd have to be as deaf as our ugly imperator here not to know your name.'

'Must you always talk in riddles?'

'You're the riddle, lad—and one I've not come across in nine centuries.'

Arthur decided the old fool was cracked in the head, and he'd been about to say as much, when the sound of shouting, followed by the tread of the returning guard, stopped him.

'The commander will see you now, lord,' the flushed soldier said, gesturing down the hall he'd come from.

They followed him along the lamp-lit corridor. A single tapestry ran the length of the walls. It depicted a lone century of legionaries, their shields interlocked in the face of an over-whelming tide of fantastical beasts. The assailants of the heroic figures had the muscled torsos of men, but the equine flanks and elongated skulls of horses. The bestial warriors charged the wall of steel with frenzied desperation etched upon their alien faces.

As they reached an ornate door with winged cherubs carved on its polished surface, Arthur prepared to learn if his trust was misplaced.

They entered a brightly lit inner chamber, decorated with tapestries that depicted scenes more common in a brothel. A suit of armour, polished to a pristine hue, hung on a wooden plinth in one neglected corner of the room. A curly-haired youth, wearing only a short tunic, lounged on a gilded divan that dominated the centre of the spacious area. Two curva-ceous slave women, dressed in flowing gowns that left little to the imagination, sat on a rug by his feet.

The youth's lips twitched with amusement at his guests as they entered, then he whispered into the ear of the blonde to his left. She giggled, worse for drink. In stark contrast, however, the black-haired woman to his right regarded them with serious green eyes. Her natural beauty made Arthur look upon her for a second longer than he intended. Unlike her buxom counterpart, she had a lithe, athletic body with appealing feminine curves. To his disappointment, her eyes narrowed on noticing his observations, and he averted his gaze in embarrassment.

'Lord Merlin, welcome to Fort Derventio—jewel of the empire,' the youth said, whilst raising his cup in mock salute. Its contents slopped over the rim onto the plush sheepskin rug.

'Who are you?' the old man replied.

The commander sat up straight, his smirk turning to a pout. 'My ancestor was the most noble Paullus Julius—'

Merlin raised a hand, stopping him mid-sentence. 'I'm not interested in which long-dead mare farted your line into existence, boy. I asked who you are.'

The blonde laughed again but stopped when she noticed the angry stare the indignant adolescent directed at her. 'Lucius Julius Cumanus, tribune of this garrison,' he stated, deepening his tone to add weight to the declaration.

'What of Caeso?'

The youth coughed uncomfortably. 'Arrested.' The flash of thunder passing over Merlin's face at the news made the boy hesitate. He glanced toward the slaves, as if for reassurance. 'I —I've been sent from the court of the prefect to replace him.'

'Why was he arrested?'

The commander took a deep swig of wine then replied, 'Treason.'

Merlin let out a weary sigh. 'Treason? Caeso Aetius, really?'

The tribune nodded hesitantly.

'Now I have yet another inbred whelp to deal with because of that paranoid fool!' the old man muttered, not bothering to lower his tone.

'Lord, I…'

Merlin took an ominous step toward the youth. 'You're going to listen—and keep your mouth shut!'

Despite his curt nod of agreement, the tribune turned such a dark shade of crimson, it masked the pimples on his forehead.

'Tell the others to leave,' Merlin ordered.

'But why?' the commander asked like a petulant child.

'Do it!'

The young officer called Lucius clapped his hands in an insipid motion, obviously unsure if he wanted to be alone with the stern Celtic lord. Not seeming to care, the guard slunk out, accompanied by the two slave girls, who left a whiff of expensive perfume in their wake. Arthur felt a stab of disappointment at their departure.

Merlin made sure the door had closed before turning back to the commander. 'I have a cart outside. There is a consignment of *deus pulvis* on it.'[1]

The youth raised an eyebrow at the news.

Arthur silently exclaimed at this information. *Deus pulvis* —god powder. It was a priceless treasure the Romans valued more than gold, and often speculated about by common folk. Some said it allowed men to do incredible things, while others spoke of its use in dark magic and the sacrifice of Celtic babes to foreign gods. The only thing most Britons knew was that its true purpose remained a closely protected secret. Only a few *pulvis* mines existed in the entire empire, one of which was in the wild lands of Kernow at the southern tip of Britannia.

The old man continued. 'You will personally make sure the box wrapped in blue-stained leather is taken from my cart, put onto a guarded barge, and delivered to Caeso Antonius Duvianus at Deva.'

'Of course, lord,' came the hasty agreement, accompanied

by a sly glint in the youth's eye. 'I'll ask the men to do it at once.'

Arthur had little doubt this urchin would have his cut of the goods.

Merlin must have shared this sentiment, because he stretched out one weather-beaten hand at the youth and commanded, '*ardú.*'[2]

The puzzled expression on the tribune's spotty face turned to terror as he floated up from his divan and drifted toward them, suspended by an invisible force. With his spindly legs scrambling in the air, the flapping adolescent halted a few feet from the old man, who eyed him with disdain. 'I said—personally.'

'But my fort! My command!' the youth squeaked in weak protest. 'Surely such an honour should go to yourself, lord?'

The old man's face grew darker at his attempt at flattery. 'My great nephew, in his infinite wisdom, decided my time would best be spent inspecting the interior defences and gathering more farmhands to fill the ranks of his army,' Merlin stated with obvious sarcasm.

'Your nephew?' the tribune stuttered, still flailing.

'The governor, you dolt!'

'Oh, I see.'

'Do you, boy?' Merlin floated Lucius closer. 'Then you will know who advises him. Have you met Quintus Caesius Bestia?'

The commanders blood-shot gaze widened. 'I know of him,' he replied in a trembling wail.

'Then you'll understand how much pleasure he'll take in flogging you when I report your men are not fit to fight off a cold, never mind the enemy!'

'I'll accompany the box myself!' the youth agreed instantly.

'Good lad!' Merlin said, slapping his cheek in approval. 'Take it straight to Caeso when you arrive in Deva.'

'Of course—yes!'

'Glad we're in agreement,' Merlin replied, allowing the shaking commander to drift earthward, much to his obvious relief.

But Merlin wasn't finished. He raised a single finger at the flying officer who halted in his earthbound journey, and added, 'One last thing.'

'Anything!'

'*Smeach*,'[3] the elder mouthed, and the squealing tribune flipped upside down in mid-air.

Arthur suppressed an involuntary snigger as the young man's tunic dropped over his face, exposing his unimpressive genitals.

'If I find out you've pilfered any of the shipment or allowed your men to take any more basilisks from the peaks, I'll ensure they crucify you. Is that clear?' Merlin's tone gave no hint of jest.

'Err, basilisks?'

'Is that clear!' the old man thundered; rocking Lucius from side to side.

'Yes, yes, please!'

Merlin flicked his wrist, dropping the commander on his head. 'You can come back in now!' he shouted to the waiting attendants outside.

The two slaves and the guard entered, and alarm struck them upon seeing the state of the tribune.

Merlin pointed at the soldier. 'You, freshen him up.' He nodded at his superior. 'I need him at the docks with an armed escort within the next two hours.'

The shocked auxiliary looked at his prostate leader lying in a dazed heap, staring at the ceiling in resigned humiliation.

'Sir, are you sure?' he asked.

'Do as he says!' the flushed tribune snapped.

'And I want my horses stabled, fed, and ready for first light.'

The soldier gave a curt nod and asked, 'What about the cargo?'

'One piece is to be handled only by him.' The old man pointed at Lucius. 'He knows which. Give the rest to the townspeople.'

The guard licked his lips, nodded again, then hurried to aid his superior.

Merlin turned to the women. 'Would you mind finding us two rooms for the night, please, ladies?' he asked politely.

'Where would you like to stay, my lord?' the blonde inquired, glancing at the dazed youth.

'Don't care, as long as it's not in this pervert's palace.'

The slave women led them back out into the fort complex, where Merlin stopped to pat his equine companions and retrieve his ever-present saddlebag.

The women took them to less grand yet still comfortable quarters nearby.

'Shall we stay?' the blonde asked, with a suggestive smirk as they entered the empty apartment.

Arthur had been about to jump at the chance when Merlin cut him off. 'No, thanks. This one's got an early start, and I'm getting too old for all that moaning and bouncing around.'

'Anything else, sir?' she added, with a slight pout of disappointment on her face. The young warrior guessed she was not nearly as disappointed as he, however.

'Would you bring us some food, girls?' he replied, turning to the green-eyed beauty. 'And please bathe this one.' He nodded toward Arthur. 'He smells like a walking corpse.'

Merlin strode off to his room.

CHAPTER NINE

The room was clean, with a comfortable bed, although its musty smell indicated it hadn't been used for some time. Arthur resisted the urge to collapse onto the sheets and sleep, his stomach growling at the prospect of a meal. While he waited, he searched for valuables worth stealing and was rewarded with a silver ring, embossed with the face of a goddess which he found in one dusty corner. Its tarnished surface was too worn to make out the letters proclaiming the deity's name. Arthur slipped the ring on his finger, and to his surprise, it fit perfectly. He suddenly recalled the strange waking dream he'd experienced the night of the ill-fated raid.

The mother and babe.

He remembered how the child had clung to its mother's hair while they screamed. It had been so vivid, so real. Something about it compelled him to understand what it meant. Who was the woman? Who was the child?

Perhaps Merlin can help me find out?

A short rap on the door broke his chain of thought. Only the dark-haired slave had returned, carrying a platter of cold meats, buttered bread, and fruit. Arthur took the plate without a word and wolfed down the food while she watched from the doorway, her arms folded.

'You're welcome,' she said coolly.

He tore into the bread and smeared it in the rich butter then crammed it into his mouth. The taste was so sublime he moaned in pleasure as the creamy mixture ran down his throat. Glancing up, he noticed she still observed him.

'Must you stare?' he asked, feeling uncomfortable.

'Must you eat like a pig?'

Arthur paused with his cheeks still stuffed and returned her disapproving pout. Secretly, however, he enjoyed the opportunity to look at her again. She appeared in her early twenties and had a soft yet determined jawline. Her pitch-black locks had been formed into ringlets in the Roman, rather than Briton, style. Again, it was her arresting green eyes that grabbed his attention. His observations lowered to the revealing dress and the shape of her figure.

'You have a sharp tongue for a slave,' he said.

No reply.

Determined not to let her frosty manner put him off his food, he continued to eat, albeit with less vigour. The awkward silence forced him to speak once more. 'What's your name?'

'Satis.'

'Pretty? That's a good name,' he concluded, trying to sound pleasant. In spite of her ill manners, he hoped to achieve a more favourable outcome to the evening.

She sniffed. 'The Roman gave it to me.'

'Oh,' was all he could think to say, cursing his luck that the blonde hadn't returned, instead. 'What's your real name?'

'Guin.'

He nodded. 'The food is good. Thank you, Guin.'

'I'm a slave. You don't need to thank me.'

Arthur's irritation grew. For the first time in his life, where he might expect deference, fate had landed him this gloomy female for company. 'Then there's no need to say you're welcome,' he said, then tore off a sliver of beef with his teeth.

Her scowl deepened, much to his amusement.

'My name is Boden,' he added, his mouth still full.

'Will you be long?' she asked, ignoring his declaration.

'Why?'

'The lord told me I was to take you to the baths.'

'I'm aware of that.' Arthur bit into a plum and allowed the juices to run into his beard. It tasted sweet and juicy.

'He said you stink like a corpse.'

Still chewing, Arthur glowered at her. 'I also know that.'

'He was right.'

This was too much for the young bandit. He spluttered with anger, nearly choking on the stone of the fruit.

'Damn it, woman! What kind of slave are you?'

To his surprise, she smiled.

* * *

AT THIS TIME in the evening, the bathhouse was unlit and empty, but gentle steam rose from the shadowed surface of the caldarium. Even as Arthur anticipated this rare treat, he wondered about the slaves who toiled in a boiling sweat box below, just to give him an hour of pleasure. The thought triggered memories of turning spit roasts for a pitiless master.

Guin paced across the tiled floor with a fire striker, lighting only a few of the oil lamps hanging around the wide room. The effect left them in flickering half shadow. A faint drip sounded from the east wall, presumably where the pipes fed fresh water into the complex. The growing glow revealed a mosaicked pool, which depicted the blue-skinned god Poseidon sitting upon a throne of kelp. Many kinds of sea creatures encircled him, as if they were courtiers paying tribute to their sovereign lord.

Arthur removed his boots and found the tiles warm beneath his feet.

'Underfloor heating,' Guin explained as he wiggled his toes in appreciation.

'The Romans are good for some things,' he said, reluctant to undress in front of this pretty slave.

A pleasant aroma drifted from the lamps.

'I wouldn't go that far.' She put the striker aside and approached him, her hips swaying beneath the thin shift. Standing before him, her gaze never left his, then with professional detachment, she lifted his tunic.

'I can do that myself,' he said, laying a restraining hand upon hers. Although he felt self-conscious, something in her intense green eyes made him want her to continue.

'Your master said I should…'

'He's not my master.'

'Oh?' she prompted, a flicker of amusement in her eye.

Realising he was in danger of steering the conversation toward his identity, Arthur decided to lie. 'Well, I'm his apprentice.'

Guin shrugged, then lifted his tunic once more, her fingers brushing against his ribs. He let her pull the garment over his head, baring his torso.

'I'll get some fresh clothes from the store. This thing looks older than—' Her words cut off.

The silence puzzled Arthur at first, then with dawning panic, he realised his terrible mistake.

The brand.

He grasped her arm as she reached to touch the wound proclaiming his shame, and her expression turned from curiosity to resigned anger. 'You're one of those types, then.' Oddly, she directed the bitter comment at the tightened fist around her slender wrist rather than at the incriminating mark upon his chest.

Uncertainty made him let go, and a fleeting look of relief passed over her face, then became curious once more. She touched the mess of raised flesh where the iron had pressed.

'It must've hurt.' Her tone was gentler. As always, the mere mention of the vicious ritual provoked memories of screaming and pain.

Does she really not know? Perhaps. It must be true that some people didn't know of the clan, but they were far from these lands.

Arthur contemplated killing her. He could slip his hands around her delicate throat and choke the life from that searching gaze, probably without causing too much of a fuss. Such things often happened in brothels. The real slight would be against her owner, in destroying his property, and Merlin had already plucked the balls from that young fool.

'It hurt,' he whispered, as his hands twitched with indecision.

He could not.

Filled with disgust at his own cowardice, he turned and plunged into the pool, but surfaced a second later, bellowing in shock.

'Hot!' he shouted, steaming tendrils rising from his head.

To his annoyance, Guin laughed.

Despite his predicament, Arthur smiled. It had been a long time since he'd heard a woman's laughter.

'You look like a cooked lobster,' she said, sitting at the edge of the pool and dipping her toes in the water. The steam clung to the hem of her white linen, turning it translucent.

'What's a lobster?' he asked, relieved to discover his feet could touch the bottom, having never learned to swim.

'A sea creature—like a giant louse.'

'I've never seen the sea.'

She swayed her legs in the water, taking pleasure in the sensation. 'I grew up in a fishing village. We'd catch lobsters in pots, then cook them till they turned bright red.' She smiled, more to herself than to him. 'The whole family would...' She trailed off, and her lips twisted into a reflective frown again—a dark cloud spoiling a sunny day.

'You can join me if you wish?' he suggested, wanting to recapture her fleeting warmth.

Her frown deepening, she stood. 'As you command.'

'I did not command—'

Guin lifted the dress above her head and stood like a pale flower in the lamplight. Her body was flawless, a supple thing of desire. The curve of her hips gave way to long, delicate legs, and her breasts were large. She stepped down marbled stairs and slid into the pool.

The green-eyed beauty dipped her head beneath the surface, then re-emerged, her wet jet-black hair streaming behind her. She closed her eyes, wincing at the rush of heat. When she opened them again, she held his gaze.

'So, how did you become an apprentice lord?' she asked, remaining upright in a way that made Arthur appreciate the view.

'Well, I'm not exactly...'

'Perhaps you are his favourite pet, then?'

'No!'

She shrugged, and to his disappointment, she stopped moving toward him.

'And why does your master travel these lands? — apprentice lord.'

'He says to inspect defences and raise troops.'

She glided forward. 'And do you trust what he says?'

'I trust no man.'

'Neither do I.' She drifted closer, very close. 'He mentioned nothing of the threat from the north—or where he is going next?' Smooth skin brushed against him, and his heart beat faster.

'Guin is a strange name,' he said, ignoring her question.

She stepped back. 'Short for Guinever.'

Sensing her retreat was due to his reticence, he spoke again. 'I know he travels to Ardotalia in the morning.'

She pondered the information, floating before him, her face as beguiling as any siren's.

'Listen, I don't expect you to...' he began.

She leaned forward and kissed him on the lips, her cheeks flushed with desire. 'Your body says otherwise,' she whispered, pressing herself against his arousal.

Arthur returned her embrace.

CHAPTER TEN

As the rising sun streamed through the shutters, Arthur raised his head from the soft goose feather pillow, hoping to get an eyeful of the slave girl called Guinever while she slept. But to his disappointment, only the scent of her perfume lingered where she'd lain.

'Bollocks!' he muttered, leaning over and inhaling. The thought he might never see her again filled him with regret.

They'd loved each other until far into the early morning. She had embraced him with a desperate urgency he'd found both alluring and disturbing. Part of him wished to go find her and persuade her to leave with him, but such thoughts were childish fancy. Most slaves freely stayed with their masters in return for a full belly and security. What could he offer but a life on the run and the ever-present risk of a lingering death?

The door to his room flew open, interrupting his melancholy reflections, and Merlin strode in, dressed and grumbling with displeasure. The old man's glare turned to an exasperated shake of the head upon seeing his nakedness. Embarrassed, Arthur pulled a pillow over his modesty.

'Good grief! I don't have all morning to wait while you play with yourself! I said first light!' Merlin shouted, then marched out again. No sooner had he left than the blonde slave popped her head around the door to giggle at the perceived indiscretion.

'I'm not...' he started to protest, but she'd already left.

'Ten minutes!' Merlin yelled, his voice echoing down the corridor.

Exhausted and muttering curses under his breath, Arthur rose and dressed in the tunic and woollen trousers Guin had laid out the previous night. He stuffed the remains of the loaf into his mouth before tugging on his boots and leaving.

* * *

A SCOWLING MERLIN waited astride Fiona outside the officers' quarters. Behind them, her white companion, Aina, stood patiently. She'd already been saddled and provisions strapped to her side, including a *gladius* with 'SPQR' stamped upon its pommel. Arthur drew the sharpened weapon.

'You may as well serve some purpose,' Merlin said.

Offended by the jibe, the bandit took a practice swing of the blade and was satisfied with how the steel edge whipped through the air. The sound was an old friend, giving him confidence in the face of his would-be benefactor.

'Thanks for the parting gift,' he said, hooking the sword under his belt then striding away from Merlin. Enough was enough, and the fact the garrison had captured one of his clansmen meant the rest of the Ravens had travelled north, passing Derventio on their way. With some luck, he could rejoin them within a few days.

He'd only taken a few strides when the old man spoke up. 'I'll pay you to be my escort.'

Arthur stopped but did not turn. 'How much?'

'Fifty denarii.'

It was a substantial sum, over two months' wages for a well-paid pleb. Truth be told, he'd been so obsessed with the likelihood of betrayal, he had given little thought to other possibilities. Under normal circumstances, he would have accepted the offer without hesitation, for it was common for wealthy patrons to take on mercenaries in these uncertain times. And a journey deep into the peaks offered many isolated opportunities to slit the throat of said foolish patron, but Merlin's motives and capabilities were far from clear. Not only that, he did not believe for a moment the wily old goat needed an armed escort, least of all one with a murky past. He turned once more, intent on removing himself from further ridiculous risk-taking.

'You dream of a weeping woman and her child,' Merlin said, his words anchoring Arthur to the spot.

Incredulous, the young warrior faced him again. 'What did you say?'

'You heard me well enough.' For once, there was no hint of a poking jest.

'Do you know who they are?'

Merlin took a deep breath as if pondering his reply. 'I can help you find the truth.'

Arthur considered this, torn between the life he'd always known, as dark as it was, and the prospect of further madness ensuing from journeying with this odd character. To his surprise, he found himself striding back to the waiting mare. 'I want half now,' he said, sheathing the *gladius* and patting Aina.

'I'll pay you when your efforts merit it. Now, for the love of Áine's tits, it would be good to leave before my arse grows as numb as your wits!'

Without waiting for Arthur to protest, Merlin cantered away, leaving the younger man to mount. Aina let out a friendly nicker. Enjoying the feel of a horse beneath him again, he patted her affectionately on the neck. 'He's a mean bugger,' he said into her flicking ear.

Arthur caught up with Merlin as they approached the outer gate. 'Why are we going to Ardotalia?' he asked. Along with Deva, it was one of the largest of the remaining forts and a place the clan avoided like the plague of Galen. 'Another inspection?'

The old man shook his head. 'No. Ardotalia is the governor's pet project, which means, unlike these useless lumps, they are at least trained. I'm to lead three hundred of them north to join the army at Luguvalium.'

This was news. 'I thought Vibius never left Camulo-dunum?' It was common knowledge that the governor rarely left the safety of his walled palace in the capital. Luguvalium was a town on the northern frontier with Pictish Caledonia, and in the territory of the Brigantes, the traditional rivals of the ruling Trinobantes. Although the Romans had forced a thin veneer of peace between the warring factions, it was still unusual for the notoriously paranoid ruler to step foot into lands nominally hostile toward him.

'True, the man is a fat toad and would never leave his nest, given a choice,' Merlin agreed.

'Then why come north?'

'Because King Talorc has overthrown his father and threatens to bring seven thousand screaming Picts our way, that's why.'

He'd heard rumours that the fierce Caledonian tribes were stirring in their mountainous lands far to the north, beyond the great wall. It was said they still clung to the old ways.

'Is he really your great nephew?' Arthur asked.

'Aye—more's the pity.'

They reached the gate, but found their progress blocked by the same guards as the previous day. This time they were occupied by the protestations of a man Arthur recognised as one of the beast handlers from Festus's execution. He wrung his hands as he pleaded with the two indifferent soldiers, 'Please, fellas, I'll pay. You know I'm good for it.'

'Fuck off, Balbus. If you think we're running after one o' them viscous lizards, you've got another think comin.'

'It's a crime! I demand an investigation!'

The larger guard, tired of the discussion, jabbed the irate protestor in the guts with his fist.

'Clean out yer ears, arse wipe. He said piss off! If you want to risk your balls hunting that monster, that's your business.'

Gasping for breath, the beastmaster took the hint and scurried off, a profound look of loss on his face.

'Everything all right?' Merlin asked the big soldier, sounding much brighter.

'Lord Merlin,' the guard greeted with a respectful nod. 'Looks like his favourite pet went missing during the night.'

'Really? How unfortunate.' Merlin's demeanour, however, suggested it was anything but.

* * *

THE FORT'S western road led into a wooded valley before turning north toward the peak district and beyond. Weathered stone walls crisscrossed the landscape where countless farmers had marked the boundaries of their land for centuries. As they progressed, the cobbled road became pitted, and they passed the familiar sight of crumbling farm buildings, abandoned after the great sweating sickness of the previous century.

The landscape rolled on, and partly from boredom, but also from curiosity, Arthur decided to talk to his mysterious travelling companion.

'You don't like Vibius Crassus much, do you?' Arthur asked Merlin, who dozed in the saddle. 'You called him a fat toad.'

'And?' the old man muttered, half opening an eyelid.

'Why do you serve him if you dislike him so much? And you don't seem to like the Romans. Why help them?'

'Why did you serve that bandit scum?' The words struck Arthur like a brick to the temple.

'You know?'

'Most people found lying in the dirt with their guts hanging out are seldom Vestal Virgins.' Merlin gave him a pointed look.

'I thought you were going to hand me to the garrison,' Arthur said, angry that he'd expected treachery, only to find it was yet another mind game. 'I could've killed you!'

'Only through the boredom caused by your incessant whining, boy.'

Arthur flushed with anger. 'You are a bleedin' old goat! You've still not explained what you want from me!'

'For you to be my apprentice, apparently.'

'That was a lie!'

'My guard, then.'

Regardless of the levity in his tone, Arthur sensed a real reluctance to answer. He brought Aina to a halt. 'I'm not taking another step until you give me an answer!'

Sighing, Merlin turned and trotted toward him. He reached a hand out, and the young man shifted backward in his saddle, unsure what was happening. The older man raised an eyebrow and tried again. This time, Arthur allowed him to press his palm against his brow, and he felt another presence within him. It was the strangest sensation, like a second figure stood in the darkness of his being, observing his thoughts. The presence delved deeper, going beyond what his conscious mind understood. It did not get far when something else, a third presence, cut off the exploration, leaving him and the old man both gasping and staring into each other's gaze.

'The same as the first time I tried,' Merlin said. 'Something shields you—something more powerful than I.'

Arthur had a sudden vision of the strange dream he'd had the night of the massacre.

'The lady,' he muttered.

Merlin's features sparked with curiosity. 'What lady?'

Arthur tried to recall the woman he'd seen in his dream, beautiful, yet terrible to behold.

'SHE... SHE WAS BEAUTIFUL.'

'Did she speak to you?'

The young warrior shrugged. 'It was just a dream.'

The old man looked him straight in the eye. 'No, there is something about you even I cannot fully understand. What did she say?'

Arthur cast his mind back, but the memory was insubstantial, like a mist he could not grasp. The more he tried to push for an answer, the more the fog thickened, blocking his attempt. 'I cannot...'

Merlin's expression hardened, and his frustration was clear to see. 'Then perhaps it was a dream,' he said, although the words did not ring true. With that, he turned Fionna and trotted on.

Strangely discomfited by the line of interrogation, Arthur followed him, but changed the subject. 'You didn't enjoy the execution yesterday?'

'No. Such cruelty makes my stomach churn.'

Arthur wasn't sure if he was referring to the butchering of Festus or the baiting of the basilisks. 'Why didn't you stop them, then?' he pressed, hoping to uncover a weak spot to aggravate his irritable companion.

'What do you mean?' the old man replied, yawning.

'They treat you like royalty, and the tribune did nothing when you dangled him upside down like a prize goose. Why not just stop the execution?'

Arthur felt a small amount of pleasure when Merlin glowered at the query. In answer, the elder pressed a finger against the side of his nose and cleared his nasal passage onto the verge of the road.

'If it bothered you so much, why not stop it?' Arthur insisted, sensing a rare chink in the old man's mental armour.

Merlin flushed, then said bitterly, 'we are still a conquered people—and don't forget it. It's one thing to rebuke the whelp of an obscure noble in private, but to challenge the empire publicly would be a declaration of rebellion. Especially from me.'

They watched as a buzzard floated on an upward draught above a nearby hill opposite. Arthur wondered how a man of such legendary renown could sound so cowed.

'How does a prince of the Trinobante become immortal?' Arthur asked, making the most of this rare moment of transparency.

'I was chosen.'

'Chosen by whom?'

Merlin rolled his eyes at the buzzard. 'It's like listening to the babblings of a child!' he protested to the uncaring bird. 'You know nothing of the Eld?'

Though he did, Arthur refused to believe this scruffy, ill-tempered vagabond was the same Merlin of legend. Every youngster learned the myth of the chosen, even one with his pitiable background. The Eld were ancient beings selected by the gods and imbued with enough power to shepherd their fellow beings in the absence of their masters.

'You expect me to believe you're a thousand years old? Ridiculous,' he scoffed.

'You're right. That would be ridiculous.'

The young warrior felt a little taller in his saddle for being vindicated.

'I'm only nine hundred and seventy-one.'

CHAPTER ELEVEN

They reached a crossroad with a crucifix driven into its centre and tilted earthward. The festering remains of a long-dead corpse still hung from it, greeting them with a rictus grin. Someone had nailed a plaque to the rotten wood above the skull of the unfortunate. It read one word: *Proditor*.

'What our masters lack in subtlety, they make up for in brutality,' Merlin said as they drew opposite the grisly message.

'*Proditor*—that means traitor, doesn't it?' Arthur ventured at the scrawled Latin.

'Aye, but it should read, "bravery is no substitute for brains," Merlin observed sadly.

'Sounds like the words of a coward,' Arthur scoffed.

'*Buachaill dúr,*'[1] Merlin muttered.

'What does that mean?'

'It means I tire of this conversation,' Merlin stepped down from Fionna and gazed more intently at the broken figure. To Arthur's confusion, he stretched his palm toward the corpse and whispered, his grey gaze turning milky white.

'Your brains really are addled, old man,' the young warrior commented, unsettled by his odd behaviour.

Merlin ignored him and continued the bizarre ritual. Nothing happened at first, other than a worm dropping from the body's weathered eye socket, but then dozens of insects followed. They scurried from every foetid orifice of the wretched thing. A tingling sensation grew in Arthur's temple, and he froze in apprehension. Beneath him, Aina's muscular haunches quivered. A sense of dread descended.

The human remains took on a darker hue, as if black light were illuminating it from within. Then, with a gargled moan, the corpse shuddered into a dreadful semblance of life, its jaw opening wide as it gasped for air.

'Shit!' Arthur called in alarm and yanked Aina away from the monstrosity, forcing her to stumble aside. She whinnied in protest at such rough handling.

'Pack it in!' Merlin shot a disapproving scowl over his shoulder. 'We are in no danger.' He turned back to the writhing corpse. 'Speak, my brother,' he said respectfully.

The dead thing's mouldering head twisted toward them, causing a flap of yellowed skin, complete with a wisp of hair still attached, to fall onto the turf below. 'My lord.' It spoke its greeting in an ethereal whisper.

'Forgive me for disturbing your rest,' Merlin said, 'but I would know who you were in life and how you came to this end.'

After a pause, the whisper returned. 'In my mortal life, I was Aed of the Coritani.' The words were but a rasp, dry and devoid of feeling. 'My kin faced starvation, so we brought steel and fire to the Roman dogs.' It took a long, shuddering gasp. 'I was captured and flayed before they brought me to this place.'

A chill ran down Arthur's spine as the dead man's gaze regarded him through empty sockets. 'So, it's true. You have entered the world of the living.' It gave a sorrowful shake of its fleshless head. 'Within the void, I have heard many whispers of your passing... but I did not believe it possible.'

Repulsed by the prospect of speaking to a corpse, Arthur remained silent, although he felt a profound sense of unease at the words.

Merlin shot him a speculative glance, then continued. 'What transpires in the world? Do you have guidance for your mortal brethren?'

The daylight darkened perceptibly. 'Evil grows in the north,' the fallen one said, its withered frame convulsing in an increasingly volatile jig.

The old man frowned at the spectre's agitation. 'Calm yourself, my friend. We will be prepared if the Picts are foolish enough to come.'

'Nay, lord, you do not understand. They have awoken a great malice!' Its whispered tone grew to a near shriek. 'In their quest for vengeance, they have blasphemed terribly against the living earth!' It writhed, its bones snapping and dropping away. 'The shadow lands are in turmoil. We fear the coming of...' Its voice rose to a roar, then descended into a screeching wail of agony.

Merlin also cried out in pain and crouched, hands pressed to his ears as if deafened. Silence followed.

The darkness lifted from the skeleton as it returned to its inanimate state. Concerned, Arthur dismounted and strode over to aid him. But when he reached his side, Merlin waved him away. Despite his dismissal, for the first time since they'd met, the old man looked shaken by the turn of events.

'What happened?' Arthur asked, relieved the impromptu show was over.

'Damn it, boy, give me a second!' the old man yelled, rubbing his temple. Another minute passed while he grumbled curses in Gaelic. 'That was unexpected.'

'What?' the younger man tried again.

'I...' Merlin replied, his brow furrowed in contemplation. 'I fear the threat to our people may be greater than I suspected.

'What do you mean?'

Merlin rose and paced in front of the cross, scratching his stubbled head. 'What could the dead fear?' he muttered, too lost in his own thoughts to reply.

Arthur posed another disturbing question. 'Why did the shade speak to me so?'

Merlin stopped and considered him with outright concern. 'I only know what my instinct tells me.

'And what's that?'

Again, the old man did not answer. He only stopped long enough to pat Arthur on the shoulder then stiffly climbed back into his saddle. The recent strain upon him was clear as he took a moment to steady himself.

* * *

THE MOON HAD long since risen to bathe the rocky peaks in its glow as the two weary travellers reached the tumbled ruins of a small *castrum*.[2] They dismounted amongst the scattered stone blocks of the dismantled outpost opposite a moss-covered gate tower. Other than a segment of wall attached to the now pointless entrance, nothing else remained. A worn set of stairs led to the parapet above the gate.

'We'll rest up there,' Merlin said, pointing at the watch platform above. 'The wall is narrow but wide enough for the horses.'

'Are you sure?' Arthur asked. 'That wall hasn't borne weight in a century. It'll crumble under us.'

'It will hold.' The old man yawned. 'Bandits crawl over these peaks like lice on a ferret's arse.' He again indicated the small watchtower above, then led Fionna toward the stairs. 'That fighting platform will protect us on three sides.'

Arthur wasn't so sure. True, it would stop potential enemies from rushing them, but it could also leave them trapped. Too tired to argue, he followed, leading a nervous Aina up the weathered steps.

They progressed cautiously, coaxing the spooked animals with soft words. Even so, Arthur had to duck when a fist-sized rock dropped from the battlements and sped past his head.

Startled, Aina reared onto her hind legs.

Merlin turned and placed a comforting hand upon the brow of his equine friend. '*Cailín socair,*'[3] he said, and she settled down.

'I am also fine,' Arthur grumbled.

'Don't worry, the rock would've bounced off your thick noggin,' Merlin retorted, chuckling at his own wit.

The circular fighting platform above the gatehouse remained stout, so it was with some relief that Arthur tied the two mounts to a rusted windlass. Regardless of the unnatural demands put upon them, the horses seemed happy enough, especially when he gave them each a well-earned grain bag and rub down.

'You've forgiven me for the rock, then, hmm?' he asked Aina as he brushed her flanks.

She nickered, half closing her eyes as she enjoyed the sensation.

Nearby, Merlin tapped his boot against a thick floor plank then lay his blanket down. 'They might be a bunch of blood-thirsty bastards, but they can build, I'll give them that.' He looked around. 'Have I stayed here before?' he speculated to no one in particular. 'Yes, I think I have. The garrison commander liked peaches, as I recall. Fat fellow he was—bad breath.'

Disconcerted by his companion's habit of casually reflecting upon events from centuries past, Arthur retrieved his bedding and settled for the night. He gazed up at the familiar sight of the star Eridanus winking against an infinite black canvas. Though he was tired, his mind refused to rest, consumed by questions about the remarkable man who lay nearby—a person who claimed to be an immortal champion of the Celtic people, no less. And what did he know about his recurring vision of the mother and child? There was no way he could guess such a thing.

'The god powder you delivered to the commander at Derventio—why is it going to Deva?' he asked, fearing more irritable mockery.

But none came, only the voice of a tired old man. 'To be transported north by sea to Alauna, then onto my sons who keep watch at Vindolanda. We may soon have need of it.'

'Then it's true the god powder is used in magic?'

'Aye. It greatly enhances the power of those with the gift. In these lands, we are called *drui*.'

The Druids of Mona, another name he'd thought belonged to myth. It was said that Merlin had formed them and they were dedicated to black sorcery and human sacrifice. Having known him for a while, however, he found that hard to believe.

'I wish I could consult with my sons and daughters, but I dare not.'

'Why? What are you afraid of?' Arthur asked, assuming Merlin could use his powers to communicate with the other drui.

'Because it would mean crossing into the spirit world for a time and that would expose us to whatever evil overpowered that shade.'

· · ·

79

ARTHUR PONDERED THIS, unsettled by the concept that Merlin feared something. 'But I thought the druids were all dead?' He asked, thinking of the tales about the aftermath of the great uprising.

There was a long delay before Merlin replied. 'Those of us who survived often wish we had not.'

Arthur had never accepted the myth of a fabled warrior queen leading the tribes into rebellion. In his experience, the disparate peoples of the Isles were incapable of uniting. Yet, around the campfire, more than one old Briton among the clan had spoken of the fire queen and the orgy of destruction her army had wielded across the land. The empire had crushed them in the end.

In an act of terrible retribution, the Romans had destroyed Tre'r Dryw, a place of worship for all the peoples of Albion and home to the druids. It was thought the entire conclave had been burnt alive among the sacred groves, even as they'd chanted in prayer. The burning of that ancient place marked the last gasp of resistance to the occupation. If true, the sad tale left many questions.

'Then why do the Romans trust you now?'

The old man gave a bitter chuckle, devoid of humour. 'They would not trust their own mothers, but these last years have been better for us—good enough, at least, to begin rebuilding the brotherhood.'

'How so?'

'They no longer see the need to persecute my kin. We are but a myth to most and a reminder of defeat to others.'

'Still...'

'We make our selves useful—it stops them from stamping us out entirely.'

'Why do you serve them after everything they've done to you?' Arthur asked, repeating the question he'd tried earlier that day. It made no sense for the druids to help their over-lords. Surely they should be the bitterest of enemies.

'The same reason you ride with cutthroats and killers—we are both slaves, boy.

'But—'

'Do you know how the Romans rose to dominate our world?' Merlin interjected.

Arthur had never considered such a thing. The invaders had simply always been present. 'They are mighty in battle?'

The old man grunted. 'Mighty, yes—undefeated, no. They have been defeated many times by many different enemies.'

'Why, then?'

'They are implacable.'

'Implacable?' Arthur was not familiar with the word.

'They don't give in—ever. They always come back for more.' Some muttered words in Gaelic followed before he spoke again. 'The first time they came to these shores, we sent them and their mightiest general, Caesar, home like a pack of whipped dogs.' His voice rose with encouragement, then fell again. 'They returned under Claudius.'

'I heard Caesar was a great general,' Arthur said, recalling an argument between two clan bandits on the subject of the best commanders in history. One, a foreigner claiming to be a native from a faraway land, had argued that a man named Alexandros was the greatest. His opponent, arguing the case for Caesar, had settled the disagreement by breaking the other's jaw.

Merlin sneered at the mention of the ancient leader. 'He was a butcher who boasted of his genocide.'

'I thought you said we defeated him?'

'We did, but our cousins in Gaul were not so lucky.' He ran a hand down his beard. 'I was in Alesia when it fell.' His anger was gone, replaced by a deep sadness. 'It was a fair city, filled with youth. I still remember that morning...' He stopped. 'Why do I always remember death, but never laughter?'

The words hung between them.

'But the Romans are weaker now,' Arthur said, convinced the man's great age had turned him into a coward. Such creeping fear was a thing he'd witnessed in once-strong warriors, bent under the weight of their years. These gelded creatures did not last long. 'Perhaps now is the time to be rid of them?'

'Perhaps, but I will not risk consigning more generations to suffering without a certain victory.'

'Nothing is certain, old man. Sometimes we must risk much to succeed.'

'Do not lecture me on bravery!' Merlin's voice rose. 'I have seen streets and fields run with the blood of men, women, and children. There is no such thing as a noble defeat, boy— only the sound of carrion flies and the rattle of slave chains.'

'You must not give in.'

'Who said I had? My kin have been forced to learn the true meaning of the word *patience*.'

Deciding not to push it further, Arthur turned and fell into a restless sleep.

HE FLEW through the air with infinite power and grace, upon mighty wings brimming with strength.

The wind rushing beneath his massive frame felt like a gentle breeze, yet he knew the pressure at this height would freeze the blood within the veins of a lesser being. His muscular chest heaved, thrusting ever faster, filling his soul with the thrill of the hunt. Far below, the outskirts of the great human city rolled into view. He didn't pity them, for a predator did not pity its prey. Tonight, he would feast upon their roasted corpses.

He dived, relishing the anticipation of splitting stone asunder, and toppling the monuments of ages. All would despair at his passage. He sped earthward, roaring his death rage.

'You are my gift to the world, young one—my vengeance,' she whispered in his ear.

CHAPTER TWELVE

A hand clamped over Arthur's mouth, and he tensed, ready to throw off his assailant.

'Be quiet. We have company,' Merlin whispered into his ear.

The hand slipped away, leaving him to shake off the last vestiges of his strange dream. Straining to hear the sounds coming from the inky darkness surrounding them, he pushed himself into a crouch, his body tense. The intrusive sound of trampling boots registered above the night breeze, as did something else, perhaps a dog's sniffing.

'It smells human flesh!' a guttural voice growled.

Merlin's expression, framed against the moonlit sky, became grim.

'Here, the spy gave us a rag. Try it,' an even deeper voice answered the first.

A pause, then more snuffling, followed by a triumphant snarling bark.

'Yessss!' the second voice roared. 'Call the others, Graak. The drui must be close. We hunt his skin!'

The shrill blast of a horn shattered the calm of the

evening. The ear-splitting din startled the horses, making them whinny in panic.

'Sneaky rats are up there!' the first voice called, filled with excited malevolence.

'Get your sword!' Merlin whispered urgently.

'What are those bloody things?' Arthur asked, reaching under his blanket for the *gladius*. Sleeping with a blade beneath him was a habit that'd saved his life on several occasions.

'Fomori.' The old man strode over to the horses to calm them. 'Shh, *calma mo milseáin*.'[1]

'More myths?' Arthur shot back in a whisper, not believing his ears. The tale of the Fomori was told to children to frighten them. They were demons from the nether world, fabled for snatching ill-behaved youngsters from their beds.

'If you doubt it, feel free to give our new friends a warm welcome!' Merlin snapped, no longer bothering to hush his voice. 'I'm sure they wouldn't dream of roasting you alive!' He patted a trembling Aina reassuringly, and then hurried into the gloom toward the stairway.

Arthur rushed after him, but he misjudged the width of the walkway and came within a hair's breadth of toppling over the side. He teetered on the brink of falling, as pebbles tumbled into the murk. Cursing, he regained his balance.

'Move your arse, lad!' The words drifted back from the silhouette of the running druid.

He gripped the *gladius* in a sweating palm, then plunged after the bobbing figure of Merlin. The old man halted, confronted by a bulky shadow, its snarls raking through the night air. Arthur jogged forward as fast as he dared upon the unreliable surface, his mind filled with terrifying images of what might await him.

'*Solas!*'[2] Merlin commanded, and a bright light splayed out in every direction. So powerful was the flash that Arthur found himself blinded. Then, as his vision adjusted, the large shadow in front of Merlin revealed itself as a fearsome brute with skin blacker than tar and coated in coarse, matted hair. It glared at the druid with murderous intent through unintelligent bloodshot eyes set within a canine skull. Saliva dripped from its fanged maw, wider than the head of the man it faced. The creature flared its nostrils, then emitted the same snort that'd announced its presence. Strangely, the thing stood on two legs like a human, towering above the old man.

The blinding spell proved timely, because the beast shook its muzzle in confusion, as if it had suffered a blow. Arthur took advantage of its temporary weakness and raced forward, then thrust his sword over Merlin's shoulder, deep into the monster's throat. Hot blood sprayed forth. The dog beast shuddered, then fell over the parapet, dead before it hit the stones below. It gave him some measure of comfort to know these terrors were at least mortal.

Three more assailants followed in its wake. The first was small and scurried on insect appendages, yet it possessed a furry torso and a weasel-like head. The unnatural thing scrambled up the stairs like a spider hurrying to devour flies trapped in a web. Its monstrous companions were tall, with the upper bodies of men, and lolloped along on hairy legs. They tossed their heads—which were hideously deformed and covered in warts, appearing more animal than human—in a frenzy of excitement. Unlike the scurrying beast, the larger duo wore crudely riven armour, black as night, except for a strange symbol of a red serpent coiled around a small white figure emblazoned on their breastplates.

Realising that Merlin was exposed to the coming onslaught, Arthur pushed past the old man, who, even in the middle of the fray, managed an irritated curse. Ignoring his companion's protests, the young warrior faced the scuttling imp. It had striking eyes, unlike any he'd seen in the animal kingdom, with yellow irises framed in a predator's snarling face. His hesitation at its bizarre appearance almost cost him dearly, for the creature snapped forward with teeth sharper and more numerous than any earthly creature possessed. He dodged, then thrust the gladius into the attacker's skull. Its body stiffened down the length of the blade.

An ugly giant kicked aside the corpse of the imp, then swung its axe above its head while screeching incomprehensible words of hatred through protruding tusks. As Arthur thrust the blade at its neck, the creature whipped out a clawed hand with shocking speed and grasped the sword in an iron grip. It leered into Arthur's fear-filled gaze, then licked its lips.

'After I skin you, I'll fuck your bones!' it growled, close enough for its foetid breath to make him gag.

It drove the axe down.

Still clutching the hilt of the *gladius*, Arthur was helpless to counter the blow and could only watch as his doom approached. Closing his eyes, he waited for death. It never came; instead, he heard a crack, then the grip on his sword went slack. Daring to look again, he saw the demon fall to its knees with what appeared to be a shard of ice driven into its forehead. In silence, the beast toppled over and fell into the gloom.

The third and largest demon retreated to the periphery of the light spell, its eyes reflecting the illumination like a cat's. It seemed hesitant to share the fate of the others, choosing instead to observe them before slinking back into shadow. When no assault followed, Arthur exhaled the breath he'd held, but his relief was short-lived, for a presence appeared at his side. He swirled, holding the sword at guard.

'Like I said—Fomori,' Merlin stated casually, eying the blade with a furrowed brow.

'Have they gone?' Arthur asked, panting warm air into the chill night.

'No, they never hunt in packs of less than a dozen.'

'What are they hunting for?'

'The answer to that is obvious. The real question is why, boy.'

'Don't call me *boy*.'

Merlin chuckled. 'How old are you?'

'Twenty-three.'

'Come back in another five hundred years and I'll think about it.' The druid patted him on the back. 'Look.' He pointed toward the road where misshapen silhouettes were forming. Although they were mostly obscured at the edge of the arc light, he could see they were a freakish collection of misfits, some clad in armour with horned skull caps upon their heads, while others were the scurrying lesser beings.

A guttural command came out of the darkness near to where the big demon had retreated. 'Take the drui alive and skin the pup!'

'That fool,' Merlin said, shaking his head in disbelief. 'Why did I not see this sooner! Talorc would bring doom upon us all for the sake of revenge!'

Arthur did not get the opportunity to question him further, for their assailants approached with frightening speed, scrambling over the shattered ruins of the outpost toward the bottom of the stairway, the only point of attack. With fascinated revulsion, he saw the smaller imps dart forward from the main pack and bite into the corpses of their fallen comrades at the foot of the wall.

The lead demon stepped back into the light and raised a nail-studded club. 'Extra flesh for the one who brings me the grey hair alive!'

The accompanying host screamed their pleasure at the offer.

A green-skinned horror with a weeping sore where its eye should be took up the challenge first. It bounded up the stairway eagerly and poked a short spear at Arthur. He parried then smashed the gladius's hilt into the creature's injured eye socket. A splurge of pus erupted from its head, and the giant clutched its face in agony. Wasting no time, Arthur pulled the sword back, then slid the blade beneath the screaming beast's chin and sheared a hole in its throat. The demon toppled like a tree into the path of its comrades, sending them tumbling. Curses uttered in a dark language echoed across the hillside as they scrambled to regain their footing.

'Enough of this!' Merlin shouted. '*Oighear!*'[3]

A layer of frost appeared beneath the feet of the Fomori, causing them to slip and tumble back once more, armour clattering loudly. Two of the scurrying imps were crushed under the weight of their larger cousins and left to scream in pain at their broken limbs.

'Fall back—you scum!' the big demon called up to the tangled group, apparently too wary to lead the attack himself.

They backed away in a tumult of claws and teeth until regaining their feet from the treacherous magical surface. Unsure what to do next, they milled around at the base of the stairs, shrieking and roaring impotently at their quarry.

'I said retreat!' the chief ordered.

The dazed Fomori grudgingly followed his command and returned to their cursing leader.

'We can't keep this up forever,' Arthur said, wiping the sweat from his brow.

'We only need to hold them off 'til daylight,' Merlin replied, grinning.

'What are you so happy about?'

'The ice spell worked rather well, don't you think?' The old man's grin widened beneath his beard.

'You won't be so happy when we've been trapped here for a week without food or water!'

Merlin rolled his eyes. 'You need to wash out your ears, lad. I said we only need to wait for the morning.'

Arthur couldn't understand such reasoning. 'The empire hasn't patrolled these peaks for a century—and most folk aren't stupid enough to travel this route.'

The old man gave his usual sigh of impatience. 'Creatures of the nether can't walk under the sun. Come dawn, our guests will die like slugs in salt.'

'They are truly from the underworld?'

'Aye. Well, what humans think is the underworld, mind.' Merlin rubbed his right hand, the same he'd used to cast the spell. 'They come from beyond the veil of our own world. Thank your lucky stars these are lesser creatures. Even their captains rank low amongst the dark ones, although they are picked for their black cunning.'

Arthur leaned against the parapet wall, aching for rest. 'Why do you think they want us?'

They peered into the gloom where their opponents now huddled around a large sack held by the lead demon.

'I cannot be certain, but I have my suspicions. What are they up to?' the old man said, interrupting himself as he noticed the demon's change of tactics.

The enemy were each handed crude short bows from the sack, which they strung with black gut.

'Shit,' Arthur said, unable to disguise his dismay at the new development. They were exposed. 'We need to go back and use the horses for cover.' He couldn't think of any other way to shelter themselves from the missiles sure to follow.

'Put my girls in danger, and I'll turn you into a cleg nut hanging from the arse of that demon!' Merlin retorted.

'Do you have any better suggestions?' the young warrior

asked, unsure which fate he feared most. 'Can't you reverse the light spell so they won't be able to see us?'

'And let them creep up on us in the dark? I think not.'

'But…'

'Trust me, boy, I've not brought you this far just to be skewered by an arrow. Now be sure to stay still and keep your gob shut!' The old man closed his eyes whilst facing the nightmarish gang that had formed into a ragged line, weapons in hand.

'Pull!' the fell captain bellowed into the night, drawing his own bow with massive biceps. A terrible moment of silence followed.

'Loose!' it called with an animal snarl, and in unison, they released a shower of death.

Arthur heard the arrows approach out of the darkness like a hive of angry bees. The clan used a similar technique on the fletching of their own arrows, and it produced a terrifying drone designed to instil fear in the unlucky targets of the barrage. It took every ounce of his will to fight his instinct to duck, but somehow, he obeyed Merlin's instruction to stay still, although his body quivered, anticipating the steel barbs about to rip into his flesh. He flinched as a flashing blur whizzed from the gloom, straight at his face.

The whistling sound abruptly stopped, but no pain followed. A heartbeat later, his guts lurched at the spectacle of a steel-tipped arrowhead suspended before his left eye. Incredibly, the missile continued to rotate on its shaft with none of its former forward momentum. As he struggled to process this strange twist of fate, Merlin murmured something beside him. Arthur turned to find the old man standing with his arm outstretched toward the deadly missiles floating in stasis before his younger companion. It was clear the demons had avoided aiming at the druid, no doubt wishing to capture him alive.

'*Cas ar ais!*'[4] Merlin commanded, his eyes rolling into his head, leaving only the whites visible.

The arrows flipped in mid-air and sped back into the murk. Arthur watched in awe as the missiles darted amongst those who'd launched them, wreaking bloody chaos. Gurgling screams rose as the pointed shafts buried themselves into their attackers. To the last, the nether host collapsed, including their champion, who lay spread-eagled with a feathered shaft sticking out from his thick brow.

'Quick, must question them,' Merlin said, heading down the stairs, only to halt with his foot poised above the treacherous frost. Swearing like a fish wife, he waved his hand to dissipate the ice and continued his descent.

Arthur followed on his heels, feeling strangely exhilarated following their near brush with disaster.

In death, the creatures had lost their colour, taking on the pasty pallor of crawling beasts more at home under the earth than above it. Even their eyes were milky white, similar to overripe fish left to rot on the riverbank. Merlin hobbled over to their remains without the usual spring to his step.

'Damn it! I wanted one of them alive!' Merlin swore after discovering they were all dead. 'I need to know who our enemy is.' He kicked the big demon in the ribs, causing its corpse to break wind. Arthur had seen the dead bodies of men do the same, again prompting him to wonder if these beings were a monstrous parody of natural creatures.

'Can't you...?' he asked the old man, wiggling his fingers above the head of a fallen imp.

'What's?' Merlin repeated the finger gesture.

'Make them talk from the dead—like you did with the other corpse.'

'Too dangerous,' the druid concluded, slumping onto the grass to rest. 'That spirit was an ally with a soul. These sewer rats are slaves with only the whips of their masters to give meaning to their pitiful existence.'

'You said "too dangerous." That means you could?'

'Could and should are two different things.' Merlin shook his head. 'I could force their tortured shadows to answer, but the wraiths of such abominations are even fouler than in life.' He sighed in frustration. 'And as I said, such an unnatural crossing risks attracting the attention of a greater evil.'

Arthur shuddered to think of anything worse than these wicked things, then noticed the symbol on the demon's armour. 'What does this mean?'

'It tells us which tribe they belong too, but not which prince they serve. These creatures are treacherous and change allegiance so often we can never be sure who they serve.'

'They have kings in hell?' He'd heard some of the new eastern religions name the nether as such.

'Hell!' Merlin spat to show his contempt. 'Mumbo jumbo spouted by the followers of Sol Invictus. Those fanatics are obsessed with punishing people for daring to have genitals. No, the nether is real.'

'What do we do now?'

'We sleep.'

Arthur didn't like the idea of staying here another minute, never mind the rest of the night. He offered his hand to the old man. 'But what if more come?'

'They won't disturb us again tonight,' the druid replied, taking the proffered aid and grumbling under his breath as he rose.

'How do you know?'

'Enough questions, boy!' Merlin snapped. Despite his usual intransigence, he leaned against his younger counter-part as they ambled back to the wall and up the stairs. Such a show of frailty from the seemingly inexhaustible druid worried him.

'Why send them?' Arthur pressed.

'I'm not sure.' Merlin stumbled as he spoke, forcing Arthur to grasp him under the elbow to steady him. 'Who knows what schemes the nether princes are toying with.' He groaned from exertion. 'The demon spoke of a spy'

'What does that mean?'

'It means, my slow-witted young friend, someone has betrayed us. They must have known our destination.'

Arthur found it hard to believe that any human would collaborate with such beings. 'The tribune?' he ventured.

Merlin sniffed dismissively. 'That useless turd would piss his tiny loincloth if he ran into one of those things. No, this is someone else. I do not know who.'

They were soon back at the makeshift camp where the horses flicked their tails in the equine equivalent of a greeting. Merlin hobbled between them, laying a reassuring hand upon their necks. 'He wanted to let the enemy stick you full of arrows, girls,' he said, tutting.

'I didn't think we had a choice!' Arthur protested.

Fionna nickered her disapproval.

CHAPTER THIRTEEN

They watched in silence as the black pall of smokebillowed fromthe wreck of Ardotalia and merged withthebroilinggrey clouds. Carrion crows circled the burning remnants of the once mighty hill fort and occasionally drifted down to peck amongst the carnage. Merlin seemed lost for words, concern written all over hisweathered features.

'What happened?'Arthur asked, wiping the persistentdrizzle of rain from his face.

'I'll consult the crystal ball I keep up my arse, shall I?'the druidsnapped. 'Come on.' He nudged Fionna into the ring of tree stumps at the base of the great mound, on which the fortification stood.

The surrounding woods had been cut back to allow the garrison a better view of the lands around them. Arthur wondered how such precautions could have failed them so badly, for the scale of thedisaster became all too clear as they approached. The cause remained a mystery but looked like a giant had descended from the heavens and smashed the defences to pieces as if it were a child's plaything. Nothing living moved among the wreckage. Arthur spat to ward away evil spirits.

'Seehow the debris lies in a wide circlearound thefort,' Merlinsaid, pointing at smouldering wooden beams and chunks of charred flesh.

'Yes?' Adiscernibleedge demarcated the outer limits of the devastation.

'It means the explosion that caused this came from within the fortress.'

'They blew themselves up?'

His companion shot him a withering glare. 'Aye. Garrison duty can be fearsomely tedious.'

Ignoring the acid comment, Arthur observed the shattered wooden defences and turf walls, which differed from the typical Roman style at Derventio. 'This was a native fort? NotRoman?'

'My nephew at least had enough brains to build his own power base. Ardotalia is…'—he paused—'*was* the biggestnative garrison in centuries.'

'Theempireallowed that?' Arthur asked, guiding his nervous mount around a decapitated head with the stag of the Coritani tattooed upon its blood-encrusted scalp. The corpse's jaw gaped, as if still shocked by the final moments of its life.

'They have little choice these days,' Merlin replied, steering Fionna to avoid body parts. 'Not a single full legion remains in the entire diocese, and our masters fear another insurrection, so they allow the governor more latitude than they would have even twenty years ago.'

The two travellers joined the roadthat ascended the hillside and followed it to the blackened main gates creakingin the crisp morning air. The wooden staves of the adjoining palisadehad been splayedoutward by the same colossal force.

'Dog's teeth! What happened here?' Arthur exclaimed, as

they stoppedatthe threshold of the broken gateway,confronted by a huge pitat the heart of what had once been a thriving community. At leastthirty feet deep, the sidesof the chasm appeared to be achaotic mixture of soil, everyday objects, and half-naked, charred corpses. The flock of birds scavenged amongst the wreckage, pluckingout glassyeyes and tearing into rawflesh.

'Bandits couldn't have done this,' Arthur said, stunned at the slaughter.

The old man stepped down from his saddle and strode to the crater's edge. 'Aye, such pests do not possess the necessary devilry.' Stooping down, he poked his fingers into the soil, dabbed it on his tongue. 'Greek fire—mixed with something I know not.' Brow furrowed in thought, he stood and searched the devastation. 'There.' He pointed at the centre of the pit where a single inhuman leg stuck up from the earth. It wasn't clearif the appendage was still attached to its owner.

'This is the work of the nether,' Merlin said, a dark look upon his whiskered face. 'Theymust've found a way inside the fort, under the foundations.'

Arthur dismounted and joined him at the edge of the hellish burrow. 'The same creatures that attacked us did this? It would take an army.'

'No.' Merlin replied. 'They exploded a device below the garrison. Ascoutingparty could've done it.'

Staring at the mangled void, Arthur had to concede the druid may be right, although he had never heard of any substance powerful enough to wreak such devastation. 'How could they burrow into the hillside unnoticed? It would have taken months of effort.'

Merlin shrugged. 'Perhaps under the cover of night. More likely, they discovered a natural cavern running beneath. These peaks are riddled with them, and imps have anaffinity for the world's dark places.'

Arthur recalled how the fallen demons' corpses had gone white soon after death. Their hideous, misshapen faces had filled his nightmares the previous night, so he found the prospect of a world populated with these beings more than a little disturbing, and even more so in the cold light of day. 'How many did they kill here?'

Merlin exhaled wearily. 'Five hundred soulsat least, not counting the women and children.'

'Shit.'

'Shit, indeed. Our journey has become more urgent. We must warn Vibius that this evil may be greater than I thought possible.'

'Why did those creatures attack this place?'

'I'm not certain, but—'

A high-pitched mewling sound came from an overturned cart.Exchanging wary glances, they cautiously approached the disturbance.

Arthur drew his blade, expecting some slavering monstrosity. 'Perhaps it's injured and seeks to hide itself underneath?' he whispered.

Merlin raised a finger to his lips.

They crept closer, traversing greatclods of earth and wreckage that made the short walk to the cart a treacherous stumble. Arthur placed his boot on what appeared to be solid footing, only for his leg to push through an upper layer of debris and into something that gave a sickening crunch. He peered down to find aflashof white bone. 'Damn!' he cursed under his breath and wiped the gore on a nearby plank.

The high-pitched cry rang out again.

They pushed forward to the vehicle. Arthur raised the sword, ready to strikeat whatever lay beneath. Merlin braced his shoulder against the side of the cart, then moutheda silent count. On three, the druidflipped it over with surprising strength, revealing more churned soil and achild'sdoll, its face streaked with dirt.

Puzzled by the object, Arthur had been about to pick it up when the doll flapped its arms and emitted another wailing yowl. 'Shit!' he said, raising his guard and stepping back as if the infant were a live serpent.

No more than a few months old, the baby gazed up at the two men in helpless bewilderment.

'How the fuck did it survive?' Arthur asked as thechild-fixed its eyes on him. No sooner had he spoken than the baby let out another squall.

'Mind yourlanguage,' Merlin said. 'The luck of the gods is with this little one.'

'What shall we do?'

'Ending the brothel talk would be a good start.'

Arthur turned the kidgently with his foot, checking its condition. 'It doesn't seem injured.'

Tutting,Merlin bent and picked up the child, his arm supporting its backside. The youngster's eyes widened upon seeing the old man's beard, and it reached out with a chubby hand to give his grey whiskers an experimental tug.

'You care for children as well as you dohorses,' the druid grumbled, placing his palm onto the infant's forehead and closing his eyes. Thechild frowned in mild surprise, then babbled.

'He says he iswell, but hungry,'Merlinreported.

'It sounded like nonsense tome,' Arthur retorted.

'Of courseitdid. He's a baby!'

'Then how…?' Arthur knew better than to finish the question. 'But seriously, it doesn't look weaned. Without a woman, it'll starve. We should leave it here.'

Merlin gave him a black glare while wincing at the aggressive tugs on his beard. 'By the—' He stopped and glanced at his tiny tormentor before moderating his reply to Arthur. 'Twinkly stars in the sky, *it* is a *he*, and he goes with us.'

'Whatare youplanning to do? Grow a pair of tits?'

'I'll grow a pair on you if you don't stop mithering me with questions!' Merlin said and trudged back to the mounts, cradling the foundling with care. 'Come on, they might be keeping a watch on their handiwork.'

Muttering, Arthur followed.

The horses nickered with relief at their return, unnerved by the surrounding destruction and unnatural stench.

'Here.'Merlinheld out the baby to the young warrior.

With a distrustful scowl, he took the proffered child, but kept it at arm's length.Rolling his eyes, Merlin grasped his saddlebag from Fionna's flank and rummaged through it.

Arthur waited awkwardly while big blue eyes regarded him with suspicion. He noticeda tiny copper arm ring around the infant's wrist, with thename 'Mordred' etched intoits shiny surface.

'Greetings, Mordred' he said to fill the awkward silence.

Thebabewrinkled its face into a sullen pout, presumably due to Arthur's less entertaining beard, then began to flap his arms and cryagain.

'Shh… shh…' the warrior said, rhythmicallyjiggingthe boy to calm him, but the ungrateful whelp didn't appreciate such placatory efforts and insisted upon continuing the tremendous caterwaul.

Wishing the ordeal over, Arthur looked to Merlin, who had thankfully fashioned a blanket into a crude sling.

'Good grief, are you trying to comfort the child or brain it!' The druid commented, before beaming at the youngster. 'The man isa meat-headedoaf,is he not?' he crooned and held out his arms. The little traitor immediately reached toward the beard again, his crying already forgotten.

CHAPTER FOURTEEN

They camped amongst the remains of ahomesteadon the edge of a disused quarry. The roof had partiallycollapsed into the interior, but the walls provided adequate shelter from the worst of the wind whipping over the cliff edge. Thankfully, the rain had subsided during the afternoon, allowing them to light a fire in the old hearth and alleviate the chill creeping into the evening.

Merlinunstrapped the makeshift cradle containing the sleeping babe from his saddle and placed him a safe distance from the roaring flames. When he rose, holding his back and groaning in discomfort as the elderly did, he took in their surrounding environment and rubbed his chin. "Hmm, I've been here before, I reckon. The house wasn't here, but the quarry was.'

'You say that everywhere we go,' Arthur grumbled, cold and out of sorts. The rain had seeped into his bones over the long day's journey.

'We dug good strong peak granite here,' the old man continued, ignoring the jibe. 'After they came, all the greedy bastards wereinterested in wastin—and the powder, of course.' Merlin seemed happy enough to converse with himself, regardless of his companion's disposition.

'Howdo you remembera thousandyears? Arthur asked, determined to irritate the druid. 'Does sorcery stop you from becoming a dotard?'

If the comment offended him, Merlin did not show it. 'Nine hundred and seventy-one,' he correctedquietly. 'And no, I don't remember everything.' The fire cast dancing shadows across his lined brow as he sat upon a stone plinth, its original purpose lost. 'The land is the easiest. It changes slowly over many decades.' He gave a small exhalation of pleasure to be resting. 'And the buildings, to some extent. But people are much harder. They are gone so quickly...' He frowned. 'The faces of those I loved above all have blurred over time. Sometimes, I wonder if it's their faces I recall, or if it's just a trick of my imagination.'

They listened to the flames crackle.

'It must be hard,' Arthur said. The melancholic response had left him in no mood to poke the druid further.

Merlin shrugged. 'You've no idea, boy.' The simple statement contained none of his usual bite. 'Our minds were never designed to last as long as my kind have endured. It is the source of much sorrow, driving many of us to madness over the centuries.' He paused for a moment. 'I am convinced it was out of the pity for the Eld that the gods made the lifespan of men so short.'

'You have brothers?'

Merlin nodded, staring into the flames. 'Aye, and sisters. There were many of us in the old days. I was one of the last.' He looked down at the baby, who slowly opened and closed his fingers while he slumbered. 'My family sees me as no older than this little one.' He smiled, placing a gnarled finger into the baby's palm. The child immediately closed his tiny digits around it. 'Some things never change, though, and I like that.'

'But you must have touchedonmany lives?' Arthur asked, surprised by his turn of mood. 'To live so long is a gift many would do anything for.'

'Hmm, I would not wish it on our worst foe.'

'Why?'

'Mortals spend so much time praying to beings that don't care, or don't even exist, begging for happiness after the end of a miserable existence. The truth is'—he gestured around him—'this can be your paradise if you make it so. Humans are lucky. They are not burdened with the consequences their actions have upon the generations to come. Trust me, oblivion is a blessing. Embrace it.' He suddenly looked fragile, as if every year had caught up with him at once. 'So, aye, I have touched upon many lives—too many.'

'Have you never been tempted to end it?'

'Many times, but while hope remains, I refuse to rest until we are free again.' He looked at the younger man pointedly. 'Even if it comes in strange forms.' The baby stirred, shaking Merlin from his reflections. 'Fetch me water from the spring yonder,' he instructed, gesturing to a tiny brook outside the moss-coveredstones of the house. It had undoubtedly supplied its previous occupants with fresh water. 'This child cannot go on looking like a filth-encrusted monkey.'

Arthur found the odd name curious. 'What's a monkey?'

'They are hairy beasts from across the seas,' the druid replied as he carefully removed the dirty rags from Mordred without waking him. 'Many years ago, I had the displeasure of meeting one. A trade galley brought the cunning wretch from the far reaches of the empire, and to my great misfortune, the fiend failed to drown on the way.'

'It was a fearsome creature?'

'A fearsomely clever thief!' Merlin spoke in low tones so

as not to disturb the baby. 'The ship's captain claimed to have trained it to play Tali.'

'You played Tali with an animal?'

'Played and lost! The wager beggared me!'

Laughing, Arthur took the bucket to fill it from the stream. When he returned the old man placed his hand over the water and commanded, '*níos teo*,'[1] causing light steam to emanate from the surface. 'Fetch me those rags inside my saddlebag.'

After receiving the makeshift swaddling from a grumbling Arthur, Merlin returned his attention to the child. He lightly placed a wrinkled hand onto the slumbering babe's forehead, and Mordred's blue eyes flickered open.

'My apologies, young master, but you smell like a dead rodent's bottom, and that will not do.' He promptly rolled back the sleeve of his grey robe and dipped an elbow into the steaming liquid. 'Perfect.' He began to wash the kid while the recipient of his aid appeared distinctly unimpressed at having his sleep interrupted. Upon completing his task, Merlin wrapped him in the fresh rags. 'Now, tell me that does not feel better, hmm?'

Mordred did not answer, for he had already nodded off again.

'What are you going to do about feeding him? He'll be dead in a few days.' Arthur yawned, having found a comfortable spot to put his feet up and doze.

That earned him another icy, grey-eyed rebuke. 'We will feed him after you've found me a goat.'

Arthur blinked. 'What? Where will I find…?'

'Use your initiative.'

'But…'

'The other option is I grow those udders on your chest. Trust me, it can be done.'

Alarmed, the young warrior held up his hands in surrender. 'Okay, okay. I'll look.'

'Good. And the horses need watering.'

With one last longing glance at the warm fire, Arthur stalked into the growing gloom.

'You'll be needing this,' he heard from behind.

As he turned, a small solid object hit him in the temple. He cursed and rubbed the offended area in annoyance. Looking down to where the missile had landed, he found a finger-sized metallic object attached to a leather loop nestled in the grass. He picked it up and examined the thing more closely. It'd been shaped into the form of a woman crowned with leaves. Inscribed along its length in Gaelic was the word '*Nimue.*' Guessing it was a good luck charm, he shrugged and placed it over his head, then continued his trek around the top of the quarry.

He searched beneath the heavens setting in crimson glory while contemplating the old man's merciful nature. The fate of such newborns in the clan was measured in hours, if not minutes, but Merlin appeared to care for all life. Something bothered him about that. Life should be simple, without inviting disaster through stupid acts of indulgent kindness. And yet, undeterred by his great age and dark history, the old man transcended those consequences in a way that made Arthur's baser instincts feel shameful.

It occurred to him that now would be the perfect opportunity to rid himself of the druid. Burdened with the child, it was unlikely even he could give chase, should Arthur simply double back, steal one of the horses, and leave. But the thought of coin and the promise of answers to questions driving him mad stopped him.

'Stupid old sod,' he muttered. 'How am I supposed to spot a fucking goat in the dark!'

* * *

HE'D BEEN LOOKING FORLORNLY for almost an hour, working his way to the base of the abandoned stone works, but hadn't seen a living thing, only mossy blocks of granite hewn from the hillside long ago and left in situ. The peaks were full of such relics of former prosperity. Realising the task was hopeless, Arthur stopped and bellowed in frustration. It did not stem from his failure, but from the consequences for the babe. The sound echoed back, enhanced by the natural acoustics around him.

The metal figurine...

Arthur lifted the object from his neck and turned its worn surface in his hand. He noticed a hole resembling an open mouth at one end.

Almost like a shepherd's whistle...

Exactly like a whistle.

He brought it to his lips and blew.

Unsurprisingly, no sound emerged, and nothing happened. A cold wind surged through the quarry, making him long for the fire all the more. Just as he was contemplating his failure, a faint sound reached him on the evening air.

He strained to hear it above the gusts, but the sound was unmistakable: a trampling stomp accompanied by bleating animal calls. Then, upon the rock face, they came. A whole herd of goats clambered toward him with astonishing agility, nimbly leaping across sheer drops and over boulders with ease, all while answering his call. Black goats, brown goats, white goats, both kids and adults.

Such was their eagerness to reach him that they hit the floor at a run. Arthur was alarmed enough to jog in the opposite direction. Only upon realising he'd no hope of outpacing them did he stop, turn to face the onslaught, and close his eyes while protectively crossing his hands over his private parts.

The wet snout sniffing loudly against the back of his hand determined he would not be savaged, so he tentatively opened one eyelid to discover a ring of the shaggy beasts gazing at him intently through yellow eyes, the pupils vertical slits.

His brief elation at the unexpected success soon turned to consternation. With no rope to snare one of his new companions, he decided to head back to camp and seek a tether there. Arthur pushed his way through the hairy throng and set off toward the trail back up. The goats followed.

'You've got to be kidding me,' he said, smiling at his own wit.

'Baaaarrrrr,' they replied in unison.

He and his newly acquired flock arrived at the abandoned structure just as the sun finally fell and found the old man fast asleep, his feet propped against the hearth's brickwork, hands folded across his chest. The child lay nearby in his makeshift bedding, also fast on. The fire crackled heartily, giving the scene a warm and inviting glow.

'Goats!' Arthur announced loudly.

Snorting in alarm, Merlin opened his eyes to regard their bustling visitors, now happily munching upon the grass atop the escarpment.

The young warrior bowed theatrically before the druid to signify the completion of his mission.

'We only need one,' Merlin observed, stretching his arms and yawning.

'Unfortunately, they declined the instruction,' Arthur snapped back.

Merlin ignored him and rose to inspect the goats, looking for a suitable candidate to act as a wet nurse.

* * *

AFTER RETURNING from watering the horses, bone-tired, Arthur found Merlin examining a large map pinned at either end by two rocks. Nearby, a rather fat nanny goat placidly munched on grass while the babe, propped beneath in his blankets, happily fed.

'It worked, then,' the young man said as he approached the oddly domestic scene.

'What?' Merlin asked, distracted from his geographic consultation. 'Oh, 'tis a trick I learned long ago. Children are actually very resilient given half a chance.'

'But the beast will slow us down.'

The old man shrugged. 'Goats are nimble creatures. It'll keep up.'

Too weary to argue, Arthur sat beside Merlin, and for the first time, noticed the striking beauty of the map he pondered. It was inscribed upon a type of animal skin in silver and gold, and featured a great island surrounded by waves upon all sides, complete with mountains, forests, and cities. Monstrous serpents decorated the watery depths of a sea to the east of its shores inscribed as 'Morimaru.' It had a curious mix of both Celtic and Roman names upon it.

'So, what's the plan?' he asked, removing the whistle from his neck and offering it back the old man.

Merlin took one look at the strange object and waved his hand. 'Keep it. Who knows, one day it may bring you your greatest desire.'

Uncaring, Arthur slipped the leather loop back over his head and watched as the druid traced his finger north from the ruined hill fort marked 'Ardotalia.' The young warrior could not understand how the ancient illustration could represent such recent destruction. 'How...?'

Merlin merely wiggled his fingers then returned to the

map. 'The governor commanded me to lead the garrison from Ardotalia and reinforce the northern army.' He pointed to the drawing of a town named Luguvalium, far to the northwest of the destroyed fort. 'But it appears the enemy is ahead of us.'

'So, we take the news to the governor. Let him deal with it,' Arthur suggested.

'You've never met Vibius, have you?' Merlin asked coldly.

'Of course not.'

'My great nephew is impulsive. He'd likely pull the army from the north and head straight here.'

Arthur wondered how many 'greats' removed the two men really were. 'And? There is a clear threat here.'

The old man's hand moved nort toward an illustration of a vast wall spanning the narrow neck of the island from coast to coast, separating the lands of the fearsome Pictish tribes from those the empire occupied south of the great divide. 'The wall of Hadrianus would be left unsupported, and any force Talorc is gathering would be free to sweep south while we chase shadows down here.'

'So, what do we do? Head back to Derventio and warn the garrison there?'

Merlin shook his head. 'No, we'd lose too much time, and you saw the state of the troops there. They're only good for torturing dumb beasts.'

'Surely we have to warn someone about those things running around?'

The druid sniffed. 'Aye, we have no choice but to tell the governor, even if it pains me to think how he'll react, but it may as well come from me first. At least that way I can advise against rash action.'

'Does he not listen to you?' Arther asked, pulling off his boots and rubbing his aching feet.

Merlin wrinkled his nose at the younger man's wiggling

toes. 'My counsel has fallen out of favour,' he snapped. 'It took me three moons to persuade the fat oaf to bring a force into the territory of the Brigantes.'

The old man pondered the map, then pointed to a small town at the edge of a hilly terrain that marked the northernmost edge of the peaks. 'We can warn the people of Cambodunum before we continue north. They can send word to the garrison at Mancunium.' He tapped a gnarled finger over a walled town further southwest.

Arthur contemplated the seriousness with which the druid regarded the situation. 'Do you really think the Picts could invade?'

Merlin peered into the flames. 'Under the old king, I would say no. I only met him once during the gathering of fealty, but he seemed more interested in boozing and whoring than in the affairs of the state. Talorc would've been a boy then, but he's a child no longer, and any man who can overthrow his own father is one to be reckoned with.' Merlin rolled up the map.

'Why do the Picts hate us?' Arthur asked. He did not believe any man would seek support from such dreaded allies.

The old druid paused in the act of returning the map to his satchel. 'They hate the Romans for the many humiliations they've imposed upon them over the centuries, but I think they hate the southern tribes more for our weakness. It reminds them how close they also came to slavery.'

The flames in the hearth crackled and spat.

CHAPTER FIFTEEN

Calder, eldest of the drui, felt a nervousness he'd not experienced for many years as the procession arrived at the ancient shore of Llyn Penrhyn. A red moon cast a sickly, ethereal light on those gathered, their hooded robes appearing drenched in blood. Another ill omen.

Where are you, Merlin? he thought, gazing upon the inky black waters, with his heart hammering in his chest. Although they'd performed the divination ritual a dozen times in his life, they had never done it without his guiding hand and never under such worrying circumstances. Again, he pondered his decision to allow the ceremony, and again, uncertainty plagued him. True, the disturbing visions they'd all experienced had demanded the ritual, but something felt wrong, not the least of which was their inability to communicate with their father.

As one, the drui clasped their hands together and chanted. In response, ripples appeared upon the mirror-like surface of the waters. The incantation was working. Ever so slowly, the inky depths swirled into patterns that formed discernable shapes. The worried throb in Calder's temple quickened. Even with his decades of training, the troubling augers were as difficult to understand as they were disturbing. The less experienced members of the congregation muttered in confusion, while the oldest amongst them maintained a stunned silence.

A raging sea…

The threads of fate speak of turmoil to come.

His jaw dropped in dismay at the next glowing symbols: a serpent crushing and devouring a child, and beside it, the form of a flying dove.

Otherworldly forces will cross the veil from below and above.

'We must find our father and seek guidance!' The panicked comment had come from Morganna, one of the novices. She was a bright girl who'd likely translated the dire warning faster than her tutors.

Calder raised a trembling hand to quiet her. Now was not the time.

No sooner had the symbols of heaven and earth dissipated than a more astonishing omen appeared.

The crown and the sword as one, yet the symbol of the nether returns to shadow its presence.

Gasps rang out around the circle. Even the newest initiate could not fail to grasp the staggering implications, for this sign had been seared into the memory of each of them from their earliest lessons.

'Silence!' Calder commanded. 'We must focus!'

The picture wavered as they struggled to maintain the incredible levels of psychic energy required to summon the mystic herald. Druce's hand tightened upon his own as he mastered his inner turmoil.

Good! Fight! he thought, swelling with love and pride for the man beside him.

As their collective will reasserted itself, the symbols coalesced. Calder gave silent thanks for the bonds of brotherhood he'd built since his rescue from a fate of abandonment and death all those years ago.

Again, the image changed against the pitch-black waters as another secret revealed itself, this one bewildering. The form was of a beautiful figure, gowned and bejewelled with starlight. A god symbol, no doubt, but the deity transformed before their eyes, becoming a misshapen, leering parody of itself.

Perhaps we should —

His own growing horror cut off the old man's thought, for the sacred waters, still as glass for countless millennia, bubbled.

Moans of terror escaped his family as a high-pitched shriek rose within their skulls. They were under attack. Calder's thoughts raced as he tried to recall a lesson that covered such a terrible blasphemy, but realised there was none. Even this dark conclusion was short-lived, for a clawed hand, attached to a scaled arm far larger than that of any man, emerged from the writhing waters. The fearsome thing uncoiled itself like a serpent while they stared in astonishment.

Following an agonising pause, the hand splayed, revealing fingers with a skewered eyeball driven onto each of its ragged talons. The deathly monstrosity flipped its wrist, then swept around the gathered circle of druids, scanning the group with a brooding calculation. The horrific intruder stopped only inches from Calder's face and searched his features with milk-white irises.

'We must end the ceremony!' he shouted, breaking the hypnotic spell. But before he could utter the words of extrication, the hand lunged and grasped the face of Galvyn, one of the oldest and most beloved of their group. Thought to be a distant relative of Merlin himself, the remarkable likeness he bore to their father had been a point of mild teasing over the years.

They could only watch in impotent despair as the foul thing dug its claws into his gentle countenance. Their poor brother called out in pain as several of the eyeballs burst under the pressure as it squeezed his skull. In an act of incredible bravery, Morganna desperately beat against the scaled limb even while it crushed the life from her elder. Her efforts were in vain, for he was lifted off his feet and left to kick beyond the reach of her outstretched arms.

'*Scaoileadh!*'[1] Calder screamed, speaking the word that risked sending them all into madness. Such was their predicament, however, that he had little choice. The backlash was tremendous. It drove the drui to their knees, and they clasped their hands to their temples in agony.

The raging lake frosted, then solidified into thick ice, severing the monstrous arm. Its guttural howl of furious pain echoed across the valley. Removed from its host, the arm fell twitching on the shore. Upon death, it turned a sickly opaque colour, the mere husk of a living thing. The drui stood rooted to their spots in the silent aftermath, reduced to frightened children adrift in a world filled with evil.

Morganna was the first to aid the sprawled figure lying crumbled amongst the water lilies on the shore. She caressed Galvyn's bloody brow and wept whilst the others gathered around, too traumatised to speak. Calder's heart beat hard and fast, close to bursting within his aged body. He feared it would fail him and leave his loved one's even more alone. The dark tidings continued, for he had tended to enough dying men to recognise that his brother's ragged gasps would be his last.

Amid his grief, a deep outrage surfaced in him. This intrusion onto their most hallowed ground was an unspeakable act not witnessed since the great massacre. In some respects, it was worse. The punitive attack by the invaders had been physical, but this spiritual assault, unconscionable in its audacity, mocked the core of their beliefs.

'Our brother is dead,' Morganna said, her voice thick with emotion. She laid his head amongst the fauna, then, in a display of kindness that made Calder choke back tears, she picked a flowering bud and placed it upon his still chest.

A collective moan of despair broke the silence. For centuries, their father had cultivated their number back from the brink of extinction. Even the loss of one was a heavy blow. More than that, they had lost the kindest amongst them, a man who had been a constant presence from their earliest days.

'Blessed be our brother...' He began the mourning incantation, not spoken aloud for twenty years.

'Blessed be,' they followed, many weeping.

On unsteady feet, Calder joined the still kneeling Morganna and placed a comforting hand on her shoulder. She did not speak but remained bent in despair. The very old and the very young often found common ground, and so it had been with these two. Despite the many years between them, they had been inseparable friends since she was a little girl. Calder removed his outer robe and draped it over their fallen comrade while the others looked on, their faces pale smudges beneath the crimson moonlight bathing the land.

'What was that thing?' Druce asked, voicing the question they all feared to ask.

'Evil,' Calder answered.

'But what could penetrate the sanctity of the grove? Our father said—'

'I do not know,' Calder replied, slumping beside Morganna. He felt every day of his eighty years. 'But I'm certain the unclean thing was searching for one of us in particular.'

Murmured words of shock followed.

'Who?' Druce asked.

'Our father.'

'But he is not amongst us tonight.'

'He looked like our father,' Morganna answered, pressing her hand upon their fallen brother's chest. Even in the depths of grief, her young mind refused to acquiesce to despair.

'How do you know? He could be anywhere in the Isles,' Druce pressed.

Calder closed his eyes and stretched his senses forth, but he only sensed the shadow of their father moving across the land.

'We know his goal is to reach the governor at Luguvalium,' he said, opening his eyes. 'We must go there, warn them both, and offer our aid, such as it is.'

He regarded the sobbing novice beside him. 'Morganna will do us the great honour of remaining here and caring for the grove. The rest of us should go.' She had suffered enough for one so young.

The decision provoked another flurry of murmured surprise. To leave the sacred heart so lightly guarded was unheard of. Feeling a crushing weariness, Calder gestured for them to be quiet.

'I will not stay,' Morganna whispered. Usually a respectful girl, she never displayed such disobedience. She hesitated. 'I would help him.' Her loyalty to their founder was fierce, even for one of his children. Merlin had rescued her from the cradled arms of her dead mother after finding the infant abandoned amongst the decimated population of a plague village.

'You are right, little one,' he replied and gently squeezed her shoulder. She had proved her courage. 'But the danger is not only to our beloved friend. The fate of all our peoples is at stake. Not since the genocide of our ancestors have we faced such peril.'

They all contemplated the difficult path ahead.

'What of the Dragon's tooth?' Druce asked. 'If the end time has arrived, we are not ready.'

He was right. No one had wielded Calesvol since the world was young. Even most of the drui considered the tale a myth. Yet their ever-vigilant leader had taught them to recognise the ancient symbol that heralded an unimaginable change.

We never found its resting place, and now time has run out, he thought.

'The great wheel guides us, as it does in all things,' he said. 'The tooth will reveal itself when it will—and in that moment, we shall be ready.'

Must be ready… he added to himself with a dread he dared not share, for if the enemy were to locate it first, death would come as a welcome reprieve.

CHAPTER SIXTEEN

'I don't want my presence here known,' Merlin said as they trotted toward the town gate of Cambodunum. 'We've enough on our plates without more midnight surprises.'

Arthur found himself agreeing with the old man for once. In fact, he'd already come up with a plan to avoid unwanted attention. 'Leave it to me,' he said, sounding confident.

'What do you mean?' came the suspicious response.

'I have a plan.'

The druid sighed. 'Heaven help us,' he said, then muttered something in Gaelic that sounded like an incantation. Curious, Arthur glanced at the druid and was shocked to see a younger man with a heavy brow and wide nostrils grinning back at him through blackened teeth. Arthur's own smile at the bizarre transformation froze, however, when he felt a sharp pain burst through his skull. He reached up to discover his own nose, broken for as long as he could remember, had snapped back into alignment.

'Shit!' Arthur exclaimed, cradling his throbbing snout. 'You could've warned me!'

'I modelled this look on your ugly mug. What do ya reckon?' Merlin presented him with a sideways profile of his new appearance.

Ignoring the jest Arthur looked to the single guard ahead, who greeted them with a scowl. The man had a blue spiral tattoo on his forehead, marking him as a warrior of the tribe, and was equipped with both a traditional conical helm and *sciath* buckler. His war garb was in the Celtic style without Roman influence. The old-fashioned armour had become popular of late, particularly among the restless northern tribes as the empire's control declined.

A palisade surrounded the settlement. Its fire-blackened tips looked fresh, the timber still green as if erected in more recent times. Whether as a deterrent against the ever-growing bandit threat, or as part of a defence against the Picts, was unclear.

'Speak your name and business,' the young guard said flatly, his hand on the pommel of his sword.

Arthur adopted the amenable expression he reserved for unwanted encounters with officialdom. 'I am Sheridan, and he is Varden of the Belgae. We've come to trade slaves.'

The ploy pleased him. Roving bands of slave traders were such a common sight across the land that two more wouldn't attract attention. Most slaves bonded themselves voluntarily, to avoid crippling taxes and starvation. This particular identity would also explain why two grown men were travelling with a motherless baby, for many desperate families sold their own children to feed the constant need for labour on wealthy estates.

But to his surprise, the introduction earned him a hard look from the warrior.

Without comment, Merlin clouted Arthur round the head with such force his ears rang.

'Forgive my apprentice,' the old man stated while his

companion sputtered in rage. 'He's a halfwit and has a habit of speaking out of turn.'

The guard's lips twitched in amusement at the altercation, but his disapproving glare did not alter.

Arthur fumed in silence. The undisclosed part of his plan had been to reverse their roles, yet Merlin had demoted him to lackey status once again.

'Tis a sorry haul,' the sentry commented, pointing at the sleeping Mordred in his makeshift crib hanging from Merlin's saddle.

'Poor business in Derventio.' The disguised druid shook his head. 'This brat was the only thing on offer.'

The guard looked far from sympathetic. 'Well, slaver, you'll find plenty of misery to filch from here.' He spat into the rutted pathway, then stood aside to allow them passage.

* * *

CAMBODUNUM HAD SEEN BETTER DAYS. Many of the stone structures, originally built under Roman instruction, had been neglected or replaced with traditional wattle and daub roundhouses. The stench of unemptied latrines permeated the air.

As the strangers trotted down the mud-clogged main street, they attracted more than a few suspicious glares from locals hurrying through the rain. Like the guard, most of the inhabitants had discarded the more Romanised southern customs and opted for tribal *braccae* trousers with brooch-fastened woollen cloaks.

'I look forward to the warm welcome your plan has earned us,' Merlin observed. 'Next time you invent a profession, I'd suggest a more popular one. Perhaps imperial tax collectors!'

Arthur began to suspect why Merlin had smacked him round the head. 'But slavers are common.'

'So is the bloody flux, but that doesn't mean people enjoy its arrival!' the old man snapped. 'Nor do they forget its passing in a hurry!'

It was true that the traders in human flesh were so hated they often camped outside of towns for fear of the locals lynching them, but such a hated disguise would better protect their real identity from discovery. After all, who'd risk a mob's wrath by claiming such a reviled profession?

They entered a covered forum at the heart of the settlement. Large parts of its colonnaded roof had fallen into disrepair, the gaping holes exposing the mosaic beneath. Open to the elements, most of its coloured tiles had cracked, allowing weed-lined puddles to form. The once elegant floor depicted Brigantia, one of the many deities worshipped in the Isles. The state of neglect and accumulated filth gave the goddess an ugly, scabrous appearance.

A few merchants dotted the forum, most with half-empty stalls on which they displayed withered vegetables. A small herd of squealing pigs rooted amidst the muddy detritus under the watch of a cross-eyed farmer, whose only role consisted of wandering amongst the swine and randomly whacking them with a crook.

'We'll stay there.' The druid pointed to the north side of the forum where a large wooden building and adjoining stable stood. A sign displaying a dancing bear hung from its gable end.

Arthur nodded, too tired to care where he lay. They'd been riding since dawn, and his stomach growled with hunger. They pressed through the herd of disgruntled pigs and into the stable yard while their unhappy owner glowered at the intrusion.

'You settle the horses, and I'll pay for the room,' Merlin

instructed and hopped from his saddle. He'd marched into the *taverna* before Arthur could object to being left alone with the baby.

Like the other buildings in town, the stable had an improvised appearance, having served a different purpose previously. The horse blocks were made of stone and far larger than needed for the modest public house adjoining them. Judging by the depicted image of balanced scales on the rear wall, it'd served as a warehouse in the past.

A brown-haired boy emerged from the back of the *taverna* and approached warily. The three painted dots on his forehead proclaimed him as still a child. As with all the Brigantes, only on his fourteenth birthday would the design be expanded to incorporate the swirling pattern of his elders, and he looked no older than twelve or thirteen.

'You paid, sir?' he asked.

'My...' Arthur hesitated to say the word. 'My master is paying for our lodgings while I wait.' To his annoyance, the kid's demeanour became cocky. Technically, this made them the same status despite their age difference. 'These mounts need to be bedded for the night.' His tone left no question as to whom the adult was.

The kid did not move. 'Where are you from?'

'The south.'

'My father says nothing good ever comes from the south.'

Arthur was in no mood to bandy words with a child. 'Then your father is a fool.'

The boy scowled with anger. 'That's not true! My dad is the smartest man in Cambodunum!'

'Good for him. Now stable these horses, boy!'

'State your business first.' The kid wiped his nose with a filthy woollen sleeve, then crossed his arms.

His defiance did not help Arthur's mood. He'd have been thrashed to within an inch of his life for such a display of insolence in his youth. 'Our business is slaves'—he pointed at the sleeping baby to emphasise the unspoken threat — 'especially kids.'

The stable boy's eyes widened in outright fear.

Arthur gestured to the horses, wondering if the lad was a halfwit.

The boy approached as if walking toward a poisonous toad.

'Thank you,' Arthur said, regretting his quick temper. Without a doubt, the kid would spread the word around town and further ruin any chances of anonymity.

The boy busied himself with his task in silence, not wishing to provoke the ire of the unfriendly stranger.

'Pass me the baby,' Arthur instructed, stepping down from the saddle. The relief to his calves was immediate and welcome.

The child fumbled with the straps attaching the tiny passenger crib to the mount.

'Here, let me.' Arthur strolled over to aid him. But this action only made the boy rush more, and he unwittingly unfastened the last knot without supporting the basket. Before either of them could react, Mordred's crib plopped onto the dung-smeared cobbles. Although a short drop, it jolted the infant from his slumber, and he emitted a squawk of shocked outrage.

'Idiot!' Arthur roared, kneeling to retrieve the indignantly flapping babe. His outburst caused Mordred to start a full-blown crying fit.

'In the name of Jupiter's fat hairy balls, what's going on?' Merlin demanded.

The fracas ended as all three protagonists looked toward the enraged druid.

'Tis nothing. The boy fumbled the straps,' Arthur interjected, then lifted the distraught infant to his breast and attempted to provide comfort by jigging him up and down.

'Please, sirs, I don't want to be no slave!' the stable hand replied, close to tears.

Merlin directed a glare at Arthur that froze his blood with dread, then turned his attention to the boy. 'What's your name?' he asked lightly.

'Peredur, sir,' the youngster answered in a small voice.

'Well, Peredur, it's your lucky day.' The old man retrieved a silver *siliquae* from inside his robe and tossed the ridiculously high bribe at the lad. Even in his distressed state, the child caught it in mid-air.

'That's too much!' Arthur grumbled.

Merlin did not bother to answer him directly. 'Ignore him. He is so tight with his money, I'm sure if we inserted a lump of coal up his arse, it would emerge as a diamond within a week!'

The worried frown on the boy's freckled cheeks changed to a tentative smile. 'My father says the same about Old Brett.'

'Aye, tighter than a noose! Which is what I intend to fashion for my foolish apprentice as soon as we find shelter!' Merlin nodded toward a red-faced Arthur. 'Now, see to the horses and our horned friend here.' The old man patted the nanny goat. 'And if you can, find me a good wet nurse. Do that and you'll get two more of these.' He retrieved another two coins from his seemingly bottomless robe.

Peredur grinned at the prospect.

'A good-natured nurse, mind. Not some mean old bag.'

'Yes, sir.'

'Good, lad. Now get to it. I fear if this little fellow has any more goat's milk, he will grow a pair of udders himself!'

The boy laughed, then led the animals inside, but only after giving Arthur a triumphant smirk.

Left alone, Merlin turned to the warrior holding the disgruntled baby. 'Would you like me to buy you a lute?' he asked in a worryingly mild tone.

'What?'

'A lute, so you may prance through the streets, singing, "The slavers have arrived!" ' he thundered. 'We'll need a guide for the next part of our journey, yet you seem determined to make an enemy of everyone we meet!'

'Sorry.'

'Aye, a sorry excuse for a man. Never mind the—' He cut himself off. 'Just give me the baby.'

Arthur did not argue, relieved to hand him over.

'You'd be safer being raised by the goat,' the old man commented to the pacified babe.

'Excuse me, sir,' Peredur interrupted, poking his head through the stable door. 'If you need a guide, my father is the best in Brigantia.'

Merlin beamed. 'Excellent! Tell him he'll find us in the *taverna*. Now settle the horses. There's a good lad.'

'Will do, sir,' Peredur replied dutifully.

'And stop calling me *sir*.'

'Yes, sir.'

CHAPTER SEVENTEEN

The air inside the *taverna* was thick with smoke and the stench of sour beer. Soot-blackened pillars ran the length of the structure, which had risen with the same organic fluidity that typified the rest of the town. Several elderly patrons sat around chipped stone tables, hewn from large building blocks, drinking from their bowls in near silence. A three-legged mongrel slept beside a poorly ventilated fire pit in the centre of the room. At the far end of the shabby establishment, a bearded man in a leather apron manned a bar fashioned from raw planks. He appeared in no hurry to clean the stack of dirty plates piled in front of him; instead, he slouched against the greasy back wall with his arms crossed.

The unusual party attracted curious glances from the drinkers as they approached the barman.

'Which one's the wet nurse?' a voice rang out.

Merlin laid a steadying hand on Arthur's arm, stopping him from responding with a suitably threatening reply.

'Afternoon,' the keeper greeted them, a spark of life appearing in his eyes at the prospect of customers.

'Afternoon, my good man, we're looking for a room for the night,' Merlin replied with his usual charm.

A toothless grin appeared on the keeper's face. ' 'Appens we have a fine lodging above, sirs. Lucky for you, it's not occupied.' He eyed Merlin's robe as he spoke.

'They must be desperate to sleep in this shit hole!' the same sarcastic voice called out.

The barman dropped his sunny disposition. 'If you want to keep watering your flapping gob in 'ere, Oran, you can shut it!'

A muttered grumble answered.

The keeper's amenable smile reappeared as his attention returned to the newcomers. 'Just the one night, is it?'

'Aye,' Merlin said, reaching inside his robe to retrieve his money with one hand while adeptly holding Mordred with the other.

Much to the barman's evident delight, the druid produced a heavy bag of coin. But as he did so, the back door of the common area flew open to reveal a hulking man, his face tattooed in the style of the Brigantes. He wore a chain-mail vest under a stag hide cloak. A thick silver torque around his neck denoted him as a nobleman. With his right hand resting on the pommel of the war axe hanging from his belt, the big man scanned the room. When his gaze settled on the newcomers, he raised a muscular arm, encircled with a brass clasp at the wrist. 'Is that 'em?' he asked the small figure peering from behind his trunk-like waist.

'Yes, Father,' the boy Arthur recognised as Peredur replied.

'Hmm,' the giant rumbled and strode toward them on long legs.

Without bothering to greet them, the nobleman nodded at the innkeeper. 'I'll have the usual,' he said, unclasping the cloak and draping it over the bar.

'Won't be a second, my lord,' the barman responded absently, still eying the coin bag in Merlin's hand.

'I want it now,' the big man added.

The barman's cheerful expression dropped at the words, and he shrugged apologetically at Merlin, before rummaging under the counter and producing an ornate bronze tankard. Unlike the other patrons' plain cups, this one was rimmed in silver and richly decorated with scenes of spear-wielding fighters engaged in combat. He filled the vessel with a foaming brew and handed it over. 'This one's on me, Lord Efrawg,' he said, sensing the tension in the air.

The burly stranger grasped the drink and drained its contents in two mighty gulps. He belched thunderously, then blew the fumes toward Arthur. 'You've got balls coming to this town,' he said, presenting the tankard for more. 'Last slavers who tried found themselves strung up—and they didn't threaten to take my son.'

The barman winced while pouring the second draught. An angry grumble resonated from the other drinkers, and the ever-helpful heckler piped up. 'Kick their arses, Efrawg!'

Tired and thirsty, Arthur was in no mood for games. 'Mind your own business,' he replied and grasped the warrior's refilled cup from the bar. He took a long, refreshing swig and wiped his lips.

So unexpected was the impetuous action, the gruff nobleman could only look on in fury. Utter silence descended upon the room, other than a single whimper emitted by the lame dog as it slept. Resigned to his fate, Arthur looked up at the big man and wondered if the throbbing vein in his temple would burst and kill him before he could retaliate. Then a vice-like grip clamped around his throat.

Arthur choked under the incredible pressure exerted on his windpipe. Reduced to instinct, he tugged with all his might at the giant's arm, desperate to remove the crushing force, but his resistance only intensified the nobleman's efforts. A second later, black dots danced before Arthurs' eyes. In a last-ditch effort to stave off oblivion, he wrenched the *gladius* from his belt and placed the edge of the blade under the chin of the enraged Brigante.

'Enough!' Merlin commanded.

Still at an impasse, both men turned to face him.

'We are not bloody slavers!' the druid said through gritted teeth.

The huge warrior blinked in confusion, struggling to replace rage with reason.

'Forgive my friend,' Merlin continued while Arthur gagged. 'A lack of rest has eroded his wits.'

The nobleman looked unimpressed but loosened his death grip.

'Did the boy speak of our need for a guide?' the druid asked.

'He did,' Efrawg replied, his jaw clenched.

'Then come up to our lodgings, and we'll talk further.'

'What of the babe?' the warrior asked, eyeing Mordred suspiciously. 'Two men do not wander the land with such a young child.'

Arthur tried to speak, only to have his windpipe crushed anew.

'A foundling, nothing more,' Merlin answered.

The tattooed hulk mulled this new information over for a long moment before releasing Arthur, who dropped to the floor, gasping for air.

'This cock's piss owes me a drink,' the giant stated.

Merlin tossed coins onto the bar, far more than was needed for the room. 'Make sure my friend here gets as much beer as he likes.'

The nobleman eyed the money suspiciously but did not reject the generous offer.

Nodding, the relieved keeper handed the druid an iron key and indicated a roughly hewn staircase to the rear of the common area.

'Good. Now that's settled, follow me.' Merlin stepped over his hacking companion and strode away, leaving him to cough under the disapproving glares of the locals.

CHAPTER EIGHTEEN

Once he'd regained his composure, Arthur followed the others up the creaking stairs to the *taverna's* only guest room. He entered the low-hanging loft and wrinkled his nose at the pervading smell of mould and damp. The only light in the confined space came from a grimy window on the east wall, giving the gathered men the appearance of grey shadows in the gloom.

Light sparked amidst the outlined figures, followed by the flickering flame of an oil lamp. The growing glow revealed a sparsely decorated area, with two square, hay-stuffed beds against each wall. The only other furniture was a plain table, surrounded by four stools.

Merlin placed the lamp on the table, then laid Mordred to rest on a bunk. Thankfully, the baby had nodded off after his impromptu dumping in the courtyard, so he did not stir. The druid then rummaged in his satchel and produced two more little oil burners, which he also lit, giving them an adequate, if subdued, glow. With the babe settled, he sat at the table and gestured for the nobleman to join him.

Having to stoop to fit his frame under the thatch, Efrawg

looked relieved to sit. Peredur came to stand by his side, while Arthur remained by the door. The big warrior drummed his thick fingers against the wooden table, eyeing Merlin's disguised face with suspicion. 'The beer earns you one minute to explain yourself,' he growled, 'and that cock's piss can keep his gob shut.' He did not bother to direct the comment at Arthur.

'We are not slavers,' Merlin said.

'So you keep saying.' The warrior drummed his fingers harder.

The old man did not seem to register Efrawg's impatience and instead pointed at the tattoo of a tusked boar inked on his muscled bicep. 'As I recall, your father had the same design.'

The warrior's stern expression turned to confusion. 'You knew my father?'

'Aye, he was a trustworthy man.'

Efrawg's bushy eyebrows narrowed, and his voice lowered ominously. ' 'Tis an easy enough claim for a trickster to make. Do not think you can play me for a fool!'

'This is no trick, son of Erwan *an Macánta*.'[1]

The nobleman looked surprised, yet guarded. 'You speak the truth, although the fortunes of my line have waned since his time.' He peered at the black-toothed man who spoke such strangely respectful words. 'Still, I am responsible for protecting this town, so I ask again, why should I trust men who come here claiming to be those we hate? The ways of the Romans are no longer practised here, and I did not lie when I said the last slavers who dared to step foot in Cambodunum found themselves strung up by their balls.'

Merlin nodded. 'You are right—this game must end.' He muttered a short incantation, and his face transformed back to his familiar weathered features.

'By the—!' Efrawg shouted, scraping his stool backward

and fumbling for the handle of his axe, before pushing aside a startled Peredur.

Merlin raised his hands in a placatory gesture. 'It's a simple trick. No need to be alarmed.'

The big man gaped at the ancient champion in awe. 'Your face is... familiar.'

The druid smiled. 'And so it should be. We met once in the governor's court, at the feast of Quinquatrus. You weren't much older than your son is now, mind.'

The nobleman's heavy brow furrowed as he recalled. 'I remember. You reached over to my ear and...'

Before he could finish, Merlin stretched out his arm to Peredur's right ear and produced a small silver ring. He offered the trinket to the boy who took it as if being handed a precious gem.

'I'll be... Merlin, is it really you?'

The old man beamed. 'Last time I checked.'

The nobleman's colour drained from hisruddycomplexion. 'Forgive me. I insulted you both.'

'Relax, man,'Merlinchided gently. 'The fault was ours. We should have invented a less objectionablestory.' He threw Arthur a knowing glance. 'I've not travelled these lands inthirty years and find myself surprised by the pace of change.'

'Hmm, even so.' Efrawg turned to Arthur. 'Forgive me, young lord.'

Any sense of smug satisfaction Arthur felt died when the druid shot him a second pointed look. 'Like he said, it was our fault.' He could not quite say *my*.

'Arthur is my apprentice,' Merlin added.

To his credit, the huge warrior gave him a respectful nod and turned back to the old man. 'Peredur said you needed a guide?'

'We do,' Merlin replied with a sigh. 'Given more time, that

L.K. ALAN

would not be the case, but I fear we must reach the governor at Luguvalium as quickly as we can.'

An unenthusiastic mutter greeted this news. 'I heard he was there.' A puzzled frown touched the nobleman's whiskered face. 'Forgive me, lord, but why the need for a guide? The quickest route by land is southeast to Ermine Street, then back north.'

'Not the quickest, my friend. It would add many miles onto our journey,' Merlin replied.

'Then why not travel to the port at Deva and north by sea? 'Tis quicker than any other way.'

The druid pondered the suggestion before shaking his head again. 'Tempting as it is, this route would leave us too vulnerable to our enemy. No, our path must take us through Darach Dorcha.'

'The Dark Oaks!' the nobleman exclaimed in alarm.

Arthur knew the rumours of the old forest. It was said to be a fay land, soured by an enchantment no man could travel through safely.

'I would not recommend such a way,' Efrawgsaid. 'None have been foolish enough to enter that evil place in twen-tyyears.'

'But I thought you had, Father?' Peredur chirped up, earning himself a wan smile from his elder.

'The boy speaks the truth, though it is not something I like to dwell on,' the nobleman admitted. He turned his left arm over to show a deep purple scar running from his elbow to his calloused palm.

Merlin inspected it. 'The wound was deep.'

'Aye, but I don't recall the weapon that caused it.'

'A blade?' the old man suggested.

'Perhaps.' Efrawg shrugged. 'We hunted a white hart—a thing of beauty she was, with a hide worth a fortune.' He

134

turned his arm back, as if to conceal the reminder. 'She darted into that wicked place, and we were stupid enough to follow.'

'What did you find there?' Merlin asked. 'It's been two centuries since I passed through the forest, and I recall a green, ancient place. I saw no malice there.'

'I do not know for certain.' The big man appeared lost in thought for a moment. 'We followed her for two days. She always stayed just beyond the range of our arrows. It was as if the very trees were cloaking her.' He paused. 'On the third day, we caught her and skinned her. Later that evening, they came upon us.'

' "They"?' Arthur asked.

'Dark spirits? To this day, I'm not sure.' The nobleman watched the lamplight dance. 'I only recall eating the sweetest of meats that night. Then I slept with a full stomach for the first time in nigh a week.' He exhaled. 'The screams woke me.'

'What then?' Merlin pressed gently.

'The rest is like a dark dream I can never quite remember.' He gestured toward his temple, as if ashamed by his own lack of clarity. 'Three of my friends died on that day—I am sure of that, at least.'

Merlin seemed to consider his words. 'I am sorry for your loss, but I can protect us against such spirits.' He placed a heavy bag of coin on the table between them.

Efrawg barely glanced at the bag. 'I don't doubt it, lord. Your reputation is, well… and I wish to know what killed my friends.' He pushed the money back toward the druid. 'Duty is its own reward.'

Merlin smiled. 'You sound just like your father.'

The nobleman shook his head. 'Nay, lord, I am not like my father. He did not bring shame upon his family.'

'How did you escape?' Arthur asked, wondering at the

man's melancholic refusal to accept such praise. Some men were cowards at heart, often at the cost of others.

'He fought his way out!' Peredur answered, indignant at the implication.

If the question had angered his father, however, he did not show it. 'I have memories of trees and fleeing. Beyond that, I cannot say.'

'Then how do you know the way?' Arthur pressed, the enigmatic answer leaving him unconvinced. How could a man forget a battle? He'd been in many and could remember every cut and bloody thrust.

'Of course he does!' Peredur interjected.

'Calm yourself, boy,' Efrawg said. 'He is right to ask. Would you follow someone who doesn't know the way?'

Turning to Arthur, however, his thin-lipped stare suggested his new-found patience had limits. 'Merlin is right that the Oaks used to be safe. When I was younger than Peredur, my father would take me hunting there. I learned every forest path, and if the old road still runs true, we should be able to follow it straight through.'

'Then it's agreed.' The druid spat into his hand and offered it to the big warrior who reciprocated the traditional gesture of a pact. 'We will meet you here at dawn.'

As if to signal his dissent, Mordred let out his usual half-hearted cry when hungry.

'And what of the child? That forest is no place for one so young,' Arthur asked, prompted by the babe's squall.

'That is why we seek a wet nurse,' Merlin said, directing the words to the nobleman while pushing the bag back toward him.

'I was going to ask Brina, Father,' Peredur said.

Efrawg glanced uncomfortably at his son. 'Oh, erm, yes.' He turned to Merlin, his cheeks red. 'My, well, my neighbour is late with child, and I'm sure she'd take the babe—if I were to ask.'He pushed the coin away once more.

'I'd appreciate that, my friend,' the druid replied without returning the money to his robe.

'Where did you find him?' Peredur asked, stepping to Mordred and curiously peering down at him.

Merlin's face turned grim. "Ardotalia.".

'Ardotalia?'the nobleman asked.

'Aye. Destroyed—the entire fort and every living thing in it. Only this little one survived.'

The big man's eyes widened in shock. 'What? The whole garrison? Caiva wept, are you sure?'

'Yes. It was a massacre.'

'But how? There must have been five hundred spears at Ardotalia, some with family in this town,' he replied, aghast at the news. 'It would take… Was it the Romans? Did those damn butchers betray us again?' He half rose from his chair in anger.

'No, not this time. I suspect the answer may be worse than you think. The attack came from beneath the hillside,' Merlin replied.

'Sappers?' Efrawg asked, retaking his seat. 'That is beyond the skill of any bandits, even those Raven scum.' He spat.

A nervous prickle ran down Arthur's spine at the remark.

'I believe they served the nether.'

It was not reassuring to see the face of the huge warrior turn pale, and Arthur did not blame him after battling those terrible creatures himself. Peredur retreated to his father's side at the mention.

'Demons? I thought them to be a myth?' Efrawg asked. 'You bring ill tidings lord.'

'If only they were the stuff of stories, my friend. No, they are all too real. We saw their wretched corpses amongst the dead.'

'Another group of the ugly beasts ambushed us in the peaks,' Arthur added. 'Fouler things than I've encountered in my worst dreams.'

'That's why we must reachthe governor as soon as possible,' the druid said. 'Theassault on the fort might be the first move in a greater game we do not yet fully understand. I fear the entire diocese may be under attack.'

The big mandigested the magnitude of the news before speaking. 'We should tell our townsfolk of the disaster. These tidings will sorely afflict some.'

Merlin rubbed a handover hisstubbled pate, seeminglytorn. 'Hmm, yes, but do not say who brought you this news. Instead, ask them to send word to the troops at Mancunium. We've already been waylaid once, and it was no coincidence.'

'How so? Spies?'

Merlin nodded. 'That worries me more than anything. These nether dogs have human allies. Those unnatural abominations could not hide in a town or village without notice.'

'Who?'

'The Picts, for certain, and perhaps others. It is a dark turn of events, the likes of which I've never seen.'

An oil lamp flickered out, leaving them to consider the implications in shadow.

'Come, lad,' Efrawg said eventually, rising and stooping away, with Peredur on his heels. 'We have much to do.'

'Efrawg?' Merlin called after him.

The big man turned, bending his head under a wooden beam. 'Yes, lord?'

'You are a good person—just like your father.'

The warrior did not answer, his face unreadable.

When they'd left, Arthur strode to the empty bed and lay down, ignoring the fusty odour permeating its thin blankets.

'A different outcome toyour earlier efforts, boy,' Merlin said from the table.

The young warrior snorted. 'Let's hope he doesn't abandon us when we need him most.'

'He would not, even if his life depended on it. Can you say the same?'

He did not reply.

'Merlin?' he asked after a time.

'What?'

'You didn't change my nose back. It was broken.'

The old man yawned. 'Aye, you are ugly enough already.'

CHAPTER NINETEEN

Arthur stirred awake to the hushed sounds of a female conversing with Merlin.

'Thank you. Without your help, this little one would have no future.'

'Do not thank me, lord. It's…' she trailed off.

'Your duty?' he finished for her. 'I've heard that already from your neighbour this evening, and no, taking this child is not your duty.'

'He's still calling me his neighbour, is he?' she said. 'For all his talk of duty, that man is adept at avoiding facts.'

'Here, please take this.'

Arthur heard coins chinking in a bag.

'Efrawg would not be happy if I did,' She replied, albeit with hesitation.

'Then don't tell him.'

She sighed. 'Very well—for the sake of the children. That and my back aches too much to argue!'

'Please, take a seat, lady.'

'Thank you, lord, but I can assure you, I am no lady.' The sound of scraping stools followed, as did a small contented moan as she sat. 'My ankles have swollen to the size of tree trunks,' she said. 'I don't believe they can be called ankles any longer—more like kankles.'

Merlin laughed. 'Efrawg is not your neighbour, then?'

She sniffed. 'He is—but the kind who pops 'round to bake buns in my oven.'

'Oh, I see.'

'Aye, it's a shame we remain only neighbours.'

'Forgive me, but that does not sound like the man I met earlier—to leave you unsupported, I mean.'

'Oh, it's not like that. No, Efrawg is a good man—the best —but he worries how Peredur would take it if he learned his father had found another so soon after losing his mother. To be honest, so do I. Ula was a good friend.

'I am sorry to hear that. Was she ill?'

'No, bandits.' Her tone darkened. 'They took her—no more than a mile outside the town walls.'

Merlin grunted in distaste. 'Did they ever find her?'

'Efrawg found her body miles to the south. He's uncertain, but thinks she took her own life rather than live with the shame.'

No one spoke for a moment.

'A sad turn of events,' Merlin said eventually, his voice hushed.

'Yes. As sad as it is common. More so because he incurred the governor's wrath.'

'The governor?'

'Didn't you know? The gossips in the town talked of little else.'

'Know what?'

'Vibius Crassus was her father. He already blamed poor Efrawg for bringing her to this backwater town. When she died, he almost had him executed.' Her voice rose with suppressed anger. 'As if he hadn't suffered enough.'

'I was not aware of that.' The druid paused to consider the implications. 'I have only met our new leader a few times recently, for I've spent the last decades with my kin, but I fear he lacks wisdom.'

'That's one way of putting it. I say the man's a pig.'

The silence between them spoke of Merlin's disquiet. It was strange to think he was distantly related to the man who controlled all their fates.

'Here, would you like to meet your new ward?' he asked, changing the subject.

'I would like nothing better!' she replied, her tone lighter.

He heard the old man rise and retrieve the improvised basket.

'Ah, a boy!' she exclaimed. 'Perfect. The canny women tell me this bump will be a girl. I'll have the best of both…well, would you look at that. He has a name bracelet—Mordred.'

'Aye, 'tis an old name.'

'Hmm, well, the gods have spoken then,' she replied happily. 'I will do my best for you, Mordred.'

Arthur did not understand why she'd willingly lumber herself with another mouth to feed.

'Thank you. This is no small request,' Merlin said.

'There is no need for thanks, you have given me enough money to keep both these little ones until they are bent with age, and I like the idea of having a full house while Efrawg is away.'

'The young are a joy, but still, I am sorry to be the one to take Efrawg from you when you'll need him most. I would not ask if—'

'I know that,' she interjected. 'It's a privilege to aid you, even in a small way.'

'Hmm, trust me—I do not deserve such loyalty.'

. . .

THE BITTER RESPONSE hung between them.

'Lord Merlin?' she asked eventually.

'Yes?'

'Mother used to tell me the old stories about you and the warrior queen fighting to save us all from slavery.'

He did not answer.

She continued hesitantly. 'It's just that I used to dream that one day I'd be brave and strong like her, like Boudica. Silly, I know.'

'There are different forms of courage, and some are more destructive than others,' he murmured. 'To raise a child with love in this hard world—that takes courage, too.'

'They say you were close?' She sounded unsure.

Merlin took some time to respond. 'We were also good neighbours.'

'What kind of woman was she?'

Arthur opened his eyes to see the shadowy flicker of lamplight against the thatched ceiling.

'I remember her sadness, but more so, her rage. So much rage, enough to sweep us all into madness. And yet, at night when she returned to me and her girls, she became a loving mother again.'

Arthur watched the shadow of an arm reach out and settle on the druid's outline.

'In the early days of the rebellion, I thought her thirst for revenge would fade, but it did not. It grew with every town we destroyed.'

'I have seen the same anger in Efrawg. It's hard for those who love someone who suffers so.'

'Aye, that is true. I'm not sure who was in more pain, me or her.'

'Because of what the Romans did to her and her daughters?'

'At first, then vengeance took her completely. Our fight for freedom turned into a bloodbath.' His voice filled with regret. 'By the time we burned Londinium, I'd lost her to thered madness.'

'But they were invaders—our enemy.'

'Hmm, explain that to the children of the settlers we burned alive as they sheltered in a temple.' His tone lowered. 'No, good lady, as I said, there are many forms of courage. Not all as benign as yours.'

'The stories say the gods opposed the rebellion?'

'They did.' His reply sounded clipped.

Another awkward silence passed between them, and he heard the woman shift uncomfortably in her seat. 'I will leave you to rest, lord,' she said, when he did not speak further.

'Thank you again,' he said.

The first stairs creaked outside the room, then stopped. 'Please bring him back to me.'

Merlin didn't answer.

A moment later, the room was quiet once more, other than the sounds of the inn below travelling up through the floorboards. He heard Merlin blow out the lamp and take his place on the pallet. Instead of falling straight to sleep, the old man sang:

'*Téann sí tríd an oíche gan réaltaí chun nascleanúint a dhéanamh ar a bealach,*

Shield maiden of the Iceni, *teacht ar ais chun solais.*

Forever does she wander the sky 'til the end of days.'[1]

Arthur closed his eyes.

CHAPTER TWENTY

Relieved that his slumber had been free of the strange dreams plaguing him of late, Arthur sat up and stretched. Merlin was already up and preparing to leave.

'Good, you're awake. Give us a hand,' he said.

Yawning, Arthur rose and packed his few belongings. 'Are you sure we can trust the Brigante?' The dilemma had bothered him deep into the night.

'As far as any man can be trusted,' came the frustrating reply. 'We need a guide and don't have the luxury of tarrying here any longer.'

'He didn't explain how he survived last time. For all we know, he could've betrayed the others to save his own skin,' Arthur grumbled.

The druid tutted impatiently as he rolled his blanket. 'We must trust someone, and his offer is by far the best we will get. Besides, my praising his father wasn't just to pacify the man enough to stop him crushing your thick skull. His line is loyal to a fault. So, unless this world has turned completely upside down since I last ventured out, we can rely on him.'

Arthur clenched his jaw at the reminder of his unsuccessful plan. 'You'd rather acknowledge the loyalty of a stranger than mine,' he grumbled.

'And there I was thinking we'd left the mewling infant behind.'

This was too much for Arthur. He tossed his bag onto the floor in a fit of pique. 'Can you not spare me the jibes for one day?' He huffed. 'I may not be a thousand years old and able to shoot lightning from my arse cheeks, but I've avoided death long enough to realise I'm not a complete fool!'

Merlin stopped his packing and strode over to the younger man, then clamped his hands either side of his arms. 'You, lad, are riddled with guilt. You carry too much.' His striking grey eyes dug into Arthur's. 'If you don't respect yourself, nobody else will, and your part in this business is too important for such navel-gazing.'

'My future is in that coin bag you keep, old man. When we get to Lugavalium, our business, as you put it, will be finished.'

'And what will you do with the money, hmm? Drink yourself stupid? Rut a few whores? Then what?'

'Then…' Arthur began but could not answer. Such considerations were for men who had a future.

'Exactly. The past is the past, and you must be ready —soon.'

'Ready for what? Be plain for once. And I do not believe for one moment you need a guard.'

Merlin grinned. 'Good. That's a start. Perhaps you're not as thick as I feared.'

Arthur's frustration bubbled to the surface again. 'You've still not answered me. You said I was important. Why? I've done nothing but watch you deal with events I've played little part in. How can I matter?'

'Really? Are you certain of that? Back at the ruined fort,

you saved my life. Without you, that demon would have taken my scalp. Your blade stopped that, my young friend.'

Arthur could hardly believe his ears. The old man had paid him a compliment.

'As for your role in this, you have my word that I do not know—yet. But what I am sure of is that you've an aura as subtle as a thunderclap. Trust me, you are important.' The druid dropped his affectionate grasp and turned back to his mundane task. 'Besides, the money is not the real reason you've stayed with me.'

There it was again. *The boy and the woman.*

'What do you know about that?'

Merlin stopped again, with his back turned. 'Sometimes, we see what we need to see, true or not.'

'More riddles, old man?'

'Only until I know more, boy. Before then, you are not ready.'

Frustrated, Arthur stalked from the room.

AFTER WOLFING down a hearty breakfast of eggs and bacon served by a *taverna* keeper unused to working at such an early hour, they left and entered the adjoining stable to find Efrawg and Peredur waiting for them in the mist-shrouded morning.

Fionna and Aina had been well cared for in their absence, for they nuzzled the boy as he brought them from their stalls, along with a grey speckled gelding and a chestnut mare. Both seemed like placid, contented beasts.

'Morning, lord,' the big warrior greeted Merlin, giving a short, respectful bow. 'We are ready as instructed, and Brina informs me the babe has settled well.'

'Good man!' Merlin replied cheerfully. 'But if we are to travel together, you must promise me one thing.'

Efrawg frowned. 'What's that, lord?'

'Enough with the bowing and lording! *Merlin* will do perfectly well. It's my name, after all.'

The big man looked confused by the direct tone but nodded regardless.

'And don't be afraid to say when I've pissed you off. I'm nine hundred years old. I can take it.'

'Nine hundred and seventy-one,' Arthur corrected him.

The druid glared at his companion, then smiled at Peredur. 'You see, I can take it, and you'll know if I can't, because I'll shrink your balls to the size of a squirrel's.' He patted him on the cheek.

The boy smirked, and Arthur found himself also smiling. The earlier conversation with the old man had eased the tension between them.

'I'll keep that in mind,' Efrawg said awkwardly, uncomfortable with a walking legend teasing him.

'Peredur, lad, would you do an old man a service and give the *taverna* keeper this,' he said, flipping a silver coin to the boy who caught it in mid-air. 'We've not paid for our breakfast!'

The youngster nodded, then hurried inside, eager to be off on an adventure with the adults.

Once he was out of earshot, Merlin turned to the big nobleman. 'I did not think you would bring the child. This won't be an easy journey.'

Efrawg, embarrassed at the question, hesitated. 'Since his mother passed, he will not stay away from my side for more than a few hours.'

'I understand, but our way could be dangerous,' the druid pushed. 'I don't want to be responsible for any harm coming to him, my friend.'

The big man ran a hand over his bearded chin. 'I know, I know. I have thought the same myself, believe me, but he will follow us, anyway, I'm certain of it, and Brina cannot stop him in her condition. At least this way, I can keep an eye on him.'

Merlin sighed as the boy returned, beaming with excitement. 'Very well, but keep him close,' he said under his breath.

* * *

THE PARTY SET off along the foggy main street. They passed the occasional workman on his way to toil in the fields or a housewife sweeping a front yard at the beginning of a long day. All would stop to greet Efrawg and his son while giving the two strangers a curious glance.

As they neared the outskirts of town and the workshops of the settlement, Merlin drew alongside Arthur and whispered, 'Someone is following us.'

'Are you sure?'

'Aye. A slim rider keeping a careful distance. He's been with us since we left the *taverna*.'

Arthur stiffened in his saddle. This could be the man responsible for the attack at the ruined fort. Worse, they might have instigated the massacre at Ardotalia. 'What do you want to do?'

'Catch him.'

'Why not just...?' Arthur whispered while wiggling his fingers. 'You could paralyse him.'

'Not here. It would draw too much attention. Besides, there are servants of the enemy who also possess the gift. I don't want to use magic unless I'm certain what we're dealing with.' He paused, considering their options. 'You will need to do this—and *quietly*.'

Arthur had a plan. 'I'll take him at the smithy ahead. I can wait for him around the corner. If you three keep moving forward in his line of sight, with any luck, he won't notice I'm gone. When he reaches the turn in the road, I'll jump the bastard.'

Merlin nodded. 'I will warn the others.'

As the old man nudged Fionna forward, a disturbing thought caused Arthur to reconsider. 'What if it's one of these magic-wielding creatures you speak of?' he whispered as loudly as he dared.

'We'll take the risk.' The less-than-reassuring answer drifted back to him through the mist.

Cursing under his breath, Arthur directed Aina into the shadows as they rounded the smithy. The manoeuvre took a split second, and unless their pursuer possessed the eyes of an eagle, he felt sure he'd avoided detection. Waiting, he listened for the telltale signs of an approaching horse, straining to hear above his own thudding heart.

The moments stretched on while his imagination filled with nightmarish visions of the monster about to emerge from the fog. Time dragged on to the point he suspected their pursuer had evaded the trap. Then came the distinct sound of shod hooves clapping against the cobbled street.

Soon after, a slender, hooded figure riding a black palfrey passed where he'd expected. Sending up a silent plea that the rider would not transform him into something unnatural, he lunged from his saddle and onto the shoulders of the mysterious passer-by. His target emitted a curiously high-pitched yelp as they tumbled to the road together. Arthur landed painfully on his chest, winding him. While he gasped for breath, the spy had already leapt onto his feet and was about to bolt into a nearby pottery yard.

Determined not to let him slip away, Arthur snatched the figure's leg and yanked him backward with ease, before grasping the stranger around the midriff and wrestling him to the ground. Just as he was going to pin him, a shadow flashed in the periphery of his vision. Arthur barely had time to react to the descending hoof, angled straight for his skull. He rolled, forcing the spy to turn with him. The horse's hoof thwacked into the grime right next to his ear, causing it to ring.

Terrified the mount would try to brain him again, he risked another look in its direction while desperately trying to maintain his grip on the wriggling enemy. To his relief, he saw a muscled arm grasp the mount's loose reins and yank it away from his prone body.

With the immediate danger over, Arthur returned his attention to wrestling their cloaked pursuer. Undeterred by the flailing kicks aimed at his face, he managed to grip the struggling spy's delicate wrists and straddle his chest. Finally, his opponent gave up and lay panting.

'Keep still, or I'll crush your skull,' he said, raising a fist in emphasis.

Hate-filled, green eyes regarded his own from above a thick cloth covering his prisoner's nose and mouth. Arthur pinned the stranger's left arm under his knee, then gripped the face mask, dreading to think of the fanged monstrosity he was about to reveal. Holding his breath, he ripped away the rag, only to recoil in shock.

The slave girl, Guinever, lay beneath him. Such was his utter confusion that Arthur loosened his grip. 'What are—'

A searing bolt of agony mushroomed in his groin. He rolled off Guin, clutching his wounded pride. Through a din of throbbing pain, he watched as she got into a squatting position and prepared to run for it.

'Oh, no, you don't, Girly.' Efrawg grasped Guinever by the waist and lifted her before she could escape.

'Let me go, you fat pig!' she cried, trying to stamp on his boat-sized feet.

'Now, now, there's no need to be like that,' he said, maintaining a stoic grip while she beat at his thick frame.

Following a few moments of futile struggle, she stopped and hung limply under his arm. 'Argh!' she screamed in frustration.

When the liquid fire in Arthur's groin had subsided, he plucked up enough courage to reach down and check for blood. Thankfully, there was none. Peredur came to his side and aided him to his feet while he huffed and puffed in discomfort.

Efrawg winced on his behalf. 'Good grief, woman. Were you never taught that kicking a man in the goolies is a wicked thing?'

She did not answer.

Merlin trotted toward the group, having watched the events unfold from a safe distance. 'Why do I know her face?'

'From the fort at Derventio.' Arthur gasped, trying not to vomit. 'The slave girl.'

The druid regarded their sullen captive sternly. 'We'll deal with her outside the town. This little romp has made our exit as stealthy as a trumpet fanfare, and I have no desire for more hysterics.'

The big warrior lifted Guinever onto his mount with surprising gentleness, then hopped on behind her, leaving no chance of escape. Meanwhile, Peredur approached her terrified horse while speaking softly. Although it shied away at first, the lad's patience eventually paid off, and he was able to grab the reins and tie them to his own saddle.

'Here,' Merlin said, tossing Efrawg a ribbon of cloth. 'Bind her wrists.'

Reluctantly, he did so.

They set off once more, with Arthur riding in considerable pain and burning with rejection. He resolved to have the truth from this spy who he'd lain with only a few nights before.

CHAPTER TWENTY-ONE

They reached the crossroads by mid-morning, where an ancient tomb of a long-forgotten Roman noble lay cracked open and empty. Judging by the sun's position, one branch of the road pointed south, and a second east. A third, overgrown and neglected, dipped toward a dark, tree-lined horizon that left no doubt which route they must take.

'We'll get rid of the spy in the forest,' Merlin said, leading them down the less trodden path.

'What do you mean?' Arthur asked, noting that Efrawg had also raised his head in surprise.

Merlin reined Fiona to a stop and turned to him, his face a picture of regret. Arthur found this more worrying than if he'd appeared angry. 'She followed us all the way from Derventio. We were ambushed, and every living thing at Ardotalia is dead. In my book, that means we are at war, and this woman is a spy. Whether we like it or not, we have no choice. Others may die because of her.'

Arthur saw Guinever's eyes briefly widen in dismay. 'We don't know that for sure,' he replied, appalled by the prospect. 'She could've escaped to join us.'

'Why?'

He shifted uncomfortably in his saddle. 'Well, erm, she and I...'

Regret turned to fury on Merlin's weathered face. 'What did you tell her?'

Arthur remembered her probing questions during their encounter at the pool, and his gut churned with realisation. 'She's just a woman,' he answered weakly.

'Well, I hope she was worth it, because dipping your wick has cost us all dearly!'

'I—'

'Tell me, young fool, would you be as merciful if this girl were a hairy-arsed docker?'

Arthur had no answer.

'My lord,' Efrawg spoke up. 'It doesn't bode well to slay a woman at the beginning of a journey. There are enough spirits ahead without more following us through that desolate place.' It was unclear if the big man's odd reasoning hid a deeper unease.

'We don't know why she followed us. It may have nothing to do with the things you speak off,' Arthur insisted, taking some encouragement from his unlikely ally.

'Certainty is a luxury a leader can ill afford,' Merlin said flatly. 'We'll have enough on our plates in there without the enemy's servant poised to betray us at every turn.'

'We could ask her?' Peredur suggested, worried by the change of events.

The druid nodded at Arthur to do so.

He trotted over to the slave girl who stared blankly ahead. 'You heard the man,' Arthur said harshly, not wishing to appear lenient. 'Why did you follow us?'

No reply.

'Speak, woman!'

She scowled back in answer, but he also saw real pain

behind her eyes. That much was clear. Merlin's words had hit her hard. 'I'm trying to save your life, you stupid cow, and all you can do is insult me!' he added in a lowered tone. 'What has gotten into you?'

'You mean apart from you?' she replied, then spat. 'Men cannot think beyond their balls.'

Efrawg coughed awkwardly. Stuck with Guinever before him, he could not avoid the heated exchange.

'I don't understand!' Arthur threw his hands up in exasperation. 'Merlin knows we were together at Derventio. You need to explain that you followed us to be with me again.'

Her lips twisted into a show of disdain. 'You really think I've suffered all I have just to get all moon-eyed over you? Believe me, you weren't that good.'

Arthur's cheeks burned with embarrassment.

Guinever looked around as if checking for spies. 'Why should I trust you?' she went on in a near whisper. Tears welled in her eyes as she gazed at him with a desperate appeal. 'Please, let me go. If I'm seen talking with you, they could be killed.'

'Who could be killed?' He asked, confused by her sudden change in tone.

She returned his gaze, as if torn, then looked away.

'You have a way with the ladies,' Efrawg muttered.

The young warrior gave him a black look that conveyed his thoughts about the observation, before deciding to renew his efforts. Despite her stunning lack of care toward him, he sensed there was more going on than what was apparent. 'That is no doddery old fool who speaks.' Arthur pointed at the ancient druid observing them with cold calculation. 'He is Merlin, and he will kill you if need be.'

Although her face drained of colour at the name, she remained resolute. A single tear ran down her cheek. 'He would be doing me a kindness.'

'I do not believe you're responsible for the deaths at Ardotalia,' Arthur said more gently, hoping to encourage her into defending herself.

She shot him a look of tight-lipped despair. 'Then, like he said, you're a fool.'

He turned to further plead with Merlin, but the druid had already ridden ahead.

* * *

'SHE'S HOLDING SOMETHING BACK,' Arthur said, pressing her case once more as Merlin stopped to observe the eaves of the forest. The shadowed canopy stretched from east to west. Faded grassland led to the tree line, forming an eerie no-man's-land. The old Roman road, on which they stood, had collapsed in places, but it still provided the surest footing for the horses into the impenetrable foliage.

'This place is wrong,' the old man said. 'It wasn't like this when I last came here.'

'But the girl?'

'What do you hear?' Merlin asked, ignoring him again.

'Nothing.'

'Exactly. Not even birdsong,' Merlin answered, hopping from his saddle and stepping over the edge of the roadway which, in typical Roman fashion, had been raised to allow better drainage. He scrambled down the embankment and plucked a sod of earth from the ground to examine it. 'Just as I thought—not even a worm. This soil is dead.'

'What does that mean?'

'I'm not sure.' Merlin slapped the pale, crumbling dirt from his hands. 'Never seen the like.'

'That gives me no comfort.'

'Nor should it, boy. But I'd say it's useful information,

nonetheless.' The old man clambered back onto the road and remounted.

Peredur trotted over, his expression curious. The initially nervous palfrey now seemed relaxed enough to follow him without coercion. 'The forest looks green and healthy, though,' he observed.

'Yes, good lad!' Merlin beamed, then glowered at Arthur in a way that made it clear who he thought should have spotted the discrepancy. 'More than healthy. Overgrown, I'd say.'

Other than where the road cut through it, the oaks were the tallest he'd laid eyes upon, and dense with creeping foliage. The over-ripeness stood in stark contrast to the dead zone around its impenetrable borders, as if the trees had drained the lifeblood from the surrounding environment.

Efrawg joined them, with Guinever wedged between his thick arms. 'We call this place *an áit marbh*, for it's said to ignore its warning is death,'[1] he said in a subdued tone. 'I ignored it once at great cost—and only in my wildest nightmares have I returned.'

'Perhaps there is another way?' Peredur asked, unnerved by his father's dark comments.

The druid lay a hand on his shoulder. 'I'm sorry, but this is our path.'

'I like it not, my lord.' The boy spoke the words for them all.

'Neither do I, lad, but I sense a greater evil is moving in this world, one that demands we must risk much. Come, let us see what this forest hides.'

Before he could lead them on, Arthur reached out and snatched Merlin's reins. 'What about the girl?'

The druid looked down at the hand as if it were of no consequence. Arthur feared he was about to push the matter into a fight he would not win. The moment stretched until Merlin shrugged, then drew his companion's *gladius* with unexpected speed. Arthur recoiled, expecting a blow to follow. Instead, the old man flipped the blade and offered its hilt. 'If you insist, we do it here, then.' His face was unyielding.

With a heavy heart, Arthur grabbed the sword and turned to the green-eyed beauty. She did not struggle. Behind her, Efrawg looked horrified.

'My lord—' he began, but Merlin raised his hand.

Arthur leaned forward and placed the edge of the blade against the same throat he'd caressed. She showed no sign of emotion, her gaze as dead as the surrounding land.

The many harsh lessons he'd learned from the Ravens demanded he push. Merlin was right—to set her free would endanger them all. A trickle of blood ran from the honed point at the apex of her neck. She closed her eyes.

In his periphery, Arthur noticed Peredur turn away. That simple act of repugnance gave him pause and made him wish he could do the same. The thought brought an overwhelming feeling of shame with it. His crippling sense of self-disgust was so great, he lowered the sword and waited for the rebuke that would follow. Instead, he heard Merlin nudge Fionna toward them.

'Look at me, Arthur,' Merlin said, compelling him to do so. The old man's gaze burrowed into his own. 'Do you accept responsibility for this woman and all of her actions?'

The question was so unexpected he did not know how to respond. Sensing the answer held significant importance, he looked once more at Guinever, hoping for a shred of encouragement, a look of longing, perhaps, or a declaration of innocence. Instead, her demeanour remained hopeless.

'Are you a man or a child? Decide!' Merlin demanded.

L.K. ALAN

'I will,' he managed eventually.

Efrawg exhaled.

'Very well,' the old man said, raising his hand to them and closing his eyes. '*Ceangail iad,*'² he said in Gaelic. Although Arthur felt no pain or physical change, a shiver of apprehension ran down his spine. 'You are joined, for good or ill. If she betrays us, then so do you. Your fates share the same path.' Merlin turned to Efrawg and added more mildly, 'This burden is not yours, my friend. Peredur, bring her horse.'

As if relieved, the druid puffed out a big sigh. 'You had me worried there for a moment, boy!' Then, before she could object, he placed his palm on Guinever's brow and closed his eyes. When she flinched away, the old man grasped her elbow to hold her still.

'I'm sorry you are in pain,' he said a second later, then directed Fionna toward the forest.

As instructed, Peredur handed the reins over to Arthur, allowing his father to lift Guinever onto the back of her mount. Without further comment, the pair followed Merlin, leaving the two former lovers to stare at each other in silence.

'Saying *thank you* wouldn't go amiss,' he said, unable to stand the tension any longer.

'Thank you, master.' Her tone was flat.

'I'm not your master.'

'That's what the old man said. I am to be your slave.'

'It's nothing to do with slavery. I've vouched for you, and we are bonded for that reason. So, if you really are working for the enemy, I'll be as dead as you.'

'Whatever you say, master. Slavery, bonding, marriage—it's all the same,' she said, but the fire in her gaze passed quickly, and became haunted once more. 'Either way, it's no more than I deserve.'

He eyed her, burning with questions, but already the

others were close to the tree line, and he did not wish to enter with only his unreliable ward for company. 'If you try to escape, I will catch you.'

'Yes, sire.'

He sighed, then led them on.

CHAPTER TWENTY-TWO

They entered a place of twilight and shadow, a world where anaemic light penetrated just enough to grow the scabrous patchwork of lichen covering the entwined branches around them. The old road appeared as a forbidding corridor, with oppressive green walls arching over it. Like the waste beyond, an inexplicable stillness dominated, as if the forest brooded upon their arrival.

'It has not changed.' Efrawg's deep voice rumbled into the murk. 'We must keep moving forward,' he added; whether to encourage himself or the others, it was not clear. A chill wind swept down the path, whipping about them. The horses whinnied in alarm. With it came a faint stench of corruption, similar to overripe fruit left to rot in the sun. The gust died down soon after.

'Does it stay like this all the way to the other side?' Arthur asked, a shiver running down his spine.

'No, it becomes less dense further in,' the big man replied.

'That is good news. This place makes my skin itch.'

'Trust me, that will be the least of our troubles.'

Arthur did not find that comforting in the slightest.

'Let us see if I can unravel this mystery now that we are within,' Merlin said, then raised his hand, palm facing the way ahead. A slight glow appeared around the edge of his fingers. Several moments passed until he raised an eyebrow. 'Interesting.'

'What is it, lord?' Peredur asked. He clung to his reins as if expecting his horse to bolt.

'I am not sure. Something familiar, and yet...' The old man knotted his brow. 'Something old. That much I can say.'

'Which is not much at all,' Arthur remarked, unsettled by the druid's lack of confidence. The muttered complaint earned him a scowl.

'Perhaps we could start a fire and burn it out?' the boy suggested.

'No, son. Look.' Efrawg took a flint and tinder from his pack, then lit a rag. A deep rumble rang out around them in response, then spread outward through the leafy canopy. He needed no further prompting to blow out the small flame.

'Hmm, very interesting,' Merlin remarked like a man commenting on the unusual weather. 'There are many forms of magic in this world, and some are alien to me. Some I have not seen since my youth. I am not certain which this is. Either way, we shall see.'

Arthur took no encouragement from that either. Regardless of the druid's dismissive display toward things that would terrify lesser men, he had still failed to disguise his confusion as to what awaited them.

'Does the road continue all the way?' Merlin asked the big warrior.

'No. It disappears about two miles in. We will have to gauge the rest by the sun.'

'Nothing is left of the road at all?' Arthur found it hard to believe. The Romans were many things, but never shoddy workmen.

'Aye. Though I do not know how or why.'

'I can find a path through,' The old druid sounded confident.

'How far does the forest go?' Peredur asked.

'Near fifty miles,' his father answered. 'We should be out in two days—if all goes well.'

'Two days in this...' the boy muttered.

They rode on.

* * *

THE AIR COOLED with every yard they progressed. What had been a mild autumn day outside the forest had descended into winter. After a few hours of sullen travel, Arthur could see his breath, and a chill had burrowed its way under his clothing, seeping into his bones.

'Why so cold?' Peredur asked.

'It will linger like this now,' Efrawg replied. 'Take out your cloak, lad. This place has no warmth to offer travellers.'

'Still no birdsong,' Arthur commented, straining to listen. Natural sounds emerged from the gloomier recesses, such as the scuttling and chirping of insects. He imagined an army of sightless, creeping things waiting for night to come, and with it the opportunity to feed upon those foolish enough to remain.

Efrawg had been right about the forest opening up further in. To the north, the ground rose toward a hazy destination dotted with tree limbs and tangled brambles. The increasingly broken road led straight into that dull landscape. Slime-covered dead leaves lay in sodden piles upon the floor. The only dashes of colour came from a red-capped fungus and translucent mushrooms that emitted an otherworldly blue luminescence.

'Unnatural,' Merlin muttered, not for the first time.

* * *

THEY PROGRESSED IN SUBDUED SILENCE, with only the clop of hooves and the constant chitter of insects as company. The once sturdy road eventually became too treacherous to negotiate. Merlin halted them at a section of upturned stone and mortar, gouged from the earth by a mighty force.

'We must use the forest floor or risk injuring the horses,' he said, eyeing the strange displacement with curious puzzlement. No one disagreed, despite the uninviting carpet of rotting vegetation beside the roadway.

They dismounted and led the five beasts onto the sodden foliage. Arthur cursed when a giant orange slug clung to his boot as he stepped into the mulch. He bent and tried to flick the thing off, but it remained stubbornly attached, forcing him to skewer the pest with the tip of his sword and sent it tumbling upon the matted undergrowth. The act caused another disturbing groan of complaint to ripple through the forest. Cursing, Arthur rose to find the others staring at him, as if he had committed some heinous crime.

'It's a bloody slug!' he protested.

Unimpressed with the explanation, his comrades turned without comment and continued. Guinever, however, remained by his side, lost in her own sorrow. In spite of her stoic demeanour, her teeth chattered through blue-tinged lips. Curious, Arthur reached for the collar of her cloak, only for her to flinch away, her expression hardening. When he tried again, this time holding her gaze, she didn't resist. He pulled aside the collar to reveal only a thin shirt beneath.

'You're cold,' he said, nodding at the saddlebag hanging from her mount. 'Have you more clothes in the pack?'

When she did not answer, he reached over and began to unstrap it.

'Don't go in there!' she said, a little too hastily. 'I mean, no —no, thank you.'

Suspicious, he continued.

'No!' she shouted and kicked his shin.

'Ouch! That hurt, woman!'

'Good!'

Pushing her aside, he removed the bag and opened it.

'You have no right!' Her panic betrayed the fact she feared more than just an intrusion of her privacy. Arthur cursed under his breath upon noticing she'd drawn the others' attention.

He found the usual collections of personal trinkets and food inside, along with a thick, sheepskin shrug. Puzzled by her inexplicable reaction, he pulled out the skin and rummaged through the pack. Nothing seemed amiss—until he came upon a small scroll at the bottom. Instinctively, he knew this communication was the reason for her alarm, as it might prove incriminating enough to seal both their fates. Not doubting Merlin's threat and silently mocking his own stupidity, Arthur searched for something else to cover the intervention, sure the old man would want an explanation for her resistance. After a moment of further effort, his luck was in.

'You really think I'd steal your money?' he asked with fake contempt, raising the coin purse for all to see, then tossing it back into the bag. It presented a tempting prize, one he'd have slit a man's throat for only a month ago.

Guinever gave him a puzzled glance but did not speak.

'When you pair are done with your lover's squabble…' Merlin said impatiently.

'Lead on. We'll catch up,' Arthur replied, trying to sound casual.

The druid rolled his eyes. 'Suit yourself, but do not tarry

too long. If we become separated in here, you'll never see the light of day again.'

When the others were out of earshot, Arthur removed the scroll, then read the spidery script:

Stay with them. We will find you. Fail in this and the tale of your little one's suffering will frighten children for generations.

The words stunned him. This was no promise of gold or a plan to disrupt their quest, but a chilling threat. But from whom? And why? She could have written it herself to coerce another, but his instinct disagreed. No, she'd shown nothing but a level of misery too difficult to fake. He was sure this ultimatum was directed at her.

'Who gave you this?' he demanded.

'I... I cannot say,' she said, her face a pale flower betraying an inner turmoil.

That look stirred something inside him, a feeling he'd been taught through bitter experience to drive aside.

'Who is the little one?' he asked more gently. 'Your child?'

She hesitated before shaking her head. Unshed tears formed in the corners of her eyes. 'My nephew.'

'They have him?'

She nodded. 'And my sister.'

Arthur's mind raced. 'We must tell Merlin.'

'No. Please,' she begged. 'I don't care what happens to me, but them... I cannot...'

'If he understood, he'd help you.' Although he sounded convincing, he wasn't so sure. Her treachery remained undeniable.

The dilemma hung between them until she shook her head once more. 'I would not risk it. Please!'

The answer made him uneasy. By remaining silent, it would only deepen his own complicity. And what if the message was an elaborate ruse to gain his trust?

'What exactly do they want you to do?' he asked, leaving aside his misgivings for the moment.

Guinever bit her lip with indecision.

'TELL ME!'

'JUST TO SPY—REPORT where you go, who you meet, and what you do.' Her hesitation suggested she was holding something back.

Although determined to get the full truth, he feared the answer to his next question. 'Were you involved in the massacre at Ardotalia?'

The tears running down her face spoke of regret. 'I did not know they would do such a thing.'

Without thinking, he wiped them away. Her skin felt cool but soft, just as it had during their night together.

'What did you tell them?' He held her cheek, caught in a swelter of emotions. It was the thought of her previous affections being false that hurt him most.

'Only where you were headed—that's all.'

His memory turned to the attack in the peaks. 'They attacked me and Merlin as well. Your betrayal could have cost us our lives!'

She sobbed. 'I had no choice.'

'And you and I? Did they ask you to bed me?' he pressed, his resentment rising. 'You must have earned your masters' gratitude then.'

Her face reddened, and she whispered, 'I'd been so alone for months, and you seemed—'

'You expect me to believe that?'

Her countenance firmed. 'I don't care if you believe me or not, Boden, or should I call you Arthur?'

'I am Arthur,' he muttered, realising he had not yet explained his own deception.

SHE JUTTED her chin in defiance, but with only a flicker of her former fire. 'Whoever you are, just know that everything I've done I've done for them.'

Not sure what to make of that, he probed further. 'Who has your family?'

'The Picts. They raided our homestead and took them north of the great wall.'

That made sense, but the threat of invasion was well known, and she could have used it to craft a story designed to gain sympathy. Was she a willing accomplice, or a desperate woman trying to recover her loved ones? He needed more answers. 'They took you, also?'

'No. I was hunting in the forest. Since father died, I was the one who gathered our food. Mother was too old. When I returned home, they were gone—except Mother.'

'They killed her?'

'That wasn't the worst of it.' Her jaw clenched with suppressed pain.

'I am sorry.' The consolation sounded weak, even to his own ears. 'How did they contact you?'

'After they took my loved ones, a neighbour came to me and told me of their fate. She said the Picts had also abducted her own family but would be returned if she agreed to aid them. Her task was to find a skilled tracker with children...' She paused, her expression twisting into fury. 'I beat her 'til I was certain she didn't know where the bastards had taken Briant and Grania. But when I realised there was no other choice, I did as they bade, wandering from one place to another.'

'That's how you reached Derventio?'

'Yes. They told me to go to the fort, seek the commander, and—' She hesitated again. 'And offer myself as a slave in return for food and shelter.' Her voice quivered with revulsion.

' 'Tis common enough for women to do so in these dark days,' Arthur said, though part of him reviled at the image of the greasy little worm laying his hands on her.

'Not for me!' she replied fiercely. 'I would rather die than allow that Roman filth to touch me, but to save my family, I will do anything.'

'There is no shame in that,' he murmured. 'You did what you must.'

'My world is filled with nothing but shame.'

Arthur bit his inner cheek with indecision. Should he tell Merlin? Looking ahead, he could see the others were moving on, a faint mist already obscuring their forms. They should follow now or risk getting lost. On the spur of the moment, he removed his *gladius*, determined to resolve this once and for all. She was either trustworthy or not. Guinever watched him without bothering to struggle, a single tear hanging from her chin.

'Keep your hands still,' he said, then cut her bonds.

She looked surprised. 'What will Merlin say?'

'I'll worry about that. Just give me your word you will not try to get away or harm us, and you will have mine that I'll help find your family.'

Guinever nodded haltingly.

Satisfied, he sheathed the blade. 'Come, we should catch up with the others. This place is bad enough with us all together, never mind if we get separated.'

They set off again.

'I keep getting the feeling that we're being watched,' Arthur said to clear the tension between them.

'These woods are strange,' she agreed. 'I've lived near

such places my entire life, but this feels wrong, like the forest is stifled somehow.'

A brown form darted from beneath the undergrowth beside them and streaked across the path ahead. Arthur reached for his sword, but Guinever placed a steadying hand on his and pointed to the emaciated piglet. It had collapsed on its side and lay panting. The animal's matted fur revealed patches of raw skin covered with sores. No sooner had it settled, too exhausted to move, than a huge orange slug slithered onto its skeletal frame.

'Come on,' he said, not wishing to tarry further.

After calming their spooked mounts, they caught up with the others. Merlin eyed Guinever's unrestrained wrists with open disapproval.

'It was my decision,' Arthur said, bracing himself for a scathing tirade. He'd already decided not to disclose why, hoping she'd soon come to trust the old man enough to tell him herself.

To his surprise, Merlin shrugged at the admission. 'If she betrays us, then more fool you.'

'She won't,' Arthur retorted, with a resolve he did not feel.

CHAPTER TWENTY-THREE

They spent the rest of the afternoon following the remnants of the road. It eventually petered out, leaving only a wan sunlight, poking through the thinning foliage, to guide them. The landscape had barely changed, and stagnant ponds choked by yellow, overripe water lilies exuded a rotten odour. Fat toads sat amongst the stinking pools, watching the travellers with lidless eyes. Another frequent sight was the grey bones of animals littering the forest floor.

As the gloom dimmed, making further progress impossible, they stopped in a wide clearing. Despite the earlier ominous warning when Efrawg had lit the rag, the penetrating cold made the prospect of a night without fire unthinkable. Not that finding dry firewood would prove a simple matter.

'We may run out of water before we get through this cursed placed,' Arthur said, peering into his half-empty waterskin. 'The filth we've passed so far is not fit for a dog to drink, boiled or not.'

'I'll take care of that if need be,' Merlin replied. 'But I'm more concerned about what will crawl up my sleeve in the night.'

'This place is one big infestation.' The young warrior kicked a long-legged bug off the pack he'd put down. 'Can you do anything about it? These pests will eat us alive.'

Merlin rubbed his hand over his bald pate, as was his habit when pondering a challenge. 'Lead the horses out of the clearing and keep back.'

Arthur and Guinever gathered the mounts and did as he said, while Peredur and Efrawg observed with interest, still inside the clearing.

'All of you need to stand outside.'

'Why?' Peredur asked absently, staring at a stick-like creature crawling up his arm. Noticing his son's visitor, Efrawg flicked the insect away. The boy glanced at him in protest, but his father shook his head.

'If you stay inside this clearing, you'll not see your next birthday, lad,' Merlin replied.

The pair required no further warning.

'Don't worry, he's like that with everyone,' Arthur said from the corner of his mouth.

Peredur gave him an appreciative look, although clearly unhappy at being reprimanded by both his dad and the ancient mage.

Once the others had gathered at a safe distance around the base of a scabrous oak, Merlin moved into the centre of the clearing, closed his eyes, and held his hands out, palms up. Wisps of steam rose from the damp foliage, creating a terrible, cloying odour that permeated the air. The druid muttered something inaudible, and the spell intensified. The detritus and wet leaves hissed, sending a plume of gas billowing into the growing gloom.

High-pitched screeches emanated from the clearing as a myriad of crawling things perished. The hissing continued until a blue flame ignited around Merlin. It spread out like a wall of destruction, incinerating the putrid vegetation. During the tumult, the old man remained calm, his body and clothes impervious to the raging torrent. The ring of fire completed its work, cleansing the entire encampment of pests and the rottenness they thrived in, with only a smoking outline and a white residue marking their presence.

'Branwen preserve us,' Guinever murmured, fingering a small talisman of the goddess hanging from her neck. 'I thought the stories were myths.'

'No, it's him,' Efrawg said. 'If I'd doubted that for even a single second, I wouldn't have risked my son's life in this wicked place.'

Just as Arthur thought they could return to the cleared area, a violent shudder ran through the oak branches above them and spread to the surrounding trees. Again, the effect reminded him of ripples upon the water, but unlike earlier, this was no pebble hitting the surface, but a boulder. The disturbance in the forest canopy travelled outward, beyond sight.

'Let's get back to…' Arthur began, not wishing to dwell beneath the branches any longer but something very large, and very angry, roared far off to the east.

'What was that, Father?' an ashen-faced Peredur asked.

'I know not, boy. If I've heard it before, I don't remember,' the big warrior replied, peering into the gathering darkness, worry written on his bearded face.

'Come on. Merlin will know what to do.'

They wasted no time in hurrying back to the purified encampment.

'I didn't like the sound of that,' the druid said, dusting white powder from the bottom of his cloak.

'You don't know what that is?' Peredur asked, aghast. His father looked just as concerned.

'Nope. Nor do I wish to find out,' Merlin replied. He strode over to his bottomless travel bag and removed a large clay jar. 'Here, lad.' He threw it to the boy, who deftly caught the container. 'Unstopper it, then trickle a line around the edge of the circle.'

'What magic is this?' Peredur asked in wonder, examining the plain pot as if it were a holy relic.

'Never you mind. Just do it quickly or my efforts will be wasted.'

Peredur scrambled over to the edge, opened the vessel, then poured the white grainy substance along the outer scorch line.

'Will he be all right, lord?' Efrawg asked, anxiously watching the youngster. 'He's not going to blow himself up with that stuff, is he?'

Merlin chuckled. 'No, 'tis only salt.'

'Salt?'

'Aye. It'll keep them crawlies away while we sleep. A good bonfire will deter anything larger.'

'But what about the forest?' Guinever asked.

The druid gave her a sullen look before directing the answer to Efrawg. 'I'd rather risk a fire than have none.'

The warrior nodded. 'We also built fires around the edge of the camp before,' he said with a reflective cast to his voice. 'It helped.'

The fact that such a towering man found this place intimidating did nothing to quell Arthur's concerns.

'Good. Then that is what we shall do.' Merlin yawned. 'And I could eat a horse.' To which Fionna gave him a disapproving nicker.

'Don't worry, my love, I'd never eat you,' he told her graciously.

She swished her tail in acknowledgment.

CHAPTER TWENTY-FOUR

Whispering stirred Arthur from a troubled slumber. As his mind emerged from the dark recesses of a sunken dream, he at first thought he was listening to a late-night conversation between his companions. Then came the chilling realisation that he didn't recognise who spoke. Flicking his eyes open, it relieved him to see Merlin whittling a stick by the central fire. He rose and strode over to where the old man sat on a stump. Also unsettled by the otherworldly murmurs, the others had risen and gathered around the bonfire. Covered in white dust, they appeared as spectral as the disembodied voices surrounding the camp in a jumble of unrecognisable dialects.

'What are they?' Arthur asked the druid, caught between terror and curiosity.

'It would seem your snoring has awakened the dead,' Merlin replied drily.

'I snore?'

'Like a pig.'

'Do I snore?' he asked Guinever, who stood clenching her fleece tight around her shoulders.

'Like an ox,' she answered distractedly, then turned to Merlin. 'What language is that?'

The old man frowned at their unwanted ward, while adding the final touches to his handiwork, a carving of a running deer. '*Languages*,' he corrected her. 'Old Gaelic for the most part. I've not heard it spoken aloud for four hundred years.'

'What are they saying?' Arthur asked, gazing into the blackness beyond the outer fires, now little more than embers.

'Promises, mainly.' Merlin blew the shavings off the stick and inspected the finished article. 'Hmm, not bad. What do you reckon?' He displayed the effigy.

Guinever did not answer, giving Arthur a pointed look.

'What are we going to do?' he pressed.

'Do? Why must people always be doing something when there is nothing to do?'

Efrawg had dark rings under his eyes, having failed to sleep. It was not difficult to guess why. 'These are the things that lured my friends into the darkness.'

'Don't worry, my friend, the circle protects us,' Merlin reassured him.

'But it's just salt. You said so yourself.'

'That's of no matter. The circle, however, is.' The druid rose to his feet with an elderly grunt. 'I have purified this ground. Anything without a living soul cannot break its bounds. We are safe.'

'But what of their powers, my lord? They can entice us with their whisperings,' Efrawg pressed, unusually questioning the ancient champion's judgement.

'While the circle remains unbroken, they have no power.' Merlin seemed confident, overly so, but there was a guarded nature to his strident demeanour.

A translucent green streak shot through the darkness beyond the northern limit of the camp. The ephemeral light darted around the circumference of the salt circle like a moth dancing before a flame. Only when the indistinct shape paused did Arthur discern its human form. Similar to the spirit Merlin had conjured near Derventio, the wraith stared at them with ravenous longing through hollow eye sockets set above a gaping jaw.

'Are they truly dead?' Guinever asked in horror.

'Aye, they are spirits. Some are ancient, perhaps as old as me,' the druid replied, popping the deer carving into his cloak pocket.

'What do they want?' Peredur asked.

'To drink our life force,' Merlin replied lightly and wiggled his fingers at the boy. 'Especially yours! For they crave the spark of youth!'

The lad leaned further into his father, not appreciating the jest.

'But why? And why here?' Arthur asked.

'That is where things become both more interesting and more troublesome,' the old man said. 'I suspect the answers lie with the roar we heard earlier. I fear these spirits serve that other presence.'

'How do you know?'

'Because I've been observing them while you slumbered like a hog, lad. These sad relics are no more than watch geese serving a greater purpose.' He paced over to the creature, then to demonstrate, he retrieved the whittling stick from his pocket and waved it in front of the spectre. The spirit followed the stick as a dog would a bone.

'See, free spirits do not behave this way. They are but shadows trying to recapture the light they once held.'

'But you don't know what they serve?' Peredur asked.

'Precisely.' Merlin beamed. 'Which is the interesting part. At my age, such surprises are rare!' He continued examining the shade. It raked a ragged claw at him, its long fingers never straying beyond the salt boundary. 'We can be sure this thing is old. I wonder if—'

Another earth-shattering bellow rang out, this time much closer. They all turned to Merlin in unison. But the old man looked up at the stars with a furrowed brow. 'Why do I get the feeling...' There was something odd about his demeanour, unlike his usual gruff condescension.

'I'm glad you find it so fascinating!' Arthur said, his patience wearing thin. Sensing danger, he strode to his bedding and slid out his blade from beneath. 'Check the horses are tethered firmly,' he instructed Peredur.

The boy did as he was asked, double-knotting the straps that connected the five spooked mounts to the charred trunk. Guinever busied herself by rebuilding the fires, the mouldy branches spluttering in protest. The renewed illumination, combined with the stark-white circle, contrasted vividly with the surrounding dark void.

'Look,' the boy said, pointing into the gloom where Guinever had yet to stoke the flames.

Other floating forms joined their lifeless comrade, streaking along the circle's outer edge, seeking a break in the line. Behind them, more substantial figures moved. Although almost invisible in the darkness, their reflective eyes blinked with the quality of night predators.

'Merlin!' Arthur called, indicating the newcomers. 'Those things are not spirits.'

'Hmm?' the druid said, struggling to comprehend.

'Do something!' the warrior pressed.

At last, the old man shrugged off his strange complacency and dug a flaming branch from the nearest fire. He tossed it into the night, above the location Arthur had determined.

'*Stad!*'[1] he called as the burning stick reached its zenith. Immediately, its progress slowed to a creeping descent, revealing the terrain below.

They waited, transfixed by the unravelling scene before them.

There stood a beautiful woman. With her long flowing hair undulating in the night breeze, she carried a flint-tipped spear in her delicate hand. More incredible still were the bird-like wings beating behind her shapely naked body. Under the unnatural light, her countenance appeared impossibly pale. Her gaze was striking, reflective like that of a cat, and burning with hatred.

'It cannot be,' Merlin exclaimed, his face bleak.

'What cannot be?' Arthur shouted, his gut sinking.

'They have not existed in these parts since my youth.'

'For the love of—what is it, old man?'

'Faerie,' he said, slumping.

'Are they nether creatures? Like those imp things?' Arthur struggled to understand what had the ancient druid so shaken.

He did not answer.

'Dog's teeth, Merlin!'

'No. Faerie folk are cousins of man—part of the natural order.'

The creature did not flinch away from the illumination, but held back, as if waiting for something.

'Like all things humans share this world with, our mastery has not been a gentle one, and yet it pains me to see them treat us like outright enemies,' Merlin said, almost to himself.

Arthur could not help but linger upon the woman's sublime beauty. Even at this distance, he longed to run his hand down the creature's supple thighs.

'Do not look too closely,' the druid said, breaking his contemplation. 'These creatures have the power to beguile men.'

'How so?' Guinever asked, glaring at Arthur. For what, he had no idea.

'They do not carry male offspring.'

'That makes no sense. How do they reproduce?'

'In ancient times, volunteers would go from each tribe.'

'Who would volunteer for that!' Peredur exclaimed.

'We considered it a great honour,' Merlin murmured. 'Only the strongest and bravest of our warriors were allowed to mate with them and live to tell the tale. Perhaps, in these dark days, they abduct men for the same purpose.' Dawning realisation spread across his face. He turned to Efrawg. 'Why did you not speak of this?'

The big man blushed. 'I did not think it relevant.'

'Not relevant!' Merlin exclaimed furiously. 'Your prudishness could cost your son his life, man!'

'You said you could protect us,' he replied weakly.

'That depends.'

'Depends on what?' Arthur asked.

Without replying, Merlin strode back to his pack and retrieved the same jar used to create the circle. He poured more salt, crisscrossing the interior of their dubious haven until he'd formed a five-pointed star within the circumference.

Observing this new measure, the faerie hissed in frustration, then gave a strange, high-pitched trill. In response, a headless spectre dived headlong at the chalky threshold, only to burst into purple flame and dissipate. A howl of agony lingered to mark its violent passage.

The floating spirits had gathered in an undulating swarm. They no longer whispered but screamed a cacophony of rage. Worse still the telltale winks of dozens of reflective eyes had appeared in the blackness behind the writhing mass.

Another roar followed, just outside the light cast by Merlin's spell. The terrified horses whinnied and heaved against their restraints in panic. A palpable sense of dread descended as something very large and heavy thudded through the forest toward them, brushing aside thick oak branches as if they were only a nuisance.

'It cannot be,' the druid said again, then stretched out his hand at the approaching thing and closed his eyes. A heartbeat later, the colour drained from his face. Merlin, champion of the Isles since time immemorial, released a deep, convulsive gasp, and then collapsed.

CHAPTER TWENTY-FIVE

'Lord Merlin!' Peredur shouted, rushing to his side.

The old man writhed on the ground, kicking white clouds into the air. His fingers had curled into stiff claws upon his chest, like a poor wretch afflicted with the falling sickness. To make matters worse, the undead had begun a frenzied assault. They pummelled the barrier in one spot, where they exploded upon its surface in waves of wild abandon.

Arthur stood frozen, struggling to comprehend what force had overcome his legendary companion. With even the towering Efrawg clearly cowed by such a disastrous turn of events, he knew it fell on him to do something. To falter now would mean the end for them all. He took a deep breath and looked around, judging just how desperate their plight had become. With a sinking sensation in his gut, he saw that the line of salt under attack by the angry swarm of spirits, had visibly thinned.

'Efrawg, carry him further in!' he shouted, indicating Merlin's prostrate form. Although he could drag the old man's wiry frame himself, the nobleman needed a distraction.

When he did not respond, Arthur lay a steadying hand on his arm. 'Please.'

'I should not have led us here,' he replied, his face haunted. 'Especially not the boy.'

'What's done is done. I can't do this alone, and the lad hasn't a chance, if you don't get a grip.'

The big warrior blinked, wrestling inner demons. Only when his worried son came to stand with him did he give Arthur a grudging nod. Slinging Merlin over his shoulder as if weighing no more than a doll, he strode to the centre of the encampment and laid him down. Although the druid's convulsions had lessened, he remained oblivious to the world.

Guinever squatted by his side and pressed a hand upon his brow. 'He's burning up.'

Arthur had no time to consider this, for the assault threatened to pierce the barrier. 'Pass me the salt, Peredur.'

The boy diligently retrieved the jar where Merlin had dropped it, but to his surprise, did not hand it over. 'He gave me the task. I should do it.'

'It's too dangerous. Let me.' Arthur looked to Efrawg for support. There was no time for such nonsense.

'It's his task. He should be the one,' the big man replied, with both pride and regret.

Without time to debate, Arthur pointed to where the tumult was most fierce. 'There.'

Peredur scurried over to the barrier and began to reinforce the threadbare defences directly beneath the ferocious onslaught. With that brave act, their plight developed into a war of attrition, with the boy's natural vigour pitted against the swirling mass of the undead. All their fates hung on the child, but he did not waver. Following several moments of tense waiting, the invisible shield held. The number of spirits joining the fray dwindled until the few remaining spectres fluttered away, howling in frustration as they winked from existence.

A brooding silence descended upon the clearing. Time seemed to slow while they waited, searching the night for the unseen menace stalking them.

'Have they stopped?' asked Guinever, holding a water-soaked rag to Merlin's brow.

'For now,' Arthur replied.

Peredur hurried back to the bonfire and his elder's side.

Efrawg unhooked his war axe from his belt. 'They do not give in.' He carried himself like a condemned man determined to make a good end.

'Father?' the boy asked.

'Yes, son?' the nobleman half turned, the shadow of flames dancing across his tattooed face.

'If we don't survive, do you think we will see Mother again?'

'Aye, lad, and she will tell you how brave you've become.' The quiet words of praise steadied the boy, and he followed the lead of his parent, unsheathing a wicked-looking dirk.

Just when Arthur had begun to hope the faeries had left them alone, a great hiss went up from every point of the surrounding forest, and the elusive forms of the woodland folk fluttered into view beyond the watch-fires. Like the first faerie, they were all beautiful, with undulating hair and their bodies naked to behold. They had wings, although none attempted to use them. The deadly intent of these strange creatures could not be mistaken, because many were armed with slender spears and stalked forward like wary hunters. A few, wearing crowns of flowers, wielded nothing but bent twigs.

The purpose of those apparently harmless sticks became terrifyingly clear when the faeries levelled their wands and shot a magical crimson fire at the barrier in several different places. The red tide hit the invisible surface like a bloody waterfall glancing off rock, then arced into the heavens. But not all the concentrated magic had been brushed aside, for residual red energy ran down the surface of the shield and pooled at its base, thinning the protective layer of salt. These new tactics rendered any effort to plug the gap impossible, for even Peredur couldn't be in three places at once. They faced being overwhelmed within minutes.

'Merlin!' Arthur shouted, not knowing what else to do. Although the old man did not respond coherently, he groaned as if trying to revive himself.

They needed more time, but how? Arthur considered their predicament. Two of the attempts to break through the barrier were close together on the south side of the clearing, while the third lay to the north. Although they could not prevent all three breaches, someone could easily flit between the two south points with the jar. That would leave only a single point to defend.

'Peredur! Take the salt and plug those gaps at the southern end. Your father and I will take the north side.'

'But—but you have no salt.' The boy's words tumbled with fear.

'True, but we have these,' Arthur replied, hefting his blade. 'We'll hold them.'

'You don't know if our weapons will work against those things.'

'There's only one way to find out.'

Efrawg bent over and quickly embraced his son, then he and Arthur ran to the northern section where a faerie with golden hair and a figure that would make Aine herself envious, blasted away the last few grains of the barrier. Her burning gaze moved from one man to the other, a cruel smirk dancing on her lips.

'You fine men would not kill a woman, would you?' she said in a husky voice and ran a hand down her rib cage.

'Shit—they speak!' Arthur exclaimed, uncomfortable at the prospect of thrusting his sword into one so perfect.

'Don't listen!' Efrawg urged. 'It's how they get you.'

'I know, but...'

With a final blast of her wand, the barrier gave a sound like cracking glass, and a foot-wide gap appeared in the salt line before the faerie's supple ankles. She let out a triumphant trill to her fellow hunters. 'Let me come and visit you both beside the fire. We will have a fine time,' she said, thrusting a shapely thigh through the opening.

Arthur imagined running his hand along that leg and caressing her skin. The tip of his gladius lowered. Would it be so bad to give in to these creatures?

'Do not listen!' Efrawg warned again, although he too sounded far from certain.

'You are a fine pair, are you not?' she whispered in a rich, sibilant tone. 'Do you crave what you see, my fine men?' She extended her arm and caressed Arthur's cheek. A wave of desire ran through his body so strong he could only see her. Faintly, he felt the blade drop from his grasp, and returning her hypnotic gaze, he reached to take her by the waist, unable to resist.

Then, as if witnessing a dream turn into a nightmare, Arthur saw from the corner of his eye a sword chop down hard across the siren's elbow. The blade cut clean through the limb and sent it tumbling to the ground. Pale green blood gushed from the stump. The faerie opened her mouth wide in shock and regarded the wound with stupefied amazement, before stumbling backward and collapsing to the sodden forest floor. Vainly, she crawled toward her waiting sisters, but the rapid loss of her essence stopped her after only a few feet. The crown of flowers upon her head, fell and became despoiled in filth. Her elegant wings spread open and took one convulsive flap, then shuddered still.

A great roar of anguish rang out in the distance.

The brutal sight snapped Arthur out of his stupor, and he turned in horrified fascination to discover Guinever standing beside him, the gladius he'd dropped in her hand, dripping blood. She watched the creature take its last breath and returned his gaze with one of disdain.

'Must men always think with their cocks!' she said, wiping the gore off the blade against his leg. She flipped the sword around and offered it back. 'If you fail again, we die.'

Arthur took the hilt, battling a welter of emotions. There was something frighteningly human in the way the woodland nymph had died, something that pricked at his conscience, yet what else could they have done?

Looking toward the southern edge, he saw that the assault had faded upon the death of their assailant and Peredur was running back to join them.

Efrawg shook his head like a man released from a spell. 'This is how they took us last time,' he said, his cheeks reddened with shame. 'Thank you,' he added to Guinever.

The forest fell quiet.

Two spear-wielding faeries cautiously approached the corpse of their fallen sister and wept. They stroked her hair and twittered gently beside her body. The ritual continued while others of their kind gathered, distraught. It was a strange scene. In the dozens of fights Arthur had witnessed with human adversaries, never had he seen such a display of loss over a single combatant.

A kneeling faerie pointed at the two men, her face streaked with tears, '*Avenge a, hathair!*'[1] she screamed.

'You were trying to kill us!' Arthur shot back, lacking the conviction he intended. 'We had no choice!'

The creatures ignored him; their grief renewed.

The sound of crashing branches and the thudding of heavy footsteps broke the lull. Exchanging forlorn glances, the party knew their misplaced hope was lost. The approaching cacophony heightened as the silhouetted tree line to the north of the camp parted to reveal a massive clawed hand. It grasped the upper limbs of a nearby oak and pulled the bulk of something monstrous into view.

The beast's head resembled a stag's, surmounted by mighty antlers but attached to a man's emaciated, fur-covered torso. From the waist down, it was animal once more, with reticulated legs, one of which appeared withered and useless. A foetid reek came in its wake, the very essence of decay. Upon seeing the crumpled form of the faerie, the giant's alien gaze widened.

With a grief-choked roar, the colossus snapped off a branch as thick as a man's thigh and leaned on the makeshift crutch to drag itself toward the mourning females. They parted, allowing him to view the fallen. The beast gently picked up the pale dead faerie with one arm, as if cradling a baby. He continued to stare at the dead creature's open eyes, lolling her lifeless head from side to side, attempting to revive her. Then, with great care, he raised the cheek of the vanquished to its maw, laid a single kiss upon her cheek, then rested the corpse back onto the forest floor.

She decayed at an impossible rate, and within moments, only slender bones remained.

The shaggy monster closed its eyes and said in a deep, rumbling voice, '*Agus mar sin filleann mo iníon ar an Domhan.*'[2]

Completing the ritual, it turned to the human intruders and gave a rage-filled growl, before pulling itself toward them, carving a furrow in the earth. Upon reaching the protective ring, the giant flicked its pointed ears as if encountering a minor irritation. 'Which one of you *francaigh* murdered my daughter?'[3] it boomed.

Arthur stepped forward, hoping to buy Merlin more precious moments. 'We only wanted to pass through,' he said, doing his best to sound apologetic. 'We are sorry for your loss, but we had no choice.'

The creature eyed him, then sniffed long and hard. Its eyes widened in renewed fury as if noticing him for the first time. 'Abomination!' it roared through foam-flecked lips. 'How dare you come to this sacred place!'

The great beast raised the branch above its head, then brought it down against the edge of the protective dome. A torrent of sparks flew off its surface as the monster battered the barrier like a blacksmith working iron. The layer of salt dissipated along with their remaining time.

With only one remaining option, Arthur raced over to Merlin's slumbering form and shook him. 'Wake up, you old arse! We need you!'

CHAPTER TWENTY-SIX

'I said wake up!' Arthur repeated.

Nothing.

Guinever crouched beside him, anxiously watching the old man. 'I should not have killed her—it's just made things worse.'

Arthur looked straight into her green eyes. 'No,' he replied flatly, still shaking Merlin, 'you saved us.'

'You're better off without—' But she did not get to finish the sentence, for a familiar voice interrupted her.

'Will you stop that, boy! My teeth are going to rattle from my skull!'

They looked down in unison to find the druid staring at the stars.

'Merlin!'

'Yes, yes. I'm still capable of remembering my name, thank you. And who called me an old arse?'

When all four of the party spoke at once, he raised his hand to silence them, then extended it toward Peredur. The boy dutifully helped him to his feet. 'Always remember rule number one, lad,' he said, rotating his neck and wincing.

'What's rule number one, lord?'

'Don't panic,' the old man replied with a grin. But his smile soon faded as he noticed the raging giant pulling his bulk through the remnants of the magical shield.

'What is that bloody thing?' Arthur asked.

The druid's shoulders slumped. 'Cernunnos,' he said with sad regret. 'We should not have come here.'

'What is it?' the young warrior pressed.

'He is the first and last of his kind,' Merlin replied, his frown deepening. 'Why is he so angry?'

'Well…' came Arthur's hesitant response. He feared the consequences of naming Guinever as the person responsible.

'Spit it out, lad. We have little time.'

'The faeries attacked us…'

'And?'

'We killed one of them.'

'You did what!'

'We had no choice!'

Merlin grimaced, then took a deep breath and steadied himself. 'What's done is done. I'll do what I can,' he said without conviction, eyeing the colossus haltingly bearing down on them, its jaundiced gaze brimming with murderous intent. 'You must all go to the eastern edge of the clearing and be ready to run. Leave the rest to me.'

'But we are surrounded!' a terrified Peredur protested.

'I know, boy, I know. Still, do as I say, for I don't have time to explain.'

'What about you? That thing will rip you apart,' Arthur said.

'He won't kill me. At least, I hope not.'

'Why?'

The old man regarded the raging beast once more, the melancholic look returning. 'Because he's my brother.'

'What?' Arthur began, unable to comprehend such a thing.

'There's no time. Go now!' Merlin left no room for argument as he strode toward the giant.

They ran to the bucking horses to untether them.

'Leave the horses,' Merlin called back.

'Leave them with those things?' Arthur asked, incredulous that the old man would sacrifice his companions.

'They won't harm animals. It's you they seek. Besides, if my girls run in the dark, they could break their legs. No, they are better with me.'

Cernunnos had stopped and was staring at the druid, a puzzled expression upon its brutish face.

Racing to the eastern edge as instructed, Arthur could only contemplate the folly of Merlin's plan. Reflective eyes dotted the darkness. There was no chance of escaping into the pitch black beyond.

'Greetings, brother!' the old man shouted.

'What?' boomed the creature. 'Who are you?'

' 'Tis me, Myrddin. Do you no longer recognise your own kin?'

'Myrddin!' the thing exclaimed in wonder, dragging its dead leg toward him. 'It has been many years, little brother. Come, your arrival is well timed! There are murderers amongst my children. You must help me catch them and skin their hides!' It peered over the druid's head and fixed the humans with a dreadful purpose. For the first time, Arthur noticed it had the same striking grey eyes as Merlin.

The old man stepped forward, regaining its attention. 'Tell me, brother, why are you here? Your new lands are far to the north. Why do you return?'

'What, hmm?' the giant responded with a distracted air. 'Oh, the northern lands are not safe for my people. The human tribes beyond the great wall no longer respect the old ways. They turned to the dark ones and slaughtered many of my—' It stopped its sentence dead and gazed into space for a long while. 'What was I saying?'

'You have returned, brother.'

The stag giant puffed out its chest with pride and straightened to its full height, standing taller than the surrounding trees. 'Aye! We have taken back our ancient heartland, and my daughters are safe once more in the place of our birth!' Its jaundiced eyes filled with a wild light. 'And now you are with us, Myrddin. It will be as the old days.' It twisted its long jaw into a bizarre smile. 'Do you remember how we danced with our sisters beneath the stars?' It stopped again and stared up at the night sky, then back at the druid. 'Shall we dance now, as we once did, little Myrddin?' It let out an unhinged cackle and began to jig on the spot. The sudden action made it stumble, and it clung to the tree limb for support. Its animal brow furrowed into a curiously human expression of suspicion. 'Why are you here, brother? And why are we speaking in the language of the invaders?'

Merlin did not answer straight away.

'*Be ready. I fear he is not himself,*' the old man's voice came unbidden to Arthurs mind.

'*Ná bréag dom,* Myrddin!' The beast drew closer, towering over the druid.

'*Iontaobhas dom mar a rinne tú aon uair amháin,*'[1] Merlin answered in the old tongue. 'I only speak the language of the invaders so the humans will understand what we are saying.'

'You are with these murderers?' the creature asked, taken aback by the idea. 'Then the warning was true. Even you would betray me, brother?'

Merlin looked at him with dismay. 'What warning? You blocked my attempts to reach out to you, and I could not tell my friends. They acted only to defend themselves.'

'Friends, you say!' Cernunnos roared. 'Friends do not

slaughter your loved ones and burn your home! Nay, such evil is not the work of friends! They must be punished, Myrddin, but for your sake, I shall make it a quick end.' He dragged himself forward. 'Stand aside!'

Merlin held out his hands imploringly. 'Your people will suffer more if you keep killing humans. Eventually, they'll come in force, and even your great powers cannot withstand an army. And what of the southern tribes? There is still respect for the gods of earth and stream amongst them. You have my word that I'll do all I can to further your cause and protect your people, but I cannot if you make an enemy of all humanity.'

"Tis you who does not see, little one.' Cernunnos shook his great shaggy head. 'The treachery of the painted ones proves we can never trust the humans. Their foolishness will bring down the fires of the nether upon their heads. But not my people. No, so-called brother, I refuse to bow my head to a prince of evil, even when his slave spirits whisper warnings that my own family will betray me!'

The druid fell to his knees. 'That is a lie and all the more reason we must stand together and fight! I love you, brother. Please, I beg you to listen!'

Cernunnos snorted in derision through flared nostrils. 'Your promises mean nothing! You have betrayed me and brought this usurper into my sacred home! I shall heed your council no longer. Even with all your guile, traitor, you've failed to sense the thing of power residing in this place—that which will protect my daughters forever and banish humans and nether creatures alike from ever stepping foot onto our hallowed ground.'

'What do you mean?' Even from a distance, Arthur could hear the apprehension in Merlin's tone.

'I felt it, even as the remnants of my people passed

through here. Do you not sense it?' Cernunnos shuddered in ecstatic rapture.

'I feel something, 'tis true, but I did not know what...'

'You don't, do you, little one? Sometimes I forget how young you are. The tooth of the Dragon has returned to the world, Myrddin.' Its inhuman eyes glittered.

'Caliburn?' Merlin replied haltingly.

'Aye, brother, I have found it here, in this ancient place. Even now it sings to me, a pure song forged in the morning of this world, when man and beast lived in peace. Caliburn will restore the grace of my daughters and protect them from the chaos that shall sweep these lands.'

'But the tooth is a gift to all the peoples of Albion, not just the faerie folk. You know this even better than I. Any being who wields Caliburn without the blessing of the gods will suffer torment. You are damning your daughters, Cernunnos, not protecting them!'

'Nay, traitor!' the forest king roared. 'I have bent the tooth to my purpose, and yet you, little brother, bring this abomination of nature!' He pointed at the four of them, huddled in fear. 'Look around you. It serves my purpose.' He splayed his withered, scab-covered biceps. 'Does it not shine with the colours and beauty of old?'

'Prepare, boy! If I am right, his madness will unbalance him. You must flee to the governor and tell him to gather all the tribes. Look to my druid kin to aid our cause in my stead. Curse the foolishness of men!'

'He's going to do something!' Arthur called to the others. 'Be ready!'

'How do you know?' Guinever asked, her face a pale moon.

'I cannot explain. Trust me.'

'You are wrong!' Merlin shouted up at Cernunnos. 'This place has become a prison of decay.' He cupped his hands around his mouth, ready to call out into the night. 'Look at your true forms, daughters of the wood!' He clapped his palms together and sent a rippling shock wave into the darkness. An instant later, feminine screams of despair rang out around them.

Two faeries staggered into the light of the dwindling fires to reveal a hideous transformation. Their shapely bodies had become little more than skin and bone covered in festering sores, and their once luxurious wings were now featherless appendages that hung from their malnourished frames.

'How dare you!' Cernunnos roared in fury. 'These are my people!' He pointed a clawed finger at Merlin. Green tendrils shot forth from his hand and latched onto the druid's ankles. They entwined around his legs, wrapping and weaving together.

Crying out in pain, Merlin raised his hands, one toward himself, and the other toward his four companions. A tongue of flame leapt from his fingers, blackening the tendrils threatening to engulf his lower body, but the creeping vegetation continued to pour at Merlin, grasping the old man faster than the fire could scorch it dead.

Helpless to intervene, Arthur watched as the druid gradually lost his battle. The forest king's power overwhelmed the flame and clasped Merlin's figure like a living tomb. Whatever his plan had been to aid in their escape, it was failing. They would be trapped and killed.

'Arrgh!' Efrawg roared in sudden pain. Arthur whirled to face him, fearing they were under attack, only to find the big man protruding his lower jaw, exposing pointed teeth.

Arthur opened his mouth to speak but couldn't as a wave of bowel-churning agony coursed through every part of his body and flowed into his fingertips like molten lead. Swallowing the scream rising in his throat, he stared at his hands in dreadful fascination as his fingers shrank into clawed stumps. The pain drove him to his knees. Silently praying for death, he remained only dimly aware of the others as they underwent the same tortuous transformation.

'Father!' Peredur wailed, the desperate plea turning into a guttural howl.

But the nobleman couldn't help his son because he'd also descended into wretched abandon, falling onto his hands and grunting like an animal. For a moment, in the extremity of their ordeal, the men's eyes met. Efrawg's bearded chin had extended into a shaggy muzzle and his gaze glowed a golden yellow. His mouth gaped open to reveal a set of deadly canines.

'*Merlin, what have you done to us?*' Arthur implored into the void.

'*There is no other way. Listen, boy. There is far more resting upon your young shoulders than you realise. You have come into this world for a purpose. I don't understand what she intends for you, but know that you will have many enemies. Like her, they will shun and fear you. For good or ill, I am not sure.*'

'*I must know who the woman and child are?*' Arthur called out, as his elbows snapped backward. Fresh pain exploded through him.

'*Forgive me, they are not—*'

Tendrils of the forest magic enveloped the druid's head, entombing him alive.

Arthur's form changed. Bones cracked and melded, leaving him in a state of burning agony for what felt like an eternity. Even amid his struggle, he became aware of new and powerful senses. The surrounding night grew brighter. The stench of sickness from Cernunnos reached an overpowering crescendo.

When the pain ended, he was left with a single thought.

Run.

CHAPTER TWENTY-SEVEN

A great tree stood where the old human had been.

The bad-smelling creature turned toward the pack, and instinctively, the wolf understood they could not win against this enemy.

'Do we run, or do we fight?' The question came from the larger black-furred male in the form of snarls. The pack leader detected no challenge to his authority and so did not bite him.

He was aware of two others in his group: a white female and a grey adolescent. The female did not smell in heat, and he sensed nothing but fear from the pup. Because these weaker pack members could slow their escape, he considered leaving them to their own fate.

'We run,' he yelped back, deciding to protect them.

As one, they sprinted toward the arms of the forest, away from the bright fires and the stench of disease. Danger circled them. Not just from the great beast, but also from other bad-smelling creatures. He led them through the danger, the others following close on his haunches. They dodged the threatening presences like night shadows.

The pack leader had already passed into the safety of the trees when the pup yelped from behind. He turned to find a diseased creature blocking the youngster. The winged female held a wooden stick, topped with something that looked sharp and capable of killing him.

'*Protect the pup,*' he snarled. They turned as a unit and leapt at the winged female endangering the adolescent. The lead wolf bit their adversary's ankles, tearing at the tendons supporting its legs. He knew he'd hit his mark when the creature screamed in pain and fell.

The white bitch and the large male snapped at the attacker's hairless hands and feet while it writhed on the ground, clutching its wound. The taste of blood ran down the pack leader's throat, making him hungry. For a second, he considered instructing his companions to complete the kill and eat, but he sensed they were outnumbered and would soon be killed if they tried.

'*We go!*' he called.

'*Yes,*' agreed the white female. '*This meat is bad.*'

They were off again, plunging into the night. He could feel the others' constant presence at his side, imperceptible to all but the most sensitive animals. They sped through the place that appeared like a forest, yet wasn't. The ground smelled rotten, like old meat not even fit for a starving wolf. And so they continued, never stopping long enough to be tainted.

On they ran.

* * *

NIGHT HAD LONGED PASSED when they reached the edge of the bad place and found signs of healthy life once more. A fresh breeze brushed against the pack leader's muzzle as they emerged into the light and padded toward green hills in the distance. Here, they would find good meat and sweet blood again.

'We must rest soon,' the other adult male yelped.

The leader snarled back, not tolerating the challenge. The black male growled before lowering his head in deference. Despite the rebuke, he knew the other male was right. Their long escape had tested even the boundless energy of their kind.

Panting, he brought the pack to a halt and sat upon his haunches. They had emerged onto a grassy plain where the faint smells of prey surrounded them. Although he licked his lips anticipating meat, he knew the hunt must wait, for their need for sleep was greater. He scanned the horizon with his powerful senses, for a place of refuge, but the only possibility was a human den atop a nearby hill.

Under normal circumstances, he would never allow them to stay in the dwelling of a hairless one, but the scents coming from that direction were devoid of the rich smells associated with man. The refuge was strangely made, projecting into the sky and formed from something hard. Deciding it worthy of investigation, he took them closer.

Upon reaching the den, he stepped over the threshold and cocked his ears, listening for danger. There was none. Just as he suspected, it was long abandoned. The others paused behind him; even in their fatigued state, they would not dare push ahead of him. Cautiously, the pack leader padded further inside and sniffed, ensuring he did not show fear. Only the faintest traces of man remained. Satisfied they were alone, he raised a leg against the nearest wall and urinated his scent. As he did, he sensed the tension lessen in the others.

'I do not sense danger here,' the white she-wolf said, echoing his thoughts.

'*Yes,*' he agreed. '*We will sleep here, then we will hunt.*'

As a group, they lay upon the floor and closed their shining golden eyes.

The leader dreamed of hunting and of lost pack mates.

CHAPTER TWENTY-EIGHT

Arthur awoke facing a cracked flagstone floor, free from pain. He was freezing, but it didn't matter because the nightmare was over. 'Merlin,' he croaked through parched lips.

'Are you awake?' The voice was Guinever's.

He turned onto his back and stared up at a blue sky framed by a collapsed roof. Guessing they were in an abandoned dwelling, he sat up to find Guinever observing him. She sat at the bottom of a broken set of wooden stairs to a small hayloft, looking relieved. Oddly, she wore a moth-eaten woollen dress.

Aware of the chill, he looked down upon his nakedness. Lifting his hand to his bare chest, he could only feel the whistle Merlin gave him, still hanging from his neck by its leather cord.

'I woke the same as you,' she said, then indicated her barely adequate clothing. 'I found the dress upstairs.'

Efrawg and Peredur were still asleep beside him.

'Shit,' he said.

'I'd say that pretty much describes the situation.'

'Merlin?' he asked against any real hope.

She shook her head. 'Sorry.'

An unfamiliar sensation of loss gnawed at him. He'd only experienced the death of comrades before—men who'd sell their own mothers for gold. But despite the maddening ways of the old man, he was the first and only person to show Arthur any kindness.

'Are there more clothes upstairs?' he asked, trying to rein in his emotions.

'There's a box of farmhand rags like this.'

Without speaking, he rose and stepped over the slumbering pair, the stone floor icy against his feet. When he passed Guinever to go upstairs, she grasped his arm.

'It's okay to miss him,' she murmured.

'I'm cold,' he replied, pulling away.

He climbed up the rough-hewn planks and emerged into the empty space, then found the plain, worm-ridden box sitting under the remaining thatch. As he pulled out several mouldering rags, the memory of Merlin being encased in a living tomb intruded upon him.

What do I do now?

With the druid gone, he could turn his back on the games of gods and kings for good and return to his old ways. Nobody could stop him. True, the old man had saved his life, but that debt no longer existed. Peredur and Efrawg could go back to their lives. And his promise to Guinever? Well, perhaps her paymasters would reward her for news of Merlin's death by releasing her family? He tried to ignore the inner voice scorning the likelihood of such an outcome.

Throwing the box back, he dressed in a faded blue tunic and ripped *braccae*, then headed down to find a newly awoken father and son bewildered by their state of undress.

'Here,' he said, tossing them the remaining rags.

When Efrawg noticed Guinever watching them, he placed

an awkward hand over his lower parts. 'Do you mind?' he said.

'You've got nothing I haven't seen before,' she retorted, a faint twinkle of amusement the in her eye.

The big man gave Arthur a look of appeal.

'Give them a minute,' he said, in no mood for games.

She shrugged and turned around.

The old clothes were woefully inadequate to cover Efrawg's muscled torso, whereas Peredur looked buried. The effect would've been comical if not for their predicament.

'Now, can someone please tell me what bleedin' madness happened last night?' the disconcerted nobleman asked, examining his new attire disapprovingly. 'One minute those... those women beasties are attacking us, and the next I'm waking up in a barn with me bollocks hanging out!'

The following silence spoke of a shared reluctance to admit what they all suspected. Arthur's own recollection of what came after the confrontation in the forest was mostly incomprehensible, other than fleeting images of running through the night with boundless energy. 'Merlin did something to us,' he said. 'Something that allowed us to escape.'

'I dreamt I was a—' Peredur began.

'It was sorcery. That's all we need to know,' his father interrupted.

Arthur shared his apparent unease at the possibility that Merlin had transformed them into something inhuman.

'So, what now?' asked Efrawg. 'We can't stay here for long or we'll starve.'

'I'll find food,' Arthur replied, knowing the task would provide the perfect opportunity to slip away and be done with this insane adventure.

'And I'll look for water,' Guinever offered. 'There's a leather bag in the loft. It might still be watertight.' She headed back up the stairs and returned a moment later with a scuffed feedbag. 'It'll have to do,' she said, also throwing more rags onto the floor between them.

'What are we supposed to do with those?' Arthur asked, not understanding.

'We've nothing on our feet and I'd prefer to keep my toes while walking through the frost.'

'We can't walk all the way to Luguvalium without anything on our feet!' Peredur exclaimed.

'We can and we will if need be,' Efrawg chastised. 'I didn't know what a boot was until I'd reached my eighth birthday, and I've still got two legs.'

'Sorry, Father.' The embarrassed boy took a couple rags and tied them around his feet. The others followed suit.

'Don't worry, lad,' the nobleman said more gently. 'I know these hills like the back of my hand, and I reckon Luguvalium is only three days' walk away. When we get to the governor, I'm sure he will treat you well.'

The look of confusion the boy directed at his father convinced Arthur he had no idea of his heritage as the grandson of Vibius.

Guinever, however, spat in contempt. 'Vibius is a useless pig. He'll not listen.'

'He is our rightful ruler,' the nobleman snapped, not taking his eyes off Peredur. Before she could respond, he rose. 'Come, boy. Let's find something to trap rabbits with.' He stomped away, followed by his confused-looking son.

'What's up with that big oaf?' Guinever asked. 'Nobody likes Vibius.'

'You don't understand,' Arthur said, no longer in the mood for company. 'I'll go forage in the wood.'

* * *

USING the tree line to hide his movement, he headed south.

The plan was to strike out east and avoid the larger settlements. Perhaps he'd be lucky and find a fat merchant with a large purse to waylay. Without the old man's protection, his predicament as an outlaw would dominate his existence once more. He pressed a self-conscious hand to the tunic covering his scar and thanked the gods only Guinever had woken before him. Ally or not, Efrawg would likely have ripped him apart upon discovering his true identity, given the fate of his late wife.

And he would be right to kill me, he thought.

Regardless of his determined stride, doubts about his intended path refused to dissipate. Friends got you killed. Betrayal inevitably followed misplaced loyalty. Those core beliefs had kept him alive for many years, and yet such lessons were difficult to apply to Efrawg and his son. In the two days since meeting them, it was clear they were moral to a fault. And Guinever frightened him most of all. He'd never trusted women. Camp followers were desperate creatures, as cold and calculating as the men they served. So he'd learned to never treat a woman as an equal, but this was what this dark-haired beauty expected. Not a thing—a person. ' 'Twas but a fuck,' he said derisively and hurried on, pushing aside memories of her sad green eyes gazing into his.

What did he see himself as in the future? A farmer? Arthur smirked at the idea, being far more comfortable with a blade in his hand. A killer, then? He imagined Merlin's disgust at the latter and his mockery of the former. So what, then? If this suicidal quest could take the life of the ancient champion, surely his paltry efforts would fail?

He strode beneath the forest's sun-dappled canopy, picking the heads off dandelions. The smells of wet earth brought back recollections of their midnight run.

I led the pack, and they followed…

'A few hours of this and I will be free,' he muttered, maintaining his pace, determined to prove he could leave them behind.

And what will you do when those things overrun the Isles?

Arthur stopped in his tracks. 'Damn it!' he roared and punched the nearest tree with a blow hard enough to make his knuckles flare in pain. He shook his throbbing hand, then raised it to his lips. As he sucked at the broken skin, he noticed a cluster of edible mushrooms at his feet.

Deciding that food would be needed no matter which path he chose, he spent the next hour searching for fungus, nuts and berries. His ability to forage had saved him from starvation many times as a child. Beyond the realm of the rancid creature Merlin had called Cernunnos, the bounty of this place was fresh and plentiful. He ripped a makeshift cloth bag from the sleeve of his already threadbare tunic, then headed south, ready to start a new life.

This is more food than you need for yourself, the thought intruded.

Arthur stopped again and shouted several curses at the uncaring trees about him, then threw the bag at the foliage in a fit of temper, spilling its contents. After regathering his foraged bounty, he marched back to the abandoned farm, fuming at his own stupidity.

The others were already sitting around a meagre fire, skinning four scrawny rabbits, when he returned in a thunderous mood.

Guinever directed a searching look at him. 'You took your time.'

Ignoring her, Arthur tossed the forage beside the fire.

'Mushrooms!' Peredur exclaimed, snatching a stray one that'd rolled out. But as he brought it to his mouth, his father clasped his arm.

'Might be poisonous,' he said, frowning at Arthur.

Meeting the big man's gaze, Arthur took one of the fleshy

treats, put it in his mouth, and chewed. It tasted good. Upon seeing his certainty, Efrawg released his grip on the boy who eagerly wolfed down his own mushroom.

Using the remains of an iron sheet as a crude pan, they dry-cooked the nuts, mushrooms and rabbit meat. Despite the earthy aromas coming from their makeshift kitchen and the fire's warmth, it remained a sobering morning for all.

'I wonder what happened here?' Peredur asked, looking around at the shell of the forest lodge. 'Whoever lived here left much behind.'

'Bandits, most likely,' Guinever replied. 'They infest these lands like rats.'

Arthur suspected the barbed comment was directed at him, but oddly, she had not looked in his direction.

Efrawg nodded. 'Aye, some gangs have grown to the size of small armies. We've hardly enough trained men to protect the walls of Cambodunum. Smallholdings such as these stand no chance.'

'It reminds me of home,' Guinever said, her eyes clouding with grief.

'Perhaps the Romans will send more legions?' Peredur suggested.

His father snorted in contempt. 'The Romans are slippery bastards—more interested in fighting each other than protecting these lands. I've heard there's barely a single legion left in the entire diocese. If it weren't for the wealth of the mines, they'd have gone years ago.'

'How big is a legion, Father?'

'Hmm? These days, a thousand men at most.'

'But that's not many at all! Why don't we just get rid of them? Fight them?' Peredur said, standing and thrusting an imaginary sword. This act of defiance earned a fond smile from his elder.

'Because the governor sits on his fat arse in Camulodunum, taking whatever scraps the emperor feeds him,' Guinever intervened.

Efrawg turned beet red at Guin's criticism of Vibius and said between clenched teeth, 'Do not speak so, woman.'

'And why is that? You are no friend of the invaders.'

'You don't know of what you speak!'

'Oh, don't I? Well, I know he did nothing to stop the Picts from taking my family, just like the poor fools who lived here.' She gestured around them. 'So why defend him?'

Arthur was beginning to wish he'd told her about Peredur's mother.

'Well... he is the governor,' the nobleman answered awkwardly, while giving Peredur a surreptitious glance.

'And?' Guinever scoffed. 'You must be soft in the head.'

'And you have a big mouth!' he shouted.

'Ha! What is it? Are you one of his bastard children?'

'No! Dog's teeth, Arthur, can you shut her up?' he called, taking his meat from the fire and biting deep into the half-cooked rabbit. 'I don't speak to spies.'

Guinever's defiance wavered at the mention. 'I had no choice.'

The big man huffed in disbelief.

'It's true,' Arthur said, deciding his promised silence no longer served a purpose. Last night's events made such deceptions unnecessary. They had all been through too much together. 'The Picts took her niece and sister, then threatened to kill them if she did not aid them.'

Efrawg's brow furrowed in concerned surprise. 'I am sorry. I did not know,' he said, the news perhaps striking a chord with his own past.

Guinever glared at them both before stomping away, leaving the men to eat in silence.

CHAPTER TWENTY-NINE

The party travelled in sodden misery through a land of great lakes and fog-shrouded peaks. Such wild places bore little evidence of mankind. During the day they only stopped to hunt, and at night they shivered beneath the stars. On the second afternoon they saw a town in the distance, but Efrawg advised against entering the place called Brocavium, for it belonged to the Carvetti, a secretive people who were smaller in stature than other Britons, but fiercely independent. Even during the height of the empire's power, they'd resisted subjugation and were hostile to Brigantes and Romans alike.

Three days and nights spent in half-frozen toil passed until they climbed a steep hill to find the small city of Luguvalium spread out across the valley below. Hundreds of fires spewed swirling smoke into the crystal-clear morning air, giving it the appearance of a mist-shrouded island. In the adjacent fields, protected by a palisade that joined the settlement, a thousand tents dotted the landscape. At the heart of the encampment was a huge golden tent embroidered with the image of a rearing horse.

* * *

LUGUVALIUM'S aged darkened gates stood as a testament to the city's long vigil against its northerly neighbours. Above the ancient entrance, the governor's majestic horse banner fluttered. In stark contrast, on either side, were the skewered remains of a dozen severed heads, their tongues lolling out of emaciated skulls. Arthur shuddered at the single placard raised above them. No words were written across it, only the splayed skin of a man's chest. The brand of the Raven clan was still visible upon its wrinkled surface. In spite of the welcome prospect of food and warmth, he regarded the unmistakable warning with a creeping sense of dread.

Two guards sporting the topknot of the southern Trinobantes manned the gate. As the party approached, the scowling duo interlocked their spears, barring their passage.

'Fack off, beggars!' a fat warrior with foetid breath said through brown, crooked teeth.

Arthur tried to remain calm despite the insult. 'We've urgent business with the governor.'

The guards shared an amused smirk, then burst out laughing. 'And what would that be? The ever-rising cost of begging bowls?' The over-fed guard mocked, pressing the shaft of his weapon against Arthur's chest. 'P'raps I will take you to Vibius just to watch 'im feed your balls to his pet Germanians.'

'I wouldn't recommend that.' Efrawg stepped forward. 'We've come with urgent news about the enemy.'

An uncertain frown appeared above the guards' jowls at the timely intervention, and he eyed the big man with suspicion.

Efrawg rolled up his threadbare sleeve to reveal the boar tattoo of the Brigantes on his arm. Only senior members of nobility could bear the symbol of their tribe. The penalty for lesser men who did so was death. The fat warrior regarded the boar for a moment, and then nervously licked his lips at the grim-faced giant towering over him.

Efrawg took another ominous step closer. 'Now, take me to the governor, and I'll consider not beating the living shit from you.'

The fat man coughed uncomfortably. 'You're truly a lord?'

'How many beggars do you see my size?'

The pair eyed each other before one gave the other a shrug. 'If he's lyin', it's their funeral.'

Brown Teeth shrugged, then nodded. 'Fair enough. Follow me.'

* * *

A SCENE of organised chaos greeted them on the other side. The cobbled streets teemed with people of all tribes, including a few olive-skinned foreigners—a less common sight in recent years. More than a few armed soldiers pushed through the crowd, eager to spend their pay on local wine and prostitutes. Hawkers crammed every spare yard of space, proclaiming their goods to the engorged population. Stinking gutters piled high with manure groaned under the strain of the extra load.

They headed through the throng toward the adjoining encampment. Like other towns, the crumbling remains of temples dedicated to Celtic-Roman deities, now fallen out of favour, lined the roadside. The many eastern mystery cults that flourished in their stead, occupied a few such ruins, including a former shrine of Bellinus, now topped by the odd sun-shaped symbol of Sol Invictus. These fanatics believed their god was born of a virgin and had miraculously returned from the dead. Arthur found such claims hard to believe.

The temple was open to the elements on three sides.

L.K. ALAN

Inside, the worshippers had stripped down to their waist and were flagellating themselves with short whips as a priest screamed at them to repent or face the fires of the place he called hell.

'Bleedin' vermin,' the guard said, observing the spectacle as they passed. 'I 'ope the governor clears 'em out. They're like rats. As soon as you get one nest, another pops up.' He spat onto the muddy ground for good measure.

They stopped at the north gate to the army camp, while their plump escort spoke to his comrades. While they waited, Peredur wandered over to watch a street juggler tossing knives into the air and catching them without injury. Guinever followed him, but not before shooting a glower of pure spite at Arthur, much to his disconcerted surprise. With little time to consider what he'd done to earn the look, he raised his concerns regarding their imminent audience with Vibius.

'Do you think the governor will believe us?' he asked, aware that they were about to meet a man who'd executed his own brother.

'We'll find out soon enough,' came the less-than-encouraging response. 'Either way, I'll do my duty.' The big man's somber look did nothing to allay his apprehension.

Arthur lost his patience. He needed to know if they were going to be disembowelled because of a domestic feud. 'Why didn't you tell the others that Vibius is Peredur's grandfather?' he asked, nodding to the boy, now grinning with innocent fascination at the street performer.

Efrawg gave him a flat stare. 'That's a private matter.'

'Your woman spoke of what happened to your wife,' he replied, certain their predicament demanded such bluntness.

The nobleman's eyes narrowed with anger, but also with a shadow of hurt. 'She is not my woman. I'm already married.'

Arthur watched the guards nervously. 'I'm not trying to pry, but we could all end up dead.'

No reply.

'Does Peredur know about the governor?'

The big man looked suddenly terrified. 'Shh, man!' he hissed through gritted teeth. 'He must never find out.'

'What?' Arthur was incredulous. The answer made no sense. The boy's royal blood was the one thing in their favour. 'But Vibius will—'

'He must not know, either.'

'But why? Surely...'

Efrawg's gaze became bleak. 'Because Peredur is all I have left. And if you speak to either of them about this, apprentice of Merlin or not, I will kill you.'

CHAPTER THIRTY

They entered a sea of mud-splattered tents, where sullen soldiers sat around fires, playing tesserae.

Most watched the sorry-looking newcomers with indifference, while some eyed Guinever, then offered their personal attention in exchange for pitiful sums of money. Used to such unwanted advances, she ignored them. Only the occasional chain-mail-clad legionary of the Victrix indicated this was an imperial army and not a large gathering of tribal militia. These full-time regulars conducted themselves with an obvious purpose the native troops lacked, striding past their inactive comrades while directing disdainful glances about them.

Arthur experienced an unwelcome reminder of his childhood when they came upon a young pot-boy perched on a platform above a huge cauldron, stirring the bubbling mix below. One wrong step and the child would be boiled alive. He found it ironic that in all the years since he had performed the same role, he'd discovered no greater security in life.

The golden tent at the centre of the camp grew ever more imposing as they neared it, so did the rhythmic music that came from within its silver-trimmed confines. The image of the rearing horse woven upon its billowing canopy appeared to run and kick in the breeze a good twenty feet above them. Arthur had never seen the like. The vast canvas enclosure could have accommodated dozens of the surrounding smaller tents.

Several towering men guarded the canopied entrance. With their mutton-chop beards, conical helms with a crude image of a white bear painted upon them, and thick fur hides cladding their bodies, they stood in stark contrast to everyone around them. Of a stature to match even that of Efrawg, the silent giants glared at the bedraggled party as they approached.

'The governor's Germanian guard,' their fat guide said through the corner of his mouth. 'Don't even think about pissing 'em off.'

'I know who they are,' the nobleman muttered, then strode over to a huge bearded man with a scar running from his empty right eye down to his throat. Unlike his comrades, he had a red bear, rather than a white one, painted on his helm.

'What you want, turd?' One Eye greeted Efrawg without looking at him. Although his tone was a bored rumble, Arthur sensed the ominous nature of the question. This was not a man people bothered lightly, and he guessed that was because of his mountainous build.

Oddly, Efrawg grinned before answering. 'To hump your woman till she calls my name, Adalric, you blind sack of shite!'

The Germanian blinked in shock, as did their brown-toothed guide, who gave an involuntary moan, then ran to the pair and sputtered a half-baked apology. As the one-eyed guard regarded the vagrant, his shaggy features lit up. 'I'll be a whore's fat nip! Efrawg! Is it really you?'

The two giants embraced each other in a hug that would have crushed the bones of lesser men. Arthur let out the breath he'd been holding.

'It must be...' the Germanian began.

'Twenty years, my friend.'

'Ja, must be,' One Eye agreed, stepping back and regarded the other man's poor state of attire with confusion. 'Why are you dressed like a beggar, my lord?'

Efrawg nodded to his equally scruffy companions. 'It's a long story.'

'I can see that.' Adalric peered at them, his deep brow narrowing with curiosity. They must have struck an odd sight. 'Then we shall drink while you tell me this tale.'

'Aye, we shall,' the nobleman said, slapping him on the arm by way of thanks, then looking at the red bear upon his helm. 'You lead the tribe now?'

The Germanian did not answer straight away, but stared at Efrawg with puzzled concern. 'Hmm? I am, but an old woman could slap these bunch of girly boys around.' He spoke loud enough for his companions to overhear and earned a few guttural laughs in response.

His demeanour turned serious. 'I did not know he lifted your exile from court.'

The nobleman shook his head. 'He has not, my friend, but I must see him today, regardless.'

Adalric's eye widened. 'Are you mad?' He lowered his voice. 'I should stick you in irons, you fool.'

'I bring word of the enemy.'

The Germanian looked surprised. 'This is why you've risked coming here?'

'Yes.'

The two men stood in contemplative silence until Adalric placed a pan-shovel-sized hand on Efrawg's shoulder. 'I heard about Ula. I am sorry. She was a good woman. After everything you both sacrificed, it was cruel luck.'

'Aye, that it was,' Efrawg replied, his expression shadowed by loss.

The captain sighed with regret. 'Then the governor must see you, but be warned, his temper has not lessened over the years, nor has his grief. Sometimes, when he is in his cups, he still blames you.' He said, gripping his shoulder tighter. 'If you go in there, he may kill you.'

Efrawg clenched his jaw. 'Yet we must. This news cannot wait.'

Adalric paused with indecision, then nodded and raised one side of the green entrance flap.

Rather than entering, Efrawg strode to Peredur. 'You will stay here.'

The boy looked shocked and confused. 'But I'd like to see the governor, Father.'

'No, you will wait.' The big warrior was unusually stern with his son. 'And if I don't return, you must go back to Cambodunum and live with Brina.'

Horrified, Peredur asked. 'But why would—'

'Enough, boy! Do as I say.'

Pale-faced, the lad could only nod. With this submission, his father kneeled and embraced him. 'Promise me you will look after them?' he said, his voice thick with emotion.

'Father, I...'

'Promise me!'

The boy turned to Arthur for support, bemused by his elder's strange behaviour. But knowing the truth, he could not offer any assurance, only a sympathetic glance. And it was a genuine one, for he had always missed the presence of his own father.

With nothing else to do, Peredur nodded, his eyes filled with unshed tears. Efrawg planted a kiss on his son's forehead, then rose and turned to the fat guard, who peered inside the tent's smoky interior with interest. Extending one muscular arm, he grasped him by the scruff of his soiled tunic and yanked him forward.

'Oi, what the fu—'

'If anything happens to him while I'm gone, I'll gut you like a pig. Is that clear?'

The guard glanced at the boy, then back at his father and nodded emphatically.

Efrawg released him and strode through the open tent without looking back.

* * *

THEY ENTERED a different world from that of the army surrounding it. Flaming braziers dotted the outer edges of the great area, casting a smoky glow over the crowd of noblemen and noblewomen lounging upon Roman-style divans. They feasted and drank while slaves, in drab short tunics, moved among them, filling empty wine cups, washing hands, or providing silver vomit buckets to participants. The stench of unwashed bodies, mixed with the rich aroma of food, tainted the cloying air.

Lithe, half-naked dancers gyrated around a great roaring fire at the centre of the makeshift hall. Arthur wondered what far-flung corner of the empire Vibius had recruited the troupe from. He looked for the musicians responsible for the outlandish tune but could only see a group of shadowy figures in one dark recess.

A plump, adolescent boy puked into one of the proffered buckets nearby, before gorging himself once more. Having once eaten his own shoe leather to fend off starvation, Arthur found such indulgence incredible. It was said that as a youth, the governor had been sent to Rome as a hostage to be raised at the emperor's palace, along with other princelings of subject provinces. The vestiges of that influence were clear.

They followed Adalric's hulking form through the revellers toward a dais at the back of the gathering. As they neared the fire, the dancing spectacle took a bizarre turn. A misshapen boy, clad in a bright red and yellow tunic, darted amongst the performers, running under their legs and slapping their buttocks. The little terror's antics earned widespread laughter from the guests, more so as the careful positioning of the sweat-drenched troupe descended into chaos. Transfixed, Arthur observed the disruptive display, until he noticed the bearded, craggy face of the tiny tormentor and realised he was a grown adult, not a child.

There was no doubt about who sat upon the large throne erected on the wooden dais. Vibius Crassus, the ruling *vicarius* of the diocese of Britannia, was a grossly fat man dressed in a purple toga. He bit hard into the flesh of a whole chicken held in one pudgy hand. Despite the levity on his face, dark bags sat beneath his narrowed eyes. He leaned forward in fascination as the little performer clung to the muscular thigh of a male dancer. Enraged at the indignity, the dancer kicked and punched at the pest, now imitating a dog humping his leg. Vibius howled with glee, spraying his mouthful of bird meat over those closest to him.

'Ha! You truly are a rare creature, Ken!' he shouted over the throng, then tossed the half-stripped chicken carcass at a huge wolfhound lying at his feet. The dog opened one drooping eye at the offering, yawned, then returned to its slumber.

To signal his gratitude of such high praise, the impish Ken darted beneath a curvaceous female, slapping her backside as he passed. She responded with a kick that sent him flying, but a well-timed, mid-air twist, stopped the tiny menace from somersaulting straight into the flames. Such a death-defying manoeuvre only increased the crowd's raucous joy.

The party reached the side of the dais, with the governor still distracted by the display. Knowing better than to interrupt, the Germanian waited for the dancers' humiliations to end.

'My lord,' he prompted, when Ken eventually scurried off, leaving his victims in a state of panting bewilderment.

Vibius lolled his perspiring jowls toward them, and his grin dropped in an instant. He peered at the arrivals through the glazed squint of a person well into their cups. 'Hmm, what is it, Adalric? Don't I pay you enough to keep every fucking beggar from my doorstep?' he slurred.

'My lord, this man brings an urgent message,' the guard captain replied stepping back and allowing Efrawg to approach.

The governor's tired indifference turned to fury as his myopic gaze landed on the nobleman.

Efrawg gave a short bow. 'Greetings, my lord, I bring you grave news.'

'You! You would dare bring me more grave news? Is that right, Efrawg of Brigantia, my so-called son-in-law?' The governor's voice rose above the music, as his bloated cheeks blazed a deep red.

'Yes, that's why I've come, lord.'

'You have a gift for bringing me such tidings, do you not, eh? Perhaps you have already forgotten the last news your actions brought to my door?'

Efrawg lowered his head. 'I have not.'

'So, tell me, what news might be graver than the betrayal and neglect that led to my daughter's death?' The governor shifted his great bulk, glowering with hatred. The last smattering of chatter among the crowd died down, as their ruler's displeasure flared in all its ominous glory.

Efrawg appeared stricken by the reprimand, no doubt believing the harsh verdict himself.

'Well, speak, you dumb ox! And if you think I'll spare you because of past leniencies, you are much mistaken!'

'My lord, can he be trusted?' The voice came from the left of the dais. A man wearing the decorated breastplate of Roman general rose from a group closest to the governor's platform. The square-jawed veteran was cleanly shaven, and despite the revelry, he appeared alert.

Vibius waved a dismissive hand at the questioner, then plucked a silver goblet from the throne arm and took a deep swig, all while eyeballing the nobleman. 'I treated you like a son!' he roared, slinging the rest of his cup at Efrawg. The big warrior did not respond, allowing the red wine to drip from his beard.

'Perhaps we should take this business into your private chamber, lord?' the Roman general warily suggested, observing the vagabonds with curiosity.

Vibius ignored the suggestion as he continued to stare at his former son-in-law's averted gaze, his head swaying. 'Mark my words, this better be important and not some sniffling apology, or I'll have you ripped limb from limb.' He pressed his palms against the throne and strained to push himself up. Immediately, two burly slaves rushed to his side and lifted him onto his bloated legs. They aided the tottering governor to wobble toward the edge of the dais, and then manhandled him down thick steps to the carpeted floor below.

The party followed under the watchful eyes of the gathered court, as he was led to a curtained-off inner sanctum at the rear of the tent.

CHAPTER THIRTY-ONE

The governor's private chamber comprised over a quarter of the tent's vast floor space. Tapestries depicting nymphs cavorting with hooved creatures disturbingly reminiscent of the forest beast called Cernunnos, covered the interior canvas walls. Ornate statues, carved in the lifelike style of the Romans, stood around the chamber. At its centre was a great canopied bed, with running horses etched upon its thick posts. Unusually, several sturdy chairs and tables dotted this inner space, giving the odd impression it served as both a bedroom and a makeshift *taverna*. An elderly slave kneeled in a corner, holding a tray with a filled wine cup on it. Two Germanians guarded the entrance curtain and gave their commander a silent nod as he entered behind the puffing Vibius and his apprehensive guests.

The governor pushed aside his aides irritably, then stomped to a padded stool in front of the bed and lowered himself with an audible groan. Panting, he glared at the ragged group, his eyes settling on Guinever. His red-eyed gaze travelled to her breasts. 'So, this is what you replaced her with, hmm?' he said. 'You thought to bring your new whore under my roof and rub your disloyalty in my face, eh?'

'No, my lord, she is just a slave.'

To Arthur's relief, she did not challenge the insult, but averted her eyes as expected of a servant.

'Pfft,' Vibius belched. 'And why are you dressed like a pleb?' He gestured at them with sausage-like fingers, thick with gold rings. 'I pray to the gods you've truly been reduced to beggary. 'Twould brighten my day.'

Efrawg hesitated, struggling to relay the unbelievable truth. 'Someone stole our clothes.'

Vibius glowered. 'You never could lie, Efrawg. I ought to have your tongue cut out, just for that.'

The Roman general came to stand by his superior. 'What news do you bring?' he asked while Vibius gave them an unsteady sneer.

'Ardotalia has fallen,' the big nobleman said flatly.

Deep suspicion sprung across the generals chiselled features. 'What nonsense is this?'

Clearly, they were the first to bring the dark tidings. Unlike his military advisor, however, a flicker of concern passed over the governor's face.

'I think a few hours of interrogation will suffice, my lord,' the Roman said.

'Hmm, I'd like to be present for that,' Vibius agreed, the threat steadying him into cold calculation. 'I don't know what form your treachery has taken, you Brigantian dog, but know I'm expecting the dotard Merlin to arrive any day with Ardotalia's garrison, and when he does, I'll have you flayed.'

The threat hung between them.

With Efrawg unable or unwilling to protest their innocence, Arthur felt compelled to intervene. 'It's true, the fort is gone—destroyed,' he spoke up.

Without looking at him, Vibius called, 'Adalric!'

'Yes, imperator?' the captain responded by the curtained entrance.

'If I don't know who this cockroach is within the next minute, I want you to pluck his eyes out.'

'Yes, lord.'

Arthur sensed the man's towering presence move behind him. Resisting the urge to turn and defend himself, his mind raced for the least damaging answer. 'Erm, I am... Merlin's apprentice, lord.'

The governor's humorless chuckle chilled Arthur to the bone. 'Well, there we have it, Quintus.' He lifted a bloated hand toward the general beside him. 'Merlin's apprentice.'

'He speaks the truth, lord,' Efrawg interjected.

'What?' Vibius snapped. Although the governor remained incredulous, Arthur saw the underlying confusion in the question. Evidently, his hatred couldn't overcome the knowledge that his former son-in-law was honest to a fault.

'This man, Arthur, arrived with Merlin at Cambodunum and sought me as a guide. They asked me to bring them here by the quickest way. 'Twas the Druid himself who told me of the massacre.'

The governor stared. 'Then you'll die thinking I'd be foolish enough to believe the word of a hedge trickster and his stooge.'

'No, lord. Merlin showed me his sorcery, and it was no trick. I am certain,' the big warrior replied, his expression stony.

Vibius gave a dismissive sniff, but it lacked conviction.

'He also told me the Picts have new allies and will attack soon.'

This prompted the general called Quintus to speak. 'Allies? Who? There is nothing but the frozen sea and the land of the dog heads beyond that cursed country.'

Efrawg surreptitiously glanced at Arthur. Talk of demons

and supernatural beasts would seal their fate. 'I'm not sure, but they could be great in number.'

'Pah! So are the crabs around my cock, but I do not fear them,' Vibius retorted.

'It is true,' Arthur confirmed. 'The entire garrison is slain.'

The governor rubbed his unkempt beard, encrusted with bits of chicken, and then turned to Quintus. 'What do you think?'

'They lie. It's not possible for such a large force to bypass our defences unnoticed.'

THE UNCOMPROMISING VERDICT prompted Arthur to silently pray for a swift end.

Vibius drummed his grubby fingernails against his vast gut in contemplation. 'If it were any other man, I'd agree with you, but this fool'—he pointed at Efrawg—'couldn't even lie about his intention to bed my Ula. Cheeky bastard asked permission to wed her while half the nobility of the Isles witnessed.' He looked around him in irritation. 'Where is my fucking wine?'

The old slave scurried over and offered the cup to his master. Vibius snatched it up and took a deep swig, splashing its contents down his already soiled toga, then continued. 'If the stupid fool had any sense, he'd have rutted her quietly in a hayloft behind my back. But no, they came to me in public, hand in hand like a pair of fucking dove-eyed teenagers.' He belched thunderously. 'Left me no choice but to give him my permission to wed her or face the shame of looking like I couldn't control my own flesh and blood.'

'That may be so, lord, but it does not explain how a small army raided the heart of Flavia Carsariensis unnoticed,' the general replied.

'Well?' the governor asked, redirecting the point to Arthur.

'They used engineers,' he answered, choosing not to mention the assailants' true nature. 'Merlin thinks they destroyed it from below.'

Vibius lolled his head to the military man again.

The general shrugged. 'Possible with sappers, but I don't know of any such tactic used on these shores before.'

More finger drumming followed. 'So, where were you when Merlin came here last?' the governor growled. 'You've the bearing of a common cutthroat. Why would he keep the company of a *cunnus* like you?'[1]

Arthur groped around in his memory for a plausible reply. 'I joined him from Mona,' he said eventually, recalling Merlin speak of his ancestral home.

Vibius yawned, and his disapproving gaze wavered. 'One of his *pedicatus* whelps, then,'[2] he muttered, appearing to be on the brink of sleep. But a hard shove from Quintus prompted him to resume his diatribe, apparently unaware of the absence. 'Fucking waste of coin if you ask me. You lot better be worth the fortune in *pulvis* we've set aside from this year's shipment!' Mention of the priceless powder brought a sly expression to his sweaty face. 'Tell me, apprentice, did your master deliver the package safely to the commander at Ratae?'

Arthur felt relieved the ploy was an obvious one. 'No, lord. Merl—my master gave it to Lucius Julius Cumanus at Derventio.'

Vibius looked to the Roman, who gave him a barely perceptible nod.

The governor considered this before speaking again. 'Then we will spare a thousand militia from the main force to go south and hunt these murderous rats. The rest of our forces shall stay with me as we push north to the wall.' He spat onto the expensive rug beneath his chair. 'I'd say 'tis about time to piss upon the lands of our enemy.'

'But...' Arthur began, recalling Merlin's objection to such a plan. A dark glare from the governor, however, made him think better of it.

'As you command, lord,' the general said, although with a fleeting frown.

'Well, that's all clear then—apart from one minor detail,' Vibius added, his face turning an unhealthy shade of puce. 'Where in the name of the holy tits of Venus is Merlin!' Spittle flew from his mouth as he roared his frustration.

'He fell, lord,' Efrawg replied, 'saving our lives.'

Stunned silence followed.

'Merlin is dead?' Quintus pressed.

'Yes.'

'How?'

'We,' the nobleman hesitated again. 'We were waylaid in the forest.'

'You expect me to believe that!' Vibius growled.

'It is the truth,' Efrawg replied with such simple conviction that the shadow of uncertainty returned to the governor's jowled features.

'What do you say, Quintus? Do we trust them?' the fat ruler asked.

'I say we torture them and compare their stories.' The verdict was pronounced with a professional manner that made it all the more chilling.

'Very well,' Vibius agreed. 'We hereby order the gentler persuasions to be administered to my former son-in-law and his vagabond companion,' he declared, then leered at Guinever. 'And it will please me to rut this *scortum* while we wait.'[3]

Arthur's heart froze.

Jaw trembling with suppressed outrage, Efrawg fell to his knees. 'We speak the truth. I swear it on the memory of Ula.'

Vibius spat in his face. 'You would dare utter her name, fucker! I treated you like a son, and you repaid me by murdering her! She should've married a prince of the empire! Instead, she ended her miserable days with a hog herder!' He clicked his fingers at Adalric.

The Germanian strode to his friend and gently lifted him to his feet by the elbows. Efrawg offered no resistance. 'I am sorry,' the captain whispered.

A second guard took Arthur by the arm far less gently.

The governor extended a grubby hand to a white-faced Guinever and gestured with his index finger for her to approach.

'Wait! There is something else!' Arthur blurted out of desperation.

'Save your bleating for your confession, turd,' the guard said, yanking him backward and almost tearing the shirt from his back, revealing the brand of the Ravens. The damning secret would've been uncovered anyhow once the torturers worked on him. Now he faced a fate worse than death.

'You have a grandson, my lord!' Arthur called.

'Halt,' Vibius commanded.

'What?' Efrawg called, shaking off the melancholic acceptance that had befallen him. 'No, you must not!' He lunged toward Arthur so violently, even his towering friend could barely contain him.

'Sorry,' Arthur said with regret. 'It's the only way.'

'No! I beg of you!'

A third guard had to race to Adalric's side to restrain the writhing warrior.

'Enough!' the governor shouted, forcing a passing calm. 'We will hear what this turd has to say,' he added, his curiosity evident.

Looking into the nobleman's pleading, enraged eyes, Arthur felt reluctant to talk further, but nothing else offered even a glimmer of hope. 'He is here, waiting outside. A boy of the Brigantes with brown hair.'

'Bastard! You have no right!' Efrawg screamed, bucking like a bull. 'I'll kill you!' Adalric and the other Germanian were ready this time, and his struggle soon subsided under the joint might pitted against him. 'I promised her...' he said, his voice trailing off.

'Promised her what? Hmm, dog?' the governor demanded. 'To never let her son know his birthright so he can till shit-covered fields for the rest of his life?'

'Aye, there's less filth in farm work than in this place!' Efrawg retorted, tears running down his face.

Taken aback by such undisguised hostility, Vibius did not respond. Instead, his piggish gaze narrowed. 'Quintus, find the boy and bring him to me.'

The general nodded and strode out of the private chamber.

They waited in silence, watching the governor drink.

* * *

'Come closer, boy,' Vibius commanded in a level tone and reached out his hand as Quintus pushed a wide-eyed Peredur in front of him. The lad's gaze sought his father's. But despite Efrawg's reassuring smile, his distress remained plain to everyone.

'Do as he says, son. He won't hurt you.'

'Are you all right, Father?' the boy asked, eyeing the gesturing governor as one would a rearing snake.

Efrawg managed a strained nod.

Vibius directed a cold smirk at Peredur 'He is overcome

with emotion, is all, lad. It's been many moons since we last met.' His tone did not speak of friendship.

Again, Peredur looked to his dad. Efrawg straightened, hesitating.

'Tell him,' the governor said flatly, his tiny eyes glittering with malice.

'This is your grandfather.'

The boy could only gawp at the fat prince before him.

Vibius beamed in a way that reminded Arthur of a pike about to devour a smaller fish. 'Come,' he repeated, gesturing more firmly.

As if walking through quicksand, Peredur obeyed.

Arthur sympathised with him, for even on the opposite side of the chamber, he could smell the stench of sour wine oozing from their ruler. When the boy was within reach, the governor grasped him by the chin. He winced as Vibius scrutinised his countenance.

'By Vulcan's fiery cock!' A look of ruddy-cheeked joy sprouted on the governor's whiskered face. 'Ha! He's one of mine, all right. See the nose?' He aimed Peredur's pinched chin toward the Roman.

Quintus kept his tone neutral. 'He has the look of you, I agree.'

'Well, well. The day grows better,' Vibius said, unhanding Peredur and leaving two greasy stains on his chin. 'Listen, my boy. A slave will take you to the kitchen so you can get yourself some grub while your dad and I catch up.' He clicked for the elderly servant to approach.

'But...' Peredur objected, turning to his father as the old man grasped his arm.

'Just do what he says, lad,' the nobleman said, looking to the floor.

They watched as the bewildered boy was led away.

The governor's pleasant demeanour dropped the instant

they'd left. 'For his sake alone, I'll let you live for now, to give me such poor service as you can,' he said, fixing Efrawg with a glare of pure hatred, 'until you help me win the boy's trust.'

Although shaking with indignation, the nobleman nodded curtly.

'Good, and when the time comes, you will fall in battle,' the governor added as if dispensing a great favour. 'Do this, and I promise he'll think you found an honourable death.' He nodded to Adalric. 'This dog can stay with your lot, but keep an eye on him, mind. Tomorrow we march the army north to Vindolanda, and he will be the first in line to greet that rabble of sheep-shaggers when they attack.'

'Yes, my lord,' the captain agreed, appearing more relieved than his prisoner. 'What of the other two?'

A bear-like yawn greeted the question. 'Don't care. I'm too tired to hump her now, anyway.' He slurred the words, drifting into a half doze.

Guinever shot Arthur a glance of grateful relief. But just as quickly, her expression set into a sullen pout.

As they turned to leave, the governor stirred to life. 'Efrawg?'

The big man halted.

'If you tell my grandson of this, I will ensure he witnesses every pleading screech of your demise. Mark my words.'

CHAPTER THIRTY-TWO

Talorc stood on the ancient rock of Dunadd and gazed upon the valley below with awe and dread, for nestled within its gentle heathland, on the eastern bank of the River Àd, the swirling black orb expanded like a growth over the skin of a dying man. It had started to pulse and shimmer in the past day, each time revealing the shadow of an alien landscape lurking behind its dark veil. His heart soared with anticipation. Soon, he'd have the means to reap a terrible revenge on the empire responsible for raiding, raping, and humiliating his people for hundreds of years. From the ashes of that destruction, he would forge a new land. To the north, the Picts shall reign as the dominant tribe for a thousand years, while the lesser peoples flocked to his banner, freed from the tyranny of Rome.

The clans had gathered on the western bank. In times past, these warriors would have sooner killed each other than their southern neighbours, thanks to the cunning schemes of the Roman elite, but he had forged them into an implacable force with his own fists. Finally, the enemy's divisive spell had been exorcised. All six thousand of his men were of strong stock and eager for the promised plunder to come. Only a few tribes had refused his call, daring to name him a tyrant. No matter. He'd punish these cowards after the coming conquest. It was a fascinating sight. A swirling mist formed within the perfect blackness of the orb, and as it grew, so did the throbbing mass of darkness. Around its edge burned a corona of fire, giving it the appearance of a black sun. Tiny figures knelt before the spectacle, genuflecting and wailing into the gusting wind. Occasionally, an enforced worshipper would panic in the face of the monstrous object and run for his life. In turn, a shaggy demonic guard would shriek with joy and give chase in the curious, bow-legged gait of its kind. Their guttural cawing reverberated around the valley until the half-starved prisoner collapsed from exhaustion, at which point their pursuer devoured them alive, as if they were trout plucked from the stream.

Finding the practice distasteful, Talorc had told the emissary to ensure such excesses were limited to the slaves, lest it unsettle the men. Not that it mattered. His nighthawk raiders had abducted hundreds of these wretches from the borderlands.

'The time has come, lord,' a rasping voice spoke in his ear, making him jump. Although he'd grown accustomed to the way the creature slunk into his presence, the habit still irked him.

'Time for what?' he snapped.

'The fist of Balor approaches, sire. He crosses with his legions.'

A crown of fire burst around the glowing corona as the slaves' chanting reached a crescendo. Then, screaming and foaming at the mouth, they collapsed as one, twitching. A profound silence fell upon the glen. The king held his breath. With a cracking pop, the orb split open like an egg to reveal a blackened parody of the rolling green hills surrounding it.

Talorc couldn't see a single living thing in that scorched place, other than swarming insects. A cloud of the pests poured forth from the dread entrance and buzzed around the demon guards standing before the threshold. Everything beyond the gateway appeared as a washed-out twin of the lands he loved, framed beneath a blood-red sun that bathed the aberrant shadow world in anaemic light.

A dark road wound through the desolation into the foreground, and in the far distance, there stood a black fortress. The king drank in the scene, wondering what could thrive in such a wasteland. Then, in front of the walls of the mighty fortification, a thicker cloud of dust appeared.

'I will greet him myself,' Talorc said and strode down the hillside, silently reminding himself of his many titles and conquests.

THE AMASSED COLUMNS marched toward his world. Rank after rank of crudely armoured demon warriors undulated across the nether landscape like a black serpent. At the head of each great column, shaggy-haired brutes rode furless steeds with pasty white skin and covered in sores. These centurions snarled and yelped at their wards, flicking nail-studded whips about them. Interspersed within the legions, huge iron cages, fixed on wooden wheels, trundled across the blighted landscape. Behind the bars of these mobile goals stood the sullen forms of massively muscled creatures, over ten feet in height, with wicked, drooling muzzles and beady green eyes.

As the first ranks drew closer, he could discern the more subtle differences in the regiments. Inscribed runes upon each soldier's black breastplate bore a mark of a serpent devouring a child, while some also bore a smaller band imprinted with a purple claw on their tall, spiked helms.

Larger demons populated these elite units and formed the officer class of their more numerous comrades. Instead of the spears held by the majority of the army, these troops carried great swords strapped to their backs, similar to those his strongest clansmen wielded. On either side of the marching columns scurried hundreds of smaller, runtish fiends armed with recurved bows, the likes of which he'd never seen.

The army was impressive, worryingly so, but even that paled in comparison to the nightmarish vision that led the force. Adorned in shining silver armour, which contrasted with the blood-red colour of his skin, Balor, sitting upon a carved throne of twinkling ebony, was a dread creature to behold. Two black horns rose above his elongated skull, and his cat-like eyes never wavered from the king. In his clawed hand he gripped a sceptre, surmounted by a severed head. The gaze of the human trophy swivelled to inspect all around it. Bearing the dark prince's litter, with eyes sewn shut and clad only in loincloths, four deathly white giants strode.

'How many spears?' Talorc asked, having lost count.

'Thirty thousand,' the emissary answered. 'Handpicked to aid our cause, mighty one.'

'Thirty thousand! We agreed on ten!' he replied, aghast. The logistics of such a large army would cripple his supply lines. Forage alone could not sustain them.

'My master is generous, is he not?' the emissary said without emotion.

'I cannot supply such a force,' the king said, sceptical of this so-called gift.

It chuckled a mirthless hiss. 'No matter. There will be many herds for us to feed upon.'

That did little to reassure him.

The white giants reached the lip of the portal, and with a crash of thunder from above, the first of the blind bearers stepped onto the green grass of Caledonia. Talorc fought down a sudden urge to vomit.

The nether guards lurking amongst the dead worshippers knelt before their approaching lord and held forth corpses of the fallen in offering. Kicking aside a demon from its path, the lead giant emerged into the world of men.

The sound of marching stopped as the sea of troops halted behind their commander. Silence reigned, as the bearers lifted Balor over the threshold like a bride on the grimmest of wedding nights. As they lowered the ebony plinth to the earth, the prince rose from his throne to tower over all but his blind entourage. His hooved feet touched Pictish land, and he opened his fanged mouth to take a deep, shuddering breath.

The waiting hordes roared in triumph.

Gazing down upon the king with slitted eyes, the demon flared his nostrils. No emotion registered on his sleek, muscled features. Talorc shifted uncomfortably at the beast's lack of deference, but the knowledge of how reliant he was on the nether prince made him stay his tongue. Instead, he forced himself to meet the creature's unblinking gaze. A fleeting recollection of his father begging him not to consult with the dark powers came to mind, but he pushed the thought into his bowels, where such contemplations of cowardice should be kept.

His own men had massed on the opposite bank to observe their new comrades. Undeterred by his misgivings, pride swelled within him, for at last his people could see for themselves the instrument of victory he'd conjured—a force to strike fear into the hearts of the gods themselves.

I will be the first king to rule the Isles since the old days, he thought.

Comforted by the promise of glory and determined to show this dog who the true master was, he maintained the game, refusing to look away. Although Balor's black lips twitched with amusement, the nether lord eventually lowered his head. Satisfied by the show of acquiescence, Talorc opened his mouth, ready to greet his ally, but the demon prince raised his face once more to reveal a weeping third eye at the centre of his forehead. The king stepped back in alarm.

As Balor's booming laugh echoed across the hills, Talorc thought he heard high-pitched shrieks emanating from within that deep tone. Then, still fixing the Pictish ruler with a cruel smile, the creature fell to his knees.

'My king, I am your humble worm,' he said, extending a blue tongue from his maw and licking the king's boot, then trailing the tip up to his bare knee. The sensation felt like a thousand crawling spiders.

CHAPTER THIRTY-THREE

In the beginning was the void—a thing of such infinite blackness, it smothered the light of creation. But an infinite thing is limitless, and so the seeds of existence wove into the fabric of the darkness, tensing every strand until it forced the void to fold upon itself, over and over. After countless millennia, the mass of nothingness became so dense, it imploded with unimaginable force, sundering the universe and forming the building blocks of life. With this profound shift came the will, an indomitable spirit melded from both the light and the dark.

In that same moment, the will birthed the nine—the original gods, and masters of all life. For millions of years, these celestial orphans wandered the stars, learning many marvels. But all was not well. Abandoned by their unfathomable mother, they longed to discover others of their kind, and as they searched countless worlds in vain, their longing became a desperate craving.

In a state of hopeless solitude, the nine resolved to usurp creation and fashion beings in their own likeness—children who would worship and venerate them, yet hold a will to rival their own. Ignoring the screams of the universe, they focused their desire upon a single planet and turned it into a cradle amongst the stars. Upon this Jewel of Eden called Earth, life flourished beyond their wildest expectations. Countless were the wondrous creations they bestowed upon this world. Then, after many ages of toil and with great joy, they birthed the first sentient peoples. The solitude of the nine had ended.

For countless generations, the gods walked amongst the mortals, guiding their every action and thought. They were beings of infinite will and resolve, imbued with the power to shape the texture of life itself. But the blessings of those fated to a mortal life were mixed, for the power of a god is matched only by their boundless capacity for rage, love, and cruelty. The thoughts and deeds of the lesser races were but a poor parody of their masters'. Doomed to taste life and never drink it fully, the mortals were forever in the shadow, nothing more than slaves enthralled by their fathers and mothers. To some, death was a wrenching loss from a beloved master, and for others, it was a blessed release from a life of servitude and misery.

Whatever the fate of their children, the ageless ones continued the never-ending game only they understood. And so, as the millennia passed, feelings of injustice grew in the hearts of the lesser, for they could never be free. The many peoples of Earth yearned for freedom.

But all things must pass.

Then the great war changed everything. Much to the horror of the gods, many of the mortal people rose and fought those who clung to the old ways. Despite the limitless power of the immortals, they feared returning to solitude above all else. The slaughter of their progeny raged unabated on both sides until their beloved children faced mutual extinction. Desperate, the nine begged their wayward sons and daughters to return under their wing, but those who had known liberty cried out, tearing at their skin and murdering their own babes in defiance.

Fearing all was lost, the gods brought the Eld into existence. These champions embodied the will of the nine, with the authority to act as both shepherd and messenger, yet were part flesh and blood, kin to the people but master of none. As mortal emissaries, they would steward the world through persuasion and guile, not compulsion. In return, the gods vowed to leave the Earth and abide by their counsel.

Only one of the nine refused these terms. Arawn, the shadow maker, swore to break the people of Earth before he'd ever see them set free. And so, his kin banished the dark one and his children to the nether, a half-formed afterbirth created in the nothing's destruction. From behind this black mirror, they could only gaze upon the beauty of the world with envy. They would fester in that cursed place, exiled from the lands protected by the remaining eight.

The arrival of the Eld created a peace not seen for generations and heralded the end of the first great age. Under their gentle leadership, the intelligent creatures of Earth thrived and multiplied for thousands of years. War faded into a dark dream, bringing much goodness to the world. But as the centuries wore on, so the memories of the gods waned in the minds of mortal kind.

The ranks of the Eld were many in the beginning, but few were born in later years, and despite their great power, their numbers dwindled because of the folly and impermanence of their wards. With the slaying of each champion, the connection between mortals and their creators lessened, and so the old bonds fell into myth, as the creatures of the world fought for dominance. The spectre of war returned to Earth many times. Mighty empires rose and fell.

The remaining Eld were forced to endure the pain of watching those they had been sworn to protect slay each other, their wisdom scorned.

The great wheel of fate continued to turn.

CHAPTER THIRTY-FOUR

Following Efrawg's ritual humiliation, they trudged in brooding silence through the encampment, the governor's cruel pronouncement having eliminated any banter between the old friends. The subdued procession didn't last long, however, as Adalric led them to two fur-lined tents devoid of the usual signs of habitation. 'These belonged to the families of Lovis and Wiltrud—good people killed by the shitting sickness cursing this place,' he said. 'They are yours now.'

Still lost in his own misery, Efrawg did not reply as he pulled the stitched leather cover of the first tent aside to walk inside. The Germanian grasped his arm, stopping him on the threshold. 'The boy will be well. I'll make sure of that.'

The nobleman half turned to the captain, his face in shadow. 'He's all I have left, Adalric.'

'Listen, you can see him yourself tonight. We will drink and share stories of the old days. You can ease his mind.'

Efrawg shrugged off the hand. 'And let Vibius treat me like a cur in front of him?' His voice rose. 'The boy must already think me mad! What kind of coward leaves his son to be raised in this place?'

'No coward.' Adalric shook his shaggy head. 'A coward wouldn't have come here to warn us.' He lowered his tone. 'And what good would it have done to spit in the governor's face or stick a blade in his fat gut? Hmm? They'd have forced your son to watch you suffer, and I'd regret that, my friend.'

Efrawg took a deep, shuddering breath. 'Still, I do not wish him to see how his grandfather regards me. Better I do not see him at all.'

'Trust me, you will not have to worry about Vibius. He's already deep into his cups. In a few hours, Venus herself could not rouse him.'

'Are you sure? I don't want—'

'The boy needs to know you've not abandoned him,' Arthur intervened, stepping forward. Speaking as an orphan, he knew this to be true.

The nobleman gave him a dark glare, still furious at the perceived betrayal.

Adalric broke the uncomfortable silence by giving Efrawg a slap on the back. 'You are tired. Get some rest and we will meet again in four hours.' He nodded to Arthur and strode toward the governor's quarters.

Efrawg entered the tent without speaking another word, a broken man.

THE TENT'S interior stank of mildew. Only a dim light emanated from the gap in the entrance flap behind them. After searching in the gloom, Arthur found that some belongings of the previous occupants remained, including sleeping furs and clothes in far better condition than their present sorry attire. Guinever rummaged through the bundle and found a plain dress. She turned away from him and threw off the rags, then slipped the dress over her head. Much to his disappointment, he didn't see her fully in the near darkness, other than a glimpse of a shapely buttock he urged to grasp. Realising he was alone with her for the first time since Derventio, he yawned dramatically, secretly thrilled at the prospect of laying with her once more.

'I could sleep for an age,' he said, hoping she'd respond suggestively.

No reply came, but he could feel her regarding him.

Deciding to play her game, he strode to the furs and spread them upon the floor. Then, removing his own filthy rags, he lay on the bedding, naked. Although they smelled musty, he didn't care, such was his need for both sleep and her. His anticipation further grew as she walked to his side and stood over him, her expression indistinct. Arthur imagined her desire growing to match his own.

'Take off the dress,' he said, closing his eyes and waiting for the touch of soft lips.

She responded by kicking him hard in the ribs. Waves of pain shot through his torso as he rolled onto his side, gasping in shock.

'Fucking pig!' she hissed, slamming another foot into his thigh.

'Argh!' he cried. Desperate to stop the onslaught, he snatched Guinever by the shin as she fired another kick and yanked hard. She tumbled to the ground. To stop her flailing arms, he tried to clamber atop her and pin her down, but she was lithe with fury and dodged aside.

'What the—!' Arthur roared. He staggered to his feet, clasping his side, fearing Merlin's concerns about her had proven true. Guinever rose to meet him. In the shadow, he could make out her chest heaving with rage.

'Bastard!' she screamed. 'To think I was fall—'

'What have I done?'

No answer.

'I thought after what happened at Derventio, you would...'

She sniffed bitterly. 'Do not flatter yourself. 'Twas pity for a dumb beast. Nothing more.'

That stung more than he cared to admit. A growing anger at her rejection replaced his pain. 'Pity had nothing to do with it. More the coin of our enemies.'

That earned him a full slap to the face. Her gaze was brimming with tears. 'I've done what I must to save those I love. What's your excuse?'

Shocked, he backed away. 'What do you mean?'

'You would flaunt that mark at me with pride?' She pointed at the brand upon his chest.

His gut sinking, Arthur realised where this was going. 'But you've seen it before.'

'Seeing and understanding are two different things,' she spat with contempt. 'You're nothing but a murdering rat. They should nail your skin to the gates next to your comrades'.' She wiped her chin, the whites of her eyes ablaze. 'I'd rather offer myself to Lucius again than bandit scum.'

Arthur suddenly understood the extent of his stupidity. She must have seen the remains of the other Ravens when they'd entered Luguvalium.

He half opened his mouth to explain, but no words came. The bitter disappointment in her voice, more than her rage, had brought forth emotions he'd suppressed since the night of the massacre. Here it was, this unpleasant thing called guilt, thrust upon him once more.

'But I thought you knew,' he forced out in a hoarse whisper.

'That's because you are a selfish bastard who only hears what he wishes,' she replied. 'What did you expect me to say? Never mind that you're a murderer, no different from the scum who took my Briant and Grania.'

'I—I have changed.' Even to his own ears, his voice sounded pathetic,

'Really? Try explaining that to Efrawg. What do you think he'd do if he knew you were of the same filth that took his wife?' She stepped toward him with her chin thrust up. 'He'd kill you, and I would cheer him on.'

'Then why haven't you told him?' All his fight had left, and only shame remained.

'You think that's because I want you—that I love you?' Guinever crossed her arms, then looked him up and down with a sneer. 'You promised to help me find my family, so I'll stay here.' She gestured at their dwelling. 'You'll keep me with this army, and after we have butchered the painted ones, and I've found my family, our business will be done.'

'But… it's true I am different now,' he said, unable to meet her gaze any longer. 'Something happened, something I cannot explain.'

'Spare me your lies, cutthroat.' Tugging away one of the sleeping furs, she stalked as far away from him as the small space would allow.

Speechless and exhausted, Arthur collapsed onto the remaining bedding, convinced it would've been better for all if Merlin had left him to rot by the wayside.

* * *

THE CREATURE SWOOPED into the night, its immense lungs sucking in air, ready to deliver pure death unto its foes. As a god of old, it would be the hand of vengeance sweeping all before it.

Soaring above grey clouds, the great beast beat its golden wings and licked its fangs in anticipation. It would use these teeth to rend the flesh of its prey, devouring them like cattle.

Soon, all would witness its birth with dread—a living nightmare.

Sensing the moment had arrived, the beast lord plummeted toward the raging battle, screaming in triumph. He had become an angel of pain, the bringer of her judgement, neither a child of the light nor of the dark. In the darkness of its mind's eye, it felt the twitch of another consciousness. The other entity was weak and close to ending its hopeless fight against a far mightier will. It groped within, like some blind thing in a hutch. The creature shrugged off this other with ease. Inside the ancient one, the last vestiges of its former self fell into the abyss of time, lost forever in the birth of its golden successor.

* * *

ARTHUR'S SCREAM trailed off as his nightmare subsided. Heart racing, he looked over at the other shadowed form in the opposite corner of the tent.

'Nightmare?' Guinever asked.

'Yes.'

'Good,' she yawned.

Someone pulled the tent flap aside, interrupting his intended response.

'It is time, apprentice of Merlin,' Adalric said, then left.

Not wishing to endure more of her scorn, Arthur rose and, shivering, stumbled over to the bundle of clothes. Through touch alone, he identified a belted tunic, trousers, and much to the relief of his blistered feet, a pair of well-fitting boots. Although a little loose upon his underfed frame, they would do. 'I'm getting out of here. Are you coming?' he asked curtly.

'I'd rather spend the night under the governor.'

Arthur cursed under his breath. 'Do you want me to bring some food back?'

'I want nothing from the likes of you.'

Shaking his head, he left without another word, determined to drown his sorrows.

CHAPTER THIRTY-FIVE

An unconscious Vibius remained seated on his throne at the head of the endless gathering, his silver cup clutched in his dangling hand. Its contents puddled upon the platform, where the hound languidly lapped it up. The musicians still played, now weaving a dreamlike tune with their instruments, while three women dressed as woodland nymphs danced sensuously around the central fire.

'Just as I said, he is dead to the world,' Adalric said to Efrawg as they stepped through the revellers, most of whom had followed the example of their leader. Of those stoic few who remained awake, some openly copulated. 'You island Celts cannot take your beer,' he added. A red-cheeked man rolled into their path, and the captain kicked him aside. The reveller proceeded to vomit. 'We will drink with the real men tonight, not these bunch of *fickfehlers!*'

He led them to the governor's private quarters, where a large group of Germanian guards lounged around the tables, playing dice and drinking foaming cups of beer served by female slaves. Adalric grasped a hurrying serving maid by the arm as she passed and kissed her on the lips. Laughing, she pushed him away. 'Get off me, Adalric, you hairy brute!'

'Mirna, my love, bring me and my friends *bier*,' he said, patting her plump backside.

'Might do,' she teased.

'Serve me well tonight, woman, and I promise you a whole foot of Germanian *wurst!*'[1]

'Pfft, a foot,' she replied, pulling a face. Then, gripping her tray with one hand, she wiggled her little finger. This resulted in a second slap to the rear.

Giving another busty chuckle, she went to fetch their much-needed beverages, leaving the three men to mingle with the scarred veterans. A young nobleman, sitting alone beside a burning brazier, rose as they approached. On second glance, however, Arthur realised the mystery lord was Peredur, dressed in the robed finery of a Roman gentile. Ignoring the others, Efrawg made straight for the lad, then wrapped his arms around him. The boy looked both terrified and relieved. Arthur joined them, hoping the big man's wrath toward him would lessen upon seeing his son safe and well.

'You look like a woman has dressed you,' the nobleman remarked, his awkward tone betraying mixed emotions.

'I was.' Peredur's cheeks flushed red. 'She kept asking me if I wanted her to undress, also!'

Two guards playing dice nearby cheered upon overhearing this lewd detail.

Efrawg looked into the boy's bewildered gaze. 'Now that people know you are of the governor's line, they will treat you differently, son.'

'But I don't want any of this,' the lad said, lifting the fancy sleeves, then dropping them in bemusement.

'You need to get used to it.' The reply was flat and uncompromising.

'Ah, boy, it is not so bad,' Adalric said, striding to their side. 'Those pieces of horse shit outside would sell their mothers to be Vibius's heir.'

'Heir?' Efrawg turned to him in surprise. 'But Oskar is the heir.'

Adalric raised the thick eyebrow above his empty socket, a disconcerting gesture. 'You don't know?'

The nobleman shook his head, concern growing on his face.

'Died last month. They declared it a hunting accident.' The captain looked around before continuing. 'In truth, the useless bastard was always too addled to mount a horse, never mind ride one. No, he died like a common drunk, choking on his own vomit.'

'He has no other nephews?' Efrawg asked, displeased by the news.

'Ja, all dead, but that is no loss. Pack of rats, the lot,' Adalric replied and spat. 'Vibius was smart enough to keep them scheming against each other.' He sliced his finger across his throat. 'Poisoned or stabbed to a man.'

'What does that mean?' Peredur asked, close to panic.

'It means if anything happens to our fat lord, you are *vicarius*,' the Germanian replied, clapping him on the back. 'Congratulations, boy!'

'Must I?' The lad looked as appalled by the prospect as his father.

'Do nothing and say nothing,' Adalric said, his expression stern. 'Keep your eyes and ears open and tread carefully, especially when he's drunk.'

Peredur had turned grey.

The captain grunted in sympathy. 'Do not worry my young *Junges*, another year and the old *schwein* will have pickled his innards enough to kill himself.'[2]

Neither the lad nor his elder seemed reassured.

The flirtatious maid returned, her tray laden with foaming

cups. Sensing the less-than-encouraging reaction of his guests to his conciliatory efforts, Adalric grasped two mugs in hands so big they made the heavy pots look like children's playthings. Then he thrust one each into Peredur's and Efrawg's hands, before repeating the gesture for himself and Arthur. 'Come, you'll feel better with a few drinks down your throat.'

Peredur peered at the beer with interest, then to his father for approval. The nobleman nodded and took a swig of his own.

'That's the spirit!' Adalric approved. 'Now we drown ourselves in *bier*!'

* * *

FOLLOWING his second flagon of the bitter brew, Arthur found a pleasant warmth spreading through his body. Efrawg and Peredur had withdrawn into a quiet corner and were deep in conversation, leaving him with the foreign warriors. Standing in awkward isolation, he watched the closeness of father and son, suppressing the old resentment he'd always experienced toward families.

'Perhaps it's better to be alone,' he muttered under his breath, contemplating the harsh fate laid upon the pair. The governor's cruel decision was as wicked as it was cunning. Vibius knew that, unlike many fathers, Efrawg would never abandon his child to save his own skin. The brave fool would keep his word, even if it meant death. Sensing Arthur was watching him, the nobleman caught his eye and frowned in disapproval. With a pang of guilt-ridden envy, Arthur looked away and sat next to Adalric, who was engrossed in a board game against a grizzled warrior with an angry scar on his brow.

'Do you play *ludus*, apprentice of Merlin?' he asked, nodding at the game board.

'Yes, but I don't recognise the pieces,' he replied. Unlike the plain black and white counters he'd seen before, the Germanians used pieces carved in the shape of woodland beasts. Their moves also appeared unusual.

'Ja, we play our own rules. Can't let the Roman fookers get it all their own way, no?'

His opponent spat into the rushes at the mention of their overlords.

'Your lands are part of the empire, then?' Arthur asked.

'Ha! Never!' Adalric replied. 'The southern tribes sold themselves like whores. Not so in the north. We eat legionaries for breakfast!'

Oddly, the veteran nodded and licked his lips. 'Ja, they taste of chicken.'

The alcohol loosened Arthur's tongue and sparked his interest. 'Then why are you here? Shouldn't you be with your people, back home?'

'Hmm, you don't know much about us, do you?'

'Well, no. I've heard you are some of the best fighters in the land.' It was true and not an attempt at flattery.

'Some of—' Adalric belched. 'Boy, we are the Rendingi,' he said as if it were explanation enough. 'The emperor's Praetorian Guard would shit themselves like little girly boys before us.' He rose and thrust his beer into the air. '*Blutjäger!*'³ he roared, and the other men returned the salute.

Arthur chose not to challenge the wild boast.

'I think the cub doesn't believe you, boss,' the veteran said, leering at the young warrior as if he were chopped liver.

It was not uncommon for men of war to test the mettle of newcomers in combat. This was not a welcome prospect.

'Show him, Notger,' Adalric said to his companion. 'Just show him mind. He is our guest.'

The veteran's growing smile drooped a little at the last words.

At first, nothing happened. The two men continued to play the game, but just as Arthur thought he was the subject of some elaborate jest, Notger's breathing grew heavier, and his head dropped forward as if weariness had overcome him.

'Are you well?' Arthur asked.

A guttural growl emanated from the other man's throat. As the Germanian raised the carved owl piece above the board, the skin of his fingers darkened, and thick black hair sprouted on the backs of his hands. Arthur stared in horrified fascination at the uncanny sight. Painful memories of his own transformation came flooding back. Lost in thoughts of the agonising change, he didn't notice the guard had lifted his head until it was too late.

The man-beast lunged, snapping its canines a hair's breadth from Arthur's exposed face. He dived backward from his stool in utter panic and fell to the ground.

'Shit!' he shouted, scrambling for a weapon to use against the monster watching him with glittering-eyed hunger. With a wide jaw and stubbed snout set within a man's skull, its features were a hideous blend of human and forest predator.

Adalric laughed, as did the other members of his tribe.

'I smell *hund*,' the man-creature rumbled, licking its lips at the prostrate warrior. It turned to his superior. '*Ich will sein fleisch.*' Although Arthur did not understand the implication, he did not like the sound of it.

'*Nien*,' Adalric retorted. No longer amused, he returned the deep growl with one of his own. '*Berühre ihn und ich reiß dir die Kehle aus.*'[4]

The shaggy man-beast snapped its jaws again, then crushed the bone game piece in its hand.

'Do not test my patience, Notger,' the captain responded coolly. If Notger's defiance concerned him, he did not express it.

With a final snarl of frustration, the creature closed its eyes and breathed deeply. Ever so slowly, the change reversed, and its elongated jaw shrank back into the guard's grizzled visage once more.

Adalric stood and offered Arthur his hand while draining his cup. Reluctantly, he accepted it, much to the cheers of the gathered men. Peredur's complexion turned white, his father already whispering hasty reassurances into his ear.

With only his pride dented, Arthur decided it was better to be in on the joke, so returned to the table and took a long swig of beer, then raised the tankard at a sneering Notger. The reason the governor had chosen such a formidable force for his personal guard was all too clear.

'You can change forms?' he asked.

'All Rendingi can. It is our gift, given by Artio herself,' Adalric replied, wiping the remains of the smashed playing piece from the board, then firing an indecipherable insult to his comrade, presumably as thanks for spoiling their game. Still, he made his next move, and the other man rubbed his chin and scowled at his new position. It would seem the owl had been at the heart of his defence.

'Doesn't the change cause pain?' Arthur asked, curious to know why the Germanian warrior had displayed nothing beyond discomfort.

The captain gave his companion a knowing look. 'That's an odd thing to ask.'

'Well, we...' Arthur began, but glanced over to Efrawg, reluctant to speak of their shared ordeal. There had been an intimacy to the experience he did not wish to dwell upon, and so he shrugged dismissively instead.

'Ah, your change was not of your own making.' The Germanian nodded in understanding.

'How did...?'

'We can smell those with the gift. With respect, apprentice, my nose had picked you out before I laid eyes upon you.'

Notger nodded again.

Arthur hesitated. 'No, I do not have any gift. Merlin changed us so we might flee the enemy.' Although he did not trust these straight-talking giants, they were the only people who'd understand.

Adalric stroked his thick beard, his single eye regarding Arthur with interest. 'And he chose the spirit of the wolf for you, no?'

'Yes.'

The captain's expression became puzzled. 'Then he must have lost his brains. Wolves are pack spirits. Such a change messes with a man's mind.'

'Ja,' the other Germanian agreed, twirling a finger next to his head. 'Fooked.'

'Why's that?' Arthur asked and gulped his beer, thankful for the steady supply making its way to their table. A short trip to oblivion was an attractive prospect on such a cheerless evening.

'Pack animals think like a unit, not like men,' Adalric said, banging his tattooed fists together. 'It is, what you say, *unnatürlich*.'

'Unnatural?'

'Ja.'

'Ja, fooked,' the other warrior concurred again, grinning at Arthur's flat glare.

The observation explained why he felt so close to his companions. It was an odd thing—a shared bond he could not explain.

'And Merlin transformed Efrawg and the boy also?' Adalric asked.

'Aye, all of us.'

'Then you are pack brothers now,' the captain concluded before sinking another cup with several impressive gulps.

Arthur contemplated this, strangely elated at the thought.

Adalric looked over to the nobleman, still deep in conversation with Peredur. 'We offered to make him one of us, many years ago, but he ran like a woman with a mouse on her tits.'

'I don't blame him,' Arthur said, suppressing a shiver. 'I've never known such pain.'

'Only the first few times,' the captain said with a shrug, his words starting to slur. In the short time they'd been here, six frothing cups had passed the captain's lips, and he was reaching for his seventh. 'We train our kids as cubs. It is easier while their bones are soft.'

'And what anim—spirit are you?'

Adalric took a deep swig, then wiped his dripping whiskers. 'You will find out soon enough, when we battle these painted north men.'

'But why do you serve Vibius? For coin?' Arthur asked, guessing it was not for any other reason. These warriors showed no affection for their lord.

Adalric chuckled. 'Why else? The truth is we had no choice, apprentice,' he replied, moving a weasel shaped board piece deep into the midst of his opponent's remaining counters. Notger muttered to himself in his native tongue at this latest tactic.

'We Rendingi travel much and are not welcomed by many,' the captain added.

It was easy to understand why.

'We are strong, but our numbers are few,' he continued, watching his companion shift a piece into the far corner of the board, an illegal move in the Isles. Adalric countered, to the evident annoyance of his game partner, who scratched at his whiskers. 'When we came here, we tried to settle in the mountains—lands where crops do not grow and only a few fools live.'

'It didn't last?'

'*Nein.* One of us got a taste for man flesh.'

L.K. ALAN

'I'm surprised Vibius cared,' Arthur replied. In these dark days, the empire only offered protection to the rich elite, and even that had become a precarious stretch of late.

'We were unlucky.'

'How so?'

'He ate a tax collector.'

'Ah, that would do it.'

'Ja, the governor sent a militia cohort to burn us out and take our families as slaves. Of course, we slaughtered them and returned their heads back to him.'

'Did he send a larger force?'

'No, he offered us gold instead. And when he learned of our gifts, he offered us more gold to become his guard.'

'He is a bastard.'

'Ja, but our alliance keeps my people out of harm.'

Notger picked up a bird-shaped counter and stared at the game pieces, unsure what to do next.

'Give up. I have you,' the captain said, taking another swig of beer.

'Fook you!' growled the veteran, dropping the piece onto the board in resignation.

Adalric smiled at the insult. '"Fook you, *sir*!" Now, where is my money, you whelping bitch? Hmm?' He extended his palm.

Notger stared at the proffered hand, as if considering declining, then reached inside the greasy fur lining his leather armour and produced a bag of coin.

While Adalric loudly counted out his winnings to the evident irritation of his subordinate, Arthur noticed the conversation between Efrawg and Peredur had become heated. The unhappy father was appealing to his son, who's crossed arms and lowered head made his disbelief clear. The big man reached a hand out to his back, only to have it

260

shrugged away. Peredur stalked from the room, his demeanour a picture of dismay.

Arthur spotted the opportunity to seek more familiar company and perhaps mend the rift between him and the noble. Although he appreciated the refreshing lack of guile from the governor's guard, they were alien to him. They also gave him the uncomfortable feeling he was being regarded as a hunk of offal hanging in a butcher's window.

'I'm going to check on Efrawg,' he said.

As he stood, the captain grasped his arm. 'He's a good man who has suffered much ill luck. Do what you can for him.'

'I'll do my best,' Arthur replied, ashamed that he'd come so close to abandoning them. 'Although he is angry with me.'

Adalric shook his head. 'Without you, he'd be dead, and his son would be weeping over his broken bones. Pride or not, he knows this.'

Arthur nodded, grateful for the kind words.

Efrawg, however, scowled at him as he approached, but made no move to leave.

'I feel like a lamb chop amongst this lot,' Arthur said in greeting.

'You get used to it,' came the sullen response.

'How do you not get eaten?'

'Don't be around when they're hungry.' The nobleman took two gulps from his tankard. Despite the light words, his pain was obvious.

They drank in awkward silence for a time, both downing beer after beer.

'The boy doesn't understand yet, but he will in time,' Arthur said eventually, his courage having increased with each pint.

Efrawg huffed. 'What's there not to understand? I've

failed him again. First his mother, and now this,' he said with a sigh.

'At least you are still alive. There is hope in that, surely?'

'Hope?' Efrawg stared at him, his head swaying unsteadily. 'No hope—that left when my son came into this snake pit.' He pointed at the entrance. 'Vibius sucks the life from anything decent. Why do you think we left?' He slumped like a man at the end of his tether. 'I wish you and Merlin had never found us.' The big man added, his eyes rolling. A moment later, he'd passed out.

The mention of the enigmatic druid reminded Arthur of his absence. He felt sure Merlin would have been ill at ease in this claustrophobic cesspit and wouldn't have returned from his self-imposed exile to serve a tyrant like the governor for no good reason. Perhaps the answer lay in the peril facing them all—a fate they'd have to confront without the aid of their greatest champion.

CHAPTER THIRTY-SIX

The dawn chorus of men coughing roused Arthur, as did a steady throbbing in his temple, and the realisation that he wanted to spew his guts. The pounding in his head increased when the shouts of officers waking their troops around the camp rang out. He groaned.

'I thought I was supposed to be the woman,' Guinever muttered. 'I need fresh air. This tent stinks like a brewery.'

Light flooded into his dark cocoon.

'Arrgh!' Arthur protested, slinging an arm over his dazzled eyes. Reluctantly, he sat up, his vision swimming for a moment. The urge to vomit worsened.

She ignored him, instead busying herself by packing her things into a sturdy canvas bag that had presumably belonged to the last occupants.

'Do we have any water?' he asked, his mouth parched.

'I do not share water with bandits,' she replied.

With his skull pounding and his threshold for insults exhausted, Arthur's temper snapped. He threw off the fur and strode over to Guinever, lifting the tunic over his head to show his scarred chest. 'Look,' he growled.

L.K. ALAN

She ignored him again.

'I said look, woman!' He grabbed her by the wrist and turned her to face his branded skin.

'I've seen it before, murderer!' she shouted in his face.

'What do you see?'

'The mark of a mindless thug and killer!'

'No, not mindless!' Although I wish I had been when they pressed the iron to my skin!'

'Save your self-pity for those you've enslaved.' Her desperate situation had blinded her to reason.

'And what do you think happened to me as a child?'

This gave her pause. She stared at him before her unreadable expression twisted into a grimace once more. 'Pity the child—fear the monster he becomes.' She attempted to tug her arm away, but Arthur held firm.

'I am no monster.'

A looming shadow appeared on the canvas opposite. Someone stood in the opening behind him.

Adalric chortled. 'You've had all night to fook her.' His voice sounded bright despite the indulgences of the previous evening.

Guinever flicked her gaze to Arthur's chest then up to meet his. Her eyes narrowed, emphasising the implicit threat.

'Morning,' he said, his flat stare daring her to speak. She did not.

'The fat one calls us to witness the augur before we march,' the captain replied, unconcerned by their standoff. 'Not that I want to see a goat have its bowels removed when my brains are this addled from booze!'

'Thanks, Adalric, I'll see you there. I just need another minute,' Arthur answered, trying to hide the tension in his voice.

'Only a minute, apprentice! The poor girl needs a real man.' The captain said, then muttered something to himself in his own tongue before adding, 'we gather in the muster field.'

As Adalric's shadow left, Arthur dropped his hand from Guinever's arm.

'Don't think I'm doing this for you,' she said, staring back at him. 'This war is my best chance to find my family. Help me, and I'll not speak of your shame. That's the only promise you'll get from me.'

'You'd be dead now if it were not for me—spy,' he replied, unable to contain his frustration.

'Tell yourself that if it eases your conscience, scum.'

THE EMPIRE'S army streamed into the muddy field, the men grumbling for being forced from their beds so early. The mustered ranks of the Legio Victrix greeted them, their collective breath dissipating into the crisp air. Dressed in chain mail, with blood red capes and each holding their kit on the end of their *spiculum*, they were prepared to march. At the head of the gathering, Vibius sat upon his throne, glaring at his troops as they poured passed. Elaborate, yet ill-fitting armour of the eastern style covered his vast frame, with his underclothes bulging through the seams. He wore a crimson-plumed helm, far too small for his skull. In stark contrast, standing to his right, the trim form of General Quintas, clad in a gleaming breastplate, appeared every inch a leader of Rome. His stony expression made it plain what he thought of the rabble he surveyed. To the left of the governor, amongst an entourage of nobles, a glum-faced Peredur stood in a fur-trimmed overcoat.

A wide circle had been cleared before the governor's dais, ringed by a dozen guards. At the centre of the space, a pure white bull chewed on a tuft of grass, unaware of its fate.

Beside the oblivious offering was a thin man in a golden robe, denoting him as a priest of the imperial cult. The old sect, dedicated to the worship of the emperor as a living deity, was most favoured by Rome and received huge tithes from the state, all paid by the taxes of the common folk. The priest's beady eyes scanned the gathered host as if they were a pack of wild animals.

Guinever had refused to accompany him to the ceremony, and if truth be told, he felt relieved by her absence, welcoming the break from her brooding hatred. He did, however, spot Efrawg standing near the sacrificial circle, with his arms folded as he watched the gathered dignitaries. Arthur strolled over to him, hoping his melancholic state had eased during the night.

'Morning,' he said, but received a dismissive glance in response.

'The Rendingi didn't eat you, then?' the nobleman observed, his focus returning to his son.

'The way my head feels, I wish they had.' Arthur rubbed his neck, not relishing the prospect of the march ahead. 'Isn't he taking a risk doing the augur in front of the entire army? How does he know the signs will favour us?'

'Why do you think the priest can afford such a fine cloak?'

By the time the last stragglers had trickled in, the field was packed with men, filling the morning air with a din of chatter and jests. The governor signalled with a bejewelled wave of his chubby hand, and the gaunt holy man raised his arms overhead to gain the attention of those gathered.

'Behold!' Arthur thought he heard him say, but the words were all but drowned out by the cacophony.

Vibius rolled his eyes, then waved to a group of scowling centurions, who in turn, lashed the crowd while shouting various insults. Following several minutes of the harsh discipline, the men quietened enough for the bird-like priest to resume his performance.

'Behold!' he began again.

'My hairy arse!' one man shouted, causing a wave of laughter to break out once more. This prompted another round of beatings, including an extra dose for the soldier suspected of shouting the lewd comment.

After waiting for the rabble to settle, the old priest removed a black dagger from within his robe and presented it to the crowd, then strutted around the circle as if his audience had never seen a blade before. Upon completing a full circuit, he stopped and raised it by the handle skyward, his expression twisting into exaggerated ecstasy. 'Here me, divine lord. Although your earthly flesh resides in the eternal city, we, your humble servants here in your poor but loyal province of Britannia, do beseech you to give us your immortal blessings!'

'Bollocks,' said a soldier near to Arthur.

'Lend us the power of your great spirit, most gracious one. May you grant your people a mighty victory against the barbarian hordes descending upon our lands!' Spittle flew from his mouth as he finished the summation and fell to his knees. Arthur saw a flash of discomfort pass across the old man's withered features as he hit the turf. While he prostrated himself, a dark cloud in an otherwise blue sky blew in on a cold wind from the north. The priest gazed up at the heavens and bit his lip.

'Get on with it, man. I want me breakfast!' Vibius grumbled.

A few guffaws rang out, the men no doubt sharing their leader's sentiment.

The priest glanced at the governor and licked his lips. 'Yes! Yes! I feel the emperor's spirit amongst us!' he declared and rose.

A freezing rain started to fall.

Striding to the grazing bull, the priest nodded to two thickset guards, who joined him and lashed ropes around its neck and forequarters. Spooked by the restraints, the animal bellowed in protest, and danced in fright, straining against the men as they braced their feet into the damp earth.

The rain turned into a downpour. Mutters of curiosity rose amongst the troops at the odd sight.

'Just kill the bloody thing, you useless piece of dog shit!' the governor called, his previous boredom replaced by caution.

The priest grasped the bull's forelock, but as soon as he did, it screamed with a high-pitched ferocity. Arthur had never heard the like from such a large beast. Staggering, the animal's red-rimmed gaze rolled into its skull, and then it dropped to the turf as if struck by an axe, all without the knife having touched it. With one final bellow of terror, it shuddered and died.

Shocked murmurs sounded around the field as the priest recoiled from the beast in confusion, his face ashen.

Alarmed, the governor half rose from his throne and roared to the cultist, 'Do something!'

The priest looked at him in utter panic, then regarded the fallen bull. 'Erm, erm... look! The emperor has blessed us!' he shouted, hardly sounding convinced. 'Yes, yes. You see, the mighty one has reached out and killed the beast. Praise be for our beloved imperator!'

Only the sound of pouring rain greeted his pronouncement.

General Quintas coughed. 'The men need to see its heart. Show us the divine guarantee of our success, priest.'

'Finish the fucking ceremony or you'll join that wretched creature!' Vibius added helpfully.

The gentle reminder regained the priest's attention, and

he knelt beside the fallen animal, his expensive cloak now spattered with mud. Following a hasty prayer to the heavens, he plunged the dagger into the bull's chest, then sawed through the tissue beneath the breast cavity. Finally, he reached inside, and after three quick cutting motions, pulled out the dripping heart from under its ribs. 'Behold! The divine spirit of our most august...' His voice trailed off as he stared at the organ in disbelief, for it had begun to beat once more. 'Argh!' he called out and dropped the gory trophy onto the turf.

'You stupid f—' Vibius began, only for the unnatural display to quiet him.

The heartbeat became ever louder, carrying across the assembled army, which could only stare in horrified silence. Lying in a pool of its own blood, the freakish organ blackened, and coarse hairs grew from its fleshy contours. The priest fell back into the filth. Eight spindly legs, each ending in a spiked claw, sprouted from the black heart. A beaked head, surmounted by a single lidless eye, followed. It turned to face the priest's crotch.

The emperor's anointed squeaked, then with his legs and hands slipping in the mud, he scuttled backward. Ever so slowly, the spider creature skulked forward, its thick pincers snapping with an audible click. Instead of helping the prostate priest, the guards hesitated, unsure how to react to this supernatural being.

'Kill it!' General Quintus ordered. Still, they did not.

The unearthly creature stopped and regarded the armed men surrounding it with its hideous eye. As if sensing their intentions, it scurried forward, its legs skittering over the mud, then plunged its deadly mandibles straight into the holy man's genitals. Arthur winced in sympathy as the priest screamed and began screeching gibberish, his neck taut. Even as his writhing descended into stunned paralysis, the onslaught upon his soft underparts did not stop. Bite by bite, the spider ate into his innards and disappeared.

Cautiously, the guards huddled around the body, swords in hand. One guardsman sliced through the thick cloak to reveal the priest's emaciated abdomen. At first, there was nothing but the noise of sucking mutilation. Then an ugly growth appeared in his stomach, bulging beneath the skin. To a man, the guards stepped back. Not a murmur escaped the gathered army.

With a blood-curdling chitter, the spider thing burst from the priest, a shrivelled testicle hanging from its snapping jaw. To the guardsmen's credit, they held their ground and stabbed down, further wounding what mercifully appeared to be the priest's corpse. But the gore-coated horror was too fast, avoiding the blows and running over the head of its former host. After scuttling between the legs of a soldier who cupped his groin and shrieked like a stuck pig, it escaped beyond the protective wall of bodies and raced toward the prodigious gut of Vibius. To the governor's left, a hulking figure darted into view and threw something at the infernal creature, skewering it to the throne's wooden leg before it could reach its target.

While his speechless commander stared in terror, Adalric grasped the hilt of the quivering dagger pinning the hellish thing and yanked it out. The would-be assassin continued to wriggle and snap its beak. Turning it this way and that, he examined the creature as one would a common cockroach, then pressed it the ground and crunched the little beast's head beneath his boot.

Muttered comments about sorcery rose around Arthur.

'The governor will dine now,' Quintus said with swift authority, and clapped his hands at the commander's litter bearers.

But Vibius could not take his gaze off the creature in its

death throes, his eyes bulging beneath the horse-plumed helm, now skewed toward his left ear. As fast as they could, the bearers carried him through the hushed ranks parting before them.

'That went well,' Arthur observed to Efrawg.

CHAPTER THIRTY-SEVEN

Staring at the alien creatures that occupied a place of honour beside his king at the feasting table, Galan, chief of the Fib Clan, wondered if his hatred for the empire would prove enough to overcome his distaste at the prospect of marching with such ungodly allies. Although he yearned to cleanse the corruption of Rome from the Isles and free the enslaved southern tribes, the mere sight of these horrors made him reach for the tiny Cailleach goddess statue sown into the lining of his cloak.

His attention returned to the imposing form of the demon lord. The massive creature surveyed all around him like a cat sizing its prey. Its yellow, slitted gaze caught his for a brief second, and although he did his best to return the look without showing fear, his soul shivered with revulsion. Perhaps sensing his disquiet, a smile played across its black lips. Galan silently prayed they would soon journey south, away from the homesteads of his kin. He also prayed only the leaders of the nether army had taken up the invitation to cross the river and feast, for he feared how his clansmen might react to these walking nightmares.

What have you promised them, Talorc? He wondered while watching an ugly, shaggy-haired brute reach across its plate and snatch up a cockroach skittering across the grand table. It fingered the insect between clawed hands before biting off its legs, one by one, with needle-like teeth. The demon examined the tiny creature's desperate struggle to flee, then instead of finishing off the bug, the brute placed it on its back, leaving it to twitch.

Galan resolved to speak to the king and persuade him that the two parts of his army should never march together; the size of the host across the river outnumbered their own by an alarming factor, more so without those tribes still loyal to the old king.

Of course, he'd considered refusing the summons, but his own lands, that of the proud Fib people, neighboured the far more populous Fotla, the ancestral tribe of Talorc, and so would be the first in line for terrible retribution should it be merited. In his youth, he'd railed against what he'd seen as his father's cowardice for swearing fealty to their old enemies. But with the burdens of leadership now weighing his own shoulders, he saw the wisdom in the decision. The gods knew his men were the bravest in all the Isles, but they were few. Even a token show of defiance would be suicide in the face of the king's infernal reinforcements. He shuddered to think of the fate of those who'd shown greater courage than himself.

A stirring at the far end of the smoky hall drew him from his brooding concerns. The nobles closest to the timber-framed entrance had risen as a figure entered through the doorway. A grey-haired elderly man with a penetrating gaze stepped in to join the feast. At first, he did not recognise Drest, former chief of the Fortriu; then he noticed the raven tattoo on his forehead. The old king had exiled the once powerful leader many years ago, while Galan was still a boy.

Having found him guilty of excesses against his own people and consorting with evil spirits, Talorc's father had gifted the disgraced lord's lands to his closest ally, Bridei, chief of the Ce.

Drest lowered the deerskin skin hood of his cloak and strode toward the king, unsurprised by their otherworldly guests. A tall, red-haired warrior, wearing the helm of a southerner, followed him. The old man caught the eye of every lord gathered around the table, his face the picture of malicious triumph rather than contrition.

Several leaders old enough to have taken part in his downfall also rose in outraged protest at the newcomer. By rights, tradition demanded his immediate execution. The king rose to greet him, ignoring the indignant outcries of the other men.

'Drest!' the king said. 'Explain yourself!' Although he delivered the command without warmth, it lacked the true outrage one would expect from such a brazen affront. It also occurred to Galan how unlikely it was for Talorc to recognise the man, having been little more than a babe at the time of his exile.

Without slowing, Drest strode toward the royal table and fell to his knees. 'My king, I've come here to beg forgiveness —and to warn you,' he said in a gravel-like cadence. Strangely, he showed no fear.

'You dare threaten me?' Talorc asked, his tone icy.

'Kill the bastard!' Old Chief Bridei demanded, but received a dark glare from his ruler. The lack of support made the chief sit back, his weathered face lined with worry.

Drest glanced in his direction, then spat. 'Nay, my king. There is a traitor in your midst,' he said, wiping the spittle from his chin.

Galan's stomach sank as he realised wicked mischief was

afoot. His own father had been on the council that banished Drest.

'And what is this treachery you speak of?' Talorc asked, rising to pace behind his gathered nobility. The last sounds of feasting ended.

'We captured a centurion of the enemy. He revealed the plot to me, my king,' Drest replied, as he surveyed his audience with an odd relish.

'And we must take your word for that, you lying turd!' Bridei shouted. He stood and raised his arms outward, ready to address the gathered men. 'My lords—'

Talorc raised a single finger, silencing him. The elderly chief flushed at the chastisement. Such a public display of royal authority was a breach of the treaties that bound the Pictish tribes. By old convention, all lords should be treated as equals during such gatherings.

Drest sneered contemptuously at his rival, then nodded at the red-haired warrior accompanying him. His tall companion left the feasting hall and soon returned with a manacled wretch, supporting him by his elbow. The prisoner could not walk unaided, so mangled was his protruding right knee. Regardless, he was made to stand beside Drest, his lolling head glistening with sweat.

'Kneel before the king!' the southern warrior commanded, forcing the man down. The disjointed knee audibly popped, and the so-called centurion howled in agony.

'What is your name, worm?' Drest asked in Latin after the whimpers had subsided.

'Gaius,' the prisoner spluttered, looking upon the demon entourage with undisguised horror.

'Gaius what?' the warrior asked, kicking his injured limb.

'Gaius Ulpius… Traianus,' the wretch whimpered. From his accent and appearance, there could be no doubt he was truly Roman.

'And you are a soldier of the imperial army, are you not?'

He hesitated, earning himself a punch to the temple. 'Yes! Yes!' the man wailed, raising his head to reveal an angry mess of swollen bruises.

'Legion and rank?'

'Victrix—Centurion!' he replied, crying in shame and self-pity.

'Now tell these lords what you have confessed to me,' Drest purred, glancing at the king who had stopped behind Bridei. He was the oldest member of the council and renowned for his sense of duty to the ruling line. Even after the imprisonment of Talorc's father, his loyalty had endured, much to the despair of the new king's opponents. But he'd also been instrumental in Drest's downfall, demanding the clan chief be held accountable for his many crimes.

Helpless frustration contorted the broken centurion's face, and he spat out the words as if ashamed of them. 'I carried coin from General Quintus... to pay a Pictish lord for promised aid.'

No one dared to interrupt.

'Who?' Drest's tone was like frost on a blade.

It took another kick to his torso to make him speak again. 'Bridei,' he gasped.

Cries of disbelief rang out.

Drest tugged a heavy bag from beneath his cloak, strode to the table of the king, and dropped it with a loud *chink* onto his plate.

'Wicked lies!' Chief Bridei protested, rising from his chair and grasping the pommel of his sheathed sword. 'If any man dares repeat the words of this Roman swine, I'll split him from crotch to skull!'

But Talorc placed his hands on his elder's shoulders and pushed him back into his seat. 'And what form would this aid take?'

Bridei's mouth opened in shocked disbelief.

'To lead a rebellion and take your crown for himself.'

'Lies!' the old lord repeated, but the conviction drained from his voice, as did the colour from his cheeks. He must have come to the same awful realisation Galan had in that moment.

The king put his mouth next to Bridei's ear. 'Is it, though, my friend?' he asked just loud enough for all to hear. Then, after savouring the other man's speechless outrage for a second, he turned to the demon lord, who observed proceedings with an air of polite boredom. 'General Balor, as a neutral party, I would seek your advice.'

'I would gladly give it,' it replied with a rictus grin.

'We have seen the damning evidence against this traitor, but for the love of my dear father, I'd spare his family,' the king said, squeezing the old man's shoulders until his knuckles whitened. The frail noble gasped in pain.

'A merciful thought, my lord,' the demon replied, his tone far deeper than that of any man. 'But treachery must be met with force, or it will spread like...' It licked its lips with a long black tongue. '... filth.'

The creature's entourage opened their maws and cackled at the apparent joke.

Talorc nodded, pretending to consider the point. 'Very well. Then I will give the traitor the chance to confess his treason and spare his daughters' lives.'

The first signs of true dread appeared on the chief's face. 'I swear to all present and to the gods, I am innocent!' he shouted through a spittle-flecked beard. 'I served you and your father with—'

Talorc grasped Bridei's thinning hair and slammed his head onto the table. 'My father lost his mind because of the treachery of those he trusted!'

Even Bridei's enemies wouldn't accuse him of such an

unthinkable thing. And yet this naked display of power illustrated the simple truth that they were at the mercy of a tyrant. With a sense of profound shame, Galan did not speak up, nor did any other lord.

'You've three daughters, is that not right, cur?' the king asked, raising the stunned man by the hair. A line of blood ran down his temple. 'Perhaps we should bring them here? What do you think?'

At this, the nether captains livened. Galan thought he heard one mutter, 'Virgin flesh!' with wicked anticipation.

'Strip them, and bring them to us,' Talorc commanded Drest's red-headed companion. The southerner gave a crooked smirk and turned on his heel.

'No, wait!' Bridei called out in anguish. Since the death of his last wife, his doting love for the three young women was well known and a source of gentle mockery amongst his peers.

The warrior stopped.

'What's that, doggy? Need to get something off your chest?' Talorc asked into his ear.

'I confess,' the old chief said in a near whisper.

'Ha! We need a bark, not a whimper!' the king said, taking a swig from Bridei's silver cup.

'I confess!' the elder shouted, tears of fury streaming from his bloodshot eyes. His pleading gaze caught Galan's own, forcing him to look away from the man who'd been his father's close friend for decades. Speaking in his defence would've meant certain ruin for his people, yet the moment still stung.

'Good boy,' Talorc said, patted Bridei on the head, then turned and nodded to the group of shaggy-haired creatures beside the demon lord.

One of Balor's foul companions, with a face resembling that of a pit bull, rose and stalked toward the prisoner with a lopsided gait. It grasped the old man by the neck with a clawed black hand, yanked him from his seat with effortless strength, then dragged him to the centre of the feasting hall, beside the slack-jawed Roman. The muscular brute lifted him to his feet with a single hand around the throat. As the elderly lord choked, it ran a finger down his jaw, causing blood to well forth. Then, in a gesture that made Galan's bile rise, it licked the red life essence with a worm-like tongue and bared its fangs, as if savouring the bite to follow. To his credit, Bridei did not call out in fear, even while suffering such indignities.

Aniel of the Cait rose from his place, his cheeks puffing with fury. He'd been a bitter rival of Bridei's for many years, so to see his enemy react so, spoke of the deep unease they all shared.

The demon prince snapped something harsh at his lieutenant in a guttural lilt devoid of elegance. In response, the beast yipped in fear and bowed at his commander, then dragged Bridei and the Roman from the hall.

'You promised to spare my bairns. I beg you, keep your word! There are witnesses!' The old man bellowed before the brute dragged him into the night.

'Have no fear. They are under my care now. I shall give them my special attentions this very evening!' Talorc shouted after him, jovially.

In the stunned silence that followed, Drest coughed, breaking the collective spell that'd befallen the gathered nobility.

'Hmm, ah, yes, my lord Drest.' The king turned his attention to the outcast and drained the old man's cup. 'You have served us well.' He shifted his gaze around the room, daring them to challenge the pronouncement. 'As the entire council is assembled here today, I propose the lands of the traitor, Bridei, be given to our reunited friend. What say you, lords?

Shall we reward his loyalty and forgive his past transgressions?' He raised his empty vessel.

No one followed suit, prompting the king to fling the cup into the rushes. 'Well? Are you all fucking deaf? Do you say "aye" or "nay"?' He glared at each chieftain in turn, but none of them dared meet his eye. 'Perhaps we have a conspiracy to deal with?' he shouted and pointed at Chief Aniel. 'You, Aniel of the Cait, do you wish to throw your lot in with a dead traitor, your sworn enemy, or your lawful ruler?'

The man rose once more, his face quivering with suppressed emotion.

Several strained moments passed while Aniel waited for others to join him. None did. He spat, then sat with a reluctance that Galan found difficult to watch. These men were the heroes of his childhood, hardened warriors who'd rather die fighting than suffer dishonour. But this doom went beyond their lives. The host gathered upon the far shore could decimate their entire people. Nothing could stand before such a force.

'Then do we say "aye"?' Talorc asked again.

CHAPTER THIRTY-EIGHT

The army of the empire snaked along crumbling roads neglected for a century. For two days, they'd trudged through a freezing sleet that whipped across the sodden hilltops of Maixima Caesariensis and seeped into the bones of those toiling through it. Unlike those he led, the governor travelled in an armoured carriage, nestled beside the treasury he insisted stay with his person. For the second time that afternoon, they had been forced to halt while slaves dug out the heavy vehicle from a deep furrow in the road. The men could only wait, stamping their feet against the cold, their collective breath steaming into the air. The plan had been to reach the great fortress of Vindolanda before dark, but this latest setback meant another morning of toil.

A curious shepherd observed the operation from his field, leaning on his crook and chewing on a raw onion. He seemed happy to allow his flock to wander to the roadside and graze beside the waiting soldiers. Bored and half frozen, Arthur wondered if the man had any idea who they were. The herdsman's detached curiosity turned to panic, however, when the imperials troops cut down several of his wards. Knowing better than to protest, he rounded up the remaining sheep while a thousand men jeered at him, some jiggling the carcasses of the animals they'd snatched from his care.

'Stupid bugger,' Efrawg muttered beside Arthur. The big man had grown more sullen with each passing day without sight of Peredur.

Not that Arthur's own fortunes were much better. Guinever's chill disdain had not lessened any, and his days had become a grind of mud, rain, and marching. But necessity pressed them on, reluctant partners in shared misery.

'Make way!' a booming voice announced from behind.

They turned to find the line of men parting for a single rider wearing the uniform of a *cursus* messenger. The imperial servant whipped his sweat-covered mount through the ranks toward General Quintus at the head of the vast column. The general was overseeing the floundering endeavour to release the governor's carriage.

Upon reaching his side, the messenger saluted his superior and handed him a scroll from his satchel. Quintus gave it a cursory scan, frowned, then passed it to a Roman officer beside him, a wiry man wearing the plumed helmet of a *legatus*.

While they waited, Adalric wandered over to them with a loaf of bread, as was his habit whenever his duties allowed. Often, he'd also bring news of Peredur. The boy now had the dubious honour of travelling with Vibius in his gilded cage.

'Who's the other officer?' Arthur asked as the captain handed each of them a hunk of the bread.

'Sertor Tullius Varo.' He replied, then emptied a nostril onto the road. 'He is Quintus's *hund*. I heard he's the cousin of a senator in Rome. The useless turd can't tell his *arsch* from his *ellbogen*.'[1]

Having shared the news between them, Quintus rapped on the side of the carriage. A bored Peredur opened the carriage door, then glanced nervously behind him. Arthur glimpsed the red-carpeted interior and soft light within. Upon seeing the lad, Efrawg stepped forward, no longer disinterested.

'What is it, boy?' the sleepy Vibius called from inside.

Peredur turned and answered, then let the two soldiers enter. They were only inside the carriage for a few minutes before the governor began a furious rant, not quite audible through the carriage's thick walls. When the tirade had subsided, the Romans emerged into the open again, both red-faced.

'Go, then, you fucking treacherous dogs!' Vibius shouted after them. ' 'Tis long since the legions were worth their salt, anyhow.'

They closed the door behind them without responding. General Quintus furrowed his brow on seeing the audience witnessing their commander's displeasure. 'We camp here tonight,' he called. 'And I want it fortified this close to the border.'

A collective groan rose from those close enough to hear. It would take hours to put up the portable palisades and erect the tents in the failing light.

A thunderstorm began to the north, driving billowing grey clouds across a dimming sky toward them.

Dawn brought respite from the rain. Arthur had spent the grey hour beneath his blanket, staring at a drip leaking through a rip in the canvas above. The march and effort to erect their shelter the previous day had been so exhausting, he'd not bothered to lay the ground sheet. Instead, he'd tossed a fur upon a smooth rock slab to keep him off the wet grass, and hoped Guinever would return to find her bedding damp, then join him. But no supple body had come that night. And so, tired and out of sorts, he'd risen and gone looking for her.

Following a miserable time trudging through the tents, he found her at the farm beyond the eastern edge of the encampment. Quintus had promised the inhabitants that he'd spare them the army staying the night in return for allowing the scouting force's ponies to be stabled there. This morning, the buildings were empty, and he guessed the scouts had already set off, perhaps to catch a warm breakfast at Vindolanda before the rest of the mob arrived.

Watching from a distance, Arthur felt a curious relief to have found her alone, brushing a chestnut gelding while murmuring calming words to the animal. Relieved and not wishing to provoke an argument, he'd been about to turn and leave when a uniformed man emerged from the stable block. It was the same imperial messenger who'd delivered the unwelcome news to Quintus. Arthur's guts rose as the other man pulled his boots on and laid an affectionate hand upon Guinever's waist. Against his better judgement, Arthur surreptitiously headed for a copse of trees within earshot of the couple.

'The stalls are all empty now. Come inside,' the Roman said, his tone leaving no doubt about his intentions.

Guinever giggled, very unlike the usual venom she'd been directing at him of late. 'No, I've already told you, only if you stay till tonight…'

'But I don't understand why we must wait. My orders are to return—'

'I need to know I'm not just another woman to you.' She planted a lingering kiss on his lips. 'I'm worth waiting for, aren't I?'

'Well, erm, I suppose one more night.' The cheeky bastard actually blushed.

'You won't regret it, I promise,' she said huskily and kissed him again.

A jealous rage gripped Arthur, and he stepped out, determined to confront the pair. The messenger's back was turned to him, but Guinever spotted him. Without any shame, she scowled and darted her gaze to the tree line. Despite his fury, something in her assertive manner made him duck behind a bush, cursing his own foolishness.

'Till tonight, my love,' she said and slipped into the copse, close to his hiding place.

He followed her in the shadows, watching the sway of her buttocks beneath her dress and hating the thought of another man touching them. Arthur wasn't sure which was worse— the fact that she'd spent the night with the messenger or her complete lack of concern at being caught. He controlled the urge to vent his mounting fury, knowing that to attack an imperial official would end with his skin being nailed to the walls of Luguvalium.

'I know you're angry with me, but rutting a Roman... that's low, even for you!' he whispered when his love rival was out of earshot, having returned to the stable.

She glared daggers at him. 'What business is it of yours? We're not married, gods be praised!'

'But a Roman!'

Guinever turned and poked him in the chest, stopping him. 'Shut up and listen, you dumb ox.' He stared back, confused. 'As much as I'd love to rub your nose in it, he's not what he seems.'

'Oh, I'm sure he's as gentle as a lamb with a bull's cock! Good grief, woman, anyone can put on an act to get into a woman's skirts.'

She folded her arms. 'Like you?'

Arthur coughed. 'Well, no, that was different. I—'

'Never mind,' she interjected. 'That's not what I meant. He's a spy.'

'What? For who?'

She tutted in annoyance. 'Who do you think?'

'The Picts?'

The reply earned him a mocking lift of her eyebrow.

It seemed implausible. Perhaps she slept with any man who could further her cause? But did he really understand what that cause was? Not for the first time, it crossed his mind that the whole story about her sister and nephew could be a lie. 'You expect me to believe an imperial messenger is one of them?'

'Yes,' she said, her smooth cheeks pale in the morning light. 'He sought me out the same as the others before him, asking questions about Merlin and the army.'

'What questions?'

She shrugged. 'Is it true he is dead? How many men does Vibius command? Things they want to know.'

'But how can you be sure he's a spy for the Picts? Maybe he reports to the emperor directly?' It was a possibility. The Augustus's paranoia was well-known, as were the lengths to which he would go to spy upon his people.

She shook her head and raised her hand, displaying the skin between her thumb and forefinger. 'He has a tattoo of a spider here—the same as the others who've approached me.'

The revelation brought back visions of the hideous monster disembowelling the priest.

An even more disturbing consideration occurred to him. 'What about the message he gave—'

'Exactly. We need to know what it said.'

'And what of the love talk? Is fucking the enemy part of your deal with them?'

The haughty look was back. 'Not that I care what you

think, but he was going to leave at dawn. I needed to keep him here longer.'

Arthur gave an unconvinced huff.

'So?' she asked.

'So what?'

This earned him a less-than-gentle jab to the arm. 'So what should we do about it? I can't help my family if our side loses.'

He considered the question while rubbing his arm. 'Adalric will know what was in the message.'

When Arthur started to lead them back to the encampment, Guinever grasped his hand. 'Wait. What if the Picts find out I betrayed him? I won't risk Briant and Grania.'

'We can trust Adalric,' he replied, hoping he was right.

* * *

THEY FOUND the captain with a dishevelled Efrawg, warming themselves by his fire pit and frying bacon. A fresh drizzle had started up, making the flames fizz and crackle. The big men had clearly been in the cups again the previous night because they reeked of stale beer.

The captain nodded in greeting. 'You pair should sleep while you can. We leave in a few hours.' He picked a sliver of meat off the pan and blew it before tossing it into his mouth.

Efrawg barely noticed them, lost in his own thoughts as was the norm of late.

'We need to ask you something,' Guinever said, cutting to the point.

The Germanian grinned. 'Sorry, girly. If you do it standing up, you still get a brat, no?' he joked, looking to his companion for an amused reaction that didn't follow.

'I'm serious,' she snapped, in no mood for jests. 'We must know what was in the message.'

'What message?'

'The one Quintus received last night.'

The captain raised a curious, shaggy eyebrow at Arthur. 'Your woman is asking dangerous questions, apprentice. It could put all of our balls on the chopper—even lady balls, no?'

Guinever flushed with anger. 'Listen, you hair—'

'The messenger is a spy,' Arthur intervened.

Adalric snorted, scoffing more hot bacon. 'Have you pair fooked each other's brains to shit? He's an imperial messenger.'

'No, he's a Pictish spy,' Arthur insisted, praying to the gods she wasn't lying.

When Efrawg snapped out of his brooding contemplation at the words and regarded them both with suspicion, Arthur realised the flaw in his plan. The unhappy nobleman already knew of Guinever's former service to the enemy.

'Merlin warned me of spies bearing the tattoo of a spider here,' he pressed, indicating the same spot on his hand she'd shown him previously.

To his relief, Efrawg did not speak up, his bloodshot gaze moving between Guinever and Arthur. Arthur returned the look with a silent plea. Adalric did not respond either, instead he scoffed more bacon, the meat juices dripping off his beard and fizzling onto the pan. 'Merlin said this?' he asked after a time.

'Yes,' Arthur replied, the man's tone making him uneasy.

The captain gave a resigned sigh, then rose, his hand moving to his sword hilt. 'Don't spoil my breakfast, apprentice.'

'He already knows about her, Arthur,' Efrawg murmured. 'We can trust him.'

'But it's not my loyalty that's in doubt, my friend.' Adalric looked Guinever up and down with his single eye. 'I'm not your love-struck whelp, woman. It will take more than a warm *fotze* for me to risk the ruin of my people.'[2]

Unperturbed, she defiantly stepped toward the Germanian towering over her. 'I spit upon the dogs who hold my family,' she said, her face etched with bitterness. 'I had no choice before. Now I do.'

Realising Adalric could reach out and crush the life from her, Arthur nudged forward, only to receive a discouraging shake of the head from Efrawg.

'I think she speaks the truth,' the nobleman said, gaining the captain's attention. 'Her grief is plain to see.'

The captain pondered this. 'Grief makes people unpredictable, my friend.'

'True, but I don't believe she'd betray their memory by betraying us.'

Guinever looked down at him, her eyes full of unshed tears. 'No, not memories. They are still alive, and I will get them back.'

Adalric's expression remained unreadable while he chewed. 'You remind me of one of my wives,' he said, eventually. 'She is a hard bitch, also, but good in the sack, no.'

Arthur breathed a sigh of relief, although Guinever hardly looked impressed by the compliment.

'The orders are no secret, anyway,' the captain added with a shrug. 'The drunken bastard is complaining about it to every slave and camp whore pouring his cups.' He drained his own drinking cup to illustrate the point. 'It was an order for Quintus to withdraw the Victrix to Eboracum.'

'But splitting the army further is madness,' Arthur said, incredulous. 'We've already lost a thousand spears to chase ghosts. Surely he can see it doesn't make sense?'

'No, it makes perfect sense to him,' Efrawg disagreed. 'The empire doesn't give a badger's shit about this province —as long as the mines keep flowing.' He gazed at the spitting fire. 'They assume the enemy will raid across the wall, raze the north, then run back over the border to rape sheep. It is of no real concern to them, only to us. It's not worth risking the only legion left in the diocese.'

'They are wrong. We must stop their withdrawal. Merlin thought the threat was greater than the Picts alone,' Arthur said.

'Too late, apprentice,' Adalric replied. 'The legion marched at dawn while these bunch of farmers still scratched their arses and dreamed of fat milkmaids.'

'Can't you send a man on horseback and ask them to come back?' Guinever asked.

'And tell them what? Our slave *frau* says the imperial messenger is a traitor?'[3] the captain sniffed at the thought. 'You saw how angry Vibius was. Quintus will think it a cheap trick to bring them back. And his loyalty to the governor stops when his real master speaks.'

'No, we can prove it. The messenger is still here.' Guinever said.

'Then he is a stupid spy.'

'He's a man, and men are all stupid,' she replied, glaring at Arthur for good measure. 'I've made sure he will stay here another day.'

Adalric's eye widened in understanding. 'Fook. You really are like my wife.'

CHAPTER THIRTY-NINE

The children of Merlin grew ever more concerned with every ill portent they encountered on their journey north. On the first day, they came upon a two-headed lamb biting at the bloody teats of its mother. That same night, a green comet streaked across the heavens, an affront to the gods themselves. Finally, came the worst blow of all. Their father's ever-present aura had disappeared without a trace, severing a bond so sacred, it almost broke them.

After days of tear-filled grief, and as abandoned orphans once more, they gathered within an ancient stone circle created by the old people, where they took what little solace they could from each other, but also to debate the way forward.

With typical caution, Druce argued that they should return to Mona and await news of Merlin. To Calder's private relief, the others overruled him, insisting they must learn more of the menace they faced and the fate of their beloved father.

'We know there's a threat in the north. Perhaps this evil stems from that?' Morganna suggested, sharing his suspicion.

'Perhaps,' Calder conceded, then sighed, knowing what he was about to ask would push them to the limit. 'We should use the power of the standing stones to reach out to our brothers on the northern defences. They may know.'

Fearful protests rang out. But Calder didn't silence them, for they were right to be worried. Activating the stones risked another assault by some nameless thing.

'What if it comes again?' Druce asked, voicing their fears.

Surprisingly, it was Morganna who addressed the man, who was far her senior. 'Then it comes again, but we need to understand who our enemy is and where we are needed most.'

'Nonsense, girl. If we must commit this folly, let us try to find our father first,' he argued in a condescending tone. 'He will guide us—as always.'

'Our father is gone!' she replied, a small sob escaping her. 'We must continue to the governor!' The sight of her obvious grief forced Calder to suppress his own sorrow.

Druce turned to him, his expression one of patronising appeal. But he could not disguise the underlying fear in his gaze. 'Brother, talk some sense into her. If we don't go back home, let us at least join our minds to search for our father and seek his guidance. I, for one, refuse to believe he is gone. 'Tis merely a trick of the enemy!'

How he wanted that to be true. For a fleeting moment, Calder considered giving in to temptation, but in his heart, he knew it was no trick. They were alone, and to range their collective will across the land in a fruitless search would leave them more vulnerable to ambush than targeting a single location. Besides, such a measure amounted to hopeless desperation. Merlin was gone. He shook his head and placed a comforting hand upon his companion's frail shoulder. The act of kindness replaced the consternation written on Druce's wrinkled brow with resignation.

We understand each other too well, old friend, he thought.

'She is right, brother. We cannot search everywhere,' he said gently. He knew Druce to be a kind soul, despite his defensive nature, and he only wished to preserve their bonds. Although second only to himself in age, it seemed like yesterday that their father had brought him back to the grove as a toddler, malnourished and crippled by rickets. Since then, they'd grown together, becoming the closest of friends, regardless of their different characters.

'And we have ways to improve our defences,' Calder stated more loudly, as if they had already agreed the decision. Such times called for desperate measures.

'The powder?' Morganna asked.

He nodded.

Many in the group looked uncertain. Again, they were right. Despite its potency, using the substance the Romans called *deus pulvis* required careful consideration. Formed from the crushed bones of long-dead magical beasts, it was a rare gift indeed. Closely guarded by the empire's elite, it was found in only a few places in the known world, and worth more than its weight in gold. The order of druids had carefully collected the powder over decades, but still only carried a small amount of the precious substance with them. They would get only one opportunity to use it, and so deciding when and why was a critical decision, and a burden they must share.

It came as a huge relief to Calder that nobody objected. They were all so afraid and uncertain, a serious disagreement could finish their order.

'Come then, let us join hands,' he said wearily.

Some followed his command straight away, including his beloved Druce, while others hesitated, their faces burning with shame. He did not reprimand them, nor did he offer comfort, for this was the individual burden of each to bear.

One by one, they filed into their places next to each stone. When the last of their number took up position, Calder's heart soared with pride for his kin and with love for Merlin. His legacy was indelible, instilling them with a loyalty so strong, it might overcome the fear of taking such a dreadful risk.

They waited in silence for nearly an hour as a spectacular sunset bathed the woods and streams of Bryn Celli Ddu in a golden blaze. Then, as twilight descended, Morganna, the red of her novice's robe fading to grey in the growing shadows, stepped forward and retrieved an unadorned leather bag from her pack. Inside, wrapped in the leaves of their most sacred oak, nestled the gift of the gods from an age when man and beast were one—*deannach na ndéithe*.[1] With it, their mental defences would be as steel-forged iron, a hundredfold stronger—strong enough, he hoped, to send their spirits further than they could hope for without.

The joining required a tranquil mind, yet turmoil beset Calder. He searched his feelings, but sensed only weakness in the face of the corruption polluting the mystic stream. Then, suppressing his revulsion at the memory of the sickening alien presence that had violated Llyn Penrhyn, he firmed himself, recalling the start of the incantation.

Feel the ebb and flow of the stream.

Let it pass through.

Become one with the stream.

'The stream binds the wheel,' his brothers and sisters spoke in unison at the precise moment required, forming the rock upon which their minds would entwine.

'The wheel and the stream are one,' he continued, glancing at the dimming figures around him. None faltered.

Morganna stepped between the participants, handing each a wrapped leaf. The weather-beaten surface of the stones, indistinguishable to the naked eye only moments ago, began to glow, revealing the ancient words of power etched upon them. The muttered prayers grew as they received their ration. Lastly, Morganna paced back to her position beside the pillar of Artio.

Calder led the group next, as eldest, sprinkling his palm with the god powder. '*Beo*,' he commanded, and the white essence stirred and swirled in the air before him, illuminating with a soft radiance. The others followed, filling the dusk with dancing lights sparkling like thousands of tiny stars. As one, the drui opened their mouths, allowing the powder to enter their bodies.

Though the nature of this joining was perilous, Calder felt a rush of anticipation, for their last ceremony had been to welcome Morganna into the order. On that happy day, they had sped across the landscape, then plunged into the ocean's depths, discovering murky wonders and strange creatures. He cherished the memory but lamented the change in times since then.

As ancient power coursed through his veins, ecstasy washed over Calder, and he gasped in pleasure, as did the others. Looking to Druce, he glimpsed his brother's eyes shining a deep blue, the colour of Boann, the river goddess. The image was short-lived, for his spirit rose from his body and up into the evening sky. His ethereal self looked down at the robed figure of his physical body, standing before the stone of Bran, eyes blazing with the green cadence of the deity. As they climbed higher, the land fell beneath them like a receding shoreline at the outset of a voyage. Calder took the lead position usually reserved for their father, allowing the spirit forms of his kin to fall behind him, appearing little more than dark shadows against the gloom.

They sped north over Mona as the last golden rays fell behind the horizon, and with it, perhaps the last sunset they'd ever see. In the blink of an eye, the drui were soaring above the crashing waves of Muir Éireann, and then in moments, they covered a distance a fast ship would've needed many hours to span. Ahead, the silhouette of the mainland appeared.

On they went, with the forests, hills, and meadows streaming below, wreathed in darkness. Only in the far distance did Calder see a hint of snow-capped mountains. How he wished they were experiencing this journey during the day to witness the beauty of the Isles in all its glory. He looked behind him and saw the pulsing auras of his brethren, who perhaps felt a similar regret. To value knowledge above all else was the guiding principle instilled in them from rebirth, but their urgent quest drove them ever northward this night. It seemed only minutes until the twinkling hearths of Luguvalium rushed beneath them in a blur of colour. They approached their destination.

Calder timed the slowing of their journey better than he'd feared, for as the land became distinguishable once more, the wall of Hadrianus loomed in the mist-shrouded gloom. Stretching as far as the eye could see from east to west, its mighty battlements stood as a bastion against the peoples contemptuously named 'the painted ones.' Even better, the great fortress of Vindolanda stood ahead, at the heart of the fortification. Sensing the presence of his siblings within, they raced toward the main watchtower, ringed by flaming braziers, sputtering in the drizzle. They slipped through its stone wall as if no more than a thin veil, and after a brief search, they found the sleeping form of their kin, sprawled in a wooden chair opposite an arched window, overlooking lands beyond the farthest limit of the empire.

Calder gazed fondly upon his brother's weary face, trying to determine which of the twins he should greet. In all these decades, he still struggled to tell Powell and Howell apart. A small birthmark on the slumbering druid's neck gave him his answer. In the soft light of the oil lamp on the table beside him, Powell's face held a faint reminder of his former youth, although his beard had greyed in the few years since his vigil began. The dark bags beneath his eyes spoke of the burden he shared with his sibling.

The twins had begged their father to help the long-suffering peoples. But Merlin's opposition to their involvement in the affairs of man had always remained vehement, so it had come as a shock to everyone when he'd conceded and let them volunteer their services.

'Wake, brother.' Calder's words emerged as a hollow whisper. The lamp flickered.

Powell bolted upright, at first regarding the shadowy forms surrounding him with horror, then with dawning realisation.

'Brothers?' he said, wiping the drool from the corner of his mouth and straightening his robe self-consciously.

'Not just brothers,' Morganna said, giving him a spectral wave of greeting.

'Little Pig?' he asked in surprise, his voice lighting with joy.

The usual warmth of her answering laugh sounded stilted. She brushed the opaque outline of her hand against his cheek. 'I've not been called that for a long time, big bear.'

The twin brothers had been something akin to surrogate parents to the girl, so when Merlin had unexpectedly allowed them to leave, the separation had caused them all great pain, especially Morganna, who'd doted on the eccentric pair.

'You fell asleep during your watch, my friend,' Calder said, causing the other man to blush. His older brother smiled, recalling how they'd tease him for his gullible nature as children.

'I'm sorry,' Powell replied, smoothing his tousled hair. 'But I still maintained the warding spell.'

'I'm sure you did.' Calder said, not wishing to cause him further strain.

His younger sibling's expression contorted into raw grief. 'Did you feel it?' he asked, tears standing in his eyes. 'Our father?'

'We did,' Calder replied, quelling his own sense of loss.

'When did you last hear from him?'

'Not since he left Mona.'

Silence settled as they pondered a thousand unanswered questions.

'How is Howell?' Calder asked eventually, knowing he must try to keep their spirits up despite such relentless ill tidings.

'Asleep. He's not rested for two nights,' Powell said with a sigh. 'The news hit him hard.'

'It is difficult for us all, my friend.'

Filled with foreboding, the elder waited for the news he feared most.

'Brother... something evil broods to the north.' Powell stumbled on the words as if afraid to speak them. 'We—we don't know what it is, but we feel it creeping toward us, like a sickness upon the land itself.'

Calder nodded, the gesture only a dancing shadow cast by the light. 'We have sensed it, too.' He paused, regretting the pain he was about to cause. 'It attacked us at the sacred glade.'

The twin gasped. 'In Llyn Penrhyn? But that is impossible. How?'

'We know not, but its vile assault took Galvyn.'

'What? No.' What little colour Powell had in his already haggard face drained. 'He is dead?'

Morganna knelt beside him and held his hand. 'His suffering is over.' The distorting effect of her ethereal form couldn't disguise the raw emotion in her voice.

Sensing they had no time to spare, even to grieve as a family, Calder pressed further. 'Sorry, brother, but you must explain everything you've learned of the evil we face.'

Powell faced him with hollow-eyed horror and pointed to the viewing window. 'It has cloaked itself in a dark veil.' He yanked his finger back, as if unwilling to move it closer to the thing he spoke of. 'It torments us, whispering in the night, daring us to reach out to it.'

'And have you reached out?'

The twin gave a jerky shake of his head, his cheeks reddening with shame. 'We dare not.'

'Then, with our combined strength, that is what we must do,' the spirit form of Sirras asserted in his heavy Illyrian accent. The middle-aged former gladiator had been reborn far later in his life than the other drui. Merlin had found him crippled after he'd lost a match. Although much of his old bloodlust had lessened, his willingness to fight had not.

Calder hesitated. Their sacred duty demanded they try to break this dark veil and see what evil approached. But the prospect of stumbling into the enemy's trap filled him with dread, making him wish this burden of leadership had fallen to another. 'I will go,' he resolved. 'But it's your decision if you'll go with me.'

An uneasy silence descended while they all tried to quell their fears.

'And what of Vibius? Has he sent reinforcements?' Druce asked, giving them a moment to consider.

The twin nodded wearily. 'The vanguard is already here, preparing the way for the larger force. They've the manners of wild dogs. I like them not.'

'War is not for the meek, my friend. It attracts such men,' his elder replied.

Powell attempted to grasp Calder's arm, only to have it pass through the wispy substance of his projected form.

'Will you come to us?' he asked, unable to hide his desperation.

'We are coming as fast as we can.' The elder tried to sound more reassuring than he'd the right to be. 'Be strong, my friend. Our father let you carry this burden for a reason. Don't forget that,' he added, not knowing how else to comfort the gentle soul.

Powell nodded again, straightening with resolve. 'Thank you.'

Unable to watch the other man's distress any longer, he turned to his spectral brethren. 'We must know more of this evil.' He held out his shimmering hands to the others. 'Who will come with me?'

Fear, steadied by strength. Strength, tempered by fear. He repeated the old mantra to himself while awaiting the decision of his siblings. And it was no easy choice. Although they had no physical bodies at present, they were still vulnerable to the arcane. If this foe was as powerful as he feared, they faced a fate far worse than death. For if the link to their physical hosts were severed, they'd be set adrift in the ether as shades, neither alive nor dead, and doomed to wander the lands forever while their mortal flesh rotted on the bone. If they refused, he wouldn't blame them. Even the demands of duty had limits.

However, the others followed, merging their hands with his, binding themselves together and becoming ever stronger. As their wills joined, an off-white flame sprang between them, illuminating Powell's gaunt features. None held back. But without their father, the brilliance of their spirit fire was dulled. They could only hope their efforts would be enough.

'May the blessings of the gods go with you,' their brother said in parting, 'but I beg you, take care. There is such darkness beyond. We have never felt the like.'

With the warning lingering in Calder's mind, they flashed

out of the parapet window and back into the night. North they sped, into the no-man's-land separating the island's southern tribes and the Picts. Although it was too dark to see, he had travelled beyond the wall in his youth. He recalled walking through thistle-filled meadows and trickling brooks. As children, their father would tell them tales of a time when the world was young, and the tribes of Albion were as one, united in their beliefs. The same stone circles of worship found in the land of the Dumnonii people in the far south could also be found in the most northerly isles, where it was said men lived in perpetual night. But the Roman invasion had created a festering sore at Albion's core, dividing the tribes and, in time, even the memory of their shared heritage.

All too soon, they reached a swathe of shadow stretching across the horizon, blocking the view of the stars above and the earth below. It appeared as a void—a nothingness suffocating the world like a monstrous cloak. Even from miles away, its oppressive malevolence radiated before it.

As they drew closer, swirling shapes could be seen darting beneath its great visage, as lice would beneath the fur of an infested beast. He slowed their approach, leading their entwined wills forward with greater caution. Although movement came from within, its outer surface remained as still as a black millpond on a winter's night.

When they came within touching distance, the veil parted, forming into a rolling funnel that invited them to enter. Calder halted their advance, knowing they'd never return if they took such bait. Instead, he peered into the mouth of the maelstrom, hoping to find a way to penetrate the shroud without risking utter ruin. The walls of the black warren transformed again, turning into grey tendrils, like that of a mighty sea creature bursting from the depths. The other druids wailed their alarm at their collective consciousness, urging retreat, but Calder held firm for as long as he dared, desperately searching the parting murk.

The tentacle lashed toward them, but they were faster. Buoyed by the power of the god dust, the spirit drui danced out of its way as a sparrow would avoid a diving eagle. Forced to plummet, they breached the veil and glimpsed the iron-clad ranks marching beneath them.

The gods protect us! Calder cried, seeing the size of the monstrous army.

They fled south.

The shroud of evil pursued them with such speed and malevolence, they could not stop and warn Powell to abandon a lost cause.

CHAPTER FORTY

They had been forced to tell General Quintus's subordinate, Sertor Varo, about the spy, with Quintus having taken the Victrix to Eboracum and the governor in a booze-fuelled stupor. After waiting almost an hour, they'd been allowed to enter the legate's tent. Only with Adalric's backing had he agreed to question the *cursus*. Guards had brought the traitor in, wide-eyed and sweating, and following the most perfunctory interrogation, it became clear he was far from an accomplished liar and lacked the most basic knowledge of Roman military structure. The tattoo had sealed his fate.

Arthur looked away as the governor's squat torturer pressed the red-hot poker against the messenger's skin. A smell like roast pork mixed with piss and excrement filled the crowded tent.

'Now, you piece of meat, who gave you the orders?' Adalric growled into his ear.

'I don't know!' the messenger screamed, spittle spraying from his mouth. 'None of us do.'

'So, you are a traitor?' Sertor asked, still half dressed. His evident concern had increased as the questioning progressed, perhaps because of his own part in delaying the plot's discovery.

'I'm just a farmhand!' the broken man replied, twisting with helpless desperation against the tethers binding him. 'They have my son!'

Arthur thought it likely the poor wretch was telling the truth, but why he possessed the tattoo and Guinever did not remained a mystery.

'Where did you get the uniform?' Sertor pressed.

The prisoner licked his lips and hesitated long enough for his tormentor to bring the poker close to his exposed elbow. He shrieked in dreaded anticipation, 'I ambushed him on Dere Street, as he left Eboracum!'

'Did you kill him?'

The spy's gaze darted around the grim faces surrounding him, like an ensnared creature. 'No—no.' He flung his head about, flicking sweat from his brow.

'Refresh his memory,' Sertor said to the hunchbacked torturer, who responded with a gap-toothed grin, then pressed the hot iron against the vulnerable flesh of their ward once more. Animal cries, wild with pain, followed. 'I had no choice!' He cried.

The legate glanced at Adalric, who shrugged.

'Answer my next question and I might grant you a quick death,' Sertor said through the scented rag he'd pressed to his nose.

The spy gibbered again, then screamed, 'Yes, yes! Anything! Please, I beg you, give me peace!'

'Did you swap the original orders of the man you murdered?'

Blubbering, he confessed, 'Yes.'

'What did they say?'

'I swear on the divines, I don't know or care!' he sobbed. 'They gave me a scroll to replace them. That's all.'

Sertor pondered this, then turned to one of the militia guards. 'Search his tent and fetch me the orders he brought last night.'

The tribesman nodded and left.

'They are trying to divide our forces,' Arthur stated, unable to keep it to himself any longer.

The legate regarded him with a cool, untrusting eye. 'Your part in this mischief is unclear, so-called apprentice of Merlin. Perhaps you and the old dog concocted this whole thing? Hmm... I, for one, don't believe he's dead.'

'You're wrong. There's no time to waste—you must bring back the legion.' The comment appeared to touch a nerve, for the redness in the legate's cheeks, deepened.

'And you expect me to believe a woman uncovered this plot.' He said in disbelief. 'And where is this wondrous patriot you speak of?' He raised his hands, appealing to a non-existent audience. In truth, they'd agreed to leave Guinever with Efrawg in case the governor insisted on using the same brutal methods on her.

'We've interrogated her already,' Adalric lied. Arthur silently thanked the captain for keeping his side of the bargain. 'She came to us. Without her, we wouldn't have known about it.'

The legate huffed noncommittally.

When the guard returned with the false orders, Sertor snatched the scroll from him and examined the message closely.

'We could send a rider south and ask Quintus to turn back. They can't be more than a few hours from here,' Arthur insisted.

The legate raised an imperious hand to silence him and continued his inspection. Only the spy's low whimpers interrupted his deliberations. 'The seal is authentic. The manner of the dictation is authentic. These orders are real,' he concluded.

'But they can't be. You heard what—'

'This vermin is a proven liar.' Sertor tossed the scroll at the head of the bound captive. 'The whole plot could be nothing more than another attempt to assassinate the governor. And these orders could still be real.'

Arthur doubted it. The spy had only stayed the extra night because of Guinever's promise.

Unless she's part of the plot and knew you'd find them... came the uncomfortable thought.

'No, they would split our army,' Arthur insisted. 'We should—'

The legate lifted a finger, cutting him off again. 'The orders are real. I'd bet your life on it.' His glare dared Arthur to argue. When no disagreement came, he softened his countenance and rubbed his hand over the stubble on his shaved head.

The traitor began to sob again. 'Please, imperator! I beseech you, I'll tell you anything, but please, no more!'

Sertor nodded at the torturer who punched the kneeling spy in the mouth. A bloodstained tooth flew from his jaw and into the embers of the portable fire, where it hissed and jiggled in the heat. 'Oh, don't worry, flower. I'm sure you'll tell us everything,' the hunchback added for good measure.

'Until we get a complete confession, the orders stand,' the legate repeated with finality and turned away to show their presence was no longer required.

Frustrated by such stupidity, Arthur followed Adalric into the fresh air, free from the reek within. 'The poor bastard would confess to being the queen of the sea, if asked,' he said, taking in a cleansing breath. 'What more do they need to know?'

The big Germanian shrugged. 'They will work on him for

hours. The legate is too much of a coward to raise the alarm without absolute certainty.'

'While the legion gets further away.'

'We've a big enough army to see off the north men.' A titanic yawn overcame Adalric, ending in a less-than-human-sounding growl. 'What about the thing that killed the priest? The Picts have unnatural allies. I'm sure of it, and so was Merlin.'

'Perhaps the north men have sorcerers who do fancy tricks. Make these bunch of girly boys shit themselves, no?'

Arthur wasn't reassured. Merlin had been convinced that evil was involved and working with the Picts. And nothing he'd seen since the druid's end gave him any reason to disbelieve it. How he wished the stubborn old arse were here now. 'I'm not sure,' he disagreed. 'We were attacked by creatures I've never seen before. They were nightmarish beasts, Adalric. Devils.'

'Devils, you say?'

ANOTHER SHRIEK CAME from the tent behind them.

'Yes. Big buggers—as big as you, with the deformed faces of animals.'

'Hmm.' The captain grunted. 'When I was a cub, our elders would tell us of the world before the great war. They spoke of the fallen ones who crave the flesh of men, not for food as we Rendingi do, but for sport.'

'They were not men—that I can tell you,' Arthur said.

Adalric tugged at his beard, then spat onto the muddy turf. 'No matter. I'll bet these creatures have never met my warriors in battle. We will devour them, ugly or not.'

The sound of pounding hooves interrupted them as a cavalry scout cantered into the camp and headed straight for the legate's quarters. Adalric nodded to Arthur, indicating they should follow.

Upon re-entering the foetid interior, they found the cavalryman nervously eyeing the legate.

'What is it?' Sertor snapped without turning from the torturer's ministrations on the spy.

'I have an urgent message for General Quintus, sir,' he said.

This got the legate's attention, and he faced the scout. 'The general has been ordered south.' He frowned, noticing the returning duo. 'What are—'

'A force approaches Vindolanda from the north,' the cavalryman interrupted, panting with exertion.

'Vindolanda?' Sertor asked, incredulous. 'Rubbish! 'Tis the strongest point of our defence. Only a fool would attack us there. Are you certain of this?'

'Yes, sir.' Although nervously delivered, his answer was resolute.

'How far away?'

'Five miles, sir.'

'Well, man, this isn't a fucking mystery play. How many?' the legate pressed.

'Sorry, sir, but their numbers are unknown.'

'What do you mean?'

The soldier cleared his throat. 'We cannot see them.'

CHAPTER FORTY-ONE

The governor's carriage became wedged in a muddy pothole only a mile from the imposing ramparts of Vindolanda. Finally urged into something approaching haste, his guards prised him from his coach like a fat tick, then clad him in gleaming silver plate and helm, before hoisting him onto a massive black warhorse. The poor beast whinnied in discomfort from having to bear such weight.

Sertor selected a hundred sullen men from the closest ranks to guard the valuable cargo within the armoured wagon.

'What are you doing, legate?' Vibius roared from his jittery mount as two slaves tried to calm it. 'I don't trust these bunch of shite knackers to guard the treasury!'

'My lord?' the officer replied, red-faced at the public reprimand.

'I want the Were's guarding it—all of them.'

'But my lord, they are—'

'Do as I say, Sertor, or I'll tell the prefect you risked half the taxes in the diocese. Trust me, you'll spend the rest of your career in a Roman brothel as the powdered favourite of a hairy-balled senator. Do you hear me?'

'Yes, my lord.'

They continued without the fighting might of the Rendingi.

* * *

THE BEDRAGGLED army reached Vindolanda's southern gate at midday, following a gruelling forced march that left many of the less healthy men vomiting by the roadside. Although constructed to a similar design, the great fortress was far larger than Derventio, possessing battle towers on either side of its northern gate, and with the added advantage of being raised upon a natural escarpment.

Vindolanda stood as an ever-present deterrent to the threat posed by their untamed neighbours. Beyond the massive fort, running east to west into the visible distance, was the impressive sight of the wall itself, named after the long-dead Emperor Hadrianus who'd founded it centuries ago. The twenty-foot-high fortification straddled the land from coast to coast for eighty miles, with watchtowers and auxiliary forts positioned regularly along its length, accompanied by deadly ballista and other machines of war. The smattering of men patrolling the lightly garrisoned battlements often stopped to peer at the northern horizon. Standing near the gate, Arthur could see the mist-shrouded outline of another, smaller, fortress to the west.

Although Vindolanda appeared large enough to accommodate a sizable force, it could not house the entire army, even with many of its wooden structures torn down to offer extra space for the influx. So, after passing through the double-arched gateway into the main courtyard, the first column of men, led by a pallid Vibius at its head, were funnelled left and right, up to the battlements as fast as the wall's narrow stairways allowed. As part of the second column, Arthur joined those reinforcing the fortress itself. The ranks behind were alternately directed up to the walls, or into the fort confines.

From the interior, it was clear the garrison had been busy storing provisions. Lining the inner walls were rows of bundled arrows for archers, piled bullets for the slingers, and barrels labelled '*plumbatae*'—darts that could be flung above an approaching enemy before raining steel upon their ranks. The condition of the walls themselves was less encouraging, with the mortar looking old and matted with ivy. Some stone out buildings had been damaged by the elements, then repaired with thatch, giving them a haphazard appearance. More reassuring were the great battle towers at the centre of the north-facing defences.

In the short time it had taken the men to file in and form up in the central yard, the light had dimmed under a thick cloud, obscuring the sky, which only an hour prior had been a cold blue. As if fleeing the growing shadow, a flock of birds passed overhead, racing southward.

Efrawg had remained by Arthur's side during the gruelling trudge without uttering a word. Now, as they stood together amongst the milling throng, he maintained his resigned air, like a prisoner before an execution. Unprepared for the impending attack, the two warriors had been forced to equip themselves with armour and weaponry abandoned in the rush. Arthur wore nothing more than a sweat-stinking *subarmalis* jacket and battered helm, but he'd also found a standard-issue *spatha*, still sharp and fit for what lay ahead. Efrawg had barely bothered to arm himself, only scavenging a hand axe, and a chipped *parma* shield.

Guinever had again disappeared. Although regretting that he might never see her again, Arthur took comfort in knowing she was probably hiding from danger, waiting for the dust of battle to settle before resuming her search for her loved ones.

Grumbled protests broke out as a harassed-looking centurion, one of the few remaining with the main force, beat and kicked his way to where they stood.

'I'm looking for Efrawg and Merlin's dog?' he barked at the crowd.

Arthur reached for the pommel of his blade, suspicious Vibius had changed his mind about their fate. Efrawg, however, stepped forward, gaining the attention of the approaching officer. 'Is my son well?'

The centurion blinked at the nobleman's question, then regarded him, before glancing at Arthur. Apparently satisfied he'd found the right men, he said, 'The governor is asking for you both. Follow me.'

Offering no further explanation, he bellowed, 'Make way, rats!' at the other militia, then pushed through the crowd to the western tower with a mixture of loud curses and elbowing. They ascended a winding stairwell lined with graffiti, some fresh and others faded to near illegibility. After a short climb, the stairs opened into a wide, sparsely decorated chamber, with arched viewing ports set into its stone walls. The soot of a thousand vigils tainted the ceiling. Heavy shutters fixed to each window had been opened to display an ominous black cloud stretching across the hills of Caledonia, no more than a mile from the imposing ramparts. This was no natural thing, for it hugged the land like a creeping fog far darker than anything seen in nature.

Vibius's hulking form occupied his portable throne, with his back to them as he faced the distant storm through the right-hand window. At first, his presence seemed a mystery, considering the impossibility of squeezing his bulk up the narrow stairs. Then Arthur noticed the winch-driven platform at the southern end of the tower. Presumably, its usual purpose was to ferry ammunition to the upper levels of the fortification, rather than hoisting an overweight prince.

Beside the governor stood Sertor Varo and two bearded, older men. They were identical twins, only distinguishable by their robes, one blue and one green. Despite their advanced age, they had a youthful look that few people took into their winter years. Half a dozen other warriors dressed in expensive war gear gazed in fascination through the left window, conversing between themselves in hushed tones. They exuded fear. Arthur guessed they were the tribal chiefs, key allies of Vibius, and, by extension, Rome. The governor's ever-present entourage of slaves remained silent, a few of the women suppressing sobs. Peredur crouched in a corner of the tower, his arms folded across his knees. He rose with undisguised hope upon seeing his father.

'It drained much of my treasury to bring you a supply of *pulvis*, yet you tell me you cannot even waft away a mist,' Vibius said, pointing a fat finger at the encroaching void. He appeared to be addressing the twins beside him.

' 'Tis more than a mere mist, lord. This blasphemy has—' The brother in the blue robe turned to Arthur, his eyes widening in shock.

'—much power,' his twin finished for him, following his brother's gaze.

'That is all you have to say?' Sertor intervened.

'Our kin promised to join us as soon as they can,' the blue-robed man added distractedly, still watching Arthur.

'Withered old twats, the lot of you! Why did I listen to that fool, Merlin? Magic, my arse!' Vibius huffed bitterly. He clicked his fingers at a female slave crouching nearby. The pale-faced woman hurried to his side, took the empty cup he proffered, and disappeared down the stairs.

The legate turned his plumed helm and regarded the

newcomers for a fleeting second, then whispered something into the governor's ear.

His superior snorted by way of reply. 'And what of Merlin's fabled apprentice, hmm? Can you penetrate this miasma?' He did not bother to face his guests.

'I...' Arthur hesitated. 'I—cannot.' He'd nothing to gain by lying.

'Ha!' Vibius barked. 'Hear that, former son-in-law? Your judgement is addled. This piss wort couldn't conjure a fart.' To emphasise the point, he broke wind.

Efrawg did not answer, his eyes on Peredur, who returned the sorrowful gaze.

They waited in silence while the sound of distant drums grew.

'Where's my drink!' the governor roared, chinking his armoured biceps against the arm of his throne. The panting slave ran back up the stairs a second later with a *calix* filled to the brim with wine. He snatched the vessel and gulped the red liquid between shaking hands. Arthur doubted his insatiable need for alcohol was the only reason for his thirst.

Vibius belched. 'We have no time to bandy horse shit. I must see the size of their force. Either you three mystic mollies find out for me, or your dangling corpses will be the first to greet these barbarians. Now do as I fucking command!' He drained the *calix* and threw it out of the window toward their oncoming foe. But his wrath did not stop the thump of marching feet nor the growing twilight.

Arthur considered running from the room or diving out of the north window, but he'd no hope of evading so many men. And if the fall didn't kill him, it would leave him crippled and at the mercy of the Picts. While he pondered this poor twist of luck, the twin brothers inched toward him as if approaching a hornet's nest. When they came within touching distance, he took an apprehensive step back, but the brother in blue fixed him with a pleading look that spoke of their shared plight. Arthur allowed him to place a cool palm upon his forehead. The sensation soon warmed, radiating across his brow. Then, in an act that bore a striking resemblance to Merlin's sorcery, the mage's eyes rolled backward into their sockets and engorged with blood.

'What do you see, Powell?' his twin asked.

The other opened his mouth and released a long exhalation. 'The touch of a god is upon him.'

'Which god?'

The blue twin twitched, as if experiencing a seizure, and his gaze widened. 'She who walks the path of tears. She who is alone.' The words emerged as a hollow whisper, alien to the speaker's wizened throat. 'She who would have vengeance. She who waits beyond the shadow.'

Nemesis. The name came unbidden to Arthur.

The second brother looked incredulous. 'That cannot be.'

'Sertor, what are they doing?' Vibius demanded, shifting in his seat to see them.

'The governor ordered you to dispel the sorcery of the enemy. Do it or die,' the legate snapped at the trio in response.

'Does he have the gift?' the green mage pressed, ignoring the threat.

The one called Powell moaned, then began to gag. 'He has power—old power. He is—'

'Centurion!' Sertor called.

'Yes, sir?' the soldier responded, snapping his heels together and giving the imperial salute.

'STAB ONE OF THEM.'

• • •

315

'Yes, sir.'

'Enough, brother!' the second twin urged. 'We must do what we can.'

The eyes of the blue mage flicked back around again and regarded Arthur with confusion, his palm still in place, even as it cooled. 'You know the fate of our father.'

Arthur nodded. 'I am sorry.' A grimace of raw grief upon the older man's features greeted the words.

THE CENTURION REACHED their side and drew his blade.

'Wait! We will do as you ask,' Howell said. 'Our father promised the aid of the drui, and we shall give it, even if it destroys us.'

The governor belched. 'Either way, you're dead. Makes no difference to me. Now get on with it!'

The two brothers gave each other a forlorn glance, then led Arthur toward a plain wooden table, on which was a wrapped package the size of a man's head—the same package Merlin had delivered to the tribune at Derventio.

'Do as we do,' Powell said and turned to his brother. 'We must use the flight of the arrow.'

'The arrow—that is beyond a novice's skill.' Howell replied, running a shaking hand down his beard, then added in a conspiratorial whisper, 'Perhaps too much for us!' He regarded Arthur with concern. 'How many lessons has our father taught you?'

'None.'

The alarm on the druids' faces gave him no comfort.

'What?' Howell hissed, glancing over his shoulder at Vibius and the gathered chieftains, all watching them. 'What do you mean, none?'

'He's told me nothing of his ways!' Arthur whispered

back. 'I've seen him do things'—he wiggled his fingers—'but I don't know how!'

'Then why are you calling yourself his apprentice?' the green-robed druid shot back. 'Are you an imposter?'

'Yes—well, no. It was only to explain why I travelled with him.'

Powell shook his head. 'No, he has a gift, brother. Although alien to us, there's a power within him. I'm sure of it.'

Arthur stared at the odd pair, torn between his urge to flee and the desire to understand their strange words about himself and the goddess. Perhaps he'd have a slim chance of escaping into the crowds below if he ran fast enough? 'Show me what to do,' he said at last, inwardly cursing his own stupidity.

Powell opened the package and removed three leaf-wrapped packets bound with animal gut. 'This enhances our power. It's our only hope against that.' He pointed behind him at the approaching shroud filling the window.

'What is this stuff?' Arthur asked, examining the packet with trepidation. The thought of having his wits addled before a battle filled him with dismay.

'It is the essence of the old world, lad, trapped in the bones of beasts who walked the Earth before men,' Powell answered. 'The gods enriched their very blood...'

Howell picked up the story on his brother's behalf. 'The gift is diluted and worthless in most, but a few of us have more of the old blood running through our veins.' He looked at Arthur with a raised eyebrow. 'Fewer still have the touch of the gods upon them.'

'Like Merlin?'

'Yes. Our father is of the Eld and more powerful than any mortal.'

'He is your father?'

Howell nodded. 'He raised all of us as his own kin. We are his ch—'

'Is this a gathering of fisherwomen or a battle? Rid me of this veil!' Vibius bellowed.

Time had run out.

Powell hurriedly unwrapped the leaf packet to reveal a mottled white powder. 'You must begin by chanting these words,' he instructed, uttering a series of Celtic phrases with his sibling. Arthur recognised a few expressions, such as fire and earth, but they were layered with others he didn't know.

Incredibly, the strange dust rose and swirled before the old men.

After repeating the sentence several times, Arthur was familiar enough with its cadence to copy them and unwrapped his own packet. At first, his inflections were off and the powder remained inert, but slowly, as he followed their lead, his own powder rose and mingled with that of the twins.

'Remarkable. I've never seen the like.' Howell's dancing pulvis faltered for a moment.

'I told you,' Powell said. 'He has the way.'

The brothers joined hands. 'Breathe it in,' they spoke in unison, then inhaled the glowing substance. Arthur followed.

Little happened to begin with, other than a tingling down his spine, then a sensation similar to intoxication came over him. His senses heightened to a degree he thought impossible, and he became aware of each living presence around him, the vital essence of every man and woman. The twins' physical forms blurred, as if they existed in two places at once. A blue glow, dulled with age, surrounded them.

Nausea gripped Arthur as his awareness floated into the ether. Panicked, he tossed and writhed as his vision tumbled like a leaf in the wind.

'*I cannot stand!*' he called in alarm, but the words emerged as a dry murmur through lungs without substance.

'*Calm yourself!*' Powell's voice was firm in his mind. '*This is normal, but we've no time. Focus on one spot.*'

With his world spinning, Arthur fought his fear and peered at the solid forms of Vibius and Sertor. They now appeared as men behind an opaque curtain, in the same space as himself, yet not; it was like viewing them from underwater. Yet, he could see colours invisible to the naked eye, for a sickly brown aura surrounded the governor. Sertor's ethereal shine possessed a yellow cast, although unlike that of Vibius, his was vibrant. Just as Powell had said, focusing his view orientated him once more.

A noise emanated from the governor, likely another threat, but in this spectral world, it sounded faraway. Arthur hoped this odd new reality lessened the pain of execution.

'*Good,*' Powell's voice came to him, although his physical lips did not move. '*You are centred.*'

'*He learns quickly,*' Howell agreed. '*But his aura is strange, though. Even our father does not display such a colour.*'

Arthur looked down and saw a golden luminescence where his hands should be. Thousands upon thousands of sparks darted amongst the dazzling radiance, and when he tried to move his arm, the light rippled.

'*Whatever gift he has, there's no other way. We need it.*' Powell sounded resigned.

'*But will his soul survive, brother?*' The question contained a pity that filled Arthur with fear.

'*Perhaps. We have no choice.*'

A growing anger replaced Arthur's fear. His whole life, others had used him for ends he didn't understand. And yet here he was again, in the final moments of his miserable existence, bereft of love and literally floating in the ether, about to face a menace he knew not. This rage gave him strength.

'*Excellent. His aura grows stronger,*' Howell observed.

It was true. When he looked again at his ethereal body, the golden fire was blinding in its intensity.

'*Yes. Use it, young one. Fight to the end!*' Powell said. '*Now imagine yourself as an arrow, notched in the bow.*'

The thought came with ease, and he felt himself taut with fury, the need to release unbearable.

'No!' the twins called together. 'Wait—we are not ready!'

But he was not willing to wait. Arthur drove himself into the air, powering, soaring, thrusting through the open window. The ground rushed beneath him. Looking ahead, he saw the creeping black swell of filth devouring the land. As the wall of gloom approached, time slowed, allowing him to pick out individual figures in the grim cloud. These spectral bodies swirled en masse—broken, pitiful things that screamed in protest at the invisible force herding them into an impenetrable barrier.

The last thing Arthur remembered before plunging into the maelstrom was Guinever's face on the night they kissed.

CHAPTER FORTY-TWO

Gareth needed to void his bowels, desperately so. But the courtyard below remained packed with a milling crowd of troops, so any attempt to relieve himself over the parapet would lead to another beating from some grizzled veteran. Nor did he wish to give the *decanus* a reason to make his day even more unpleasant.

Only a few months ago, his life had been so simple. Hard, true, but without the imminent prospect of death. Yet here he was, standing on a faraway wall, staring at what could only be described as a tide of marching darkness, while surrounded by men who treated him with less care than he'd given his flock. His dread grew with the sound of every drumbeat and tramp of feet emerging from the approaching veil. The hardest thought was that he'd volunteered for a year of this misery in return for the promise of seventy-five denarii. Hands slippery with sweat, the young shepherd adjusted his grip on his spear and shield, and then wrinkled his nose at the rotten stench blowing from the north, making his guts churn again.

Although it did not extend beyond sight, the black tide

was still an awesome thing to behold, stretching several miles from east to west. But what did it obscure? The *optio* had assured them the enemy had never fielded an army larger than one half their own, and this sorcery was merely a ploy to disguise the barbarians' weaknesses. But the oncoming darkness left him with little confidence in such promises.

Men prayed around him and spat to ward off evil spirits. What subdued conversations he could hear, speculated on the true nature of what approached them and the ill omens they'd witnessed, not least of which was the grisly fate of the Roman priest. The man's dying shrieks had filled his nightmares ever since that day. His only comfort came from the high walls he stood on and the artillery pieces to his right, fixed upon the mighty towers of the fort. These were deadly looking machines of war, capable of tossing a solid stone ball over a great distance.

The ill wind picked up, whipping his homespun cape about his shoulders. The smell, like a festering latrine, worsened. A second later, a buzzing swarm of fat carrion flies flew at them from the dark mass, quickly covering the distance to Vindolanda. As the insects buzzed around the men's heads, a pest settled on his elbow and bit him, sending a needle of pain burrowing into his joint. Repulsed, he swatted the little blighter away with his spear shaft. Unperturbed, it came back again and stung him in the same spot.

'Little bastard!' he exclaimed, letting his shield clatter onto the stones, and crushing the bug with the flat of his fist. He examined the mess of squashed bug guts on his skin, then scraped it off on the battlements. Already his arm felt sore from the nasty nips.

The flies were causing serious disruption amongst the ranks as they settled on any exposed flesh with a relentlessness that went beyond mere nuisance. A few paces along the line from his post, a boy younger than himself flailed with such vigour at the buzzing host, he lost his footing and fell between the crenulations. The unfortunate tumbled over the north face of the wall and thudded into the stake-filled ditch below. To Gareth's dismay, the lad continued to scream, even with skewered limbs. As if sensing his helplessness, a cloud of the parasites converged upon the prone figure.

'The gods are angry!' shouted an old man with Brigantian tattoos, standing next to where the boy had been. Dropping his spear, the panicked auxiliary pushed his way toward the stairs, muttering and cursing. He'd almost reached them when a burly centurion grasped him by the throat and tossed him over the northern face to join the unfortunate who'd unsettled him.

'Anyone else abandoning his post will get the same! Now stay in position!' he ordered. The grand army of the empire was too busy swatting themselves to argue.

The black mass grew until it obliterated all before it—grass, sky, and sun. As it crept forward like rolling death, its surface was discernible as a swirling, dancing thing, streaked with greys and browns. At first, Gareth thought his eyes were playing tricks on him in the dimming light, for he saw figures flying amongst the gloom. Then a chill ran down his spine as he realised he was not mistaken; these spectral beings formed the very fabric of the looming cloud. Thousands upon thousands of them screamed and howled with looks of horror on their cadaverous faces.

Growing calls of dismay arose from the warriors, as they also comprehended the unholy spectacle. What was this foe? He'd been promised an easy victory and the spoils of the vanquished, but this? This was something his entire being told him he should flee. Several others in his unit did just that, all rushing the centurion at once. They pushed him aside then raced down the steps.

The air grew oppressive, like the sticky mug before a

storm. Such was their trepidation, the calls of the men subsided to a morbid silence. A cold sweat broke out on Gareth's forehead. The sound of marching thundered on.

A golden shard of light sped from a northern battle tower of the fort and arced out over no-man's-land, toward the heart of the encroaching gloom. It was a shimmering spear of pure sunlight—a thing of beauty that contrasted perfectly with its dark destination. He wondered if the artillery had unleashed a missile against the enemy, but on turning to the ballista crew, he saw they were as awestruck as the rest of them. Whatever it was, it gave him hope. The light plunged into the black mass, which rippled as water hit by a stone. The surface of the veil shimmered, then, with a deafening boom of raw energy, it shattered.

In the aftermath, wails replaced the rhythmic thump of marching, as if many souls had cried out in release; better still, the tormenting plague of flies dissipated. Just as Gareth began to hope the gods had saved them, an evil vision unveiled itself. The army before them was a sea of howling horrors—things conjured from his worst childhood nightmares. Shaggy-haired brutes filled the columned ranks mostly, taller than men, with muscular frames and animal-like muzzles. Clad in black armour, they had the appearance of crawling beetles. Their fluttering pennants were blood red, with crude designs and symbols he didn't understand. In their clawed hands, they wielded wicked cleavers, pikes, and clubs. Other creatures stalked amongst them—beasts so horrible he could scarce comprehend.

A dozen siege platforms trundled ahead, pushed by emaciated human figures, naked but for the filth that covered their bodies. As he looked on, one of these wretches collapsed. A crookbacked guard with a lolling tongue stabbed him to death, then cut him to pieces on the spot and tossed the remains to the front ranks. The soldiers, if that's what they could be called, jostled to catch the grisly bounty and gnawed upon the bloody offering, yowling through slavering mouths lined with sharp teeth. A looser and less numerous group of human kilted warriors surged toward Vindolanda's sister fort to the west. Even at a distance, he saw men with blue war paint on their faces, many wielding two-handed swords or short stabbing spears.

As the dread army resumed its advance like the maw of a great beast, Gareth regretted that he'd never again see his flock.

CHAPTER FORTY-THREE

Refusing to miss her opportunity for revenge, Guinever had slipped away from Arthur in the night to join the coming battle. But because the arrogance of men would never allow a female to fight with them, she'd stolen the clothes and bow of a forest hunter, then sheared her long hair and dirtied her face, hoping to pass as a wild boy of the wood—one of the many cutthroats enticed into the ranks for money. Although her appearance wouldn't fool determined scrutiny, the surrounding men were so distracted by their approaching doom, none had questioned the presence of the slender, soft-cheeked lad amongst them. Part of her now wished they'd spotted the ruse and sent her back to the other camp followers.

The black veil had been bad enough, but when the golden missile had revealed the terrible truth, her legs had trembled in terror. Not so much for her own fate—she resented her own existence—but at the thought her family might be amongst the pitiful wretches forced to serve such vile things. Lined like shackled animals and whipped beyond endurance, the only respite she could offer these lost souls was a quick death. Her heart quailed inside her, begging her to leave this place to the men and never come back, but rage and hope drove her on. Perhaps if she fought well, the gods would reward her and spare them? She raised the bow and nocked an arrow to the string.

A command rang through the ranks. 'Aim for the slaves pushing the engines!'

Guinever wiped away the tear running down her face, then took up the stance learned from her father.

In the interminable moment while they waited, she contemplated the events that had led her to this forsaken place. On the same night she'd lain with Arthur, a voice came to her in a dream, promising she'd find her loved ones again if she went north with him. But he'd failed her—just another corrupt man in a land full of such men.

She hated herself for knowing her attraction to him remained, despite his wicked past. Arthur—nothing but a common thug, guilty of the same evil her kin had endured. And yet he'd shown her no sign of the cruelty he must surely possess. She recalled that first night, when they'd loved each other with a passion born from the affinity of two lost souls. Only her recent sense of betrayal equalled the intensity of those feelings.

No matter. This will end us all, she thought, taking aim at a hideous monster flogging a poor wretch covered in red welts.

Just before she loosed the arrow, a memory came to her of a summer day spent catching butterflies with her sister in a forest clearing. She tried to recall the sweet fragrance of wild-flowers above the rotten stench coming from the horde, but the sight of the dark tide soon crushed any memories of goodness or light.

Guinever let the arrow fly and watched the shaft sail true and bury itself deep into the beast's neck. It clutched at its throat, then collapsed to its knees with black blood pulsing through its hairy fingers. As it twitched, the prisoner's pasty face looked to the battlements before reaching down and unsheathing a dirk from the felled monster's belt. Her hopes soared. Perhaps the unfortunate would take advantage of the coming chaos and escape? But when the slave plunged the wicked implement into his own throat, a sense of dark abandon seeped into her being. Sobbing, she rained deadly barbs upon the horde below.

* * *

EFRAWG RETURNED his son's gaze, his heart filled with shame. First, he'd failed his mother, and now he'd led their only son to ruin.

They will not have him while I still draw breath, he thought.

Although he'd pledged to die during the battle, he hadn't promise when.

Not 'til he is safe. Then we will be together again, my love.

He smiled at the boy, determined to show him how a true warrior faced death.

CHAPTER FORTY-FOUR

Arthur tore through the black void with ease, freeing the trapped souls forming the fabric of the shroud from unspeakable bondage. Never had he experienced such limitless energy. A great battle joy filled him as he surged forward with naked power. Nothing could stand before him.

Then another conscience joined his own, one even greater than himself—a soul capable of shaking the very pillars of the earth. She who was divine and full of infinite fury. She who would have vengeance on her betrayers. The lady had come.

'Yes, my son,' she whispered in his ear as he drove deeper into the black chasm, tearing its remnants to shreds. Her voice was a pure single note that drew him, filling his soul with a longing to become one with her forever and lose himself in his eternal mother's bosom. 'Now is the time of your birth,' she rejoiced. 'But do not forget that you forge your own destiny. I cannot protect you from the forces of this world without risking the return of my kin and the ruin of all. Look for signs of my favour, for they will aid you. Now go! Reap me a harvest of bones!'

And then she was gone, leaving him bereft and alone as a

child ripped from the womb. For a time, his senses drifted in the ether while he yearned for her.

* * *

WHAT COULD HAVE BEEN moments or centuries passed until he opened his eyes and saw the granite flags of the fortress tower once more. A thudding pain to Arthur's stomach greeted his return to the world of the living. He gasped, his lungs emptied of air, then looked up to find the centurion snarling at him. Although he could see the man's lips moving, his words emerged as a muffled echo. A second blow followed, sending him sprawling, but with the pain, the sounds of the present also came crashing back.

'The governor told you to rise, turd!' Despite the harsh delivery, a note of alarm accompanied the soldier's command.

Arthur spluttered, clutching his ribs. 'It would be easier to rise without your foot in my guts!' He tried to stagger to his feet, but the exertion of destroying the veil overwhelmed him, and he slumped. But to his relief, instead of receiving another kick, he felt a big hand reach under his armpit and lift him. A grim-faced Efrawg greeted him with his axe drawn.

'I hope you are planning to put me out of my misery with that thing,' Arthur said, wincing from the pain in his side.

'I'll end us both, if it comes to that.'

He clasped the nobleman's thick waist to steady himself. 'You're as chirpy as ever.'

'Come, the enemy is upon us,' Efrawg said, leading him to the throne of a now silent Vibius, who seemed mesmerised by the approaching force. His chubby hands gripped the arms of the reinforced chair.

'Well?' he asked, turning his sweating face to Arthur.

'Well, what, my lord?' he replied wearily.

'What can you do about that?' the governor shouted, pointing at the window.

Arthur followed his arm and staggered back in shock, for he looked on a vast army of the same demons that had ambushed him and Merlin.

To see a dozen of the monsters had been harrowing, but these were legion, thousands upon thousands of unholy brutes poised to assault Vindolanda. Shaggy-haired Fomori captains wielding whips and staves surmounted with skulls headed the square formations, while other creatures with reptilian snouts, yellow eyes, and human-like faces dotted the host. These lithe auxiliaries did not appear to be organised into regular units; instead, they bobbed amongst their fell comrades on serpentine bellies, their backs armoured by scales. Smaller imps scuttled under the legs of their larger cousins and clambered up their torsos to gesticulate at the defenders.

Carried on a huge black litter in the heart of the throng was a red-skinned figure clad in silver. Except for its deathly pale bearers, the creature was twice as large as any of the surrounding force. A great evil emanated from it.

'Do you need more of the *pulvis*?' The governor urged him, his small eyes darting to the table where the twin druids leaned upon each other, panting with fatigue. They regarded Arthur with slack-jawed awe.

'No,' Arthur replied, a strange calm coming over him. 'There is nothing more I can do. We must fight.' Somehow, he knew it to be true. Stunned silence greeted the pronouncement.

'You… you… cockroach! I'll have—'

A severed head flew through the window and squelched across the flagstone. It rolled to a stop at the feet of Vibius.

The grisly trophy opened its eyes and leered. 'Little Pig!

Little Pig! Let me in,' it said with a hollow growl and licked its lips.

'Arrgh!' the fat man groaned in horror, trying and failing to pry his plump backside from the throne.

Arthur drew his blade, skewered the head, and slung it back to where it came from. Needing no further encouragement, the gathered chieftains scurried to the shutters and slammed them shut, plunging the chamber into gloom. Only slivers of light filtered through narrow slats in the protective covers. It did little to quell the screeching horde outside.

'Summon my bearers!' Vibius wailed.

'My lord?' Sertor asked, incredulous.

'The office of governor is too important to risk on this, erm, skirmish,' he called, his eyes bulging with fear at the bloody pool where the head had sat. 'I'll bring reinforcements to relieve the siege.'

No sooner had he spoken than half a dozen slaves raced to pulley the platform back into the tower, realising their master's cowardice could be their salvation.

'You're leaving?' Arthur asked, unable to believe his own ears. 'This is no siege. They are about to attack!'

Although he did not reply, the governor at least had the good grace to avert his eyes in shame.

'My lord, how long do you wish us to hold them here?' Sertor asked, his face ashen.

'Oh, err, not long. I will gather a force at Eboracum and return. A few weeks at most.'

The tribal commanders looked askance at the prediction, then began to argue amongst themselves. A top-knotted southerner spat at Vibius, then hurried from the chamber. Nobody tried to stop him.

Efrawg marched to the governor's side while slaves dragged his bulk onto the platform. Vibius regarded the axe in his clenched fist with apprehension. 'On your daughter's memory, you will take the boy with you.'

'What? Hmm… yes, yes. He will come with me,' a pale and shaking Vibius said, gesturing for Peredur to join him.

The boy took one horrified glance at the wild-eyed fat man, then pleaded with his father. 'No! I want to fight by your side.'

Efrawg strode to him and gripped his arm. 'Goodbye, son,' he said, his voice thick.

'No, please!'

His father dropped the axe and scooped Peredur into a bear hug. They clung to each other before he set him back down.

A guttural chanting grew outside.

The nobleman grimaced at the shuttered window, then regarded his son once more. 'You will go with your grandfather—now.'

The boy's shoulders slumped. 'Please, I…'

Head bowed with regret, Efrawg turned his back on the desperate plea.

A single sob escaped Peredur at the rejection. But he straightened a moment later, wiped away the tears streaming down his cheeks, and paced to Vibius's side on the platform.

The governor did not meet the eyes of the assembled chieftains as his attendants strained to lower him. The remaining slaves rushed through the door to the stairwell. Unable to ignore the cold glares of his subordinates any longer, he spoke. 'Erm, mark my words, they will not dare a frontal assault on the wall. Order your men to hold their ground!' And he was gone.

As soon as Vibius, and the boy disappeared from view, a rhythmic twang rang out from above. Arthur strode to a shuttered window and looked through the slats. A ballista had fired into the massed ranks, piercing the breast of a club-wielding fiend and pinning its torso to the creature behind it. The hellish duo collapsed in a heap of flesh and bone.

A roar of anger erupted from the nether army, followed by a cacophony of howling war cries.

'Who gave the order to fire?' Sertor shouted. He raced to the slats and peered through. Slamming his fist upon the frame in frustration, he turned to the chieftains. 'Go. Tell your men not to provoke the enemy. We need to buy time.'

The nobles needed no further prompt to leave.

CHAPTER FORTY-FIVE

'I'm glad Peredur will be safe,' Arthur said to Efrawg, as they jogged along the tower steps to the adjoining battlements.

The nobleman grunted, his expression set like stone. 'It would have been kinder to put a blade through his ribs.'

'You don't mean that.'

'Don't I?'

A terrified boy clad in a leather jerkin far too large for him barrelled into them from the opposite direction.

Irritated, the big man grasped him by the scruff of his neck as he tried to scramble around them. 'Pack it in, you bleedin' idiot!' he roared. 'If a centurion sees you running off, he'll jab your guts.'

The panting boy blinked. 'We're going to die!' he whimpered.

Efrawg stilled his wriggling captive with one bone-rattling shake. 'If you wish to see your mother again, walk, don't run.'

The youth licked his lips and nodded jerkily. 'Ye-yes, sir!'

'Go, and be sure to warn who you can on your way back home,' the nobleman said, lowering the lad to his feet.

After giving him a nervous glance, the boy continued his descent with a more measured stride.

'You'd help a coward?' Arthur asked.

Efrawg shrugged. 'Children have no place on the battlefield. They'll suffer enough, anyhow, if this lot pushes south.'

'More reason to fight,' Arthur said, needing to seek solace in the red mist of battle.

The big man hefted his axe. 'Come on, let's spill some blood. I'm sick of this life, anyway.'

They ran up the remaining steps, then emerged into a world of flying missiles and screams.

The siege towers had resumed their onslaught, triggering a withering arrow fire from the defenders. The enemy's intention to attack head-on was undeniable. When the foe came closer, the imperial infantry threw rocks and plumbatae darts at them. The deadly shower crushed the rounded helms of the dark soldiers and left many in twitching heaps upon the field. Against the unarmoured slaves, however, the effect was even more devastating. Regardless, the inexorable progress of the machines barely halted, for demon warriors trampled over the bodies of the fallen wretches to take their place, like dogs clamouring for cuts of meat.

It soon became terrifyingly clear what purpose the reptilian beasts served. For following the initial efforts of the imperials to repel them, the columns of troops parted behind the first ranks, exposing their mysterious comrades. In turn, the lizard men bent backward at an impossible angle before whipping their heads forward as one and spitting barbs at the auxiliaries lining the wall. The missiles rose to a high zenith, then descended, producing an unearthly wail in their wake. Seeing the oncoming wave of death, the defenders raised their shields or crouched behind the thick parapet crenulations. The barbs hit and exploded on impact, spraying a bright green goo onto the bodies beneath.

Hundreds of men screamed as the steaming effluvia melted through armour and burned into flesh. Maddened with agony, many threw themselves over the side, only to be seized by the horde below and torn asunder. Their indignities did not end there, for their bloody remains were tossed backward and chewed upon by the creatures awaiting their turn to assail the wall. It sickened Arthur to see such hellish glee on their foe's screeching faces, despite the losses they'd endured.

The siege machines crashed against the battlements in unison, along the length of the defences. One tower, with the emblem of a severed head painted in red upon its thick planks, smashed into a section only ten feet from Arthur's position. A wooden drawbridge dropped onto the parapet, crushing an auxiliary beneath its weight. Even as his comrades rushed to aid him, a terrifying new menace emerged from within the tower. A muscular squat thing with beady eyes and a wide muzzle, like that of a toad, strode onto the connecting bridge. Strapped to its back was a steaming cauldron etched with alien incantations. Animal gut tubing led from its sloshing contents to a hollowed horn held between the creature's clawed hands. With a wicked sneer, it pointed the nozzle at the tribesmen pulling their comrade free.

'Farrack!'[1] it commanded and shot fire from the contraption at its unwitting targets, engulfing them in a bright blue flame that stripped both clothing and flesh from their bodies. Screaming, the men threw themselves to their deaths as flaming torches. The still trapped soldier, now burning, could only writhe in the extremes of his agony.

This same terrible tactic played out along the battlements as more stormtroopers emerged to clear wide sections of wall for the waiting reinforcements. Arthur's hopes sank at the devastating cruelty of these new monstrosities. They threatened to overwhelm the entire garrison, despite the fight having just begun. Drawing his *spatha*, he pushed through retreating auxiliaries and ran straight at the hulking flame wielder cackling maniacally at its blackened victim.

Although a rational part of him warned of the folly of his actions, a deep revulsion drove him on. He tried to rush the unclean being before it noticed his presence. By some infernal sense, however, the demon turned to face him before he could plunge his sword into its fat, bulbous stomach. The nether soldier snarled in disdain, drool dripping from its yellow canines.

'I roast your man skull, worm,' it growled and raised the nozzle.

Arthur dived, using his momentum to carry him, then stabbed the blade forward, feeling it connect. A piercing heat rolled along his back, bringing memories of his branding with it. The sensation soon lessened, leaving him shrouded in a stinking fume. Choking, he scrambled to gain his footing, desperately squinting through the concealing smog. An acrid whiff filled the air.

Following a heart-stopping moment, the fog dissipated, and he made out the beast once more. It swayed upon its bowed legs and toppled to its knees. The movement jolted the pot on its back, and its contents sloshed over the lip. The demon howled as the boiling black substance frazzled the coarse skin of its cheek.

Intent on finishing the creature, Arthur rose to his feet. But another flame-wielding trooper emerged from the siege engine, already raising its fire-breathing contraption at him. With no energy left to resist, he could only raise his hand in a futile attempt to defend himself.

A large figure leaped into view, grasped the kneeling demon, and, with a roar of strained fury, tossed the creature into the path of its comrade. They tumbled back into the ladder shaft of the engine, squealing. Just as Arthur glimpsed Efrawg standing in front of the engine's mouth, a great whump erupted from its depth, knocking him off his feet once more. The wall's foundation vibrated with the shock wave.

Once the initial cacophony had passed, he pushed himself to his hands and knees. The nobleman lay beside him, his eyes closed, and his beard singed from the blast. Arthur nudged him.

He stirred, then winced.

'Are you injured?' Arthur shouted, his voice sounding muffled in his ringing ears.

Efrawg opened his eyes and grinned for the first time in many days. Despite the throbbing in his skull, Arthur also smiled. Without hope, one was left with a choice to either fight or skulk away. They had chosen to spit in the face of fate and die gripping a sword.

Helping each other onto unsteady feet, they peered over the battlements upon the utter destruction beneath them. The siege engine lay in a smoking wreck, crammed with the bloody corpses of its former occupants. The few remaining auxiliaries on their section joined them to witness the minor victory amidst relentless ill news. Although their intervention had brought a brief respite for themselves and the surrounding Britons, most of the line had fared poorly, allowing the black tide of the nether army to pour onto the wall.

CHAPTER FORTY-SIX

The nether army charged along the wall, tearing men limb from limb with a ferocity that would make hardened veterans piss in their boots. The farmers and townsmen of Britannia stood no chance against such visceral hate. All along the northern defences, the imperial troops dropped their weapons and fled in droves. Those upon the walls east and west of the fortress streamed toward the woods south of their position, while the men upon the battlements of Vindolanda retreated into the dubious safety of the inner compound. But these unfortunates found themselves funnelled into the congested roads between the stone barracks and the fort's workshops. The few remaining officers maintaining discipline were overwhelmed. This was no orderly withdrawal, but a rout.

While surveying the growing disaster with fading hope, Arthur spotted Guinever, only fifty feet away, amongst one of the last bow companies still loosing upon the enemy. She'd disguised herself as a man, but with the residual power of the god powder within him, he could sense her presence, brave and angry to a fault. With dismay, he realised the terrible plight she faced.

A jostling pack of demons pressed the handful of defenders standing between them and the bowmen, with more of the dark army streaming from the siege towers to join the attack. Unlike the other archers who'd now fallen back, Guinever appeared consumed by her deadly task, unaware, or uncaring, of the approaching mob.

'Look,' he said to a panting Efrawg, pointing. 'Guinever.'

'What!' the big warrior replied, narrowing his eyes at the bowmen. 'I don't see a woman.'

'She's dressed as a man. Trust me, it's her.'

'Shit,' the nobleman said, wiping the sweat from his blackened brow.

Below, in the fortress, auxiliaries clambered over each other to reach the narrow arches of the southern gate, which acted as a bottleneck, stemming the growing exodus.

'I won't leave her here,' Arthur said. 'Are you with me?'

The nobleman nodded in resignation.

'Come on, then.' Arthur strode forward, swinging his sword arm to release the kinks in his muscles.

'Wait!' Efrawg said, stopping him. Arthur feared his friend's courage had failed in the face of such poor odds, but he turned to find him strapping a discarded battle shield to his arm. 'I'm coming, you hairy bastards!' The nobleman roared, charging toward the nearest demons, brandishing the shield before him like a battering ram.

Arthur went with the plan and sprinted on his comrade's heels, ready to strike. They crashed into the exposed backs of the nether troops. Using his momentum, the big man sent them shrieking to the inner fort below, where the milling humans stabbed them to death, eager to exact a small measure of revenge upon their foe.

Progress along the ramparts became more difficult as the blood-slickened stone made for a precarious, adrenaline-fuelled sprint. They hit the next couple of enemies full pelt. One fell to its doom, while the other avoided them, dancing backward with surprising agility for such a heavy creature. The quick manoeuvre unbalanced Efrawg, forcing him to halt and adjust his stance. Sensing its opportunity, the Fomori leapt at him, directing a wicked dirk at his exposed brow, but Arthur was quicker. He drove his sword past his comrade's head, straight into its biting maw. The fiend crumbled to the flags, twitching.

'Thanks,' Efrawg said.

'Save that for the *taverna* afterward.'

'There will be no after for me,' came the somber reply.

Arthur sighed. The mad fool still intended to keep his bargain with the governor. But there was no chance to argue, for the last men defending Guinever were fighting a hopeless battle. At any moment, they'd flee or be cut to pieces.

The two warriors made steady slaughter, until a huge demon warrior with an angry red scar running down its hairy cheek stepped in their way. Rather than evade them, it planted its feet wide and swung a gore-encrusted flail above its horned helmet. 'Come, bring me your flesh!' it growled.

They charged, screaming their defiance. But the creature was ready for them and whipped the flail against the shield with lightning speed, its iron barbs biting deep into the wooden rim. With a hellish grin, the beast wrenched its arm backward and tore the shield from Efrawg's grasp. Worse still, the two men's momentum worked against them, sending the pair tumbling at the feet of their snarling foe. Arthur flipped onto his back and found a mailed foot poised above his face. He rolled, and the stonework disappeared beneath him.

Flinging his arm up, he managed to grip the ledge with his left hand, not daring to drop the blade in his right.

Although Arthur's death had been momentarily checked, he was at the mercy of the brute looming over him. It raised an iron-shod foot, ready to crush his skull. Without a chance of avoiding the attack, he jabbed the *spatha* upward and pierced the heel of the descending boot. Black blood spewed into his mouth. Howling, the demon staggered away, leaving Arthur to spit out the vile stuff with disgust. Even the unnatural thing's life essence tasted like a foul parody of real blood.

Efrawg's thick bicep wrapped around the creature's neck and squeezed. The nether captain choked, raking its filthy claws down the big man's arm, jerking and twisting to dislodge him. But the warrior did not relent, and with brute strength alone, he crushed its windpipe until its slitted yellow eyes bulged from its skull. The creature gargled its last breath through grime-covered teeth.

Efrawg kicked the corpse over the side and pulled up his comrade with ease. 'I reckon that makes us even,' he said, doubling over to catch his wind.

Too exhausted to banter, Arthur simply said, 'thanks.' A ragged cheer rose up from the crowd below at their victory.

But they had no time to tarry, for the siege engines spewed forth the enemy like towering burrows filled with creeping insects. The news further afield was no better; Arthur could see the Picts had taken the fort west of Vindolanda and had raised banners upon its pinnacle. The total collapse of the empire's forces was at hand.

Efrawg reached for the demon's flail. 'This is butchery, not war,' he said wearily, familiarising himself with the weapon's weight.

Arthur took a deep breath, bracing himself to assault the final group of creatures hacking at the raised shield of the single brave soul holding them off Guinever. She stood no more than ten feet away now, continuously nocking and releasing arrows in a death trance.

Creeping upon the unprepared enemy, they unleashed a force of nature, ripping and hacking as they went. The death-wielding duo took the demon company with such surprise they fought until the last demon had fallen and only the lone auxiliary remained.

Arthur hooked his finger over the trembling rim of his shield and dipped the edge enough to see a single eye peering at them, at first with terror, then confusion. 'Erm, hello there.'

The soldier lowered his defences to reveal a fair-faced youth not much older than Peredur. Pale and shaking, his sweat-matted blond hair poked out from under a rusty helm.

'I'm not dead?' he asked, unshed tears standing in his eyes.

'Not yet, but you will be if you don't move your arse,' Efrawg replied, aiding him to his feet.

Regardless of his obvious fear, Arthur admired the lad's tenacity. Behind him, Guinever continued to draw and shoot. 'If you value your life, leave,' he said.

'But the centurion ordered us to stand our ground.'

'No, lad,' Efrawg said. 'Trust me, this fight is finished. Only death can be found here.'

The youth gaped at the towering nobleman with a fraction less fear than the warriors of the nether. Still, he shifted on his feet, then hefted the shield again, unconvinced about abandoning his position.

'What's your name?' Arthur asked, forcing a patient tone. Even if he was daft in the head, he owed him much.

'Gareth,' he replied unsteadily.

'Well, Gareth, you are as brave as you are stupid.'

The lad blinked.

'Just stick with us,' Efrawg said, giving him a friendly slap on the back that drove him to his knees.

While the big man helped up the youth once more, Arthur

strode to Guinever. 'What in the name of the gods are you doing?' he shouted, unable to curtail his frustration.

She reacted with frightening speed, aiming the taut bow at him, poising the arrow tip at his throat.

'It's me!' he said while sheathing his sword, dismayed by her flat glare.

'I know who you are.'

Arthur exhaled in exasperation. 'We don't have time for—'

The arrow tip nicked his flesh.

Efrawg approached them, his hands spread before him in a calming gesture. 'Woah, lass. If you need to take one of us, take me.'

She shot him a puzzled glance, then switched her attention back to Arthur. 'Does he know of your past, yet?' she asked, her face a tumult of hopeless rage. 'Do you think he'd try to save your sorry hide if he did?'

The pressure from the arrow tip increased, and her slender arms quivered from the strain of maintaining the draw.

'I did not take them,' he said, making no attempt to move the tip aside. 'We'll find them together. You have my word.'

'Ha! Your word!' she spat. Her face hardened as she pulled the gut string back further. Her expression turned to grief. 'They must be dead.'

Arthur winced at the thought she might skewer him. 'You don't know that.'

'It's the hope I cannot stand.' Her voice quavered. 'Part of me wishes I found them here—just so it would be over.'

'They might still need you.'

She lowered the bow, then raised it again. Arthur closed his eyes and heard the twang as she loosed.

He was not dead.

When Arthur re-opened his eyes, he found Guinever

staring over his shoulder. He turned to see a demon collapsing, the shaft of an arrow piercing its brow.

'I… thank—'

'Just remember your promise,' she said, her green eyes hard.

He nodded and was about to reply, but Efrawg called out in alarm, 'Peredur!'

The nobleman pointed toward the southern gate where an almighty tumult had erupted. His son clung to the side of Vibius as their dais was jostled through the crowd of fleeing men. But their progress had become increasingly precarious as the surrounding troops reacted with fury at their leader's obvious cowardice. The wobbling platform came to a halt as the baying mob swept aside the slaves carrying it. The throne tilted, toppling its occupants into the arms of those screaming for their blood.

'No!' Efrawg cried, leaping off the southern side of the parapet, the bodies of the many corpses below breaking his fall. Apparently uninjured, he stood and bounded toward his stricken child.

'Efrawg!' Arthur called after him, knowing the man would only add his own sacrifice to his son's.

But even the lust for revenge against the governor didn't stop the frenzied rout for long. The enemy had captured the wall-mounted ballistae and turned them against those they were intended to defend. The war machines blasted bloody runnels of death through the throng below. Vindolanda ran with blood, and the last vestiges of order disintegrated. Every man had become a hunted animal.

CHAPTER FORTY-SEVEN

Following the collapse of the imperial army, the blast of a deeply resonant horn rang out, and as the signal thundered over the battle lines, the nether's forces halted and gave a great victory roar. A thousand drums beat a slow rhythm that quickened until another blood-curdling cheer erupted. Then, their ranks parted like the tides of a black ocean, and the white giants strode down the living corridor, carrying their dread general. Even those demon warriors upon the walls stopped the slaughter to hail their lord. The enemy fell into a brooding silence, with only the screams of the dying greeting the passage of the conqueror.

From his position west of the northern gates, Arthur could see the wall beyond was overrun with scuttling imps, which had joined their larger cousins to gnaw upon the limbs of the fallen. To try this way would be suicide. Their best hope of escape lay in retreating to the main battle towers, then continuing east along the wall, and past the fort, where the hammer had dealt the lightest blow. Many imperial troops had reached the same conclusion and were escaping via this precarious route. He guessed that once back at ground level, they might stand a chance of re-entering through the southern gateway to assist Peredur and Efrawg. Whether such aid would prove futile, however, he knew not.

'Come on!' he said to Guinever and the boy Gareth.

They ran for their lives.

The brief respite provided by the impromptu triumph of the enemy only added to the panic of those within the fort. Men scrambled and clawed at each other to get out, but slowly, with great loss of life, the pressure perceptibly eased around the southern gates and more imperials fled into the relative safety of the dense woodland beyond.

The way to the central towers remained mercifully unchallenged, and they'd soon sprinted to the steps that led to the towers, where Arthur brought them to a halt. The only nether troops he could see nearby were the two creatures operating the ballista atop the tower, and they appeared distracted by the spectacle of their approaching leader.

Arthur raised his finger to his lips. 'Wait here,' he whispered to the frightened pair, then sneaked down the steps and through the arched doorway.

Something white-hot skimmed across his cheek and burst into shards upon the stone beside his head.

'Hold!' He called at the sight of a terrified Powell, his arms outstretched toward him. Howell stood next to his twin, gripping his arm. Only the two brothers remained in the command centre.

The druid lowered his trembling hands. 'I nearly liquefied your skull!'

'We can't stay here,' Arthur said, holding his knees and panting. He looked around the empty chamber. 'Where's Sertor?'

'Gone,' the blue-robed mage replied bitterly.

Arthur spat onto the flags. 'We never stood a chance.'

Guinever and Gareth ran into the chamber from above, alerted by the loud bang the ill-timed attack had created.

The two groups eyed each other warily.

'I think the monsters above might have seen us,' the boy said, his face filled with alarm.

'Just follow us,' Arthur ordered the sorcerers and strode to the far exit.

Despite his obvious fear, Powell crossed his arms. 'Our place is here. We promised our father...'

Arthur half-turned to glare at him. 'I'm sick of all this noble self-pity! There's nothing glorious about becoming a corpse. Come with us or not, I don't—'

A red-helmed demon with a face disfigured by warts burst through the doorway facing him. The beast screeched its hate and sprang at the distracted warrior, the bloodied club in its hand raised for the kill. Another blinding flash shot from Powell, striking the thing in its widening jaw. The intense heat of the magical bolt ripped the creature's mandible apart, flecking the chamber with black blood. Gargling, the brute fell.

Arthur regarded the aftermath, his heart pounding, then turned to his elderly saviour. 'Your aim's improving.'

Powell sheepishly retracted his extended fingers. Needing no further prompting, the group raced through the eastern doorway.

'Wait!' Howell called at the threshold and darted back into the tower chamber. He returned a second later, wheezing and clutching a handful of leaf-wrapped god powder packets. 'We might need these.'

With a muttered curse, Arthur led them on.

They were lucky. The battlements remained untainted by the enemy, and as they reached the stairway leading down to the countryside beyond, Arthur stopped to look at the plight of those trapped below. The compound of the inner fort had emptied, with only the dead or wounded left behind. Amongst the terrible scene, the governor lay upon his back like an upended crab. Incredibly, Peredur and Efrawg were leaning over him.

'Stupid fool!' Arthur murmured in disbelief. Instead of taking the boy out of harm's way, the nobleman had joined his son's efforts to remove Vibius's heavy armour and give him a chance to flee. 'Bloody idiots!' he barked in frustration, intent on leaving them to their stupidity.

Fearing they would soon run out of time, he looked over the north side, where the demon lord's procession had stopped at the locked gates. If their predicament hadn't been so dire, Arthur might have been tempted to linger and admire the magnificent thing sitting upon its ebony throne. With a mantle of glittering gold on its horned head and its black gaze fixed ahead, it appeared as a living relic. Raised high upon the shoulders of its bearers, it towered above all and did not gesture to its troops, which averted their eyes in reverence as it passed.

The blind giants knelt as one, allowing the demon prince to step down with a languid, unhurried motion. Now stood at full height, the nether general was a thing to behold, mighty as it was terrifying, a mass of muscle and horn. The death lord regarded the barrier before it, its clawed hand still upon the skull of the giant supporting its descent. A visible wisp of smoke rose where its palm touched the pasty white scalp. In its other hand was a sword the colour of midnight. It raised the dark blade above its head. 'Hear me, Father!' It spoke in a beautiful, yet dreadful tone that carried perfectly to Arthur. 'For too long we have been cast to shadow!'

The following roar was deafening.

Its glassy, mirror-like eyes glittered with malice. 'We shall harrow this land in your name!' the dread general called to its nameless god. 'We will honour your flesh by partaking in theirs!'

A mighty cry of 'For the body of our father!' answered the dark benediction. The *Fomori* surrounding him groaned and fell to their knees.

An evil power gathered in the tip of the general's sword, drawing streaking lights from every corpse surrounding the gate. The fallen howled in agony as their dying souls were extracted from their broken vessels.

'Come, my dogs!' the demon lord called as his blade burst into purple flame. 'Now is the hour to gorge yourselves upon our new cattle!'

It pressed the blade's fiery radiance against the ancient wooden trunks of the gate. A huge explosion rocked the world, and a great shudder passed through the wall with thunderous force, throwing Arthur onto his back. All went dim. Then as he returned to his senses, Guinever was screaming. Sitting up, he saw the blast had thrown her down the stone steps. She lay at the bottom, clasping her knee. The twins and Gareth scrambled down after her, their ashen faces speaking of terrified exhaustion.

Arthur regained his feet then risked a final look at the gate. Although damaged, even the mighty blow had not shattered its massive frame. But the respite would not last for long, for the demon prince was already raising his blade again, leeching further force from the dead. The unearthly howls of the tormented rose, this time with less vigour, prolonging the horrific process. He staggered down the steps and scooped Guinever into his arms. She pressed her head against his neck, yelling pain-filled curses.

'Quick!' he shouted to the others, stirring them from inaction.

They pounded along a muddy track skirting the eastern wall of the fortress, made treacherous by those fleeing before them. By the time they rounded its southern extremity, they were breathless. The south entrance loomed a short distance away. Ahead, the remnants of the imperial army routed as fast as their injuries allowed. Arthur shuddered to think of the fate awaiting those unable to extricate themselves. But there were still no signs of the pursuing enemy—yet.

'What about Efrawg and Peredur?' Guinever asked, as he set her down to rest his aching arms.

Bent with exertion, Arthur held her questioning gaze.

'Well?' she pressed.

'Damn it! Wait here!' he said and strode toward the gate.

'Where are you going?' Powell asked.

'To get myself killed over a pair of bloody fools,' he called over his shoulder. 'If I'm not back soon, drag her to the woods.'

'What then?'

'Keep running! And don't forget to remind her why my corpse is resting in the guts of some fucking monster!'

Arthur jogged into the inner fort, deserted but for the groans of the dying. Several of the outbuildings had been set alight, presumably by the arching flames of the fire-wielding horrors that had started the devastating attack.

Efrawg and Peredur were close. He raced to where they toiled, desperately stripping the mud-caked armour off the governor. Vibius seemed dazed, froth bubbling from the corners of his mouth. The noblemen looked up at him with surprised gratitude. 'Help us!' he said, loosening the straps on the massive breastplate.

Arthur spoke low into his ear, not wishing to panic the nearby child. 'They will be through the gate at any second. We've no time!'

Frowning, Efrawg looked at the boy removing his grandfather's right greave with shaking hands. Then without pausing his struggle to unstrap the governor's armour, he said, 'I won't have Peredur burdened with this mess. They already know he is heir Vicarius. If Vibius dies, he'll never be free of this!'

'None of us will be free of this, man!' Arthur yelled.

This brought some sense to the nobleman, for he stopped and grasped his son's arm.

The boy gave his father a hopeless look, tears running down his cheeks. 'Mum won't forgive us if we leave him here!'

Efrawg hesitated, struck by the plea.

'I mean it!' Arthur said through gritted teeth. 'We don't have ti—'

Another explosion blasted the northern gate to pieces. Timber and stone burst into the air, forcing them to cower. A whistling sound alerted Arthur to the object descending toward them, and he shoved Peredur's crouching form out of its falling path. The heavy wooden stave missed the boy's head by a hairs breadth, but plunged into Vibius's plump thigh. The pain must have roused the governor from his stupor, for he bellowed like a stricken bull.

CHAPTER FORTY-EIGHT

'We must leave him!' Arthur yelled at Efrawg once the cacophony had subsided.

The nobleman didn't listen, returning to Vibius's side to continue his hopeless task. Peredur followed his lead.

'Are you both mad? They are coming!' he implored, grasping Efrawg's arm. 'Vibius has done nothing for either of you. Leave him!'

'I swore an oath!' the big man replied, shrugging off the hand. Redoubling his efforts, he unsheathed the governors gilded dagger, then began to saw through the straps of his breastplate.

'What about your son, man?'

Efrawg stopped as if shaken from a dream, then regarded the boy as he worked at a blood-spattered left greave. 'Take him,' he said, his face set in grim resignation. 'Go. Get him out of here.'

'What?' Peredur called, his fingers slipping from the straps. He looked at the men, his eyes filling with fresh tears.

Arthur ran to the lad and grabbed him by the waist.

'No!' Peredur screamed, struggling as he was lifted away.

'Listen to me, son!' Efrawg shouted, seeing how he resisted. 'You must go back to Brina. Take her south, as far from here as you can.'

'My place is with you!'

'No, my time is done. You must protect her now.'

The boy searched his fathers face, uncomprehending.

Efrawg lowered his head in shame. 'She is carrying your brother or sister.'

Peredur stopped fighting. 'What? Why didn't you tell me?'

'Because—' A towering figure rounded the corner of the *principia* behind them.

The dread lord strode with the gait of a nightmare predator, while regarding Vibius's prone form with glittering eyes darker than the pools of the dead. A great company of huge demons garbed in blood-red armour, trudged in unison behind it, all with black swords held aloft to their brows, the blades longer than a man.

On they came, things of the pit.

The soulless gaze of the demon prince flicked from the fallen governor to Arthur, and the awful leer upon its blue lips twisted into a sneer of apprehension. It flared its nostrils, sniffing the air.

'Why are you here, unclean thing?' it asked in a tone that froze Arthur's blood.

He did not answer.

The demon's pace quickened, until it stood before them, taller than Efrawg by three feet. In its tightened grip, the pommel of the soul sword shone with a shadowy glint. Crooked runes adorned its blade. The general sniffed again, and a cunning smile spread across its face. 'Ha! You are but a baby!' It flashed its razor-like teeth. 'Tell me, little one, do you still suckle upon your mother's teat?' A black tongue snaked from its mouth and licked its lips.

The governor interrupted its cruel contemplation with a strangled groan. Noticing his pain, the nether lord's smile widened with infinite malice. 'My lord, 'tis my pleasure to accept your invitation into this fair land.' It reached down with one hand, grasped the timber shaft in the stricken man's thigh, and scooped him into the air. Vibius screamed.

Efrawg charged the nether prince, but it kicked him aside as if he were nothing. Crying out in shock, Peredur twisted with such fury, he wriggled free from Arthur's arms and rushed to the side of his stunned father. The monstrous creature regarded them no further. Instead it eyed Vibius greedily while jerking his body upon the stave like a curious cat playing with a wounded mouse. Such was his agony, the governor attempted to draw his sword, but the blade fell from his grasp.

Then, ever so slowly, the demon opened its maw to an impossible angle and placed the fat man's sweating brow between its gleaming white teeth. Vibius squealed, urine seeping through his armour to join the blood spattering onto the cobbles below. His cries only caused his tormentor to pose in mockery for the humans before it bit deep into the governor's head, crunching through helm and skull alike. After chewing on bone, hair, and the mysterious white matter residing within men's heads with great relish, it said, 'Hmm, not bad, though a little fatty.'

The red general dropped the remains, then regarded Arthur with curiosity through glittering orbs. Reaching a decision, it pointed its sword at the warrior watching him aghast. With their gazes locked, Arthur imagined countless treasures and the caress of beautiful, passive women. 'Join us, pup, and I, Balor, shall be your master.' It extended a finger with a single silver ring upon it. A deep green emerald surmounted the band. 'Kiss it, and be my grateful slave.'

'I do not...' Arthur hesitated, his world filled with soft scents and the tinkling of gold.

The nether prince grinned, and the wonders offered to Arthur grew even more magnificent. He saw great feasts, rich with delicate meats and sweet treats. Best of all, a limitless power that would forever free him from his shameful past. For none would dare challenge an ally of this red demi-god. Unable to resist, he fell to his knees before the overwhelming presence of the colossus.

'No!' Efrawg cried.

He glanced at the nobleman to see disgust written upon his face. Beside him, Peredur looked on with a smoke-streaked expression of undisguised terror.

The image in his head changed. The lusting beauties and wealth transformed into the golden-haired woman carrying a crying infant, surrounded by encroaching flames. She looked him in the eye. '*The choice is yours, my son,*' she said.

Arthur grasped the nether lord's icy finger, and as he touched the immaculate crimson skin, he saw a vision of a vast lake brimming with blood. In its inky depths, countless souls gasped and fought each other for breath. Upon its bone-lined shore sat a great, golden being, with a sceptre resting across its lap. He sensed the figure was infinitely alone, consumed by an unquenchable craving for more souls to fill the void within itself. Arthur longed to be with it, and as he peered through the veil at this splendid sight, he became enamoured with the shining being. It beckoned to him, willing him to regard a face so wondrous his mind would shrivel upon seeing its countenance.

Join us. The call was distant, yet tugged at his core.

A great battle raged within him as two, immeasurably superior forces, ripped at his soul. On it went, with a relent-less energy that reached an unbearable intensity. Unable to stand it any longer, he screamed, clutching his head.

The world stilled again.

Blinking, Arthur saw Vibius's sword resting at the demon prince's cloven feet in a pool of its former owner's viscera. It was a good blade, old and notched, an heirloom of the Trinobantes for many generations. An image of a set of scales stamped on the sword's pommel caught his eye.

The scales of Justice.

And the scales of the lady…

Nemesis.

Casting aside the fog within, Arthur tightened his grip on the demon's finger, then grasped the sword and thrust it into the outstretched palm of the nether prince. The thing calling itself Balor growled furiously and tried to wrench its hand back, but the old steel was strong. He slid the blade in further, sawing through tissue and bone. The demon howled, no longer in anger, but in pain, then raised its rune blade, ready to strike down.

Arthur wrenched the governor's sword free of the demon's palm, and with his remaining strength, he swung the blade up at the wrist of the dread general as it was about to deliver the killer blow, slicing clean through it. Balor roared in stunned agony as both his hand and the sword it held dropped to the ground. Through pure instinct, Arthur released the governor's blade and snatched up the twitching limb instead, which still held the dark weapon. Upon the pommel of the nether sword appeared the visage of a contorted face—a poisonous, unnatural thing. Its very presence sickened him, yet he sensed it was also a relic of great power.

Repulsed, he threw the cursed object aside, not caring where, but by some strange twist of fate, the blade clipped the lip of the nearby garrison well and disappeared into its depths.

Balor stumbled backward, its black eyes wide with

dismay, even as a gout of blue blood spurted from its arm stump. 'I will have you dragged down to the stone to watch those you love flayed for an eternity!' it screamed, staggering to the well and smashing through the surrounding brickwork with its muscular legs.

One of the general's red guard ran to its aid, carrying a flaming torch. Balor grasped it by the neck with its remaining hand and squeezed until the lesser creature's head popped from its body in a fountain of gore. The demon lord cast aside its servant's limp form, then picked up the torch and pressed it to its wound, fizzling the gushing blood. Then the general screamed in agony but did not remove the flame from the stump.

Eventually, it had cauterised the mass of flesh into a smoking deformity. Then with a heaving chest, it turned back to the well and clawed the earth with its single hand. Undeterred by its grievous injury, it still possessed incredible strength, and burrowed into the earth surrounding the shaft in a desperate bid to reclaim the shadow blade.

The show of weakness had unsettled the other nether elites, for they did not move to attack. Instead, they snarled with indecision. Behind them, the silent dark army lined the walled ramparts, watching.

You are not yet strong enough to withstand such devilry. Run while you have the chance, boy! It was Merlin's voice that came to him.

Seizing the moment, Arthur ran to Efrawg and Peredur. 'Come on!' he cried. Wide-eyed, the pair looked at him. 'I mean it!'

They ran.

* * *

ONLY AFTER THEY had raced through the south gate and found

the others still waiting did a great roar arise from within Vindolanda.

'They are coming!' Arthur called to the druids and Gareth. With no time to be gentle, he scooped Guinever onto his back. She groaned in pain but managed to wrap her arms around his chest and her legs around his waist.

'What happened?' Howell asked.

'I think he made them angry,' Peredur said, panting.

'Oh, dear,' the druid replied, his face gaunt with fear.

They ran for the woods to the south, but halfway, Guinever shouted a warning. Arthur turned and discovered that the red guard were already pouring from the southern gateway and running with greater speed than any armoured human could manage. In their eagerness to catch their prey, some had discarded their weapons and were galloping on all fours, like wild hunting beasts.

With dismay, Arthur realised they'd lost any hope of escape. The demons would overwhelm them long before they reached the relative safety of the trees. He looked to the canopy rustling in the gentle breeze and found such proximity to their salvation a bitter fate to swallow. The grunting sounds of pursuit grew behind them. The pack was closing in for the kill.

He looked to his left and right. The two young men were fine, their bodies able to take the exertion, and Efrawg was as steady as ever, but the twins were puffing and blowing like landed fish. Soon, they'd be spent.

In those final moments, with his body close to exhaustion, Arthur's thoughts turned to Merlin. What had the wily druid seen in him? Much of what he'd demanded of him made little sense, yet he'd always been making a point, even though the purpose of such lessons remained a mystery. Despite his impending doom, Arthur could not help but smile, as he recalled the time the old man gave him that ridiculous whistle to summon a herd of goats. Perhaps as a final salute to the old fool, he felt the hard outline of the goddess-shaped object under his filthy padded shirt.

Keep it, boy. Who knows, one day it might conjure…

He let one of Guinever's legs slip, then took out the whistle and turned it in his fingers.

'There's no time to play with trinkets!' she shouted and shifted her weight to look behind them. 'They are nearly upon us!'

'Merlin gave me this!' he gasped. 'He said it can bring me what I most desire!'

'Whatever you're going to do—do it now!' she cried.

Arthur raised the whistle to his mouth, but fumbled it from his grip as he stumbled over a clod of turf. Cursing, he barely stopped Guinever from toppling away. Placing his lips around the whistle's worn tip, he blew, then fixed his gaze upon the oaks ahead.

Nothing.

He blew again.

Still nothing.

Merlin, you mad, old bastard, help me!

He tried a third time.

A hundred naked Germanians emerged from the shadows, their tattooed muscles rippling as they strode from beneath the canopy.

'Mother of—we need to talk!' Guinever called, half in wonder, half confused.

With a relieved smirk, Arthur redoubled his efforts to run.

She shifted again in his aching arms and called with excitement, 'they've stopped!'

The nether must have spotted this new approaching force and decided to regroup.

They ran on, closing the distance to the Rendingi.

'Do you plan to scare them off with the size of your

cocks?' Arthur asked, as loudly as his burning lungs would allow.

A big grin appeared on Adalric's bearded face. 'Your woman does not look so scared,' he replied lightly, as if out for a stroll in the woods.

Upon reaching their unusual saviours, they fell to the ground at their feet, heaving for breath.

'This fight is lost,' Arthur gasped, his lungs ready to burst. 'You are too late to save the governor.'

'Ja,' the captain said, then spat, the gesture expressing the depths of his grief.

'He's right. You cannot win here,' Efrawg said, his arm clasped about Peredur. 'Tens of thousands follow behind this vanguard.'

Adalric patted his old friend on the shoulder while he gasped. 'We'll still give these bastards a greeting worthy of the Rendingi!' His grin widened to reveal sharp, elongating teeth. 'Oh ja, we will have good times while we hold them. Give you girly men the chance to run away, no?'

'Adalric, I have seen enough needless sacrifice this day,' the nobleman replied. 'You should retreat.'

The captain changed the pat into a fist upon his friend's shoulder. 'Do not worry. We are fierce, not stupid.'

His gaze shifted to regard Arthur. 'Now go, apprentice!' he said, delivering a bone-shattering slap on his back. 'But know that the next time you blow a dog whistle at me, I'll ram it down your throat!' He turned to face the mass of demons standing before the entrance to the fortress.

The nether creatures snarled at this new nuisance and smashed their great swords upon their crimson armour.

Adalric took a step toward the nightmares and cracked his neck from left to right. 'Fook me, they are ugly!' He raised his fist above his head. '*Komm, brüder, wir jagen!*'[1] he called, the words ending in an ear-shattering roar.

The were-guard charged, transforming as they ran. Their biceps and skulls lengthened, lending their swirling tattoos an undulating quality as their limbs pumped with power. Animal hair sprouted over their sweating bodies, obscuring their human forms. Even their bones gained girth, becoming thicker and stronger.

The Germanians began their attack as men, but hit the line of demons as great bears, taller than the largest human, even on all fours. Although outnumbered, they tore into the enemy's front ranks in a flurry of black blood and the audible cracking of bones. They bit, clawed, and crunched through the first ranks as if they were rag dolls, then fell upon the second like a force sent by the gods to cleanse the earth of vermin. The display was a bewildering torrent of gore on the senses. Nothing could stand against the onslaught of the Rendingi. The nether elite faced decimation.

But even as Arthur's heart soared at the glorious spectacle, the desperate nature of the counterattack soon became clear. With each passing second, more of the dark army spilled through the fortress gateway, faster than his fierce allies could quell them. Worse still, seeing the challenge arising against their cause, the enemy horde still on the walls of Hadrianus, streamed toward the stairs, threatening to flank the brave Were.

Then, to his further dismay, the twins walked out toward the last stand, each carrying several packets of *pulvis.*

'What are you doing? We must flee!' Arthur called after them.

Smiling, they turned to him as one and said, 'Now we understand our purpose here.'

'But we—'

'He'd be proud of you this day,' Powell added. 'Remember that in the dark times to come.'

Arthur moved to stop them, but Efrawg placed a

restraining hand upon him. 'Come, you are needed with us, my friend.'

The siblings took each other by the hand and strolled toward the bloody tumult as if young children facing a shared nightmare.

They stopped halfway to the battle, set the packets down, and unwrapped each while muttering incantations. The powder swirled into the air. Still clutching each other's hands, they allowed the *pulvis* to enter through their open mouths. The two old men rose from the ground, hovering a few feet above the field.

'They've taken too much,' Arthur muttered, somehow knowing it to be true.

The twins pointed toward the southern gateway. A grinding rumble rose, followed by the sound of cracking rock. The keystone, topping the archway above the gate, fell onto the heads of the demons emerging through it. Then, with a great crack, the entire edifice collapsed, burying those beneath it and stemming the tide of the enemy passing through. Taking advantage of the lull, the Rendingi made quick work of the Fomori remaining on the southern side of the broken gate.

The exertion had utterly drained the twins. The pair fell against each other, lifeless husks of their former selves.

'Now is our chance!' Efrawg called out, grasping Arthur's arm.

'But the were—'

'Can run as fast as horses,' the nobleman replied. 'We are most at risk.'

Arthur nodded. With his senses reeling, he picked up Guinever once more. The exhausted company ran into the protective embrace of the woods and an uncertain future.

CHAPTER FORTY-NINE

Framed by the burning fortress behind him, King Talorc strode amongst his exhausted men. For the first time in many months, a grin appeared on his chiselled jaw. The crushing victory had been swifter and more complete than he could possibly have hoped. His people had been humiliated for too many centuries, compelled to fawn at the feet of an insurmountable enemy, but he, Talorc the great, would be hailed as their saviour and that of all Albion for generations. Finally, it would be the turn of those effete southern bastards to beg at his table, forced to leave their arrogance at the door of the great feasting hall he'd build on this very spot.

Although eager to hunt the fleeing Vibius, he could not resist taking a moment to enjoy the adoration of his countrymen as they gathered around their clan banners staked into the mud-churned ground south of the wall. No matter. The fat man would not get far before Talorc personally ran a blade into his overripe guts. Now even those who'd doubted him—especially those who'd doubted him—must accept the brilliance of his strategy.

As he neared the men of the Fib, his pace slowed. Their

peoples had been bitter enemies of old, prior to the ascendancy of the Fotla. Only the scheming obedience of their less numerous neighbours had prevented them from being crushed years ago. He firmed his resolve and headed for Galen, their lord, as he shared a drink with his warriors.

Talorc considered if now was the right time to conclude their ancient blood feud, having more than enough power at his command to make short work of these so-called allies. He'd always disliked Galen, the cur's loyalty only came from fear. They'd only met a few times in person, mainly as children, but he'd never forgotten resenting his easy manner with the other boys. A lord should project strength, not sit with inferior folk, talking to them as if equals.

Seeing his ruler approach, the soot-covered lord stood and inclined his head enough to avoid any accusation of disloyalty. 'My king, we of the Fib offer our congratulations on a great victory.' He spoke the ancient greeting without any hint of disrespect as he raised his drinking cup and gestured for his men to stand and do the same. They followed his lead with an air of relaxed camaraderie that irritated Talorc. Still, he rewarded them with a cool smile, then fixed his gaze upon his rival. To his further annoyance, Galen did not avert his eyes. The fool had no idea how close he was to ruin.

'Your men fought well, Galen, but why are they not plundering Vindolanda? Have the Fib lost their legendary appetite for gold?'

If the veiled insult offended the lord, he did not show it. Instead, he thumbed over his shoulder at the fortress behind him, where smoke billowed into the air, accompanied by the distant shrieks of demons. 'We thought it only proper to allow our new allies to take their fill first, my king.'

Talorc was about to comment on the delicate nature of Galen's men, when he noticed how many of the warriors surrounding him, and not just the Fib, were glancing nervously at the once mighty fort. The nether army swarmed over the bastions, butchering the bodies of Britons and tossing them around like playthings.

'No matter. Your men will be richly rewarded for their loyalty when we march south tomorrow,' he said, raising his voice to ensure it carried further. 'The fat lands of the empire lay before us. Nothing will stand in our way!'

A muted cheer greeted his stirring words. The king froze his smile in place, although he longed to sneer at their cowardly response.

'What's this? One battle has transformed you all into exhausted old milkmaids!' Talorc called with feined levity. From the shared barrel of the Fib, he poured himself a frothing beer in a spare cup and raised it. 'What say you? To victory!'

A better cheer followed, this time led by Galen. Talorc took a deep swig, satisfied for now. As he drank, the Fib lord looked over his shoulder and frowned. 'My king,' he said, nodding.

Talorc turned to find Drest riding toward them. The remains of something bloody hung from the saddle of his gnarled steed. The old man raised his hand upon seeing the king, then picked his way through the resting men, many of whom gestured to ward off evil as he passed.

The decision to invite Drest back to favour hadn't been an easy one, so deep was the hatred in which most of the nobility and commoners alike regarded him. But his role in gaining the aid of the nether had been critical to their victory and the reason Talorc had agreed to his demands of restoration.

'Finally, you return!' the king called. He had sent the reinstated lord of the Fortriu to seek news from the nether army, as the dark emissary had failed to report back to him. 'I thought one of those hairy bastards had eaten you. Not that you'd make much of a meal!' he said, pleased the nearby men chuckled at his derision.

Drest glanced in disdain at Galen, then stepped down from his mount and poured himself a drink. 'General Balor sends you a mighty gift,' he said, taking a sip.

The king was interested enough to ignore his lack of formality. 'Gift?'

The necromancer gestured to the bloody object attached to his horse. Scowling in distaste at the contents of the cup, he poured the liquid onto the mud.

Curious, Talorc strode to the broken thing and grasped the mass of matted hair and shattered bone. It looked like something gnawed by a dog. 'The general should learn the ways of men better,' he muttered, unable to fathom such a pointless trophy. 'We'll see enough dead southerners tomorrow.'

'Look closer,' Drest said.

Talorc turned the head over again, this time noting the size of the skull and the fat cheek flap drooping from an exposed jawbone. A single piggish eye glared at him. 'Vibius?' he asked, rage blooming in his chest.

'Aye, 'tis him.'

The king dropped the head, then strode to the old man and grabbed him by the collar of his cloak. Drest did not resist being pulled forward.

'We agreed that I—!' Talorc roared, then checked himself, noticing the watchful eyes of his men. 'We agreed I'd be the one to kill the governor!' he finished in a lower tone.

Drest looked around him as if drawing the king's attention to the undignified spectacle he presented. 'The general sends his apologies. In battle, not all things go to plan.'

Talorc spat his disappointment, but released the other man, his cheeks still burning with indignation. 'You'd do well to remember who you serve and to whom you owe your change of fortune.'

The old man stared back. 'I have no doubt about that.'

The king forced himself to adopt a calmer demeanour. 'Very well. Tell the general I thank him for his gift and will offer him and his troops a generous share of the riches to come.'

Drest's white whiskers twitched into what could have been amusement. 'He has no doubt of that, either, my lord.' He strode to Vibius's remains, drew a black dagger from beneath his cloak, and sliced the leather thong attaching it. The head of the former governor dropped to the earth.

He paused before turning back to the king. 'General Balor has instructed me on a personal matter.' There was a surreptitious air about him, as if he were uneasy with the subject. Talorc found such an uncharacteristic display of weakness intriguing.

'What matter?'

Drest frowned, reluctant to speak. 'An agent of the enemy he would have me find.'

'Merlin? I thought your spies said he was dead?'

The necromancer shook his head. 'I no longer sense Merlin's presence.'

'Well, who then? I've no time for the riddles of an aged fool!'

A flash of anger passed over Drest's gaunt features but disappeared as quickly as it came. 'There was one among my men. A...' He hesitated again. 'A man who showed signs of other powers.'

'What powers?' Talorc's curiosity deepened, and he took another drink of the poor brew.

The necromancer grunted. 'We are not sure. Something hid his true nature from me.'

Smiling, the king understood why the unfathomable sorcerer was behaving so. 'You lost him, didn't you?'

Drest scowled in the face of his ruler, the raven brand

upon his brow appearing to undulate for the briefest second. Then in a tone as cold as winter, he said, 'sometimes, much is hidden from us. Our own arrogance often makes it so.'

The king's grin froze, for a fleeting vision of a woman standing on a great bonfire, screaming in agony, came to him. She stared back with such hatred he gasped in dismayed shame. For Talorc, conqueror of the Isles of Albion, saw his mother. Not the broken shell of a person left by his father, but the young woman who'd raised him.

Drest didn't speak another word, but instead hobbled to the black haunches of the creature he rode and lifted himself into his saddle.

'Drest!' Talorc called as the necromancer trotted away.

The old man stopped, his head angled toward the man responsible for returning him to power.

'You didn't ask my permission!' the king shouted.

Ignoring him, the necromancer rode toward the mounted warriors of the Raven clan, now gathered at the southern end of the makeshift camp.

Having watched the ungrateful bastard leave, Talorc cast the drinking cup aside. 'I want your men ready at first light,' he ordered Galen, hoping for even a hint of defiance, so great was his sudden urge to throttle someone.

But his rival's reply remained respectful, 'Yes, my lord.'

Talorc regarded him for a second, then strode away to find less cowardly company. The nether army had cleared the rubble from the main gates of Vindolanda by now and were pouring through it in numbers already matching his own force. The sight prompted him to decide not to finish the Fib just yet. It would be better to wait until the conquest was complete and their allies had returned to their own dark realm.

CHAPTER FIFTY

Arthur's vision swam from sheer exhaustion as he lay Guinever upon the bracken of the forest clearing. In the failing
light, her eyes appeared as white ovals, regarding him with
an intensity he found uncomfortable. She'd not spoken
during the long afternoon since the defeat, but had clung to
his back like a broken creature, taking what comfort she could
from the closeness of another. During their arduous flight
south, they'd kept to the woods and shadows avoiding roads,
never coming across the were or other survivors.

Spent, he threw himself down beside her, not bothering to
check for enemies. The others did the same, and the sound of
snoring followed soon after.

'How's your ankle?' he whispered in the dark.

'Throbbing,' she replied, her voice strained.

'Then we'll make a litter in the morning and find horses, if
we can,' he said, riven with indecision about their next move.
Every choice seemed to merely postpone the inevitable.
Perhaps it would be better to kill themselves than face such
implacable enemies?

'I saw you,' she said, cutting through his dark thoughts.

'Saw me?'

'I stood at the gates, watching you fight the red devil.'

Arthur sniffed into the cold air. 'It was hardly a fight. I caught a lucky blow, that's all.' If Guinever knew how close he'd come to joining the enemy, she'd rightly slit his throat during the night.

'It was brave,' she said with a yawn.

His guilt stopped him from accepting the compliment. 'Are you cold?' With his body cooling after the day's exertion, he'd begun to shiver.

'Freezing.'

He sat up, piled foliage on top of them, then lay back and pulled her slender waist close to his own. She didn't object as they warmed each other.

'Arthur?' she said.

'Yes?'

'Do you think my family is dead?'

He sighed, knowing the truth would crush what little hope she had left. 'Perhaps they are with the Picts rather than with...' He paused, not wishing to name their enemy in the growing darkness. 'And if they are, they may still be alive.'

'Will you keep your promise to help me find them?' she asked.

'Yes,' he replied, already drifting to sleep.

DAWN'S early light crept through the canopy, bringing bird-song with it. Arthur woke with stiff limbs and bones as chilled as the grave. He opened his eyes and looked upon Guinever, her chest rising and falling. Her pale beauty was like that of a snowdrop flower upon the forest floor. Such was his concentration that it took him a moment to register the approach of crunching boots.

Bolting upright, he grasped a small rock and threw it at Efrawg. It bounced off his stomach and plopped onto the moss-covered turf beside him. The big man flicked his eyes open, first in furious confusion, then in alarm as he registered the unmistakable sound of danger.

Arthur shook Guinever.

'What?' she uttered, stretching her arms.

He placed a hand over her mouth, then whispered into her ear, 'shh… we're not alone.'

Her green eyes widened at the ill news.

Realising they could not flee quickly, he covered her with leaves until only her face remained visible. 'Don't move,' he added, then rose and drew his sword, before gesturing to the others to hide amongst the nearest trees.

Efrawg nodded, already wielding a gnarled branch as a makeshift club. Peredur and Gareth followed their silent lead and slipped behind the thick trunk of an oak.

The cause of the disturbance became clear when a group of ten armed men strode into the clearing. Much to Arthur's relief, however, they sported the close-cropped hair and gold earrings of the Corvanni. By the look of their dishevelled appearance, he guessed they were fellow orphans of the army.

'Take another step, and my men will fill you with barbs,' Arthur called out.

The grim determination upon the faces of their unannounced guests transformed into panic. They froze as one, but a younger lad turned to run.

'If he runs, you all die,' Arthur added.

'Hold up, Morgan!' a heavyset man with a rusty mail shirt shouted, grabbing the youth by the back of his neck and wrenching him to a stop.

Their quick compliance emboldened Arthur to push the bluff further. 'Now drop your weapons!'

L.K. ALAN

'Just wait a—' their leader began, but a towering Efrawg stepped from behind the tree and smashed the branch against his open palm while fixing each of them with an ominous glare. That, and his torque of nobility, made him an imposing figure. The newcomers dropped their weapons.

The self-appointed spokesman of the militiamen licked his lips. 'Who are you?'

Arthur strode into the light and sheathed his sword. He'd cowed these farmers enough. Experienced warriors would never have fallen for such a cheap ploy. 'If we were the enemy, you'd be roasting on a spit by now.'

The plump tribesman gave him a curious stare. 'You've come from Vindolanda?'

'Aye, and we are nearly as sorry a sight as you lot,' Efrawg answered, slapping the man on his blood-smeared cloak.

The Corvanni smiled. 'Our apologies, lord, but while the rest of the army fled, we fought till they outnumbered us.'

Efrawg chuckled. 'I'm sure you did.'

A rustling in the undergrowth caught everyone's attention. Many of the southern tribesmen uttered their shock and stepped back. Guinever sat up and regarded them with annoyance, then spat out a twig. 'When you men have finished congratulating each other on our defeat, do you think we might have a fire! If I stay here any longer, I will stick to the frost!'

Morgan gasped and clasped the arm of the man next to him. 'By the gods, she's a nymph of the woods! We must kill her before she beguiles us!'

Guinever narrowed her gaze at him while brushing dirt from her body. 'Come near me, and I'll rip your balls off!'

Arthur strode to her side and sat her on a nearby log. 'I can vouch she speaks the truth of that,' he said, earning a glare from his unimpressed ward.

'Where are the rest of you?' a Corvanni asked.

Peredur and Gareth stepped out and waved sheepishly.

'Oh, for fuck's sake!' the militia leader exclaimed, realising the extent of the ruse.

Arthur grinned.

The plump tribesman reddened with resigned embarrassment. 'My name's Reagan, and this bunch of turnips is all that's left of our unit.' He looked at the others about him, rolled his eyes, then tutted.

* * *

'WHERE ARE YOU HEADED?' Arthur asked Reagan as they sat around the fire, feeding upon the Corvanni's rations. Regardless of their own desperation, the retreating auxiliaries had proven surprisingly generous.

The other man shrugged, wiping biscuit crumbs from his whiskers. 'Back to our families at Deva and the fort—strongest in the Isles, they reckon.'

'That's what they said about Vindolanda,' one of his comrades, a reedy fellow with protruding ears, piped up.

Reagan shot him a disdainful look. 'Thanks for reminding us of the bleedin' obvious, Weylin. P'raps you'd prefer to meet those things again in a straight scrap? How'd you think that'd turn out?'

'He'd shit im sen again!' a black-haired northerner answered, much to the amusement of the others.

The man called Weylin crossed his arms and glowered. 'You lot can take the piss all you want, but I'm done with fightin' for one lifetime! I'm getting as far away from those things as possible. Mark my words, you won't see my arse for dust!'

'Aye, well, that goes without sayin'!' Reagan snapped back, then muttered to Arthur, 'And to think my people used to be warriors.'

'That's just a matter of training,' Arthur replied distract-edly, noticing how Morgan didn't take his eyes off him or Efrawg.

'Are you ill, lad?' he asked, irked by the unwanted attention.

The youth winced at the challenge. 'Oh, err, forgive me, sir, but...'

'But what?'

'Well, aren't you the same men who destroyed the enemy's battle tower?'

Arthur exchanged a surreptitious glance with Efrawg.

'I'll be—the boy's right!' Reagan said, looking at the pair with surprise. 'We watched from inside the fort while you cut through those... those... whatever they are and blew the tower to the heavens. Damnedest thing I ever saw!'

'They are Fomori,' Arthur said. 'From the nether.'

Many of the gathered men made signs to ward off evil.

'We are truly buggered,' Weylin muttered.

'That's nothing!' Peredur spoke up. 'He and my father fought the demon general and won!'

The Corvanni looked at them in sceptical amazement.

'You took on that red giant?' Reagan asked, his hand paused halfway to dipping his biscuit into the thin mush-room broth they'd cooked.

'No!' Efrawg chided his son. 'I won't have that.'

The men turned to him as one.

'Arthur cut off the general's hand—not I. Speak the truth, boy!' the nobleman added.

'Sorry, Father.' Peredur looked suitably chastened.

Weylin stood. 'Pah, what rubbish! Next you'll be telling us you fired that golden missile from your backside!'

Arthur shifted uncomfortably. 'Well, it didn't come from my arse, I can tell you that much.'

'What? You're a liar!' Weylin said, looking to his comrades for support. When none came, he sat again, his face flushed.

'Wise choice,' Efrawg rumbled.

Reagan glowered at his ill-mannered companion, then turned back to Arthur. 'Not that I would doubt your word, lords, but it's quite a tale.'

Peredur stood, his chest puffed with indignation. 'It's true —he did send the missile. I saw it!'

The men looked at the defiant youth as if he'd cracked.

'And he's Merlin's apprentice!' he declared.

The incredulous stares the auxiliaries directed at Arthur showed this last revelation had not helped matters.

Knowing how such incredible claims must sound, he offered the men a placatory hand. 'Look…' he began, but just as he did so, a ball of light rose from his palm and swirled into the crisp morning air.

The Corvanni cried in shock and scrambled away from him, leaving Arthur to stare in wonder at the glowing thing that had emerged from his outstretched limb. As it climbed, the sphere's light coalesced into a golden wyrm, its muscular haunches bunched with majestic power. The beast's maw opened to reveal deadly teeth.

'By the divines, 'tis a dragon!' Reagan said with awe.

A great wind swept through the woods, and with it came a female's voice, both beautiful and terrible. 'By this sign you shall follow him,' she said, the words shaking the ground.

The men gasped, and some fell to their knees. No sooner had she spoken than the golden beast winked from existence.

Shocked silence followed.

It alarmed Arthur to see that even his companions gawked at him.

'What would you have us do, lord?' Reagan said after a time, the front of his cloak covered in the breakfast he'd just spilled over himself in shock.

Almost unable to speak, Arthur gestured for them to rise. 'You can stand for a start. I'm not the bleedin' emperor!'

They rose.

Although his mind raced with questions, he pondered his next words, sensing much hinged on them. 'Go back to Deva and warn them. Tell them the new governor is raising an army and will come to their aid.'

Reagan's brow knotted in puzzlement. 'New governor?'

'Vibius is dead,' Arthur stated flatly, then pointed at Peredur. 'He is the new governor.'

When the plump auxiliary's look of confusion only deepened, Efrawg came to stand behind his son and placed his hands upon the fine cloth of his shoulders. 'He is Peredur, son of Ula, daughter of Vibius Crassus, and the rightful Vicarius of Britannia.'

More astonished looks followed. This time, the men bowed before the boy.

'And where will you go, erm, lord?' Reagan asked.

'First to Eboracum. We will warn those we can on the way,' Arthur replied, returning Efrawg's uncertain frown. 'We must have the legion. They are the best troops left in the Isles.'

'What of the Rendingi?' the nobleman asked.

'We'll find them—if we can.'

Efrawg nodded. 'And then?'

Arthur stared into the flames of the fire pit, remembering Merlin's voice calling to him during the battle.

TO BE CONTINUED...

AUTHOR'S NOTES

I would like to start by offering the caveat that I do not pretend to be a professor of antiquities, nor an expert on the legend of King Arthur. I am a fiction author who's done as much research as I deem necessary for the purpose of telling the tale I wish to convey. Any qualified person claiming to know more than me, probably does. However, as some of you may at least will be curious to understand a little more about the subject of Arthur and other general points of interest, here are my thoughts...

On the legend of King Arthur

One of the most common questions pondered about Arthur is: was he real? When considering the answer, it's almost impossible to overstate just how important literature has influenced the perception of not just who Arthur was, but when he existed. The tradition of writing Arthurian tales alone has a recorded history that dates back at least twelve hundred years.

The earliest known reference to a warrior with a variant

name of Arthur was made in a series of sixth century Welsh poems called The Gododdin. However, as these were transcribed from oral histories, scholars can't agree if the legendary name was added later. The first concrete mention of our protagonist came in 830 AD in the Historia Brittonum, a text attributed to a Welsh monk called Nennius. Interestingly, this source also did not refer to Arthur as a king but as a sixth century warrior who took part in many battles, including the battle of Badon hill.

These early texts are the reason many of the more "authentic" retellings of the legend depict Arthur as a late fifth century or early sixth century Celtic war lord, fending off the encroaching Saxons in a post Roman world of growing darkness. Some scholars think Arthur was in fact part of a dwindling Roman nobility in the British Isles, clinging onto the remnants of empire in the face of overwhelming odds.

Why the Welsh connection with the earliest tales? Much of the cultural difference between Wales and its larger neighbour today stem from its Celtic rather than Germanic roots. This is because Wales, Cornwall, Ireland, the Isle of Man, and Scotland, all carry a greater tradition of the earlier Celtic peoples who pre-ceded the Anglo Saxons i.e. the Brittonic people who formed most of the population during the Roman occupation. The traditional view is that these post imperial Britons retreated west in the face of constant Germanic invasions, hence the 'Celtic fringe' formed on the westerly side of the British Isles.

If Arthur existed, the most likely explanation is that he was a warrior/war leader (perhaps not a King) of renown, who had some success fighting off the ever-expanding Anglo-Saxons. Again, I have to emphasise that this is merely my opinion, and I would happily defer to anyone who has a greater understanding of the subject.

Much of what many modern readers associate with

Arthur comes from the later works of Thomas Malory. Published in 1485, Le Morte d'Arthur was a re-working of older Arthurian tales and influenced by French literature, as was the fashion of the time. Thus, the chivalric tradition was introduced, as was the romantic love intrigue between Arthur, Guinevere and Lancelot. We also experience the quest for the holy grail.

There are many modern retellings of the King Arthur story. My personal favourite is the "Warlord Chronicles" by Bernard Cornwell. I would highly recommend this gripping version of the saga, written by a true master of the craft.

Like many of these iconic figures of antiquity, the true Arthur will remain an enigma, and largely a construct of the human imagination; an irresistible mixture of fact, fiction and national pride. In the same way that Thomas Malory re-imagined Arthur as a paragon of fifteenth century chivalric values, I have retold his story as a dark fantasy, complete with magic, gore and bad language. I'm not sure what that says about today's society (probably more about me).

Perhaps in some far distant, or maybe not so distant, post-apocalyptic future, some half-starved survivor of world war five will pick up a dog-eared copy of this version of the tale and conclude that men once had the ability to change form, and Britain did indeed suffer a demon invasion! Regardless, I can only say that it is a real privilege to offer my own humble, albeit rather fanciful, slant on one of the great tales of all time. I'm sure I won't be the last.

How realistic is The Dark Isles Chronicle re-telling?

Putting aside those things that are obviously not factual… (please remember to check your meds, those of you who were wondering about the existence of 1000-year-old druids. Erm, sorry Merlin, I mean 971).

The Dark Isles Chronicle places Arthur even earlier in the timeline than other Arthurian literature, during the period when Rome withdrew from the diocese (more on that term later). There is no historical evidence to place Arthur during this tumultuous time. I made the decision to start the story at this juncture for purely dramatic purposes. Not only that, I reserve the right to change the timeline or nature of any historical event to suit the story. So, having made that unnecessarily belligerent sounding statement, suffice to say that I've done my best to weave in some key historical events, such as the invasion of Albion by Caesar and later, Claudius.

I'm not aware of any evidence that suggests the Britons reverted their dress styles and customs back to "the old ways" toward the end of the Roman occupation. In fact, the opposite is likely to have been true i.e. south of Hadrian's wall the population was thoroughly Romanised by the early fifth century.

To digress for a moment, I recently heard one interesting revisionist theory that proposed the Anglo-Saxon invasions did not actually occur in anywhere near the numbers traditionally believed. It went on to say that evidence of a growing Germanic influence during the fifth and sixth centuries can be explained merely as changing trends within the native population, spurred by interactions stemming from trade. The point was illustrated by asking: if we were to dig up the remains of modern Britain in 1500 years, could we conclude there had been a Swedish invasion because of all the Ikea stores?

Whilst I'm not sure I buy into this theory, I only reference it to highlight the fact that the centuries immediately after the Roman era are some of the least well documented in history, and that people far more qualified than myself question some of the common beliefs about the period. Although the term the "Dark Ages" is generally frowned upon now, it does still accurately convey our relative lack of knowledge for the time.

Now we've established that T.D.I.C is not the most accurate of historical texts, neither would it be true to say that readers of my re-telling are being entirely hoodwinked. For example, there are several places we encounter as the tale progresses that did in fact exist and that I've made some effort to represent as realistically as possible.

Yes, there was a small fort and accompanying vicus at Derventio (modern day Derby). Sadly, in more recent times, local town planners destroyed its archaeological remains and replaced them with a car park and a tennis court. Similarly, a series of forts did exist in the peak district, which included Ardotalia. Although, I'm pretty certain none of these suffered destruction by a force of demon sappers. I can also confirm that having travelled through the peak district, I did not encounter a single Basilisk. Perhaps if this book series becomes a commercial success, the town planners of the region may be tempted to shave the local Badger population, then paint them blue and green (no doubt after first demolishing their sett's and replacing them with car parks).

However, you may be pleased to know that there are places in the UK that are rather better at preserving their cultural heritage of the Roman period. To reference two examples, I would recommend a visit to Chester (Deva) and the museum at the remains of fort Vindolanda (Yes, it really exists).

Our very own Peredur is loosely based on his better-known incarnation of 'Percival.' I'm not sure yet how much this information will influence the story as we progress, but we shall see! Similarly, Efrawg was noted as Peredur's father in the original text from which I derived their names: The White Book of Rhydderch. However, it is important to note that although a Welsh tale, this 14th century story, is again influenced by French writings. I find the fact that our friends across the channel came to steer the perception of a British legend so much, an interesting reflection of just how complex the history of Arthurian literature is. And perhaps an example of how strong the British Isles traditional ties are to the continent (before you ask, I will not be venturing my opinions on Brexit).

The terms "Diocese" and "Vicarius" are historically accurate to describe the province and the title given to the post-holder governing it. The Christian church later adopted these phrases and adapted them for their own purposes.

The map posted at the start of the book is a semi-realistic rendering of the diocese, complete with authentic tribal locations, and the Latin names attributed to each administrative region. However, there are a few fantastical embellishments added, such as the forest of "Darach Dorka" (translated as "The Dark Oaks"). Again, I have added these to suit the story.

Speaking of translations. Although I wrote the story in English, there are three other languages referenced: Irish Gaelic, German and Latin. These are only designed to highlight cultural differences between characters. The actual languages of the period would have differed greatly from anything spoken today (other than Latin), and subject to a level of academic study well beyond the limited realism intended by myself.

I realise that some of you may be horrified upon reading the above paragraph i.e. Irish, not Welsh?! I can only offer the following poor excuse. As stated above, the actual languages used in antiquity would have been very different, regardless of which later descendent was used. For the record, I happen to think Welsh is a fine language, it's just that the particular words required seemed to resonate better in Irish Gaelic (for the purpose of telling the story) to my poorly trained Anglo-Saxon ear. I don't speak a word of either language, btw.

Here is a quick example. You might recall Merlin referring to himself as "Amadán" (fool in English). The same word in Welsh is "Ffwl." The Irish pronunciation simply sounds more like an actual name to a reader lacking the familiarity with either of the other dialects.

I can only offer my humble apologies to any disappointed Welsh readers and can assure you that I have no desire to be tarred and feathered on the streets of Cardiff! Also, having established the French influence upon the Arthurian legend, I would like to think I can be forgiven for invoking the Goidelic strand, rather than the more technically correct, Brittonic strand of the Gaelic language.

Merely as a point of interest and to illustrate why a little leeway on this topic may be appropriate, it's worth considering that according to my extensive research (Wikipedia), there are presently a healthy sounding 562,000 Welsh speakers in Wales, as opposed to less than 30,000 native Irish speakers in Ireland.

Like it or not, translations are available after this section.

So, have I ticked off the points I wished to cover during this diatribe? Wait a second while I get my list…

1. Insult local town planners. Tick.

2. Insult the great nation of Wales by not using their language in a story that almost certainly derived from them. Tick.

3. Patronise the people of Ireland by suggesting they need the help of an Englishman to save their language. Tick.

4. Inadvertently promote the abuse and ethnic cleansing of innocent Badgers. Tick.

5. Imply that Arthurian legend is more of a French construct than British and thereby insulting the English. Tick. Full house! Oh, wait a minute, what about the Scots? Hmm…. Hold on, I've got it! Lots of readers will think they are the bad guys in the book!

6. Insult the fine people of Scotland by creating the impression they are the bad guys in my book. Tick. Definitely a full house now! (Actually, the Scots were based in Northern-Ireland during the period I set the story. They don't get a single mention in the entire book. Put that in your fact pipe and smoke it!).

7. Promote smoking. Tick.

8. Mention Brexit. Tick.

Awesome. Success!

I think I've rambled on quite enough. Now, onto that small matter of book two…

L.K. Alan. 2019

TRANSLATIONS

CHAPTER 3

1.
The carter: *Codladh.*
Sleep.
2.
The Carter: '*Ionúin, Airmed,*' he called, raising his head to the sky. '*le do thoil cabhrú leis.*'
'Beloved Airmed,' he called, raising his head to the sky. 'Please help him.'
3.
The Carter: *Fuil.*
Blood.

CHAPTER 4

1.
The Carter: You can call me *Amadán.*

You can call me fool.
2.
The Carter: *Baois óige.*
Youthful folly.

CHAPTER 5

1.
Ploughman to the Carter:
Tighearna Myrddin!
Lord Merlin!

CHAPTER 7

1.
Merlin: *Conas an mighty tar éis titim.*
How the mighty have fallen.
2.
Officer: *Ex aequo et bono.*
According to the right and good.
3.
Officer: 'I therefore sentence you to death—*executio juris non habet injuriam!*' the officer concluded with the ancient customary proclamation, not disguising his enthusiasm. The two guards restraining the prisoner drew wicked–looking hatchets from their belts. More cheering followed.
'Paratus!'
'I therefore sentence you to death—the execution of the law does no injury!' the officer concluded with the ancient customary proclamation, not disguising his enthusiasm. The two guards restraining the prisoner drew wicked–looking hatchets from their belts. More cheering followed.

'Ready!'

4.

Decanus: 'Crus!' the officer demanded, and the guards shoved a deathly white Festus onto his back, upon a platform awash with gore. One pinned his blood–drenched torso to the ground while the other lifted his left leg and stretched it out. 'Tres!' the scruffy decanus shouted with relish.

'Leg!' the officer demanded, and the guards shoved a deathly white Festus onto his back, upon a platform awash with gore. One pinned his blood–drenched torso to the ground while the other lifted his left leg and stretched it out. 'Three!' the scruffy decanus shouted with relish.

5.

Merlin: Codlata dearthāir beag.

Sleep little brother.

CHAPTER 8

1.

Merlin: Deus pulvis.

The dust.

2.

Merlin: Ardū.

Rise.

3.

Merlin: Smeach.

Flip.

CHAPTER 11

1.

Merlin: *Buachaill dúr.*
Stupid boy.
2.
A small *Castrum.*
A small fortification.
3.
Merlin: *Cailín socair.*
Calm girl.

CHAPTER 12

1.
Merlin: *calma mo milseáin.*
Calm my sweets.
2.
Merlin: *Solas!*
Light!
3.
Merlin: *Oighear!*
Ice!
4.
Merlin: *Cas ar ais!*
Turn back!

CHAPTER 14

1.
Merlin: *níos teo.*
Hotter.

CHAPTER 15

1.
Calder: *Scaoileadh!*
Release!

CHAPTER 18

1.
Merlin: *An Macánta.*
The honest.

CHAPTER 19

1.
Merlin: Téann sí tríd an oíche gan réaltaí chun nascleanúint a
dhéanamh ar a bealach,
Shield maiden of the Iceni, teacht ar ais chun solais.
She goes through the night without stars to steer her way,
Shield maiden of the Iceni, come back to the light.

CHAPTER 21

1.
Efrawg: *an áit marbh.*
The dead place.
2.
Merlin: *Ceangail iad.*
Bind them.

CHAPTER 24

1.
Merlin: *Stad!*
Stop!

CHAPTER 25

1.
Faerie: *Avenge a, hathair!*
Avenge her, father
2.
Shaggy monster: *Agus mar sin filleann mo iníon ar an Domhan.*
And so my daughter returns to Earth.
3.
Shaggy monster: *Francaigh.*
Rats.

CHAPTER 26

1.
Cernunnos: *Ná bréag dom, Myrddin!*
Do not lie to me, Merlin!
Merlin replies:
Iontaobhas dom mar a rinne tú aon uair amháin.
Trust me as you once did.

CHAPTER 31

1.

Vibus: *Cunnus.*

A very rude word. I think you get the idea!

2.

Vibius: *Pedicatus.*

Sodomite.

3.

Vibius: *Scortum.*

Prostitute.

CHAPTER 35

1.

Adalric: Germanian *wurst*!

Germanian sausage!

2.

Adalric: My young *Junges*, another year and the old *schwein* will.

My young pup, another year and the old pig will.

3.

Adalric: *Blutjäger*!

Blood hunters!

4.

Notger: 'I smell hund,' the man–creature grunted, licking its lips at the prostrate warrior. It turned to his superior. 'Ich will sein fleisch.'

'I smell dog,' the man–creature grunted, licking its lips at the prostrate warrior. It turned to his superior. 'I want his meat.'

Adalric replies: 'Nien,' Adalric retorted, no longer laughing, and returned the deep growl with one of his own. *'Berühre ihn und ich reiß dir die Kehle aus.'*

'No,' Adalric retorted, no longer laughing, and returned the deep growl with one of his own. 'Touch him and I'll rip your throat out.'

CHAPTER 38

1.

Adalric: The useless turd can't tell his arsch from his *ellbogen*.
The useless turd can't tell his arse from his elbow.

2.

Adalric: *Fotze.*
The same very rude word as chapter 31, only this time in German.

3.

Adalric: Slave *frau*.
Slave woman.

CHAPTER 39

1.

Calder: *Deannach na ndéithe*
Dust of the gods

CHAPTER 45

1.

Demon: *Farrack!* (please note that this is a fictitious word).
Fire!

CHAPTER 48

1.

Adalric: *Komm, brüder, wir jagen*!
Come, brothers, we hunt!

PLACE NAMES

Alauna = Maryport, Cumbria
Cambodunum = Huddersfield
Camulodunum = Colchester
Derventio = Derby
Deva = Chester
Darach Dorcha = Fictitious
Dunadd = Dunadd Fort, Lochgilphead, Scotland
Eboracum = York
Fort Ardotalia = Located in Gamesley, near Glossop
Fort Vindolanda = Near Bardon Mill, Hexham
Llyn Penrhyn = Lake Penrhyn, Anglesey
Londinium = London
Luguvalium = Carlisle
Mona = Anglesey
Ratae = Leicester

ALSO BY L.K. ALAN

Visit www.lkalan.com for progress updates on book 2 of *The Dark Isles Chronicles*.

Lightning Source UK Ltd.
Milton Keynes UK
UKHW020907271222
414464UK00016B/1012